JAN 1 6 2013

Pra...

THE DUKE'S

"The Duke's Perfect Wife i...
was captivating from the fi...
—*Joyfully*...

"The unforgettable Mackenzies return as Ashley spins the fourth in the series into another mesmerizing, intensely emotional romance that steals readers' hearts and minds. With her innovative plots and characters, Ashley pushes the boundaries of the genre and creates 'keepers,' because they touch readers on many levels." —*RT Book Reviews* (Top Pick)

"It's all such a seductive world, you'll get swept away, just as I did." —*DemonLovers Books & More*

DISCARD

PROPERTY OF :
RANCHO MIRAGE PUBLIC LIBRARY
71100 HIGHWAY 111
RANCHO MIRAGE, CA 92270
(760)341-READ(7323)

... sexy, ... p...
... writing ... —*Booklist* (starred review)

"...ssionate, well-drawn characters, breathless romance, and a memorable love story. —*Library Journal*

"Innovative as ever . . . a beautifully written, tender, touching romance that will leave readers breathless. Her strong characterizations and poignant yet sensual storytelling draw readers into her unforgettable love stories."

—*RT Book Reviews* (Top Pick)

"Readers will love Ainsley." —*Publishers Weekly*

continued . . .

Berkley Sensation titles by Jennifer Ashley

The Mackenzies

THE MADNESS OF LORD IAN MACKENZIE
LADY ISABELLA'S SCANDALOUS MARRIAGE
THE MANY SINS OF LORD CAMERON
THE DUKE'S PERFECT WIFE
THE SEDUCTION OF ELLIOT McBRIDE

Shifters Unbound

PRIDE MATES
PRIMAL BONDS
WILD CAT
MATE CLAIMED

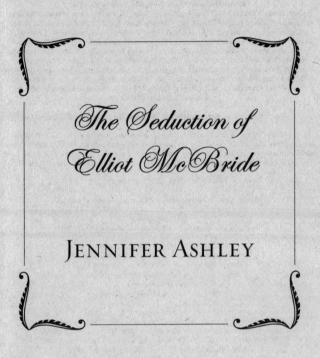

The Seduction of Elliot McBride

JENNIFER ASHLEY

BERKLEY SENSATION, NEW YORK

THE BERKLEY PUBLISHING GROUP
Published by the Penguin Group
Penguin Group (USA) Inc.
375 Hudson Street, New York, New York 10014, USA

Penguin Group (Canada), 90 Eglinton Avenue East, Suite 700, Toronto, Ontario M4P 2Y3, Canada
(a division of Pearson Penguin Canada Inc.) • Penguin Books Ltd., 80 Strand, London WC2R 0RL,
England • Penguin Ireland, 25 St. Stephen's Green, Dublin 2, Ireland (a division of Penguin
Books Ltd.) • Penguin Group (Australia), 707 Collins Street, Melbourne, Victoria 3008, Australia
(a division of Pearson Australia Group Pty. Ltd.) • Penguin Books India Pvt. Ltd., 11 Community
Centre, Panchsheel Park, New Delhi—110 017, India • Penguin Group (NZ), 67 Apollo Drive,
Rosedale, Auckland 0632, New Zealand (a division of Pearson New Zealand Ltd.) • Penguin Books
(South Africa) (Pty.) Ltd., Rosebank Office Park, 181 Jan Smuts Avenue, Parktown North 2193,
South Africa • Penguin China, B7 Jiaming Center, 27 East Third Ring Road North, Chaoyang
District, Beijing 100020, China

Penguin Books Ltd., Registered Offices: 80 Strand, London WC2R 0RL, England

This is a work of fiction. Names, characters, places, and incidents either are the product of the author's
imagination or are used fictitiously, and any resemblance to actual persons, living or dead, business
establishments, events, or locales is entirely coincidental. The publisher does not have any control over
and does not assume any responsibility for author or third-party websites or their content.

THE SEDUCTION OF ELLIOT MCBRIDE

A Berkley Sensation Book / published by arrangement with the author

PUBLISHING HISTORY
Berkley Sensation mass-market paperback edition / January 2013

Copyright © 2012 by Jennifer Ashley.
Excerpt from *The Wicked Deeds of Daniel Mackenzie* by
Jennifer Ashley copyright © 2012 by Jennifer Ashley.
Cover art by Phil Hefferan. Hand lettering by Ron Zinn.
Cover design by George Long.
Interior text design by Laura K. Corless.

All rights reserved.
No part of this book may be reproduced, scanned, or distributed in any printed or
electronic form without permission. Please do not participate in or encourage piracy of
copyrighted materials in violation of the author's rights. Purchase only authorized editions.
For information, address: The Berkley Publishing Group,
a division of Penguin Group (USA) Inc.,
375 Hudson Street, New York, New York 10014.

ISBN: 978-0-425-25113-3

BERKLEY SENSATION®
Berkley Sensation Books are published by The Berkley Publishing Group,
a division of Penguin Group (USA) Inc.,
375 Hudson Street, New York, New York 10014.
BERKLEY SENSATION® is a registered trademark of Penguin Group (USA) Inc.
The "B" design is a trademark of Penguin Group (USA) Inc.

PRINTED IN THE UNITED STATES OF AMERICA

10 9 8 7 6 5 4 3 2 1

If you purchased this book without a cover, you should be aware that this book is
stolen property. It was reported as "unsold and destroyed" to the publisher, and neither the
author nor the publisher has received any payment for this "stripped book."

ALWAYS LEARNING   PEARSON

Many thanks go, as usual, to my editor, Kate Seaver, for all her help and patience as we journey from manuscript to finished book. Also to Katherine, the best assistant editor ever, for keeping everything on track; and Erin, my fantastic publicist, who is always there with enthusiasm and support. And to my husband, who puts up with the ups and downs, joys and despair, dirty house and potluck dining that goes with living with a writer. Love you, dear! And as always, a special thanks to my readers—you are the greatest!

Chapter 1

Juliana St. John's fiancé was an hour late to his own wedding. While Juliana sat waiting, resplendent in satin and yellow roses, various friends and family members were dispatched through rainy Edinburgh to find out what was the matter.

The matron of honor, Ainsley Mackenzie, tried to keep up Juliana's spirits, as did Juliana's stepmother, Gemma, in her own way. But Juliana knew in her heart that something was terribly wrong.

When Grant's friends returned, embarrassed and empty-handed, and Ainsley asked her husband, a tall brute of a Scotsman, to go, the result was different.

Lord Cameron Mackenzie opened the vestry door wide enough to stick his head around it. "Ainsley," he said, then shut the door again.

Ainsley pressed Juliana's hands, which by now were like

ice. "Never you mind, Juliana. I'll discover what has happened."

Juliana's stepmother, only ten years older than Juliana herself, was angry. Gemma said nothing, but Juliana saw rage in every movement she made. Gemma had never liked Grant Barclay and liked Grant's mother still less.

Ainsley returned in a short time. "Juliana," she said, her voice gentle. She held out her hand. "Come with me."

When a person spoke in that tone, terrible news was certain to follow. Juliana rose in a rustle of satin. Gemma tried to follow, but Ainsley held up her hand. "Juliana alone, I think."

Gemma, of the volatile temper, started to protest, but Gemma was also intelligent. She gave Juliana a nod and squeezed her hand. "I will be here for you, dear."

Juliana had a temper of her own, but as she stepped out into the gusty rain of the church's courtyard, she felt nothing but a curious numbness. She'd been engaged to Grant for several years now. The wedding had always been so comfortably far away that it had come as something of a shock to finally reach the day. And now . . .

Was Grant ill? Dead?

Mist and light rain cloaked the city, obscuring the sky. Ainsley led Juliana in her finery out and through a tiny yard, mud soaking Juliana's new white high-heeled boots.

They reached an arched breezeway, and Ainsley started down this, away from the main church. Thank heavens, because all the guests were in the church, waiting and watching, speculating about what had gone wrong.

Under an arcade, but still in the chill, Lord Cameron waited alone, a broad-shouldered giant of a man in a Mackenzie plaid kilt. When Ainsley and Juliana reached him, Cameron looked down at Juliana with flint-hard eyes. "I found him."

Still Juliana felt nothing but numbness. None of this

seemed real, not Cameron, not the lowering skies outside the church, not her wedding finery.

"Where is he?" Juliana asked.

Cameron gestured with the silver flask in his hand. "In a carriage behind the church. Do you want to speak to him?"

"Of course I want to speak to him. I am going to marry him . . ."

She noticed the look Ainsley and Cameron exchanged, caught the glimpse of anger in Ainsley's eyes, the reflected anger in Cameron's.

"What is it?" Juliana squeezed Ainsley's hand. "Tell me before I go mad."

Cameron answered before Ainsley could. "Barclay eloped," he said, syllables blunt. "He's married."

The arches and the courtyard, solid Edinburgh stone, spun around and around her, but no, Juliana was standing upright, staring at Cameron Mackenzie, Ainsley's warmth at her side.

"Married." Juliana's lips were stiff. "But he's marrying me."

She knew that the last thing in the world Lord Cameron Mackenzie had wanted to do this day was hunt down Juliana's groom and then tell Juliana that the man had run off with another woman. But she kept staring at Cameron, as though if she looked at him hard enough, he'd change the story and tell her a different one.

"He married yesterday afternoon," Cameron said. "To a woman who was teaching him the piano."

This was mad. It had to be a joke. "Mrs. Mackinnon," Juliana said without inflection. She remembered the woman with dark hair and plain dresses who had sometimes been at Grant's mother's when Juliana arrived. "She's a widow." A choked laugh escaped her lips. "Not anymore, I suppose."

"I told him he needed to have the decency to tell you himself," Cameron said in his voice like rough gravel. "So I brought him. Do you want to talk with him?"

"No," Juliana said quickly. "No." The world started spinning again.

Cameron shoved his flask into Juliana's hand. "Get that inside you, lass. It will lessen the blow."

A proper lady did not drink spirits, and Juliana had been raised to be so very proper. But the turn of events made this a highly *un*-proper occasion.

Juliana tipped back the flask and trickled a bit of burning Scots whiskey into her mouth. She coughed, swallowed, coughed again, and dabbed at her lips as Cameron rescued the flask.

Perhaps she should not have drunk it. What Cameron had told her was starting to seem real.

Two hundred people waited in the church for Juliana St. John and Grant Barclay to wed, two hundred people who would have to be told to go home. Two hundred gifts to be returned, two hundred apologies to be penned. And the newspapers would certainly enjoy themselves.

Juliana pressed her hands to her face. She'd never been in love with Grant, but she'd thought they'd at least formed a friendship, a mutual respect for each other. But even that . . . Grant hadn't given her even that.

"What am I going to do?"

Cameron tucked the flask into his greatcoat. "We'll take you home. I'll have my carriage pull up in the passage at the end of this walk. None need to see you."

They were kind, Ainsley and Cameron—they were being kind. Juliana didn't want kindness. She wanted to kick and rage, not only at Grant, but at herself. She'd been so secure in her engagement, rather smug that she was in no danger of being left on the shelf. Not only that, she'd wanted the stability of a normal life, something she'd fought for all her life.

Her future had just crumbled to dust, her safe choice ripped from beneath her feet. Shock still rendered her numb, but she sensed regret coming hard on its heels.

Juliana rubbed her arms, suddenly chilled. "Not yet.

Please, give me a moment. I need to be alone for just a moment."

Ainsley glanced into the courtyard, into which people were now emerging from the church proper. "Not that way. There's a chapel down here. We'll keep them out."

"Bless you, Ainsley." Juliana could not unclench herself enough to give Ainsley the hug she deserved.

She let Ainsley guide her to the door of the chapel, which Cameron opened. Cameron and Ainsley stepped back, and Juliana went in alone, the door clicking closed.

The chapel was chilly but dim and peaceful. Juliana stood for a moment in front of the bare altar, looking up at the plain cross hanging above it, alone and unadorned.

Grant, married. To Mrs. Mackinnon.

Juliana now realized things she'd seen in the past few months but had paid no mind to at the time—Grant and Mrs. Mackinnon side by side at Grant's mother's piano, their exchanged smiles, the looks between them. Grant gazing pensively at Juliana as though he wanted to speak to her about something important, and then making some joke or inane remark instead.

She knew now what he meant to say. *Miss St. John, I've fallen in love with my piano teacher and wish to marry her, not you.*

Scandal. Humiliation.

Juliana balled her fists, wanting to shout at Providence for being so aggravating. But, even in her agitation, blasphemy in a chapel seemed wrong.

She settled for storming into a pew, her ivory skirts billowing around her. "Blast!" she said and slammed herself into the seat.

On top of something that moved. A man with long legs under a woolen kilt, a broad body that heaved up onto strong elbows. A man coming awake to find a hundred and twenty pounds of young woman in wedding garb sitting on his thighs.

"What the devil?" Gray eyes the same color as Ainsley's flashed in a face that was too tanned to have been in Scotland long.

Elliot McBride obviously had no compunction about blaspheming in a church. Or sleeping in one.

Juliana swiftly rose, but she couldn't move out of the pew. She stared down at Elliot as he levered himself partway up and leaned back into the corner of the pew, his booted feet still on the bench.

"Elliot?" Juliana asked, breathless. "What are you doing here?"

"Trying to find some quiet," he said. "Too bloody many people about."

"I mean, here in Scotland. I thought you were in India. Ainsley said you were in India."

Elliot McBride was one of Ainsley's many brothers, a man the girl Juliana had fallen madly in love with about a hundred years ago. He'd disappeared to India to make his fortune, and she hadn't seen him since.

Elliot rubbed a hand over his stubbled face, though he smelled of soap and water, as though he'd recently bathed. "Decided to come home."

Laconic, that was the way to describe Elliot, the untamed McBride. Also large and strong, with a presence that knocked the breath out of her. It had been so when she'd been a child and he'd been the wild brother of Ainsley, and again when she'd been a proud debutante and he'd attended her coming-out ball in his army regimentals.

Juliana sank to the pew again, at the end of it, beyond his feet. High in the tower of the main church, bells rang, striking the hour.

"Aren't you supposed to be in there, lass?" Elliot asked. He removed a flask from his coat and sipped from it, but unlike Cameron, he didn't offer her any. "Getting married to whatever his name is?"

"Grant Barclay. I was to have been Mrs. Grant Barclay."

The flask stopped halfway to his mouth. "*Was to have been?* Did you jilt the whey-faced bastard, then?"

"No," Juliana said. "Apparently, yesterday, he eloped with his piano teacher."

It was all too much. Strange laughter welled up inside her and came pealing out of her mouth. Not quite hysterics, but a hearty laugh she couldn't stop.

Elliot lay still, like an animal deciding whether to attack or run. Poor Elliot. What must he make of a woman who'd jolted him out of his sleep by plopping down on him and then laughing uncontrollably because her fiancé had abandoned her?

Juliana's laughter eased off, and she wiped her eyes with her fingertips. Her dark red hair was tumbling down, one of the yellow roses Ainsley had tied into it falling to her lap. "Stupid flowers."

Elliot sat frozen, his hand gripping the back of the pew so hard he was surprised the wood didn't splinter. He watched as Juliana laughed, as her glorious hair fell to her bared shoulders. She smiled though her blue eyes were wet, and the hands that plucked the flower from her lap were long fingered and trembling.

Elliot wanted to put his arms around her and cradle her close. *There now*, he'd say. *You're better off without the idiot.* An even stronger instinct made him want to go find Grant Barclay and shoot him for hurting her.

But Elliot knew that if he made the mistake of touching Juliana, he wouldn't stop at comfort. He'd tilt her head back and kiss her lips, as he'd done at her debut ball, the night she'd permitted the one kiss.

They'd both been eighteen. Before Elliot had gone to hell and back, that chaste kiss would have been enough for him. This time, it would not be enough, not by a long way.

He'd kiss down her pretty throat to her bosom, nuzzle her gown's neckline with its points of lace, and feather kisses to her shoulders. Then he'd lick his way back up to her ripe lips, seam them with his tongue, coax her to let him inside.

He'd kiss her with long, careful kisses, tasting the goodness of her mouth while he held her and did not let her go.

Elliot would want to take everything, because Lord only knew when he'd have the chance again. A broken man learned to savor what he could when he had the opportunity.

"It will stay with me forever," Juliana was saying. *"Poor Juliana St. John. Don't you remember? She'd already put on her wedding clothes and gone to the church, poor darling."*

What did a man say to a woman in this state? Elliot wished for the eloquence of his barrister brother, who stood up in court and made elegant speeches for a living. Elliot could only ever speak the truth.

"Let them say it, and to the devil with them."

Juliana gave him a sad smile. "The world is very much about what *they* say, my dear Elliot. Perhaps it's different in India."

Dear God, how could anyone think that? "The rules there are damn strict. You can die—or get someone else killed—by not knowing them."

Juliana blinked. "Oh. Very well, I concede that such a thing sounds worse than people expecting me to hide in shame and knit socks for the rest of my life."

"Why the devil should you knit socks? Do what you like."

"Very optimistic of you. Not fair to me, but I'm afraid I will be talked about for a long while now. *And* I am now on the shelf. Thirty years old, and no longer an ingénue. I know that women do all sorts of things these days besides marry, but I am too old to attend university, and even if I did, my father would die of shame that I was such a bluestocking. I was raised to pour tea, organize fêtes, and say correct things to the vicar's wife."

Her words slid over Elliot without him registering them,

her musical voice soothing. He lay back and let her talk, realizing he'd not felt so at ease in a long while.

If I could listen to her forever, if I could drift into the night hearing her voice, I might get well again.

No, nothing would be well, never again, not after the things he'd seen and done, and what had been done to him. He'd thought that once he took refuge in Scotland again, it would stop. The dreams, the waking terrors, the utter darkness when time passed and he knew nothing of it. But it hadn't, and he'd known he had to put the next part in his plan to work.

Juliana was studying him, her blue eyes clear like a summer lake. The beauty of her, the memory of those eyes, had sustained him for a long time in the dark.

Sometimes he'd dreamed she was with him, trying to wake him, her dulcet voice filling his ears. *Come on, now, Elliot. You must wake up. My kite's tangled in a tree, and you're the only one tall enough to get it down.*

He remembered the day when he'd first realized what he felt for her—they must both have been about sixteen. She'd been flying a kite for children of her father's friends, and Elliot had come to watch. He'd retrieved the kite from a tree for her and earned a red-lipped smile, a soft kiss on his cheek. From that day forward, he'd been lost.

"Elliot, are you awake?"

His eyes had drifted closed on memories, and now Juliana's voice blended with the remembered dream. He pried his eyes open. "I think so."

"You did not hear me, did you?" Her face was pink in the dim light.

"Sorry, lass. I'm a bit drunk."

"Good. Not that you're drunk, but that you didn't hear me. Never mind. It was a foolish idea."

He opened his eyes wider, his brain coming alert. What the hell had he missed?

The darkness did that to him sometimes. Elliot could slide past large portions of conversation without noticing he had done so. He'd come back to himself realizing people were waiting for his response and wondering what was the matter with him. Elliot had decided that avoiding people and conversation was the best solution.

With Juliana, he wanted to know. "Tell me again."

"I don't think I ought. If it were a cracking-good idea, you'd have leapt on it at once. As it is . . ."

"Juliana, I swear to you . . . I drift in and out. I want to hear your cracking-good idea."

"No, you don't."

Females. Even ones he'd been secretly in love with for years could drive him insane.

Elliot sat up and moved closer to her, his feet on the floor. He stretched his arm along the back of the pew, not touching her but close enough to feel her warmth. "Juliana, tell me, or I'll tickle you."

"I'm not eight years old anymore, Elliot McBride."

He wanted to laugh at her haughty tone. "Neither am I. When I say *tickle*, I no longer mean what I did then." He touched her bare shoulder with one finger.

A mistake. The contact shot heat up his arm and straight into his heart.

Her lips were close to his, lush and ripe. She had faint freckles across her nose, ten of them. She'd always had them, had always tried to rid herself of them, but to Elliot, every one was kissable.

Her eyes went still, and her voice was a whisper of breath. "What I asked, Elliot, was whether *you* would marry me."

Chapter 2

Elliot sat still, his eyes as gray as winter skies and just as cold.

Juliana realized that, when she'd blurted her question, she'd been thinking of Elliot, the teasing, warm-eyed young man of her youth. This Elliot McBride was a stranger. His light hair had been cropped close, his face hard, and thin scars laced his cheek.

This Elliot had tracked and killed other men, had been captured and held prisoner for so long that they'd all feared him dead. The ten months he'd been missing had been the worst of Juliana's life. He'd returned to his brother's house for a time to recover, but Juliana had not seen him. He'd visited no one, had let no one visit him, and had disappeared back to India again.

"As I say, a foolish idea," Juliana said quickly. "You look a bit green, Elliot, so never mind. I didn't mean to frighten the life out of you. Return to your cozy doze."

Elliot's gaze flicked to the bare altar and back to her, his fingers at her back hot in this chill place. "Not so foolish. I think it a grand idea."

"Truly, pretend I said nothing. You didn't hear me the first time anyway."

Elliot moved his hand to cup her shoulder through the satin, his strength rippling heat through her too-cold body. "I cannae pretend I didn't hear the second time, lass."

"Well, I take it back. I shall remove to my father's house and start returning the gifts. I kept meticulous notes, as I always do. Gemma smiles at me for my lists and notes, but she will thank me for them now."

Her smile was wide, her eyes too bright, and Elliot's heart beat so hard he was surprised it didn't echo in the quietness.

He wanted to charge out of the pew shouting for joy, tow Juliana back into the church, and command the minister to get on with the ceremony. His family and Juliana's were residents of this parish, they were both of marriageable age, and there would be no impediment. He knew people who could issue a new license quickly, and it would be done.

Elliot had traveled to Edinburgh to find her today, to continue plans he'd put in motion. The interminable wait in the crowded church had started to unnerve him, so he'd slipped away to be alone in the chapel. A few sips of whiskey, and his tired body—he never rested well at night—had taken him to sleep.

To be awakened by the delicious weight of Juliana in her satin and tulle, the scent of roses, the sound of her voice. Yes. This was *right*.

"I won't be going back to India," he said. "I've purchased a house, th' old McGregor estate about thirty miles north of Aberdeen. McGregor's my great-uncle on my mother's side, and was in need of a bit of cash. You might as well marry me and have the run of th' place."

Juliana still stared at him, her lips parted enough for him to want to taste the moisture between them. If she said no, or that she wanted to wait, he had more plans for that.

Elliot might be mad, but he intended to be very, very persuasive.

"That's a bit of a journey," Juliana said, her voice faint.

"Aye." Trains made traveling much easier these days, but even so, the north of the country was remote, a peaceful retreat against the noise. Elliot needed so much peace.

Juliana's blue eyes held trepidation. Under their scrutiny, Elliot felt his lassitude trying to descend once more, wanting him to lapse into a stupor again, to lean against the satin warmth of her and breathe her scent . . .

"Are you certain, Elliot?" Juliana's voice brought him awake again.

Of course he was certain. Elliot needed her with him so he could be strong and well.

He shrugged, pretending nonchalance. "I told you, 'tis a grand idea. Everyone is wanting a wedding. You're in the bridal clothes, and I'm not likely to stay in finery long."

Her eyes widened. "You mean that you want to do this *today*?"

"Why not? Your guests are here, the minister is waiting."

Juliana pursed her lips, the little gesture heating his blood. "It would be quite a scandal."

"Let it be. While they talk, we'll be at our estate, far away."

Juliana hesitated, then her smile took on a hint of wildness. "All right. As you say, why not?"

Elliot's heart thundered, elation rising to choke him. He needed to finish this, take her home, *be* with her.

Elliot pulled her to her feet and propelled her out of the pew. Juliana half tripped in her high-heeled slippers, but he steadied her with a strong hand. The nearness of her, the feel of her soft arm beneath his scarred fingers, urged him on. He needed to seal this bargain before the darkness returned, and he didn't mean the darkness of the nighttime.

They were at the door. Elliot stopped her, his grip on her too tight, but he couldn't make himself ease it. "Stay with my sister while I go explain to the minister that the groom will be a different man. Will ye be ready?"

"Yes." Juliana wet her lips. "Indeed."

"Good."

She reached for the door handle, but Elliot drew her back. "Wait."

He slid his arm behind her, as solid as a tree branch, and drew her closer. So close she saw the pattern of white scars on his cheek, the thin lines that ran across his cheekbones and ended under the line of his hair. A thin, jagged blade had made those cuts.

He was going to kiss her. Juliana's breath caught as she waited for the cool touch of his lips, the press of his mouth. She'd dreamed of his kiss so many times, after the one he'd stolen from her so long ago.

It never came. Elliot drew her hand to his lips, turned it over, and pressed a long, burning kiss to her palm. Any disappointment dissolved in the heat that swept down her arm and the wicked fire that streaked through her body.

Elliot opened the chapel door, propelled Juliana out into the cool mist of the courtyard, and closed the door behind her. Juliana found herself facing the concerned Ainsley, the bulk of Lord Cameron, and her stepmother, Gemma, hurrying out to see what had become of them all.

~~~~~

That was how Juliana St. John came to be married an hour later to Elliot McBride, in the church in which she was to have married Mr. Barclay that same day.

The guests watched in either shock or great enjoyment as Elliot, in formal black coat and McBride kilt, stood ramrod straight at Juliana's side and said his vows. When Juliana's father put her hand into Elliot's, Elliot closed his fingers over hers in a hard grip. It wasn't letting go, that grip.

The service was brief and simple. Ainsley had retied the

roses in Juliana's hair, and Juliana's wedding finery cascaded across the plain floor of the church. Her bouquet was still fresh, thanks to Ainsley and Gemma, with a sprig of heather tucked into it for luck.

Elliot continued to clamp down on Juliana's hand as the vicar moved through the service, not releasing her even after he slid the wedding ring onto her finger. They'd had to borrow the rings from Elliot's brother Patrick and his wife, Rona. Rona's ring was a bit too big for Juliana, and she had to squeeze her fingers together to hold it in place.

Now the vicar was pronouncing them man and wife. Elliot turned Juliana to face him, tilted her head up, and kissed her.

It was possessive, that kiss. A Scottish laird of old might have kissed his won bride like this, and Elliot was not so many generations removed from those lairds of old.

He raised his head after the kiss and looked down at her, his hands firm on her arms, gray eyes filled with triumph. And Juliana was married.

Several hours later, during the wedding feast at the St. John town house—Gemma seeing no reason to let all the preparation go to waste—Juliana escaped the laughter-filled public rooms and the scrutiny of her friends with the excuse of having to use the necessary.

She breathed a sigh of relief when she stepped into an empty back hall. She was glad people were enjoying the banquet she and Gemma had meticulously organized, but the congratulations and the questions had begun to weigh on her. What she'd done would be a nine days' wonder, and the first day of it was already wearying.

A strong hand landed on her shoulder, and Juliana bit back a startled cry. Elliot put his finger to his lips, leaned down, and kissed her cheek.

"Time to go," he said.

She wanted to—restlessness gripped her like a fever—but Juliana mouthed the correct words. "That would be a bit rude, would it not? My stepmother has gone to all this trouble."

Elliot ran his hand down her arm to lace his fingers with hers. "Do you want to go home, Juliana?"

Juliana closed her eyes, breathing in his warmth. "Yes."

"Then we go."

Without waiting for further argument, Elliot led her down the servants' staircase and through the kitchen to the back door, where an Indian man in white clothes and turban waited with Juliana's summer coat and two valises. The Indian man helped Juliana into her wraps without a word and just as silently opened the door and ushered them out of the house.

~~~

The ride to Juliana's new home took a long time. They boarded a train that chugged slowly north and west, into the heart of the Highlands. In a private compartment, the wife of Elliot's Indian servant helped Juliana change from her wedding gown into a traveling dress. Her valise proved to have been packed with sensible traveling clothes— Ainsley and Gemma looking after her to the end.

As they traveled, the day's remaining clouds broke into tatters before a strong wind, the sun emerging to bathe the world in warmth and glittering raindrops. High summer was coming on, which meant, this far north, the sun would linger well into night.

At Stirling, they took another train toward the coast, heading north of Dundee toward Aberdeen, where they boarded yet another train on a smaller line. They finally disembarked at a tiny station in a village called Highforth, thirty miles north of Aberdeen, tucked between mountains and the sea. The late afternoon sun silhouetted hills to the west and reflected on the stretch of sea to the east and north.

The station was nothing but a small building on the side of the track, the platform so short that passengers had to disembark one train car at a time. Elliot and his party were the only ones who descended, in any case.

Elliot went in search of the stationmaster, leaving his manservant and manservant's family clustered around Juliana like colorful butterflies. A highland wind blew across the empty platform, swirling the colorful silks of the Indian women's clothing, the creamy brown skirts of Juliana's traveling frock, and the bright blue and green plaid of Elliot's kilt.

The manservant, Juliana had learned during the journey, was called Mahindar, and he had brought with him from India his wife, Channan, mother, sister-in-law, and a small child who seemed to belong to the sister-in-law.

Mahindar's mother calmly tucked a fold of her silk head scarf around her neck, looking neither left nor right as they waited for Elliot. Mahindar's wife, Channan, plump and cylindrical, her shape emphasized by the narrow skirt and silks that wrapped her body, looked around with more interest. Channan's younger sister—her half sister, if Juliana understood aright—held the little girl's hand and shrank into Channan's side.

Only Mahindar spoke English, though Channan, he'd said proudly to Juliana, was learning. Channan's poor widowed sister spoke only a few words of English, and his mother, none at all.

Elliot, in his kilt, boots, and flyaway coat, was the only one of them who looked as if he belonged in this wild place. While he'd been in India, though, Juliana had heard stories about him *going native*, as people called it, staunch disapproval in their voices. Elliot had eaten Indian food, worn Indian clothing, and had even taken up with Indian women, it was rumored. He'd spent so much time in the sun that his skin was baked quite brown, and he'd hardly looked Scottish at all anymore.

Elliot turned and strode back to them, wind lifting the coat from his McBride tartan kilt. If Elliot had gone native in India, he'd certainly changed back to being fully Scots in his homeland.

"They have no transport," he announced, no concern in his voice. "A cart is coming from the house to fetch us, but it won't seat us all. Mahindar, you and your family will have to wait here for it to return."

Mahindar nodded without worry. His mother didn't look worried either as Mahindar translated, and she turned to study the mountains, the sky, and the cluster of buildings that made up the village.

Channan's sister—Nandita—when she understood that they would be left behind for a time, chattered something in a terrified voice. She clung, trembling, to Channan, her dark eyes wide.

"She is afraid soldiers will come to arrest us if we stay here," Mahindar said. "It is what happened to her husband."

"Oh, the poor thing," Juliana exclaimed. "Mahindar, please explain to her that such things do not happen in Scotland."

"I have tried," Mahindar said in a tone of long-suffering patience. "She does not understand. But we are strangers here, and she cannot know."

Juliana held out her hand to Nandita. "She can come with us. We'll squeeze. We'll take the little girl too. Come along. I'll take care of you."

Mahindar rapidly translated. Nandita didn't much like the arrangement of leaving her family behind either, and started to cry.

Mahindar's mother snapped two words at her. Nandita dropped Channan's hand and scuttled to Juliana, dragging the child with her, though silent tears continued to trickle down her face.

The child, a little girl of about three, seemed undaunted by any of this. She gave Juliana an adorable gap-toothed smile then watched with interest as the dogcart clopped into the yard.

The cart was driven by a thick-muscled lad with brilliant red hair and a face awash with freckles. He stared with unabashed curiosity at Juliana and Mahindar's family as he pulled to a halt a foot away from Elliot.

Elliot helped Juliana and Nandita into the cart's narrow seats then took the rear one, which would be the muddiest. Nandita had to let go of the little girl to adjust her wind-whipped veils with shaking hands, and Juliana reached for the child.

She happily climbed into Juliana's lap, and Juliana closed her arms around her. The little girl had dark hair and brown eyes, and her body was warm as Juliana gathered her up.

"What's her name?" Juliana asked Elliot.

Elliot closed the rear door of the dogcart. "Priti."

"Priti." Juliana tried out the name, and Priti looked up in delight. "Fitting, because she is pretty."

"Yes, she is," Elliot said in all seriousness.

The cart jerked forward. Mahindar lifted his hand in a wave while his wife and mother continued to look about at their new surroundings.

What must they think of this place? Juliana had seen photographs and paintings of India, and this isolated corner of Scotland must be vastly different for them—cold woods climbing up high hills, farmers' fields between mountains and the sea. No slow rivers, elephants, tigers, or jungle.

Priti gazed around with much more interest than did Nandita. The child's skin was not as dark as Nandita's, and strands of brown laced her black hair. Juliana wondered whether the girl's father had been European, and if that was why Nandita had agreed to leave India with her sister and Mahindar. If her European husband was dead, perhaps Nandita had no one to turn to except Channan.

But Mahindar had said that Nandita's husband had been arrested by British soldiers. Puzzling. Juliana would have to pry out the entire story later.

The dogcart bounced up a steep road paved with broken

stones. The road turned to hard earth as they climbed into the hills, the track lined with rocks, heather, and greenery. The sea stretched to the east, sun touched and breathtaking.

The red-haired lad, who said his name was Hamish McIver, talked at them over his shoulder as he drove.

"The village is down there, m'lady." Hamish swiveled in his seat, gesturing with a long whip. "Not much to it, but it does for us. There's a pub, of course, and a brewery that used to belong to old McGregor. He sold it a few years back to some English people, and Mr. McBride, of course, has bought the house. The McGregors have been in these parts six hundred years, but McGregor's skint and everyone knows it."

The cart listed into the mud on the side of the track, and Nandita made a noise of terror.

"Watch the road, lad," Elliot said in a quiet voice.

Hamish made an adjustment to the reins without concern. "My great-aunt, old Mrs. Rossmoran, lives down there." Hamish nodded at a gate that sagged, half open, between two trees. "Half out of her mind she is, with only my cousin, her granddaughter, to look after her. She'll be expecting a visit from you, m'lady, now that she knows the new laird's taken a wife."

Juliana stared at the gate as it dropped behind them. "Goodness, how does she know? We only married this morning."

Hamish grinned over his shoulder. "Came over the stationmaster's telegraph, didn't it? Stationmaster's son found me in the pub and told me, and we had a drink to your health, begging your pardon, m'lady. Someone would have gone out and told my cousin, who was doing her shopping, and *she* would have run back and told my great-aunt."

The cart gave a large heave and dropped over a bump, and Hamish swung to face front again. Nandita squealed, and Juliana cried out with her, but Priti only laughed with the joy of a child.

They'd gone through an open gate and dropped down a foot from the eroding road to a wooden bridge. Hamish clattered the cart over this, while a river rushed below them in a great freshet.

Nandita grabbed the side of the cart, her eyes round, her veils fluttering about her face. The cacophony of the wheels on the boards along with the rush of river were loud, but Nandita's voice rose above them. The young woman looked no older than the lad Hamish himself, perhaps nineteen or so, much younger than her sister, Channan. And she'd already lost a husband. No wonder she was so frightened.

"It's all right, lass," Hamish said as the cart clattered off the bridge. "No need to be afraid of the stream. There's good fishing there."

Nandita's cries ceased now that they were on solid ground again, but her eyes remained huge.

"Elliot, can you tell her?" Juliana asked. "Tell her she's safe."

The cart hit a wide hole in the road just then, rocking them all. The latch on the door beside Elliot came open, the door flapping wildly.

"Elliot!" Juliana cried. She couldn't lunge for him, because she had Priti, and Nandita was screaming again.

A less athletic man than Elliot would have been thrown free. Elliot gripped the cart, sinews standing out through his tight leather gloves. He maintained his balance, grabbed the flailing door, and closed and latched it again.

He turned to Nandita as though nothing remarkable had happened and began speaking to her, unhurried, in a language Juliana knew not one word of. Nandita listened, at last comforted by whatever he said. Her cries wound down, the road quieting as the river dropped behind them.

They came out of the woods and started downward, the road hugging the side of a steep hill. At the bottom of the hill was wide field of green, bordered by mountains marching in the distance and a sweep of sea far to the east.

At the end of the road sat the house.

It was was gigantic. And rambling. And ramshackle, crumbling all over in complete and utter disrepair.

Juliana put her hand to her throat, half rising in her seat. "Oh, Elliot," she said.

Chapter 3

Five stories of house shot straight upward from a rectangular base, the wall covered with a fantastic arrangement of crenellations, windows, arrow slits, and little round towers that swelled out from unexpected places. A mansard roof, punctuated with tiny dormer windows, rose high into the sky.

This wasn't a medieval castle. It was a wealthy man's fantasy, built to impress the neighbors—a fairy-tale castle. Except that now the fairy-tale castle was a hundred and more years old, crumbling, stained, and moss covered, windows broken, bricks from the roof littering the yard before it like gray snow. The clearing that had looked immense during the drive down the hill now revealed that it once had been twice that size, with new-growth woods invading the previously extensive park and gardens.

Hamish stopped the cart close to the house, the horse stepping carefully around the fallen stones. Elliot opened the cart's rear door and stepped down. He surveyed the colossus with his hands on his hips, a new light in his eyes. He looked . . . satisfied.

Hamish leapt to the ground from his high seat, and the mare lowered her head and started cropping grass. Elliot turned to help Juliana out of the cart, his hand warm in the cooling evening air.

Nandita took longer to climb down, fearful of putting her foot on the little step, even with Elliot to steady her. Finally Hamish reached past Elliot, slung one arm around Nandita's body, and lifted her to the ground.

Nandita stared at Hamish in complete shock and brought up her veils to cover her face.

"Hamish, lad," Elliot said in a quiet voice. "An Indian woman is not to be touched by anyone outside the family." His tone was stern, but the look he gave Hamish was almost amused. "It could be the death of you."

Hamish's eyes rounded. "Oh aye? Sorry." He looked at Nandita and said in a loud, slow voice, "Sorry, miss."

"She's widowed," Elliot said. He reached for Priti and swung her down from the cart. "Not a miss."

Hamish's voice got louder. "Beg your pardon, ma'am." He left her and climbed hastily back to the driver's seat. "I don't want to cause no one's death. Especially not mine."

He turned the dogcart and slapped the horse into a fast trot, careening back out of the clearing. The cart slipped and slid on the narrow track as Hamish drove up the hill, the wheels rocking perilously close to the edge.

The front door was not locked, and Elliot pushed it open. The vestibule beyond was empty, its once-ornate ceiling covered with cobwebs. Muddy boots, likely Hamish's, had tracked the flagstone floor as recently as today.

Elliot walked inside and opened the door on the other end of the vestibule to the house proper. The top half of the vestibule door held stained glass, but the glass was now so grimy that every pane was black.

The inside of the house was much worse than the outside. In addition to the dust hanging thickly in the air, the walls were coated with cobwebs, and the grand staircase, winding upward from the great hall, was missing spindles and stair treads. A chandelier, a giant of a thing, all its candles gone, hung from a thick chain down through the middle of the open staircase.

Doors led from the great hall to rooms both large and small. Juliana glanced inside a few, seeing that some contained furniture covered in dust sheets, others no furniture at all. The grimy windows and waning light made the house darker, and Juliana tripped.

Elliot instantly steadied her. Juliana caught his arm, finding it hard as steel under his coat. "Good heavens, Elliot, what on earth made you purchase this house?"

"Uncle McGregor needed the money," Elliot said. "I didn't mind helping him out. I stayed here off and on as a boy. Always had a fondness for the place." He looked up the staircase. "I had Hamish fix up a bedchamber for us. Shall we go find it?"

Priti darted around them for the staircase, Nandita calling out desperately to her. Elliot stepped into the little girl's path and swung her onto his shoulder, saying, "Uuup we go."

The child's English seemed to be better than Nandita's. She clapped her hands. "Yes, yes. Up!"

Elliot took the stairs to the next floor, in no way unbalanced by his burden. Juliana followed, watching anxiously, but the stairs were solid. The entire house was very . . . solid. Nandita came close behind Juliana, and thus they all ascended.

On the first floor, Elliot walked around the gallery and headed down a wide hall. This house had once been very grand, with high, ornamented ceilings and intricate carving on dadoes and cornices. Elliot started opening doors, revealing more furniture under dust sheets like crouching gray humps. The fourth door he opened finally emitted light and warmth.

A fire danced on a brick hearth of an old-fashioned fireplace, the most cheerful thing Juliana had seen since entering the house. A massive bed stood in the middle of the floor, rather than against a wall, the mattress a bit sagging, but at least it was whole, and covered with a clean quilt. The floor had no carpet nor the bed any hangings—nor did the windows have drapes—but compared to the rest of the house, the room was palatial.

Before Juliana could step inside the welcoming room, a door banged open down the hall. Nandita shrieked, and even Priti let out a squeak of alarm.

A stentorian voice roared down the passage at them. "What th' devil are ye doing in my house? Get out, the lot o' you. I have a gun, and it's loaded."

The small, wiry, elderly man who strode into the hall did indeed have a shotgun in his hands, and he stared down its long barrel at them. He had a white beard and thick sideburns, and from this hairy face blazed dark eyes with plenty of life in them.

"I'll shoot you, I tell ye. A man's allowed to defend his own household."

"Uncle McGregor," Elliot said in a loud voice. "It's Elliot. I've brought my wife."

The man lowered the gun but didn't put it down entirely. "Och, so it is you, lad. Thought it might be burglars. This is herself, then? Little Juliana St. John?" Mr. McGregor came down the hall toward them. A kilt hung on the small man's bony hips, topped with a loose shirt and a tweed coat that had seen better days. "I knew your granddad, lass. Last time I saw you was at your christening. You yelled the church down. Far too loud for a girl child, but then your mother was a madwoman."

Juliana choked back the first retort on her lips. He was

elderly, she reminded herself, with the bluntness of the old. And he did still have the shotgun. "How are you, Mr. McGregor?" she managed.

"I'm sixty-nine years old, young woman. How do you think I am?" McGregor looked past Juliana to the terrified Nandita hiding behind her. "Ye've brought your natives back with ye this time, then?"

"You'll like them," Elliot said. "My manservant is a fine cook."

"Cook, eh?" McGregor kept staring at Nandita, who was trying to shrink into Juliana. "That reminds me, I'm hungry. Where's that blasted lad with my supper?"

"Hamish has gone back to the station to fetch my manservant and the rest of his family. And our baggage, with any luck."

"He couldn't have fed me before he left? My family works this land for six hundred years, and now the laird is foisted off without a crust of bread?"

"I'll rummage for ye." Elliot put his hand on the small of Juliana's back and guided her toward the bedroom.

McGregor's outraged expression gave way to a sudden laugh. "Can't wait to be at it, can ye, lad? Lovely bride like that—I don't blame ye at all, m'boy." Chuckling, he uncocked the gun and retreated to the room from which he'd sprung. He slammed the door so hard that bits of plaster floated down from the ceiling.

Elliot remained in the hall, Priti still perched on his shoulders. "You rest," he said to Juliana. "I'll go down to the kitchen and fix Uncle McGregor some food."

"I thought you said you'd bought the estate from him," Juliana said, confused.

"Aye, but the rest of McGregor's family are dead, and he has nowhere to go. He'd never manage in one of the estate cottages on his own. I told him he had a home here until he chooses otherwise."

Juliana let out a breath. "I understand, though I wish you had warned me. I thought my heart would stop. I suppose his staff won't mind looking after us as well?"

Elliot set Priti on her feet. "Uncle McGregor has no staff. Just Hamish."

"Oh."

Juliana had been raised in a house with no less than twenty people to take care of two. This place was immense and tumbledown, and Mahindar and his family couldn't be expected to do everything themselves. Juliana saw, stretching before her, a great deal of planning and work.

Elliot turned away. Priti jumped away from Nandita, who was trying to get her to stay in the bedroom, and ran for Elliot. "Kitchen!" she shouted.

Elliot scooped her up again. "All right, Priti. Let's go explore the kitchens."

He didn't seem to mind the girl hugging him around the neck while he carried her down the hall, heading for the stairs.

Juliana closed the door and looked at the bed, a monster of a thing crouched in the middle of the room.

"Why put it there?" she asked out loud.

Nandita stared at her, not understanding. Something in the corner caught Nandita's attention, and she cried out, pointing.

Juliana followed the young woman's outstretched finger, then heard the rustling and skittering. "Ah," she said. "That's why."

A string of mice raced across the edge of the room from one corner to the other before plunging behind the skirting board. When Juliana turned back to Nandita, she found the young woman in the center of the bed, her arms curled around her knees, her colorful scarves covering her body.

One of the mice chose to make a daring dash across the carpetless floor, heading right for Juliana. Juliana shrieked as loudly as Nandita had and scrambled to the center of the bed. Nandita reached for her, the two ladies hugged each other, and Juliana began to laugh, peal after peal that wouldn't stop.

~~~

Elliot found the kitchen easily enough at the end of a long passage. An echoing room, it had been kept in some repair—the stove shiny and the coal bin stocked, the cabinets fitted with latched doors to keep the mice from the food.

The room was gloomy, the sun finally setting behind the mountains. Elliot lit candles, reflecting that he'd have to send Mahindar back to the village for kerosene and some lamps. It would be a long time before gas was laid on at the McGregor house.

Two worktables ran the length of the big kitchen, the end of one cleaned and sanded enough for using. Elliot set Priti down on one of the two stools there and began rummaging for food. He could at least take McGregor some toasted bread and cheese if nothing else. A good bottle of whiskey or a pint of ale might ease the man's temper as well.

The dismay in Juliana's voice when he'd told her there was no staff but Hamish had been sharp. When Elliot had first visited this house, he'd seen its potential, not its flaws. A place where he could retreat from the world and lick his wounds.

He could restore it himself—he didn't mind hard work. He also knew that the villagers would welcome the extra wages for helping him. Elliot had enough money to employ them all. The fortune he'd amassed in India, which had continued to build even when he'd been in prison, was now vast.

When Elliot had picked this house, he'd pictured himself sharing it with Juliana, the only woman he'd have considered marrying, even though she'd been betrothed to another.

What I asked, Elliot, was whether you *would marry me.*

The question had dangled in front of him like a lifeline. He'd clutched it, desperately hanging on, not letting go.

He'd never let go.

Elliot sliced bread with a knife that had only a few crumbs clinging to it. He handed one slice to Priti, who gnawed on it then made a face. The child didn't like English or Scottish food, but she'd have to put up with it until Mahindar could make his marvelous butter naan or delicious roti.

Mahindar and family had not accompanied Elliot on his first trip up here to buy the estate, and Elliot knew that the state of the kitchen would draw Mahindar's dismay. But Mahindar had worked miracles before.

Elliot found another knife and a square piece of yellow cheese. The stove wasn't stoked, so McGregor would have to eat his bread cold.

The knife went through the hunk of cheese at the same time Elliot heard a faint step behind him. A stealthy step of someone who did not want Elliot to know he was there. It wasn't Juliana, who smelled of rose water, nor was it Mahindar or one of his family. Nor was it McGregor, who pounded about like a troop of soldiers.

All this flashed through Elliot's thoughts before his mind went blank. Heat came rushing at him, the flat heat of summer in the dry lands. There was no shadow, no concealing cover. He had to run, run for his life, but it was all open, nowhere to go.

And someone was behind him. There was no getting away—Elliot had to turn and fight. Bile rose in his throat. He'd have to kill or die.

Elliot shouted as he spun around, grabbed the muscular intruder, shoved him across the kitchen, and plunged the knife at his attacker's throat.

Chapter 4

Elliot's captive yelled. And yelled and yelled. Over the noise came the familiar voice of Mahindar.

"No, no, no, no, sahib! You must not!"

Yes, he did. Elliot had to kill, he had to get away . . .

A big hand landed on his arm, stopping the knife. "No, sahib. You are safe now. This young one, he is a friend."

Elliot blinked. And blinked again. Mahindar's dark face swam to him through the gloom, the man's kind brown eyes full of distress.

Under Elliot's hand, a body struggled, and someone gasped for air. Elliot's vision cleared, and he found that he held young Hamish, the bread knife about to nick the skin of his throat.

Mahindar stood beside Elliot, one hand on his arm. Behind Mahindar were his mother and wife; beyond them, Priti, still chewing her bread while she looked on with round eyes.

And then the clatter of feet in the passage, and Juliana's worried voice. "Is everything all right? I heard shouting. Elliot?"

Damn, damn, and damn. Why the devil had Hamish tried to creep up on him like that?

"Sahib, you really must give me the knife."

Elliot growled. He shoved Hamish away from him and tossed the knife to an empty table, then stormed out the kitchen's back door into the gathering dusk of the Scottish evening.

~~~

Juliana remained in place for one moment, then she started for the open door. "Elliot . . ."

Mahindar stepped in her way. "It is best to let him go, memsahib. One never knows what he might do when he is like this."

"But what is the matter? Hamish, what did you do?"

"Nothin'!" Hamish adjusted the collar of his shirt, his eyes still huge. "I didn't do nothin', promise ye, m'lady. I came in same as always. Then I saw Himself, and I thought, Mr. McBride, he's a rich man and a gentleman, and I work for him now. So maybe I should walk a bit quieter than I usually do. Mr. McGregor says I'm like a drum brigade. I was tryin' t' be dec'rous."

"He does not like anyone walking softly behind him," Mahindar said. "Better you be a drum brigade."

"Why doesn't he?" Juliana asked. "Mahindar, what is the matter? Please, tell me."

Mahindar looked sad. "The sahib is very ill. He is much, much better now, but when we found him after he escaped his jail, he was a raving madman. We cared for him for a long time before he was able to speak to us and tell us what happened. The poor man went through a great ordeal. He is very strong, and very brave."

Juliana looked past Mahindar to the overgrown path outside the open back door, night at last falling. "Will he be all right?"

"Yes, indeed. The best thing for him is to walk about by himself. He will come back, as you British say, right as rain."

"You'll make certain?" Juliana asked.

"Yes, memsahib. I will do that. Now, my wife will take you up and put you to bed. Nandita, when she is terrified, is useless, but I will make her and Priti go to sleep. Things will be well in the morning."

Juliana was not certain they would be, but she consented to walk back upstairs with Channan, who made her way robustly through the dark and dirty house. Mahindar's mother—Komal—came behind, saying nothing but looking about her with the same interest as she had all day.

They found Nandita still in the middle of the bed, hugging herself. After a few words from Komal, Nandita scrambled off the bed and scuttled from the room. Juliana heard Mahindar calling Nandita from downstairs, and Nandita's running footsteps, heading toward him.

Channan went at once to Juliana's valise and began unpacking with competence. She must be used to being a lady's maid, Juliana decided, because she knew which garments to hang in the heavy armoire and which to fold away into the drawers of the high chest.

Komal walked around the room looking things over. She pushed back the silk covering on her head, showing that her hair was gray mixed with black. Channan's hair was jet-black, and her face was plump and unlined.

Channan finished putting away Juliana's clothes and came to unbutton her dress. Komal ignored them to approach the bed. She put her palms on the mattress, smoothing it, then she said something to Channan and laughed.

Channan laughed as well, while Juliana stood between

them, bewildered. "She says you have much luck," Channan said. "A husband so rich and handsome. The sahib is a good catch."

Juliana blushed, which made both women laugh again. Komal brushed her hands over the mattress and talked at some length. Channan nodded and answered, then turned back to Juliana.

"She says she'll give you a charm. So you have many sons."

Juliana thought about Elliot wandering about the McGregor grounds in the dark, and wondered if she would have the opportunity to have sons at all. Channan must have understood her expression, because she said, "Do not worry. The sahib will be well. My husband takes care of him."

Elliot still had not returned when Channan tucked Juliana up in bed in a clean night rail, with a wrapped brick to warm the sheets. Channan and Komal made quite a lot of noise quieting each other, then they finally slipped out of the room, leaving Juliana alone.

On her wedding night.

The sky darkened, the open windows cooling the summer air. The house grew quiet, the walls thick enough that sound didn't carry from the floors below. Outside, the silence was broken by frogs croaking frantically for mates and wind sighing in the trees. The quiet here, when Juliana was used to the noise of the city, was deafening.

The moon rose, its silver disk broken by the trees, and shone on the bed where Juliana lay waiting. And still, Elliot did not come.

Well past midnight, Elliot heard a branch break in the woods behind him. This was followed by a loud rustling and the voice of Mahindar. "Do not worry, sahib. It is me."

Elliot stood atop a rock that overlooked the rushing river below. Moonlight glittered on the water's surface and also on the spires of his new house, a false castle built on the the site of an ancient one.

Mahindar slipped and slid on the path, flailing for balance. Elliot put out a hand and pulled the man up onto solid rock beside him.

Of course Mahindar would come to find him. The man had made it his task in life to look after Elliot, ever since Elliot had taken Mahindar away from another planter who'd hired him as a valet then treated him little better than a slave. Elliot had visited the planter one day and found him beating Mahindar.

The planter had apologized—to Elliot—for Mahindar's behavior, and had gone on about Mahindar's shortcomings, until Elliot had said, "If you don't like him, he can come to work for me." The planter had been surprised then looked grateful. Sikhs, the planter had said, couldn't be taught proper humility, and he'd been a fool to take one on.

Kindly Mahindar had looked upon Elliot as his savior forever after that.

Mahindar peered up at him now. "You are all right, sahib?"

"Better. How is the lad?"

"Oh, you scared the piss out of him, no mistake. But he will recover."

"And Mrs. McBride?"

"Put to bed. My wife looked in on her before I came out, and she is sleeping, as you say, like a baby."

"Good." Elliot couldn't forget the look on Juliana's face when she'd walked into the kitchen and seen him with his knife at Hamish's throat. Her bewilderment had turned into astonishment and then worry. But not fear. Juliana wasn't afraid of him.

"Will you join her, sahib?" Mahindar asked.

He sounded eager. But then, Mahindar enjoyed weddings and marriages and the possibility of children. He and his wife had borne five sons, all of whom had married and now started families of their own. Mahindar liked to take care of people, which was why he'd brought his mother and Nandita, Channan's young sister from her father's second marriage, to Scotland with him. Mahindar had saved Elliot's life and believed it his duty to make sure Elliot was well so that his effort hadn't been in vain.

"You will have to share her bed in any case," Mahindar said. "There is no other."

Elliot jumped down from the big rock, helped Mahindar scramble down, and started along the path to the house.

When they reached Castle McGregor, all was silent within. Hamish and Mahindar's family must have gone to their beds.

Mahindar stopped Elliot before he could make his way out of the kitchen. "You must not go to her like that, sahib. You must be presentable."

He had a point. Elliot was dusted with soot from the train journey, and his climb in the woods had rendered him muddy. Mahindar pumped water into the kitchen sink—clean from a well—and instructed Elliot to strip to his kilt.

The water was freezing. Mahindar dunked Elliot's head all the way in, using the cake of soap that he'd brought from Edinburgh to scrub Elliot's hair and body clean. Mahindar had bought glycerin and rosewater soap, which had made Elliot's brothers and sister laugh. At least it got him clean, if smelling a bit like a lady's boudoir.

Mahindar brought out Elliot's thick dressing gown and the Indian silk drawers in which Elliot usually slept. Elliot donned these and climbed the stairs, taking a candle himself, refusing Mahindar's offer to light the way.

The candlelight wavered on the Gothic arches in the hall, making the place cavernous, decorative stone finials hanging like strange stalactites. As a boy, Elliot had felt a tingle of fear walking in this place, but it was peaceful to him now. This was nothing more than an old house, through which had passed its share of families—births, marriages, deaths, laughter, sorrow, lovemaking. No terror, horror, or fear so deadly it made a man wrap up in himself and weep.

Elliot pushed open the door of the bedchamber, at the same time blowing out the candle. Moonlight spilled through the unshuttered window, a beam spreading over the bed in the middle of the room.

Juliana lay on her back in the bed, the covers pulled up to her chin, but she wasn't asleep. Elliot heard the quick breath that told him she was wide awake, never mind how tightly she'd closed her eyes.

He deposited the candlestick on the nearest table and went to the bed. Juliana lay like a princess in a storybook, waiting for the prince to waken her with a kiss.

Elliot thought of the heady taste of her lips when he'd kissed her at the altar. Her skin had been damp with warmth and agitation, the taste of her like honey on his tongue.

He rested his hand on the bedpost, leaned down, and brushed a soft kiss to the dimple at the corner of her mouth.

Juliana's eyes flew open. She looked at him with no trace of sleep in her eyes. "Is young Hamish all right?"

Elliot straightened up, his hand still on the bedpost. "He will be."

"I hope he wasn't too frightened."

"He's recovered." Elliot tried to move from his fixed stance and found he couldn't.

Juliana's color deepened, and she cleared her throat. "Are you coming to bed, Elliot?"

Her high-necked nightgown was prim, but this was the first time Elliot had seen her without the barricade of stays, bustles, skirts, and tightly buttoned bodices.

Elliot finally let go of the bedpost to untie his dressing gown and let it fall from him. He watched her gaze go to his bare torso, then drop to the silk drawers that rode low on his hips, a drawstring holding them closed. The under-breeches reached his calves, leaving the rest of his legs bare.

"An unusual garment," she said, her voice soft.

"They're Indian. I prefer them to English clothes."

"Do you? Why?"

"Much more comfortable." The cool air from the window touched his skin. "More practical in a hot climate."

"I can imagine."

Elliot remained rigidly beside the bed. He wanted her with a desire so hard it gripped him, but still he couldn't move.

Juliana cleared her throat again. "It's been quite a day, hasn't it? To think, tonight I was to a have been in a hotel in Edinburgh, with . . ."

She pressed her hand to her mouth and squeezed her eyes shut. Moonlight glittered on the tears that slid down her cheeks.

"With . . ." Her voice caught on a sob.

With Grant Barclay, damn him, the blithering fool who'd decided to improve himself with piano lessons. Elliot wanted to strangle the man, first for trying to steal Juliana from him, then for making her cry about him while she lay in Elliot's bed.

And Elliot knew how to. Exactly how to get a man's throat under his hands, where to press to cut off the air, to make sure Grant Barclay never breathed again . . .

Juliana tried to wipe away her tears. Elliot unfroze, lifted the covers, and swarmed into the bed beside her.

Chapter 5

Juliana hadn't meant to cry, but she'd suddenly realized that she could be lying in a hotel bed with Grant tonight, instead of far from home in a run-down fairy-tale castle next to the strong warmth of Elliot McBride. What a lucky, blessed escape.

Elliot's lips touched her cheeks, kisses taking away the tears.

"I'm sorry," she whispered.

His kisses moved to her lips. Strong, sure kisses, brushing the pad of her lower lip, tracing the curve of the upper. It was warm in the close room, warmer under the covers, and Elliot's body in the bed drew sweat.

He licked the perspiration from beneath her lip, scraping her hair back with a strong hand. Something primal beat through Juliana's body, erasing all Gemma's instructions for her first coupling. This was to have been a dutiful night with Mr. Barclay—now she was with Elliot, the man she'd loved from girlhood and never dreamed she'd be with.

His lips caressed hers open, tongue sweeping into her mouth. Elliot closed his eyes as he kissed her, cradling her head with fingers, thumb caressing her temple.

The button at the top of her nightgown loosened, the placket parting. Elliot slid his hand inside, moving across her damp skin to close over her breast. Juliana arched to meet the cup of his hand, all the while kissing him, their lips parting and touching.

Elliot swept his tongue inside her mouth again, more insistent this time. He nudged her into response, making her lick across the warm friction of his tongue.

A lover's kiss. Elliot McBride, her lover.

He closed his callused hand around her breast, caressing, kneading. Two fingers caught her nipple between them and gave it a little tug. Sensations Juliana had never experienced before spiraled around the areola, the point rising, hardening.

She couldn't breathe. The bed was too warm, Elliot's mouth on hers pressing her down into it. He tugged her nipple, building the sensations to fire.

Fire built from there to her heart. The collar of the nightgown grew wet with her perspiration, and she was going to die.

Juliana pushed against him. Elliot's tongue filled her mouth, and she couldn't speak. She tried to close her lips, but he wouldn't let her.

She pushed again, both hands on his chest. Elliot at last broke the kiss, his lips hovering close to hers.

His half-closed eyes were dark in the moonlight, the silver gray glinting through. One droplet of sweat trickled down his throat.

"I can't breathe," Juliana whispered.

Elliot said nothing. He took his warm, wonderful hand from inside her nightgown, unbuttoned the rest of her placket, and loosened and opened the nightgown to her waist.

Sliding down her body, Elliot lowered his head and

closed his mouth over the breast he'd stroked to life with his hand.

Breath rushed into her lungs. Here was the air she missed, but now she had too much of it. Heat raced down her body, incandescent at the beautiful point of Elliot's mouth on her breast.

He suckled her, eyes closed in concentration. He gently squeezed her breast with his callused fingers to make the nipple rise higher, then pursed his mouth to suck and tease, nibble and tug.

Juliana squirmed under him, her heart pounding. Between her legs was a point of white-hot fire, a yearning to rub that place against him.

"Elliot, what are you doing to me?"

Elliot didn't stop to answer. His mouth moved more insistently, making her ache, the opening between her legs widening and heating.

"I need . . ." Juliana bit back the words. She had no idea what she needed.

Elliot released her breast and played the tip of his tongue over the nipple. Juliana rose to him, seeking his mouth, but he lifted away, and she made a noise of disappointment.

But then Elliot slid his hand down her body to glide two fingers between her legs. Juliana sucked in a breath, her eyes widening as he touched her hottest place.

As Elliot sank his fingers into her moisture, he closed his eyes again and drew a long breath. He could scent her longing for him, honey in the darkness.

In this bed, enclosed in her heat, Elliot was safe. The empty blackness, the cold, the stifling airlessness, were gone. They couldn't touch him here. Juliana was all that was safety, light, and warmth.

She was also a woman longing for the touch of a man, and not understanding her longing. Elliot would teach her. Whether it took a year or ten years, he'd teach her everything.

He gently thrust a finger into her. Juliana bucked against Elliot's hand, and he closed his palm over the berry that was tightening with her need.

"What are you . . . ?" Juliana's words ended on a sob.

"Getting you ready." Elliot didn't know what endearments women liked, or how to soothe her. He only knew how to touch her, her body and his communicating in silence.

Her wiry hair curled against his hand, the depths of her hot and moist. She'd never done this before—he knew by the way she started in surprise when he began stroking her. This was a new sensation for Juliana, and it was new to Elliot, because it was *her*.

I've waited for you all my life.

In the darkness and through the hunger, he'd dreamed of her, but his dreams had been incomplete. Elliot hadn't known the full scent of her, the warmth of her skin, the feel of her beneath him.

He withdrew his fingers and touched them to his tongue. He hadn't known the taste of her either. Sweet nectar. He needed more.

Elliot licked between her breasts, tasting salt, then he kissed his way down her belly, yanked open the nightgown the rest of the way, and pressed a burning kiss to the join of her legs.

As she drew in a sharp breath, he tasted her, licking where he'd touched, his tongue entering where his finger had.

Beautiful, sweet honey. Elliot licked and drank, the tightness in his body easing.

Feast on her, drink of her. *If I have enough of her, I will never be afraid again.*

Juliana's hands went to his hair, furrowing as he licked. Her little cries drove him wild. His body started to move, hips to roll with the rhythm of his tasting, his hardness digging into the mattress.

"Elliot!"

As her cry rang out, he felt the little pulses in her sheath, the female need, the headiest pleasure of all.

She was a virgin, and Elliot knew it would hurt going in. But she was wet and open, her body already releasing.

Elliot would love to lie here and lick her while she came into his mouth, then bring her to readiness again. And again. All night.

But his own body cried out for release, his cock so tight it ached. Elliot took his mouth from her beautiful place, untied and wriggled out of his silken breeches, and slid up her body.

He had one instant of enjoying the softness of her under him, and then he thrust inside her.

Her eyes widened, beautiful Juliana, her cry turning almost to a wail. But not in pain. She closed over him, wanting him, her passage so slick that the barrier vanished with one push.

Crazed with need, Elliot took one, two, three strokes inside her, before his seed released, and his shouts mixed with hers.

He kept pumping, hips moving, needing her, unable to have enough of her. Wind slapped at the window, sending the old casement banging open, and a gust of wind poured over the bed.

It cooled Elliot's skin and made Juliana shiver. Elliot's thrusts slowed, and he curved protectively over her.

Always protect her. Juliana was his. She'd stood in the church today and declared that she belonged to him. Forever.

～～

The sun rose early in high summer this far into the Highlands. Juliana opened her eyes as sunshine poured in through the eastern window and brushed the body of her husband beside her.

Juliana felt odd—exhausted and exhilarated, and yet at

the same time pliant and relaxed. Gemma had explained what a woman was expected to do on her wedding night— lie back, breathe deeply, and remain calm.

She'd not mentioned a man licking, exploring, touching, and drinking. Gemma had said that the first time hurt. And it had, but in a wild, need-filled way that hadn't been pain at all.

And yet, Juliana was sore, and she knew without doubt that she could no longer be called a maiden.

Elliot slept facedown next to her, his cheek crushed against the mattress, nowhere near a pillow. His long legs poured out the bottom of the bed, the covers thrown half-way off in his sleep.

His hair was half folded, half sticking up, the light brown burnished with gold from the sun. His lashes were golden too, resting against a face that had been Scottish fair before tropical sun had burned it brown.

One broad hand lay near his face, his bent arm showing her thick muscles that came from hard work. A design had been inked on his right bicep, a flowing vine that wrapped all the way around his arm.

Juliana stared at the tattoo, fascinated. She'd never seen anything like it. She'd heard of sailors being tattooed on their voyages to faraway places but had never seen a gentle-man with one.

Then again, Juliana had never seen a man without his coat, waistcoat, shirt, high collar, and cravat, not even her own father. Athletes stripped to shirtsleeves or short sleeves to run, row, or play ball games, or so she'd heard tell, but Juliana had never attended a sporting exhibition. Quite a lot of gentlemen might have tattoos in places a lady would never see.

Part of Elliot's backside was exposed, his knee hooked over the quilt. Juliana studied his tight hip, letting her gaze move to the wiry hair that traced down his leg.

He was a well-formed man. God had quite nicely put him together.

Elliot had scars on his back, random white lines from long cuts, similar to those on his face. He'd hurt, those scars told her; he'd bled. The cuts had been made deliberately, by someone who'd wanted to hurt him.

Juliana put out her finger and traced one of the scars that snaked to his shoulder. The skin was smooth where it had been cut, and she glided her touch over it, then down his arm to the delicate leaves of the tattoo.

She expected Elliot to wake at her touch. He'd open his gray eyes and smile at her, and perhaps—her heart beat faster—he would roll her onto her back and continue kissing and tasting her. The marriage bed was a fine place indeed.

Elliot didn't stir. Not to be surprised—yesterday had been excessive.

Juliana leaned down and pressed a kiss to the vine on his arm, then another, and another. Her hair tumbled forward, loosened from its braid, brushing Elliot's back, and still he did not wake.

Juliana lifted her hair out of the way, leaned to Elliot's cheek, and kissed it. Then his lips.

She wanted him to open his eyes, to smile, as he had when he'd come to Juliana's debut ball and stolen a kiss from her on the terrace. That young Elliot had been laughing, teasing, a man with whom she'd talked and danced for hours.

This Elliot was quiet, his smiles gone, with a tattoo on his arm and knife scars on his face and back. She kissed the scars.

Elliot still didn't move. Juliana sat up and looked at him.

The covers fell from her bare body. Elliot slept on, his breathing quiet and shallow, no snoring. *All* men snored, Gemma had assured her.

"Elliot?" Juliana gently shook him. His skin was hot, his body limp, and he didn't wake.

"Elliot." Her alarm grew. He might be a sound sleeper, yes, but she'd feel better if he opened his eyes and growled at her for waking him.

Her father had always done that when startled from his nap—he'd insist he hadn't been asleep at all, never mind his head was thrown back on his office chair, his mouth open, his spectacles askew.

Elliot did nothing so amusing. His body moved with her shaking, but he never opened his eyes, never stirred.

Juliana kicked off the covers, found her nightgown and slid it on, buttoning it with shaking fingers. Channan had hung her thick dressing gown over the chair, and she slipped this on too and looked for a bellpull. Part of one did hang on the wall, but it had been chewed through by the mice, and Juliana couldn't reach the attached half of it to ring for anyone.

First thing that was fixed tomorrow . . . no, today—the bellpulls.

Juliana went out into the hall to find the house deathly silent. She had no idea where Mahindar and his family had found to sleep, no idea whether Hamish lived in or trotted home to his mother every night. Shouting might only bring Mr. McGregor flying out of his room with his shotgun again.

She hurried down the hall toward the large staircase. The gallery was dark, the only light coming from windows in the hall below. The chandelier hung dark and empty. Second thing to repair—the lamps.

As Juliana started down the stairs, a door banged somewhere in the bottom of the house, and red-haired Hamish strode into the hall. He looked up the stairs, gave a startled yell, and dropped the armload of wood he'd been carrying. It clattered loudly to the floor, and his voice rose over it.

"Haunt! Banshee!"

"Hamish," Juliana said sharply. "Don't be silly. It's me."

Hamish pointed at her with a shaking finger. "How do I know you're really the missus? Demons wile and beguile."

"Do stop that. Where is Mahindar?"

Hamish gulped, but lowered his hand. "Downstairs. Are ye sure ye're not a ghost, m'lady?"

"Quite certain. I will change my dressing gown from white to purple and red striped if it will make you feel better. Now, will you please fetch Mahindar? Tell him I'm sorry to disturb his rest, but Mr. McBride needs him."

Hamish gave her a salute. "Right, m'lady."

He charged off, jumping over the wood he'd scattered. Before Juliana could ascend again, Mahindar came rushing out of the back of the house, followed by his wife and mother.

A door banged above, and Mr. McGregor stomped out, sure enough, with his shotgun. "Can't a man get peace in his own house? Hamish, lad, what ails ye?"

"It's all right, Mr. McGregor," Juliana called.

McGregor tramped his way to the gallery and peered over the railing. "Why is there a woodpile all over the floor? And who is *that*?" McGregor brought his shotgun down, aiming at Mahindar. "Good God, it's savages from Khartoum."

Mahindar put out his arms and stepped in front of the ladies, trying to protect them. Juliana rushed back to the top of the stairs.

"No, Mr. McGregor. They're Mr. McBride's servants. From India."

"Even worse. Thuggees. I know about them. They strangle you when you're not looking."

Juliana walked swiftly down the landing to him. "They're friends. Put away that gun."

To her relief, McGregor lowered the butt of the gun to the railing, the barrel pointing upward, away from all human beings. "Don't patronize me, lass. I've been handling a gun, man and boy, these nearly seventy years . . ."

The last of his words were lost in a bang and a roar. The shotgun blast hit the ceiling high above the gallery. Juliana screamed, as did Mahindar and family, and Hamish.

Plaster, dust, and mud slammed to the floor below, and the huge chandelier started to sway . . .

Chapter 6

Juliana held her breath as the chandelier went back and forth, back and forth, like the giant pendulum in the terrifying story by the American Mr. Poe. The others watched it with her, frozen in place as they tracked the chandelier's path.

The chain groaned against the ceiling, but slowly, slowly, the giant chandelier eased back to its resting place.

Juliana let out her breath and heard McGregor's loud exhale at the same time. She turned to him and held out her hand.

"Give me that gun, *if* you please, Mr. McGregor."

McGregor, looking sheepish and defiant at the same time, eased his finger from the trigger and handed her the weapon. Juliana broke open the gun with the competence her father's gillie had taught her and held it safely over her arm.

She opened her mouth to tell Mr. McGregor to dress himself, for heaven's sake, when Mahindar's mother came charging up the stairs, shouting before she hit the first step. Komal held her fluttering silks in one hand, and raised the other, not at Juliana, but at McGregor. She bore down on him, her raised hand moving back and forth like an angry bird while she railed at him in rapid speech.

McGregor retreated several steps, arms high in defense. "Don't ye be screechin' at me, woman. A man has a right to defend his own home."

Komal continued to yell, her meaning clear even if Juliana didn't understand her words—*Get back to bed, you daft old man, before you shoot the house down.*

McGregor turned and ran, Komal chasing him, her voice growing louder as she followed him down the hall. Mahindar called to her from below, but his voice was faint, nervous, and Komal didn't pay the slightest attention.

"Mahindar," Juliana said over the railing. "I can't wake Mr. McBride. Can you help?"

Mahindar stopped pleading with his mother and came upstairs, Channan with him. Channan left him at the head of the stairs and went after her mother-in-law and Mr. McGregor, a determined look on her face.

Juliana led Mahindar back to the bedchamber. Surely they'd find Elliot on his feet, demanding to know what all the noise had been about. But when Juliana opened the door, Elliot still lay on his side, sleeping his deep sleep.

The look on Mahindar's face renewed her alarm. "Mahindar, what is wrong with him?"

"I hoped, I so hoped . . ." Mahindar trailed off as he approached the bed. "Be careful, memsahib. Sometimes he does this, sleeps like a dead man for hours and hours. But when he comes awake, he can be violent. He doesn't know where he is, and thinks I am his jailer."

"But he's safe now. He knows that."

"Yes, yes, when he is awake and fine, he understands this." Mahindar touched his forehead. "But inside his head, sometimes he is still confused. You must understand—he was left alone in the dark for a long, long time. Sometimes they fed him, sometimes they didn't bother, sometimes they left him alone, sometimes they beat him for nothing." Mahindar looked sad. "I know they must have done much more to him, but that is all he has told me."

Juliana looked at Elliot, lying so quietly on the bed, his chest barely moving with his breath. His body was whole, only the scars on his back and face attesting to his ordeal. But perhaps healing outside and healing inside were two different things.

How did a man face such horrors and then return home to normal life? He'd never be the same, would he? How did he speak with people who'd never known his horror, people who'd lived in comfort and safety all their lives, who could never understand?

Such a man did what Elliot did. He kept to himself, bought a run-down house in a remote corner of the High-lands, and lost himself in the depths of sleep.

"What do I do?" Juliana's question came out a whisper.

Mahindar, with his thickset body and intelligent eyes, gave her a look of vast sorrow. "I do not know, memsahib. I have tried everything to heal him. I hoped that when he came here to this country he loved so much, he would get better. Maybe now, that he is married to you, he will."

Juliana drew her dressing gown more tightly about her and looked at her husband, her marriage one day old. "I barely know him, Mahindar. Not this Elliot."

The Elliot of her youth, who'd helped her retrieve a kite from a tree, who'd smiled in triumph when she'd kissed his cheek, had vanished into the past. This Elliot was hard, marked with scars, and had been through more than any man should face. The world expected him to shrug it off, to keep a stiff upper lip, to ignore his pain, but how could he, in truth?

She'd have to get to know him all over again before she could even hope to understand him.

"I will help you, memsahib," Mahindar said, with a quietness like a deep river. "You and I, we will bring him back together."

~~~~~

"Ah, you are awake at last." A voice swam out of the darkness to Elliot. "Thank all the gods. Your sister, she is here."

Elliot peeled open his eyes to see a face hovering mere inches above him. He experienced a moment of panic— *What now? What now? Couldn't they leave him alone?*

Then he realized that it was Mahindar's kind and worried countenance studying him, thick brows drawn together under his white turban, the man's beard tucked neatly inside his tunic.

"Damn it, Mahindar."

Mahindar's distress did not abate. "Lady Cameron has come to visit the memsahib. Your sister-in-law, she is here too, and she insists she see you."

Rona and Ainsley. Elliot's redoubtable sister-in-law and pretty, lively sister. Not what a man needed to face when he'd awakened feeling like he had a three-day hangover.

Elliot rubbed his face, finding it full of bristles. He must have been asleep for a long time. Another spell must have taken him, leaving him no idea how long he'd lain in darkness.

And where the hell was he? He squinted at the bedroom empty of drapes and filled with large, square furniture, the bed in the middle of the floor. "Is this McGregor's place? How did we get here?" Only Great-uncle McGregor's house could look solid and falling apart at the same time.

The last time Elliot had come here, to purchase the house, he'd bunked down in the warm kitchen—much more comfortable.

Mahindar looked troubled. "Do you not remember? Yesterday, you were married."

Yesterday was a blank; all days for a long time had been a blank . . . except . . .

"Married? What the devil are you talking about? Tell me you brought me whiskey."

"No, indeed. Her ladyship, your sister, forbade it. She said I was to get you up and down to the drawing room by any means necessary, except whiskey."

"Ainsley said that?" Elliot wanted to laugh. He'd always been close to his little sister, who knew him in ways no one else ever could. That was the old Elliot, though. No one knew the Elliot of now.

Elliot threw back the covers. He was naked, but Mahindar neither noticed nor cared. "Draw me a bath. I'm not fit to be seen by decent women. Not even my resilient sisters."

As Mahindar bustled around preparing the bath with ewers of steaming water, Elliot fought his way from the dense fog of his sleep. Mahindar was speaking, and Elliot struggled to focus on his words.

"I have put them in the morning room with the memsahib," Mahindar said, "and there they wait."

"The memsahib?"

Mahindar looked up, the water dribbling, unheeded, to the floor. "Yes, the memsahib," he said in careful tones. "Until yesterday she was called Miss Sinj."

Mahindar, who'd worked for Britons all his life, prided himself on getting British titles correct. He did have some difficulty pronouncing the names, however—*and who can blame him? Some are bloody impossible.*

Elliot rubbed his face again. "Miss Sinj? I've never heard of anyone called Sinj . . ." His eyes slammed open, letting in too much light. He rolled out of the high bed, landing hard on his bare feet, and the room spun.

"You mean Miss *St. John?*"

"Of course."

"Bloody hell, and damn everything."

Snatches of yesterday came to him—Juliana plopping down on his lap in a billow of white, her hopeful smile, her beautiful blue eyes.

The memory of her skin under his fingertips, the kiss he'd pressed to her palm. Elliot had drawn her warmth into him, which he'd clung to as though he hadn't felt warmth in years. He'd longed to kiss her lips there in the chapel, but couldn't bring himself to with a mouth sour with whiskey.

Then he remembered standing at the front of a packed church, almost panicking at the press of bodies, all those eyes staring at him as he promised to be a good and true husband to Juliana St. John.

Bits and pieces came to him of the journey here, too slow when all he'd wanted was to be with Juliana. Then they'd been at the run-down house, Elliot coming to himself with his knife at the throat of the terrified Hamish, Juliana's voice cutting through the darkness.

His mind gave him back the next thing, the bliss of Juliana's heat, her touch, the scent of her surrounding him. A moment, that was all, of drowning in her and forgetting *everything*.

But the darkness had decided to rob him of even that. It wanted to take Juliana away from him, snatch back peace as Elliot reached for it.

No. I need this.

He plunged into the bath, letting it bite his flesh and the scars on his back. Mahindar knew better than to try to wash Elliot or help him into or out of the tub. Elliot soaped himself down, getting plenty of water on the floor, then curbed his impatience to lie back and let Mahindar shave him.

Mahindar finished as quickly as he could, unhappy he couldn't wrap Elliot's face in a hot towel and perhaps finish with a massage. Elliot ignored the man's complaints, rubbed himself dry, and dressed.

Hamish was clattering around the hall below, making a great deal of noise when Elliot descended, but Elliot couldn't stop to decide what he was doing. He noticed that a fist-sized hole had been punched into the lacy stonework of the ceiling, only a few inches from the big chandelier.

Elliot barreled into the morning room to find three elegant ladies in the act of lifting teacups. A clock somewhere in the house chimed three. Ainsley smiled at him, and Rona, his prim sister-in-law, gave him a look of appraisal.

Juliana studied Elliot over the rim of her cup, then she set the cup back down, her eyes full of concern.

Did he look that much like hell? He should have glanced into a mirror, but the bedchamber had none, and Elliot had learned to avoid mirrors. He trusted Mahindar to make sure his clothes were straight but never bothered anymore with anything beyond that.

"Here you are, Elliot," Ainsley said, her voice overly bright.

"Yes, here I am. Where else would I be?"

He heard the growl come out of his mouth, but he couldn't stop it. Ainsley, his tomboy sister, was resplendent in some creation of cloth that subtly changed hue when she moved. Rona, plump and regal, wore a dark dress she'd assumed befitted her age of fifty-odd, with a cap of ruffles, bows, and floating lacy bits. All his life, Elliot had seen Rona in some kind of cap—plain ones and Sunday best, caps for calls and for receiving calls, for visiting one's doctor and for shopping. Whenever he thought of Rona, his first vision was of caps.

He took all this in swiftly, then observations were shoved to one side of the room, and the only being who existed was Juliana.

Her lawn gown was cream colored with thin black piping outlining her bodice, placket, collar, and cuffs, the skirt deeply ruffled down the front. A high collar framed her chin, softening her face and emphasizing the slight dimple in the left corner of her mouth. She'd woven a cream-colored ribbon through the dark red of her hair, little ringlets left to float from her forehead and the back of her neck.

She resembled the china figurines he'd seen in shops throughout Europe, elegant ladies frozen forever in time, their porcelain hands plucking at swirling porcelain skirts.

Except that Juliana didn't have the coldness of porcelain—she was warm flesh, breath, and life.

She watched him with blue eyes that reminded him of cornflowers, or maybe the sky in springtime. Only the women of Scotland had eyes that color. Juliana was of this place, Elliot's home.

"Elliot," Juliana said. Her sweet voice rushed at him. "Rona has come for the rings."

Rings. Elliot looked at his left hand, which sported a thick gold band. He remembered pushing Juliana's ring onto her hand, telling her he plighted her his troth. His truth, his fidelity.

As though he could conceive of touching any woman but her. Ever. For any reason.

"I presume," Ainsley broke in, still speaking in that overly cheerful sickroom voice, "that you thought to order rings for yourself."

He had. He now remembered telling Mahindar, before going into the church to wait for Juliana, to send to the family's jewelers for rings to be made. Remembered Patrick, his kindhearted brother, pulling Elliot aside and closing into his hand two cool rings, which had not left the fingers of Patrick and Rona since their marriage thirty years ago.

"It's taken care of," Elliot said. He tugged the wedding band from his finger, went to Rona, dropped it into her hand, and pressed her fingers closed around it. "Thank you."

Rona's eyes shone with brief tears, then she tucked the ring into a little pouch. It clinked against another, and Elliot saw that Juliana's finger was already bare.

"We thank you," Juliana said, pouring out a fourth cup of tea. "It was kind of you."

"Entirely logical," Rona said, pretending the tears had

never manifested. "Nothing else to be done. Elliot, *what* are you going to do with this awful house?"

Elliot watched Juliana pour his tea, her hands competently balancing the cup on the saucer, steadying it perfectly under the stream of hot liquid. She set the fat teapot back on the tray without wincing from its weight and lifted the dainty silver tongs from the sugar bowl.

Here she faltered—a woman ought to know what her husband took in his tea, but Juliana and Elliot had never had tea together. At least, not since they'd both been fourteen.

Rona leaned forward and whispered, "One lump, dear."

"Actually, I prefer it with no sugar at all now." Elliot reached for the cup in Juliana's hand.

She held the saucer so daintily that his big fingers were in no danger of touching hers. He changed that by folding his hand over hers and slipping the cup and saucer out of her grasp.

Juliana's lips parted, and heat swam in her eyes. It matched what was in his blood. The entirety of last night was returning with a vengeance.

Elliot needed to sit down—next to her. But Juliana was perched on the front edge of a narrow armchair, her bustle filling the rest of the seat. There was a perfectly good love seat in the room, but that was occupied by Rona and Ainsley, sitting side by side. Two more chairs and an ottoman completed the circle around the tea table, the rest of the furniture in the room covered with dust sheets.

Elliot hooked his leather-shod foot around the ottoman and dragged it close to Juliana's chair. He sat down on it, settling his kilt, his knee firmly pressing Juliana's, and balanced the delicate cup and saucer in his big hand.

Ainsley and Rona watched him intently, but Elliot was only aware of Juliana, her warmth, her nearness, the rightness of her.

"Where did you dig these up?" Elliot said, lifting his cup

to study it. The porcelain was fine and almost paper-thin, the flowers painted on it with a skilled hand. These teacups had been turned out in some factory in England or Germany at great expense. "They were never in Uncle McGregor's crockery cupboard."

"A wedding gift," Juliana said. "Lovely pieces, do you not think?"

Elliot took a sip of tea, which wasn't bad, but it needed more whiskey. He turned his head so he could see Juliana, nothing else. "I thought you were returning the gifts."

"She is," Ainsley said. "But this is a wedding gift from *me*, so it's entirely relevant. And you have no need to worry about the others, Juliana. Rona and I and your stepmama are taking care of sending back the gifts with necessary letters of explanation. No need for you to hie back to Edinburgh for that."

"But I ought," Juliana said. "It's kind of you, but I should truly be there to help, not to mention pack the rest of my things. Gemma must be going mad with it all. If you stay the night here, I can take the train back with you tomorrow."

"No." The word was so loud that the three women froze, teacups raised, three pairs of feminine eyes widening at the masculine power of Elliot's voice.

Elliot moved his hand to Juliana's thigh, closing over it and clamping down before he could stop himself. "Juliana can't leave."

"What?" Ainsley asked, the lightness in her voice forced. "Never?"

Chapter 7

Elliot tried to soften his grip on Juliana and couldn't. "No," he said.

Juliana's gaze was for Elliot alone, but she didn't look at him in fear. More in surprise, and with a sparkle in her eyes that might be defiance.

"Elliot has a point," Juliana said to Ainsley. "There is much to be done in the house. I certainly wish to be here for the work, if you take my meaning."

Both his sister and sister-in-law nodded, still watching Elliot, as though they reached for lines they'd rehearsed. "Quite understandable," Rona said. "There must be someone with sense to organize it all."

Ainsley's eyes twinkled. "I believe there is a bit more to it than that, Rona. Remember what it was to be a newlywed?"

"Ah yes." Prim Rona softened into a smile. She and Patrick had always doted on each other, and Ainsley and Cameron were very attached to each other. So much so that even through Elliot's fog, he wondered why Ainsley was out of Cameron's sight now, and why Rona had left her beloved Patrick behind.

His eyes narrowed in suspicion. "Where have you left your husbands? In the village?"

Rona flushed, though Ainsley, very good at dissembling, only took another sip of tea. "They're at the pub," Ainsley said. "You know gentlemen."

"I know my sisters," Elliot growled. "You weren't certain what you were going to find, and you came to smooth the way. You weren't sure I was fit to be seen."

"Well," Rona said, her voice gentle in the same way Ainsley's had been bright. "You must admit that you've been unwell, Elliot. We did try to call earlier, but your man couldn't wake you."

"I was tired," Elliot said in a hard voice. *"Remember what it was to be a newlywed?"*

Juliana's face went bright pink, which made her eyes starry. "No matter," she said quickly. "We were somewhat at sixes and sevens earlier today. Best to let Elliot sleep anyway."

Elliot felt the snarl in his throat. "Don't try, Juliana." He let his gaze skewer his sister then sister-in-law, who both looked guilty. "Coddling doesn't help, Ainsley. Leaving me the hell alone is best."

"Is it?" Ainsley said, her *let us comfort my poor, sick brother* tone vanishing. "Is that why you bought this house in the middle of nowhere? Helping Uncle McGregor is your excuse, but if you bury yourself here, you will never get better. There's many a fine house to be had in Edinburgh, or even London, for a man of fortune. Which I know you have. A fortune, I mean."

"I like the countryside."

"A countryside difficult to reach, no matter how determined your family."

"A countryside where a man can find a little peace and quiet." His voice went up in volume.

"But now you've dragged Juliana up here," Ainsley said. "Is it fair to her to pull her into your prison with you?"

Juliana leaned forward to set her cup on the tea table, her movement decisive. The angle made her brush Elliot's broad shoulder, her reaching arm letting that shoulder contact her breast. She wore stays, but even the stiff touch of them was intimate.

Elliot would have Channan make Juliana a sari, so he could wrap her in silks and nothing else. Then he could touch her without undressing her, his hands sliding over the fabric warmed by her body.

"Elliot is my husband now," Juliana said, with the slightest emphasis on *my*. "And this is our home." Again a slight emphasis, this time on *our*.

Ainsley and Rona looked at her, blinking a little as they rearranged their ideas.

What had they expected? That Elliot had run off with a struggling Juliana over his shoulder to ravish her in a castle in the woods? To keep her prisoner here, the poor, naive beauty who hadn't the faintest idea how to handle Elliot the beast?

They did think that. Dear God. Their faces made that plain enough. Elliot's temper rose, but Juliana's quiet, clear tones cut through.

"I quite understand." She poured more tea, every movement connecting with Elliot's body in some way. She dropped in two lumps of sugar and topped the tea with a dollop of cream, her arm, side, or bosom touching him at any given moment. "You are concerned for your brother, and our marriage was very hasty." She gave them a little smile. "Well, it was hasty on Elliot's part. I was for marriage, obviously, no matter which groom turned up."

Ainsley raised her teacup in salute. "Bravo, Juliana. May

Mr. Barclay's wedding bed be filled to the brim with bed-bugs."

"Ainsley," Rona said, though it was apparent she agreed. "For shame."

"Nonsense, Mr. Barclay is the one who should be ashamed," Ainsley said. "How lucky that Elliot turned up to save the day."

"Not luck," Elliot rumbled. "Mahindar and whiskey."

"Then thank heavens for Mahindar and whiskey," Ainsley said.

"My point is that everything has turned out for the best," Juliana broke in. "Elliot and I live here now. Pity us if you like, but there it is."

The two ladies blinked again. Ainsley and Rona had come rushing out here, like fairy godmothers to Cinderella, to rescue the fair maiden, only to find the fair maiden sitting before them, her back straight, primly telling them to go away. Juliana faced his sister and sister-in-law like a terrier confronting bloodhounds, and the bloodhounds weren't quite certain what to do.

Elliot stood up. He didn't want to, because he liked the warmth of Juliana against him, but this circle of femininity had gone on long enough.

"Fetch your husbands," he said, "and either stay for a proper visit or scuttle back home. I will remain here, Juli-ana with me."

Ainsley gave him a look of exasperation, while Rona merely raised her brows.

Elliot saw from their expressions that their next strategy would have been to bring Patrick and Cameron in on the matter. *Elliot isn't well*, they'd say, *and shouldn't be left up here on his own. Do talk to him.*

"But only if Patrick and Cam want to play billiards, shoot, or drink. I don't need to be mollycoddled by the men of the family either."

"Did you want us to leave on the moment, dear brother?" Ainsley asked. "I haven't finished my tea."

Elliot growled. The windows had been opened to let in the breeze, but he could feel nothing of it. The indoors sometimes pressed in on him, and it started to press in on him now.

They could never understand—and Elliot couldn't make them understand—the little piece of darkness that gnawed away in the back of his brain and never went away. It had started while he was buried underground, in a place where time was nothing, where hunger and thirst were the only indication he was still alive. In a place where the strongest of men became raving lunatics, the darkness crouched, waiting to drag him back down to it.

I am not there. I am here.

Mahindar had taught him to say that when the darkness started to come. Elliot repeated it silently now, his jaw clenched, while the three ladies stared at him in consternation.

He had to leave. Now.

Elliot realized he still held his untouched teacup. He thrust it at Juliana, who took it quickly, before he strode out of the room.

He knew the ladies would put their heads together after he was gone and discuss what had just happened. Juliana's defense of him warmed him a little—she'd been eager to go back to Edinburgh with Ainsley, but she'd changed her intent the moment she'd realized that Elliot wasn't ready for her absence.

Elliot knew, logically, that they couldn't stay at Castle McGregor forever, but he could make decisions about that later. Much later.

For now, he only wanted to walk.

As Elliot entered the kitchen, Hamish jerked up from where he was pumping water into the sink, blue eyes widening. Mahindar was busily going through the pantry, making disparaging noises, and Channan sat quietly at the table, cutting up vegetables and plopping them into a bowl.

"Rest easy, Hamish, lad," Elliot said. "I don't have any knives. But I want a gun."

Any other time, he might laugh at the way Hamish first relaxed then went ramrod straight with fear again. But he didn't have the patience.

Mahindar backed out of the pantry. "Memsahib took it from Sahib McGregor and had me lock it away," he said.

"Then unlock it." To Hamish's continued stare, Elliot went on, "For rabbit, or game birds. There's not much to eat, and my brother and brother-in-law might be joining us for supper."

"Supper for six?" Mahindar rubbed his bearded chin as he always did when agitated. "That is much to ask, sahib."

"Send to the pub for the meal then." Elliot waited, and Mahindar hurried to a cupboard, unlocked it, and lifted out the shotgun and a box of shells. Elliot tucked shells into his sporran, checked the barrels and mechanism, laid the unloaded gun over his arm, and walked out the back door.

No one followed him, thank God. The wind was brisk, the sun high, clouds gathering above the towering mountains. Rain would come later, but not now. Wild country was what he needed. To be alone in it, what he wanted.

A small, muddy figure darted at him as he passed the garden gate. "Come!" Priti held up dirty hands to him, an eager smile on her face.

Something inside Elliot untwisted, and the darkness receded a little, snarling in frustration.

He reached down and scooped up the little girl, settling her on his shoulder, keeping her well away from the gun.

Priti balanced herself without worry, happily holding on to Elliot as they started up the path to the hills.

This child had never known fear. Elliot swore with everything within him that she never would.

⁓

When the ladies finished their tea and rose to leave, Juliana said, "I think you should return to Edinburgh. Today, I mean. Without dining with us."

"Nonsense," Rona said briskly, but Ainsley, with eyes so like Elliot's, gave her a nod.

"I think I understand." Ainsley came to Juliana, took her hands, and kissed her cheek. "He's my brother, but he's your husband now, and you need to learn the lay of the land. But if you ever need us, you telegraph. And I promise we will come for a nice long visit once you have settled." She gave Juliana a grin. "You've married into a very large family, and this house, unfortunately for you, is big enough for all of them."

More kisses, and a stout hug from Rona. "Look after my lad," she said. "And make certain he looks after you."

Juliana said a few more reassuring things then walked with her guests out the enormous front door and down the overgrown walk. The two ladies had come on foot, the skies so fair, though Juliana cast a wary glance at the thunderheads on the horizon. The weather could change quickly in the Highlands.

She waved her guests away at the gate then turned alone to her new home, pausing to take it in.

The castle and grounds truly were beautiful. Sunlight touched the pile of house, rendering it golden and hiding the gaps in the stone. Behind the house rose the mountains, liquid light shimmering in their folds, and to the east lay the slice of sparkling sea.

Time to make the place livable. Juliana had kept house for her father since the tender age of eight, when she'd realized that her flibbertigibbet mother, who preferred shopping, gossiping, and dosing herself with laudanum to running a household, would never be able to cope. Juliana had learned much from the butler and housekeeper, who'd become her friends, and after Mrs. St. John's death when Juliana had been fourteen, Juliana officially ran the household. Gemma married Mr. St. John right after Juliana's twentieth birthday, but Gemma had been wise enough to let Juliana carry on, never ousting her from doing what she loved.

The McGregor house would be more of a challenge, certainly, than her father's elegant town house and small manor house near Stirling, but Juliana could do it, she thought. It was all a matter of organizing, and Juliana was most excellent at organizing.

She'd already begun making lists of things they needed to do, subdividing those lists into what must be purchased, what jobs could be left to ordinary laborers, and what jobs would take an expert's skill, such as the bell system, which was in a complete disarray. To repair it, they'd have to find every rope in every pipe behind the walls and untangle the lot. But no matter—on the list the task went.

Juliana's bravado flagged slightly as she walked back into the castle's dusty interior. Hamish had tracked another layer of muddy boot prints in since the day before, but otherwise, all was as it had been yesterday—which meant a chaotic mess.

Because of the broken bell system, Juliana either had to shout for the staff when she needed something or go in search of them. As she reentered the morning room, she decided to do neither this time but carry the tea tray back to the kitchens herself. The empty things weren't heavy, and Mahindar and his family had so much to do already.

She gathered up the cups and saucers, piling them neatly on the tray. If she fingered Elliot's cup a little longer than the others, there was no one to see, was there?

When she entered the big kitchen with her tray, she was assailed by pungent aromas of food she couldn't identify, the scents odd but somehow mouthwatering. A pot simmered on the stove, Mahindar tending it, and Channan sat on her heels next to a large clay pot in the fireplace, poking at something inside.

Hamish was at the sink, scrubbing pots.

"Where is Nandita?" Juliana asked as she set the tea tray on the kitchen table. "Is she all right?"

They'd found her this morning, after a frantic search of the house, hiding in the boiler room. McGregor shooting off the gun had frightened Nandita badly—she'd been certain that soldiers had come to take them away. Channan and Mahindar had to talk to her for a long time before she'd come out again.

"She is with my mother," Mahindar said. "She will be well."

Juliana thought of the way Komal scolded Nandita, not to mention the way she'd chased McGregor back to his bedroom, and wondered.

"They are looking after Priti, then?"

Channan looked around from the fireplace. Mahindar shook his head. "No, Priti left with the sahib. He went walking in the hills."

"With the shotgun." Hamish didn't lift his arms from sudsy water, but he cranked his head around for the announcement.

"Oh." Juliana rolled her lower lip under her teeth. "Is . . . she all right with him?"

"Yes, indeed, certainly," Mahindar said without worry. "The sahib always takes care of Priti."

Juliana relaxed. Elliot did indeed seem to like the child, and she'd seen how gentle he could be with her.

"He is very good to her," Juliana said. She lifted one of the teacups from the tray, admiring its fineness. Ainsley had been sweet to give them the set.

Mahindar looked surprised. "But that is only natural, memsahib," he said. "After all, Priti is his daughter."

Chapter 8

The teacup slid out of Juliana's hands and fell down, down, to smash into fragments on the flagstone floor.

Juliana regarded it in dismay, while her heart pounded in her chest, and her face grew hot.

Channan said something admonishing to Mahindar, and the man looked unhappy and bewildered.

"His daughter?" Juliana said, swallowing on dryness. "With Nandita?"

"Nandita?" Mahindar looked surprised. "No, no. Nandita is not Priti's mother. She is her ayah—as you say, her nanny—but we all look after Priti. No, her mother is dead, poor thing."

"Oh." Juliana's thoughts fluttered around each other. She'd assumed Nandita the mother, because the young woman had been so attentive to Priti, and Channan had made clear her only children were grown sons. But Juliana had had no notion that Priti was *Elliot's*. Elliot and . . . who?

She wet her lips. "Mr. McBride. He was married? In India?"

Channan and Mahindar exchanged a glance. Channan said, "He was not."

Mahindar tried to drown her words with a string of Punjabi. Channan answered him as forcefully, then she turned back to Juliana.

"The sahib was not married to the lady," Channan said. "She was the wife of someone else."

Juliana couldn't breathe. Her eyes begin to burn, her heart to beat painfully.

"You knew nothing of this?" Mahindar asked her in a faint voice.

Channan spoke to him rapidly and firmly in their native language, and Mahindar grew more and more embarrassed.

A lady did not break down in front of her servants in the kitchen, Juliana admonished herself. A lady shouldn't even *be* in the kitchen, should never pass through the green baize door that separated the servants' quarters from the rest of the house. Even though they were living rough here, and any green baize had worn to gray tatters long ago, Juliana should have observed the sanctity of the custom.

She held on to this idea, pounded into her head by her upbringing, to keep Mahindar's revelation from overpowering her.

"You weren't to know, Mahindar," Juliana said. "Hamish, fetch a broom and sweep up the broken teacup."

She walked away from them, her heel catching on one of the porcelain fragments and grinding it to powder.

⌒

Mahindar knew Channan was going to scold. And scold and scold. His wife was good at scolding him, but she only did when Mahindar deserved it, so it smarted doubly.

The sahib had never kept secret the fact that Priti was his child. But the man spoke so very little to anyone that most people did not realize that he'd fathered her. They assumed, as the memsahib had, that Priti was a servant's daughter. Mahindar never spoke of it to anyone himself, because both he and Channan knew how the English felt about half-caste children. The sahib, and Priti, would have an easier time of it if people didn't know.

But Mahindar had assumed the memsahib would know. Mr. McBride had spoken of her often, describing her as a childhood friend, a young woman to whom he'd never had difficulty talking about anything and everything.

Mahindar braced himself for the scolding, but it didn't come. Channan simply turned back to her tandoor and stirred the vegetables inside.

"I know, I know," Mahindar said in Punjabi. "I am a fool."

"I said nothing," Channan said without looking at him.

"But you are right. I want him to be happy. I *need* him to be happy."

"What happened to the sahib was not your fault. I have told you."

Mahindar turned back to his pots of spices, reflecting mournfully that his supplies were too low. He'd become acquainted in London with another Punjabi who knew where to find the best Indian spices in the city. Mahindar had started sending the man money and a list of needs, and the man sent back, by special delivery, lovely jars of turmeric and saffron, the mixture called masala, and peppers that Mahindar could not find in the English or Scottish markets. He would have to write another letter to his friend and post it soon.

As always when Mahindar thought of what had happened to the sahib, and the enmity between Sahib McBride and Sahib Stacy, he felt remorse. He might have prevented the fight, might have prevented the journey into the wild lands during which the sahib had been stolen.

Mahindar had searched and searched after the sahib had disappeared, but hadn't been able to find him. He'd searched every day. Those long months had been the worst time of Mahindar's life.

"Not your fault," Channan repeated.

Hamish, not understanding a word of what they said, swept the floor in a rush of energy, as he did everything else. "So Nandita doesn't have any children?" the lad asked.

"No," Mahindar answered, switching to English. "She was married very young—fifteen or sixteen she was, but her husband was a soldier. He was arrested and killed, sadly."

"What had he done?" Hamish asked, the broom slowing.

"Nothing at all," Mahindar said. "He saw someone else doing something they shouldn't, so they came for him one night and pretended to arrest him for treason. They shot him like a dog." He shook his head. "Poor little Nandita."

"That's terrible." The broom stopped altogether, and Hamish leaned on it, his red brows drawn. "Is that why she was hiding in the boiler room?"

"She is afraid of soldiers and guns. They mean grief to her."

"Poor thing." Hamish's sympathy glowed from him. "Does she speak any English?"

"She knows a few words only."

"Well, I'll just have to teach her then." Hamish looked down at the broom, realized it was at a standstill, and began sweeping vigorously again.

Mahindar noticed Hamish hadn't offered to teach Channan or Komal English. He went back to his spices, smiling to himself, feeling a little better.

Dinner was slightly delayed because when Elliot and Priti returned, they were covered from head to foot in black mud.

"What on earth happened to you?" Juliana asked, coming into the flagstone passage to discover the source of the delay.

She found Priti in the laundry room, standing inside the huge metal sink, Channan pumping water over her and scrubbing her with a large sponge. Elliot, stripped to the waist, was standing at a smaller sink, with Mahindar scrubbing just as hard.

"Riverbank," Elliot said, spluttering as Mahindar squeezed a giant sponge full of water over Elliot's head. "I slipped in, and Priti fell in trying to rescue me. The bank we climbed out onto was this color." He pointed to the tar-like mud on his kilt.

Juliana fought back the urge to laugh, and at the same time she didn't know what to say to him. Elliot seemed relaxed, happy about his escapade with Priti and the comic way they looked.

Mahindar kept slopping the sponge, which was at least two feet wide, all over Elliot's body. Elliot gleamed, wet, his arms glistening with water that pattered to the floor, the tattoo stark on his skin.

He grabbed the sponge from Mahindar. "Enough. Get Priti upstairs and dry."

Mahindar relinquished the sponge with a sigh, as though realizing the limit to which Elliot would put up with his ministrations. Elliot scrubbed himself over, sloshing water onto his face and torso.

His kilt was drenched, and so were his bare legs, his boots left outside the back door. He snatched up a towel and rubbed his hair vigorously as he started out of the laundry room.

Juliana flattened herself against the wall in the passage between laundry room and kitchen as Elliot strode out, wearing only his kilt. He halted when he saw her, and he stepped close to her, his gray eyes glittering in the dim light of the hall.

Despite the toweling, Elliot was still wet, water beading on his lashes and dripping from the ends of his short hair. He said nothing, only leaned closer, closer. Now Juliana's bodice was wet, the front of her skirt smudged with mud from his kilt.

His breath heated her lips, and his hands, one still holding the towel, went to either side of her. His gaze swept downward, then he skimmed his lips from her forehead to her chin.

The light touches sent warm shudders through Juliana's body, heat curling in her belly. She wanted to latch on to him and pull him close, despite her still-spinning thoughts, and rise to him for more of his kisses.

"Did you have a nice walk?" she babbled. "You and Priti? Besides falling into the river, I mean?"

Elliot didn't answer. He skimmed kisses down her face once more then came to her lips, parting them with his. Juliana's head went back to the wall, and Elliot slanted his mouth over hers, his heat and his body covering her.

He licked slowly into her mouth, coaxing her tongue over his in return. She tasted the water on his lips, the salt of his sweat, the excitement of him. The length of his hardness, firm through the wool of his kilt, unashamedly pressed her skirts.

Elliot eased the kiss to its close then touched his lips to the corner of her mouth and the tiny dimple there. Still saying nothing, he straightened up, hooked the towel around his neck, and walked away.

Juliana's heart pounded, the heat between her legs incandescent. She clutched the wall, the only thing supporting her, while she watched his kilt swing against his bare legs as he strode back through the passage to the main house.

Juliana was still standing there when Channan came to her with a stiff brush, to clean the water and mud from the front of her frock.

Elliot came downstairs again fifteen minutes later, dry and fit, feeling better than he had in a long while. He'd put on one of his formal kilts and a jacket, and had jerked a comb through his damp hair.

Juliana emerged from a room below, every sleek hair in place, her gown none the worse for wear after his impromptu kiss. Stopping to taste her while she'd stood against the wall in the kitchen passage had been impossible to resist.

Elliot reached the bottom of the staircase and held his hand out to her. Juliana looked a bit strained about the eyes as she took it, her face too pale.

Next time Elliot went for a walk, he'd take her with him. Juliana would love the beauty here, and there was so much of it to show her. And if he had to struggle up a riverbank again, he couldn't think of more enjoyment than getting muddy with her.

As Elliot started with Juliana toward the dining room, Hamish came barreling out of the kitchens. Something that looked like a dead bird dangled from under his arm, its legs swinging. Hamish pushed past Juliana and Elliot, ran up three of the stairs, whisked the dead bird out from under his arm, put one of its spindly legs to his lips, took a deep breath, and blew.

Elliot lunged for him. "Hamish, for God's sake, no . . ."

But the lad had already filled the pipes' bag with air, and it came out again, a groan and a squeal that filled the hall and tore at Elliot's eardrums.

Juliana clapped her hands over her ears. Hamish went on blowing, his face red, his thick fingers finding the holes in some semblance of a pattern.

Elliot took Juliana's arm and quickly propelled her down a long passage to the dining room. Hamish came behind them, piping the laird and his lady to their banquet feast.

As soon as they reached the dining room, Hamish threw down the pipes, which died with a squawk, and ran to hold out a giant wooden chair for Juliana.

Elliot made for the other end of the long wooden table, which had been scrubbed until it gleamed. At his place were pewter plates, scrupulously clean; a goblet and tumbler also of pewter; and thick glass decanters of water and whiskey.

Elliot waited until Juliana was seated, Hamish pushing in her chair enthusiastically, then he smoothed his full kilt and sat down on the carved wooden chair at the head of the table. The back of the chair rose well above Elliot's head, the square cut of the seat hard against his backside.

Hamish retrieved the pipes, which emitted another squawk, and ran out of the room, the spindles of the pipes slapping his kilt. Mahindar came forth bearing a giant bowl, into which he dipped a giant spoon. He ladled food first onto Juliana's plate then walked down the table to spoon it onto Elliot's.

Only the two of them dined. Uncle McGregor had made it clear he preferred to eat in the comfort of his room, without the nonsense of formal service. Elliot was happy to let him—dining alone with Juliana was preferable.

Fragrant steam rose from the chicken and vegetables Mahindar put onto Elliot's plate, which he covered with a piece of flat, teardrop-shaped bread called naan. Mahindar set a little crockery bowl next to Elliot's plate, which was filled with what looked like oil and smelled like butter—ghee.

Juliana picked up her fork. She moved a small piece of chicken out from under her bread, eyed it suspiciously, and took a bite.

Elliot watched her face change as the spices filled her mouth. He'd approached his first Punjabi meal with the same suspicion, until the savory flavors had made him understand what true beauty was.

He hid his smile and scooped the chicken smothered in garam masala onto his fork, enjoyed a mouthful, then tore off a bit of bread and dipped it into the ghee.

Down the table, Juliana said, "This is wonderful, Mahindar. What is it?"

"We call it tikka, memsahib. It is made with chicken and spices."

"And this?" She pointed to her crockery bowl.

"Ghee. It is butter that has been boiled down and the fat skimmed from the top. You put it on your bread."

Juliana took another bite of the tikka. "It is most excellent." She dabbed her lips. "Highly unusual." She reached for her goblet of water and took a long drink. "And quite spicy. Elliot, you did not tell me you preferred native food," she said a little breathlessly.

Elliot shrugged as he swallowed another large mouthful. "Rona's cook wanted only Scottish food in her kitchen, much to Mahindar's distress. I told him that here, he and his wife can cook whatever they like."

"Well." Juliana drew another breath. "I will be eager to taste what you come up with, Mahindar."

Mahindar did not look convinced. "Perhaps the memsahib prefers haggis?" His expression said that he'd rather die than have to prepare such a thing, but Mahindar always wanted to please.

"No, no," Juliana said quickly. "This is lovely."

"The sahib, he was so kind to us when he had his plantation. He let me tempt him with many a Punjabi dish, and did not insist on boiled mutton and very soft peas. He is so kind, is the sahib. Always kind to everyone."

Juliana saw Elliot look up from his food, brows drawn, then he went back to shoveling the tikka into his mouth, tearing off pieces of the bread to accompany it. Nothing wrong with Elliot's appetite.

Juliana knew exactly why Mahindar was emphasizing Elliot's kindness. Kindness to Mahindar, to Mahindar's family, to Priti . . .

"Thank you, Mahindar," she said. "That will be all for now."

Mahindar looked from her to Elliot. "But there is more in the kitchen. I can bring more."

"No, you and your family should enjoy some food and

a time to eat. When we finish, or need anything, I will ring . . . I mean, Mr. McBride will shout for Hamish."

Mahindar looked to Elliot for confirmation. Elliot glanced up briefly and gave him a nod. Mahindar, resigned, set down the tray and walked quietly out of the room, shutting the door carefully behind him.

Juliana pushed her fork through the red orange savory sauce and tried to decide how to broach the subject.

Ladies were supposed to expect their husbands to take lovers outside marriage and even to have children with said mistresses. A wife was not supposed to mention this or bring up the fact, even if the children were brought home to be raised in her house.

This situation was different, perhaps, because the lover in question was dead, the affair conducted years before Elliot's return home or this marriage. Indeed, because the woman had passed away, perhaps Elliot was more to be pitied than censured. But still, a lady was not to notice these things—she was to look the other way at her husband's goings-on.

But Juliana had never been one for looking the other way at anything. She'd had to keep her eyes firmly open growing up with her kind but distant, ever-so-respectable father and her self-indulgent, rather indolent mother.

"My stepmother," Juliana said. She had to stop and clear her throat.

Elliot looked up, his black coat and white shirt elegant, yet his skin brown with his outdoors life, his hands blunt and worn from work.

Juliana coughed and took a drink of water.

"I'll tell Mahindar not to make it so spicy next time," Elliot said.

"No, no. It's fine." She dabbed her lips with her napkin. "As I was saying, my stepmother can be very blunt. Discusses things quite frankly. When she comes to visit, she will want to know all about Priti, and her history. What shall I tell her?"

Elliot looked faintly surprised. "Tell her anything you like. I'm not ashamed of her."

"Yes, but, my dear Elliot, I'm not sure myself of the story."

He frowned. "I've told you."

"No." Juliana dragged in a breath. "No, you haven't."

His frown deepened. "Haven't I?"

"No."

"Mmph." Elliot reached for the whiskey decanter and poured a large measure into the goblet. He took a generous sip then ran his tongue across his lower lip. "Sometimes I can't remember the things I've said or not said."

"I understand. It must be painful for you."

Elliot stopped in the act of taking another drink, the goblet halfway to his mouth. "Don't pity me, Juliana. I'm sick to death of pity."

Juliana held up her hand. "Not pity. Interest. I'd be quite curious to hear the story."

Elliot drank the whiskey. He set down the goblet, keeping one hand on it. "It's not pretty. Not fit for young ladies at a drawing room tea."

"We're in the dining room. And I'm a married woman now." Juliana's face heated as she remembered the weight of Elliot in the dark last night, the pain-pleasure when he pushed his way inside her for the first time. "In all ways married."

Elliot's expression didn't soften. "There's a chance she's not my daughter," he said. "But a much better chance that she is."

"Which do you hope?" Juliana held her breath for the answer.

"That she's mine. But it doesn't matter. Her mother is dead, Archibald Stacy is dead, and Priti will live with me, no matter what."

Chapter 9

Juliana let out her breath again, little by little. "Mr. Archibald Stacy was the lady's husband?"

"Stacy was a Scotsman I helped settle on a plantation. I'd known him in the army, given him some training. Stacy came to me when he resigned his commission, and I helped him find a plantation near mine."

Juliana knew from Ainsley that after Elliot had left the army, he'd become a planter, and then made a business of showing other Europeans how to live and prosper in India.

"We were friends," Elliot went on. "Stacy had a Scottish wife, a young woman he'd gone back to Glasgow to marry, but she grew sick and died within a month of their arrival."

"Oh dear. Poor lady."

"Illness can take one swiftly in India," Elliot said, not without feeling. "Stacy grieved, then took a fancy to an Indian woman called Jaya."

A courtesan, Juliana supplied silently. She knew that respectable young women in India were ferociously looked after to prevent them having out-of-wedlock affairs with European men—with any man, for that matter.

"It was a casual affair," Elliot said. "And I . . . had an affair with her too. But Jaya fell for Stacy. She feared he had no true affection for her, was using her to soothe his feelings. So, to move things along, she told him she preferred me, packed her bags, and arrived at my house. Stacy was incensed and came to fetch her back. I don't think he realized his affection for her until she left him." He turned the goblet with stiff fingers. "When I returned to the plantation after my capture I found that Stacy had married Jaya, she'd borne a child, and she was dead. Stacy had abandoned Priti, and Mahindar and Channan had taken her in. I paid them for Priti's upkeep, including what expenses they'd incurred while I'd been gone. Priti was just old enough that the lady could have started her when I was taken."

Juliana tried to decide what to feel. First, jealousy, her failing—a large, painful dose of jealousy. In her mind, Elliot had always belonged to *her*, ever since the ten-year-old Elliot had kissed her cheek in order to slip a frog into the pocket of her pinafore.

She'd been willing to marry Grant because she'd known it would be useless to pine away for Elliot, who'd preferred India and adventure to this tame side of the world. But the fact that Elliot had gone to this unknown woman, that he'd been willing to do so, burned in her heart.

Second, pity—for Priti, left alone and not understanding, and for Elliot, who'd returned from a horrible ordeal to find the woman he'd had a child with dead. Anger at Mr. Stacy for abandoning the little girl no matter whom she belonged to.

"Is Mr. Stacy still alive?" Juliana asked.

Elliot shook his head. "I don't think so. He left his plantation and went to Lahore, according to Mahindar, and Mahindar heard that he died in an earthquake there." Elliot sloshed more whiskey into his goblet. "I told you, not a pretty story."

"You are correct. Not for young ladies in a drawing room."

"It is in the past. Gone."

"I know."

Elliot drank the whiskey and returned the glass to the table, obviously intending to say no more.

"Well," Juliana said briskly. "Priti is a sweet girl, and I'm happy we can provide a home for her. I will have to look into clothes for her, and a governess, and we must make certain a nursery is put in order for her. Nandita is kind to look after her for now, but Priti should not live like a servant."

"She doesn't."

Juliana set down her knife and fork exactly parallel across her plate. "What you mean, my dear Elliot, is that she lives the way you do, which means a bit rough. I don't intend to break her spirit, if that's what you fear, but she does need to learn manners, and English, and a good many things."

"I'll ask her," Elliot said with a straight face.

"You should begin acknowledging her as a McBride right away, so that there is no question how you view her as she grows up. I warn you, it will not be easy for her, having an Indian mother, but we will do our best to smooth her way."

"Thank you."

The quiet gratitude sent a shiver down Juliana's spine. Not Priti's fault at all that she was the daughter of a courtesan two men had loved. The jealousy prickled again. Juliana would have to decide what to do about that—the affair had been so far in the past, after all. That Elliot had planned to take care of Priti no matter whose daughter she turned out to be mitigated the jealousy a bit.

"Yes, there is much to be done." Juliana took refuge from her emotions, as always, by organizing. Organizing was such a comforting thing. "Not only for Priti, but for us as well. As soon as we are able, we must pay calls to everyone in the area. It's our duty, and also our duty to host a gathering, perhaps on Midsummer's Eve. That will indicate to the neighbors that we plan to settle here, and are not simply city dwellers looking to spend an idle week in the country. We'll have a fête, and a ball. I shall have to find out what fiddlers to hire and where to obtain the food, which will all have to be local, of course. Perhaps you could . . ."

She noticed that Elliot had frozen in place, staring at her with an unfathomable look.

"Elliot?" she asked quickly. "Are you all right?"

"I don't do well around people," he said in a hard voice. "Not anymore."

No, he didn't. She'd seen that already, even with his own family. "That is the beauty of having a wife," she said. "You have to do nothing but stand looking laird-like and letting the whiskey flow. *I* shall have to greet everyone and make sure they're entertained. Trust me, much better for us to endure such a thing for a few hours than be talked about up and down the countryside. Don't worry, Elliot. I will take care of it."

She had no idea, Elliot thought, how absolutely beautiful she looked at this moment. Her blue eyes were shining under the light of the candles, her hair glistening as she moved her head. She talked rapidly and gestured with her plump hand, so happily dooming him with neighborly calls and a midsummer fête.

Easy to confess to the world, even to gentle and proper Juliana, that he'd sired a child on Jaya, who'd kept him warm when the cold winds came off the wall of mountains separating northern India from the world. Easy to admit he and Stacy had shared her between them at first.

That sin was so far removed from the terrible nightmare of being captured and displayed as a prize. So far removed from what the men of that fierce tribe had done to him, and had taught Elliot to do for them. He'd experienced slavery firsthand, when a human life was considered less important than an animal's—when the whole of his history, from birth to present, meant nothing.

Elliot also couldn't explain to Juliana that when he'd been their prisoner and slave, he'd forgotten all about Jaya. His time with the woman and Stacy, his years at the plantation, his friends there and in the army might have never existed. The only person he could hold on to, the only face he saw, was Juliana's.

Juliana kept on chattering about the fête and jumble sales and conferring with the minister's wife, but Elliot couldn't hear her words. He was aware only of her voice, clear like a fall of rain.

He pushed aside the whiskey he drank too much of these days and rose from his chair. Juliana looked up at him in surprise, because of course a gentleman never left the table until the lady decided it was time for the women to retire to the drawing room.

Elliot reached the end of the table and pulled Juliana's chair back. As she looked up at him in astonishment, he lifted her out of the ridiculous throne-like chair and set her down on a vast blank area of the table.

"Elliot, I don't think . . ."

Elliot silenced her by kissing her. He drew his hands up under her heavy coil of hair, fingers loosening the silk of it.

In the dark cells he'd imagined this, remembering the soft of her hair when he'd touched it the night of her debut ball, before he'd shipped off the next day to join his regiment. He'd recalled he exact shape and touch of her lips from that brief kiss, the scent of her rose-soft breath.

She'd sustained him in the dark, and now he needed sustenance again.

Elliot drew his tongue across her lips, touching the moisture behind them when they parted. Juliana's hands came up to cup his elbows, fingers sinking into his biceps through his coat.

He kissed across her lips, every inch of them, then moved to her cheek, kissing the skin he had the privilege to touch. In the darkness, in the pain, the memory of her kiss had wound comfort through the agony. She'd never know— he never would find the words to explain—how many times she'd saved his life.

I need you.

Elliot moved to the shell of her ear, brushing it with the tip of his tongue. Juliana made a soft noise in her throat as he closed his teeth on her earlobe.

He was seducing her again, but she'd seduced him every night of those months he'd been lost. He'd longed each day for the torture to cease, for his captors to ignore him for stretches of time, because then he could sink into a stupor and be with his visions of Juliana.

They never could make Elliot forget her, because they didn't know about her. Her name had never crossed his lips. Juliana was his secret, his soul.

And now she was real.

He sucked her earlobe gently into his mouth, liking the way she shivered under his touch. He loved the scent of her, the taste of her, and he'd never be able to have enough.

Elliot kissed his way back to her mouth, one tiny kiss at a time, until he opened her lips and stroked across her tongue. He loved her tongue. He trapped it with his teeth, then he gently suckled it.

Juliana made another quiet noise of pleasure, and Elliot kept suckling, liking the friction, taste, and heat of her mouth. He let her go and reached for the whiskey decanter, pouring more into his goblet.

He touched the goblet to her lips until she took a little into her mouth, then he plunged his mouth across hers and scooped up the whiskey with his tongue.

Her eyes were soft when Elliot drew back. "What are you doing?" she asked.

"Savoring you."

"Oh." Her flush, the little word, made his body tighten.

Elliot touched the goblet to her lips again. This time Juliana sipped then closed her eyes as Elliot imbibed the whiskey from her.

Again and again he slid the best McGregor single malt into her mouth; again and again, he drank from her. He was a man dying of thirst, and Juliana was his vessel.

When the goblet was empty, Juliana smiled up at him, her blue eyes warm, her hair mussed. "You're going to get me tipsy."

Elliot kissed her one more time without answering. He skimmed his fingers down her throat, bare for evening, the creamy silk bodice hugging her shoulders and bosom. Female fashion had always baffled him—ladies were buttoned up to their chins during the day but décolletages might barely cover their nipples at night.

All the better for him. Elliot unhooked her bodice in the back and took the half sleeves down her arms, revealing the bow at the top of her corset, the coy lace of chemise beneath that.

Juliana's father was a wealthy man, and Juliana wore rich clothing, all the way down to her skin. The silk of the bodice he parted caught on the rough tips of Elliot's fingers, the lawn of the corset cover smooth and embroidered with silk flowers.

Elliot loosened the corset's laces and pulled them out, opening the cage and lifting it away. The chemise beneath billowed free, its lawn folds as soft as the gown's silk.

Easy to untie the ribbon holding the chemise closed and slide it down, bunching the fabrics of chemise and bodice at her waist.

Juliana watched him more in curiosity than trepidation as Elliot poured another measure of single malt into the goblet. He lifted it to her and trickled whiskey across her collarbone, the amber liquid trailing down to her bared breasts and abdomen.

Juliana gasped. "Elliot, my gown . . ."

Elliot barely heard her. He leaned down to her, licking the whiskey from her skin, following it to the heat between her breasts. He tasted and drank, closing his mouth over her breast to suck.

He left marks where his teeth and tongue had been, decorating Juliana's bosom. She'd have to wear higher-necked gowns now, but Elliot didn't care. She could wrap herself in a sedate package that she unwrapped only for him.

He licked her clean, slowly easing her backward onto the table, until she lay on the tabletop, her small bustle squashed to one side, her skirts rucked up.

He upended the rest of the goblet, lifting it high so the whiskey splashed down on her. Juliana squealed, then laughed.

She stopped laughing when Elliot leaned on top of her, licking, tasting, kissing her lips before moving back to lick every droplet from her breasts.

He paused at her nipples, light pink brown against her creamy skin. He scooped up the droplets there, then closed his mouth over each nipple in turn.

Juliana clung to the edge of the table, her legs parted around Elliot's hips, a wild feeling building and building inside her. She felt it most between her thighs, but the hot tingling under his mouth made her almost as insane.

His eyes were half closed, his brows drawn in concentration. The hand over her right breast was scarred and hard, the back of it crisscrossed with scars and sun-streaked hair.

Juliana stroked the hair on his head, liking how the bristly ends caressed her fingers. He was more beautiful now, she decided, after being banged about and repaired, than he had been in his untouched youth.

Elliot raised his head, his eyes a flash of hot gray. His next kiss pressed her hard onto the table, Elliot coming full length on her.

He kissed her thoroughly, every stroke of his tongue,

every caress of his lips deliberate, taking. Juliana chased his tongue with hers, wanton and not caring.

Just when she thought he'd back away, perhaps help her dress enough so they could go upstairs, Elliot pulled her upright by the wrists. He took her all the way off the table, standing her against him, while his hands went to the back of her skirt.

"I want this off," he said. "All of it. I can't touch you with this stupid bustle in the way."

Juliana fumbled with the catches that fastened her bodice to her skirt, overskirt to underskirt, skirts to bustle.

The bustle itself Elliot loosened with impatient jerks to the hooks, and Juliana knew she'd be sewing them back on again later. He dropped the wire form to the floor, where it settled with a clatter much as Hamish's bagpipes had.

Next came the drawers; easy to unbutton and slide off. Now Juliana was bare, in her dining room, exposed by the light of the few candles. She still wore her stockings, white silk tied with silk garters, and her favorite beaded slippers.

Elliot set her on the table again. His hand went to his waistband, and he unpinned the yards of tartan that wrapped his waist, to reveal himself hard and fully extended beneath.

He spread the plaid on the table behind Juliana and lowered her onto it, then he scooted her hips to the edge of the table, positioned himself, and slid straight into her.

Chapter 10

Again the sensation of rightness filled Elliot, rising over even the excitement of the sex. Not that entering Juliana's heat and moisture didn't pleasure him. Mindlessly so.

She was desire and goodness, and she smelled of her glycerin soap, a touch of French perfume, and a woman wanting. The sight of his cock disappearing inside her, her wiry red hair damp around him, made Elliot's blood and body scalding hot.

Juliana's eyes grew heavy with passion, her breasts rising with her quickening breath. She had such beautiful breasts. Creamy and pale, her areolas like silk.

Juliana clung to him with fingers and thighs, their bodies twined and locked. Elliot was safe at last, in his haven inside her. If he could stay here always, he'd be well. Everything he'd done in the past would be erased, and there'd be only Juliana.

He rocked inside her, loving how her face softened in pleasure, how her hair tangled across his kilt on the table.

She was spread for him, delectable, naked, his Juliana. He'd thought of her so many times, imagining doing just this, but the reality was a hundred times better than the fantasy.

The reality meant he could feel her around him, every texture and the temperature of her skin, and scent her longing, which drowned out every thought in his brain. He could taste her lovely skin, the smooth warmth of her areolas; hear the pretty noises she made that meant she found pleasure in what he was doing.

Every sense brought a different delight, but the whole of her was more beautiful than anything he could ever have imagined.

Cold suddenly poured over him, but it was only the sweat on his roasting-hot skin, the shaking deep in his body that meant release.

Elliot didn't want release. He wanted to hang on, to be held in the cradle of Juliana forever.

He groaned, unable to stop what his body wanted to do, sorrow that it was over mixing with shuddering joy. He pulled Juliana to him as soon as he spilled his seed into her, and wrapped his arms around her, holding her as she clung to him.

"Elliot," she whispered.

One word, quiet in the candlelit room, but it was enough.

Juliana was never sure how long they held on to each other. Her head rested on Elliot's strong shoulder, and his heart drubbed and bumped beneath her ear. She kissed the skin beneath his lower lip, tasting salt.

He held her with arms that shook but would not let her go, or let her fall. Juliana wasn't sure how she knew that, but she knew.

One of the candles hissed as burned wick fell into the wax, and rising wind outside rattled the old casements.

Other than that all was silent. Juliana felt like a fairy-tale princess in this old, false castle, and the knight who'd brought her here was showing her a world she'd never known. Locked away in his palace, she'd learned more in the last two days than she had in the first thirty years of her life.

Elliot's body was as solid as the foundations of this house. And yet, she sensed his fragility. He could crumble at the right touch to the right place, just like some of the walls in this old place. Juliana had to make sure that the touch never came.

The passage outside the dining room suddenly filled with noise. An impossibly loud bang and crash of glass sounded, followed by pounding footsteps, then a shrill voice shrieking in Punjabi, and a man's bellow.

Juliana raised her head in alarm. She and Elliot were both naked down to their socks, Elliot's kilt spread like a table-cloth where he'd laid her down. Their clothes were scattered over the floor, and the room had only one door. Hiding or flight was impossible.

McGregor's voice rose right outside the door. "You leave that be, woman! A man can't be stifled in his own house."

More invective coming from Komal, because that was the only person to whom the stentorian female tones could belong. Footsteps hurried along the passage, followed by the voice of Channan, obviously trying to quiet them down.

Elliot's arms tightened around Juliana. "Don't worry," he said into her hair. "Mahindar will keep them out. He's on guard outside the door."

Juliana's face heated. "Outside the door? But I sent him back to the kitchens."

"Mahindar guards any door I am behind. He knows what might happen if I'm disturbed."

"What might happen?"

He shrugged "I might hurt whoever comes charging in. If I'm not in my right mind, I can lash out."

His mouth thinned to a hard line, resigned, as though

he'd already decided it was useless to fight his madness. He'd accepted it and was doing what was necessary to live with it.

Somewhere inside the hard, scarred Elliot was the laughing youth Juliana had fallen in love with so many years ago. He was still in there . . . somewhere.

Juliana had no illusion that she was special enough or wise enough to save him. She only knew she had to try. The man crying out to her in silence needed no less.

~~~

The bang and crash turned out to have been a glass-doored breakfront in the drawing room, now lying facedown, the glass smashed. Juliana gathered the story in bits and pieces.

McGregor had been searching the cabinet for a stash of cigars he'd sworn he left there fifteen years ago. Being of small stature, he'd stood on a chair to search the upper shelves, then decided to climb on the breakfront itself to search its top recesses.

Komal, entering the drawing room on some errand, had seen McGregor on the top of the breakfront, and started scolding him. When McGregor had tried to jump to the ground, his kilt had caught on a finial on the breakfront's top. His weight had jerked the cloth free, and he'd sprung clear, but the breakfront had overbalanced and the entire thing had come crashing down.

Komal had started shrieking at McGregor, and the two had stormed through the halls, shouting at each other, neither understanding a word of what the other was saying.

"I've been laird here forty-five years," McGregor said, poking the air with a finger partly bent from rheumatism. "Forty-five years. I will nae be chased around me own home by a pack of godless, screaming savages."

"We are Sikh, sahib," Mahindar said, offended. "We have a god."

"You cannae deny that *that* woman is a screaming savage."

"She is old, sahib."

"Old?" Behind all his white hair, McGregor's face turned chartreuse. "She's no older than I am. Do ye mean that people of my age are raving mad? Say so and be done, damn ye."

Juliana stepped forward. "Mr. McGregor . . ."

"And don't ye try to placate me, young woman. I know all about the ways of beguiling women. My wife, God rest her soul, excelled at turning a fellow up sweet. I know all the tricks of females."

"Uncle McGregor." Elliot's strong voice rolled through the hall as he emerged from the dining room, having resumed his shirt and kilt, his coat slung over his arm. "There's a fine stash of whiskey down in the cellar. Why don't you come and help me sample it?"

McGregor drew himself upright, his voice winding down to mere loudness. "Now *that* is the first sensible suggestion I've heard all evening."

He turned and stalked down the hall. When Elliot caught up to him, McGregor said in what he thought was a quiet tone, "Got a leg over in the dining room, eh? Mrs. McGregor and me, we favored the conservatory. Had many a fine night under the moonlight there." His chuckle faded away as Elliot ushered him into the cellar stairs and shut the door behind them.

～～～

He knew they were searching for him. He'd found a place to hide, down in the bowels of the earth, in a part of their warren-like prison even they didn't know about. Some tribe had carved these caves deep into the hills in a time forgotten, and Elliot took refuge in them now. The doors he'd been locked behind were ancient and rusted, the locks easy to break, but there was no way out of the tunnels, and his captors knew it. The only opening to freedom led to a guard with a rifle.

Early on, Elliot had watched one poor fellow prisoner struggle out into the light and air, only to hear the crack of a rifle and the man's muffled scream. The gunshot hadn't killed him instantly. He'd lain under the baking sun and slowly bled to death over the next full day, begging for water or, for God's sake, for the guard to shoot him again.

His had been the last human face Elliot had seen for weeks after that. His captors ignored him, occasionally remembering to throw in bread and some fetid piece of goat meat to keep him alive.

The head tribesman wanted Elliot alive, though, because he wanted to play with him. The head man hated all Europeans, blaming them for any and all chaos he could see from his mountain perch.

Elliot had found places to hide in their own tunnels, holes so tiny and foul that no one but the desperate could live in them. They knew he was in there, trapped like a fox in his den, and they knew he couldn't get out. They'd hunt for him when they wanted him, and they were hunting him now. Elliot heard them calling, passing above his hiding place, their voices filling the spaces.

He crouched into the hole, feeling no glee at evading them, wanting only peace. But the pain kept knocking at him. His kilt warmed him, but his fingers were cold, bloody cold.

They'd pulled off his nails, one by one, for the enjoyment of it. Elliot had refused to scream or make a sound, which had disappointed them, so they'd thrown him back into the cell and taken away his water.

Thirsty, he was so thirsty.

The search went on above, until the voices trailed off. They'd leave him alone now. Alone to heal until thirst and hunger drove him out again. But until then, Elliot would have days of darkness and silence to himself.

~~~~~

Juliana's worry when Mahindar and Hamish emerged from the cellars the next morning without finding Elliot rose to near panic.

Morning had dawned fine and fair. Elliot had dropped into bed beside her very late last night and very drunk, having helped Mr. McGregor "sample" much of the whiskey. He'd gathered Juliana into his arms for a whiskey-flavored kiss, then snuggled beside her and dropped into a limp sleep.

She'd left him asleep when she'd risen and gone down to breakfast, having enough experience with Scotsmen and whiskey to know he would remain in bed awhile. Likewise, thankfully, there was no more noise from Mr. McGregor.

As she ate the breakfast of eggs and more naan brought by a cheerful Mahindar, Juliana planned her calls.

She'd questioned Hamish about her neighbors, the lad knowing everything about them down to the last detail. The Englishman Mr. Terrell, who'd purchased McGregor's brewery, and his wife were gentlefolk, Hamish told her, the man being the son of a gentleman. They would be near the top of her visiting list, but heading them would be the Highlander in the neighboring estate, Ewan McPherson, a crony of Mr. McGregor's.

Mrs. Rossmoran, while not as wealthy as the Terrells, was a daughter of Scotland, whose family, according to Hamish, had been in this area longer than anyone. Juliana would be sure to visit her among the first as well.

When she finished breakfast she went in search of Hamish again. She had no luck finding him until she went down the flagstone passage, calling his name.

He popped out of the kitchen, looking worried, but Hamish generally looked worried, so Juliana thought nothing of it at first. "Hamish, please spread the word that builders are desperately needed. Any kind of builder, plumbers, glaziers, and drapers. They may begin assembling here today, and Mr. McBride will speak to them."

Hamish listened in all seriousness then said, "Aye. If we can find him."

Juliana stopped. "If you can find who? Mr. McBride?"

"Aye." Hamish nodded, his worried look becoming more pronounced. "He's gone, m'lady, and there's no trace of him."

Chapter 11

"What do you mean, no trace of him?" Juliana stared at Hamish, cold fear wiping out any plans of calls or house rebuilding. "He likely went for a walk. He and Mr. McGregor did imbibe fairly heavily last night, and Mr. McBride no doubt needs to clear his head."

"No, m'lady. We thought of that, but he's not gone for a walk. Mahindar says he's gone into hiding."

"Into hiding? What on earth does that mean?"

"Mahindar says that sometimes, when it all gets too much for him, he disappears. Mahindar says he sometimes can't find Mr. McBride for days. But he says he hasn't done it in a long time now."

"Where is Mahindar?" Juliana demanded. "I want to speak to him."

"He's out looking. He and his wife and Nandita and the little girl are all hunting high and low for Himself. I was too, except you called me."

What did Elliot fear? This was the Highlands, his home. He was safe here.

Juliana pushed past Hamish and dashed to the kitchen, never mind her strictures of the lady of the house never entering the servants' quarters. "Mahindar?"

Mahindar popped out of a darkened corner so quickly that Juliana squeaked. He began an apology, but Juliana cut through it. "Have you found him?"

"No, memsahib. But we are looking. You should go out and make your visits. I will find him. I always do. Eventually."

"Don't be silly. I cannot tamely sip tea and talk of the weather while wondering if Elliot is all right. He might be hurt. I'm not leaving until we know he's safe."

Mahindar spread his hands. "Very well, but it might be days."

"Days?" Her heart squeezed. "I don't understand. Why should he do this? This is his home."

Hamish loomed at her shoulder. "Because he's a madman, ain't he?"

Juliana swung on him. "Hamish McIver, don't you ever say that again. If you do I'll . . . I will speak to your mother about it. Mr. McBride is *not* mad. He was held for a long time against his will, and that is hard on people, isn't it? It stands to reason he still has bad dreams about it."

"But he's awake now."

Hamish had a point, and Juliana hardly understood it at all. But she thought of some of the things Elliot had told her: *I drift in and out . . . Sometimes I can't remember the things I've said or not said . . .*

"The lad is right," Mahindar said. "The sahib is a bit mad now. He never quite recovered from his imprisonment, the poor man."

"Stop," Juliana said in a loud voice. "No more talk of madness. My husband is not mad. But we must *find* him."

Both started at her tone and scurried away to resume the search.

They hunted everywhere. Mr. McGregor joined in, for once not arguing, scolding, or shouting, despite his obvious fragile condition from imbibing the night before.

The man put a bony hand on Juliana's arm. "There is a place he could be. I used to go there when I was a lad, pretending there were ghosts."

Hamish paled at the word *ghosts*, his freckles standing out on his white skin.

"This house is too new for ghosts," Juliana said briskly, even as she let McGregor lead her away.

"But it was built over the old castle," McGregor said. "Which was th' McGregor stronghold for six hundred years. Before that, it was a keep to defend this little valley against all comers." He climbed down the stairs from the scullery and led her along the passage to the boiler room, where they'd found Nandita cowering the morning before. "There's still a way to get to the old McGregor castle—the ruined cellars below it, anyway. Found it when I was a boy."

Mr. McGregor moved to the other side of the boiler room and pried a piece of grimy paneling from the wall. Behind this was a narrow niche that looked like a broom cupboard, empty and unused. McGregor shone the candle lantern he'd snatched up onto the flagstone floor.

"Trapdoor," he said.

"Where?" Juliana stared at the floor but saw nothing that looked like a trapdoor.

McGregor chuckled. "My nanny and tutors could never find it either." He set down his lantern, dug his fingers under at what looked like a haphazard crack in the floor, and pulled.

The entire piece of flagstone came up and away, revealing a hole into dank blackness.

"Come on," McGregor said cheerfully. "It's not deep. A sturdy Highland lass like yourself will find it no trouble."

He dropped through the hole and landed on hard-packed earth five or so feet down, enough room for the small-statured McGregor to stand upright. A tall man like Elliot, though, would find it a tight fit.

McGregor helped Juliana down then reached back up for his lantern.

"I thought these were the dungeons, when I was a lad," he said, flashing the light on the irregular walls, the old, old stones still a solid foundation for the house above. "But they were the wine cellars. I found a plan of the whole place once."

The darkness was vast, the many walls forming a maze. Juliana crept close behind McGregor, hoping his memory for the place hadn't failed him.

She heard a noise. Movement.

McGregor heard it too and stopped, shining his light into a corner of two thick walls. The lantern caught on something that glittered. Eyes.

A powerful form lunged out of the darkness. McGregor's lantern went flying, and the candle extinguished as the lantern clattered to the floor. McGregor cried out, then Juliana heard the thump of a body slammed against stone.

She ran toward the sound and found the hard-muscled figure of her husband kneeling on the floor, McGregor kicking and flailing under him. McGregor's breath grated, and any words he tried to form were incoherent.

"Elliot!" Juliana shouted as loud as she could. She grabbed Elliot's shoulders and tried to pull him away.

Elliot resisted, twisting to loosen her grasp while keeping hold of McGregor, but Juliana clung fast. She put her lips to his ear and begged, "Elliot. Stop."

He didn't respond. Juliana wrapped her arms all the way around him, tears filling her eyes, her voice breaking on a sob. "Please." She kissed the line of his hair.

Elliot froze. All movement ceased, Elliot's body becoming immobile as a marble statue. Beneath him, McGregor coughed.

"Juliana," Elliot whispered, bewildered, uncertain.

"I'm here."

Elliot turned, swiftly, almost violently, his hands finding her arms, her shoulders, her face. "Juliana."

"I'm here," she repeated, trying to keep her voice steady. "You've given poor Mr. McGregor quite a fright."

"I'm all right." McGregor coughed again and cleared his throat. "Lad, you have a powerful grip. We'll have some Highland games, and I'll put my money on you to win every round."

Elliot ignored him. He ran his hands over Juliana's face and down her arms again. Juliana touched him in return, their only connection in this dark place. She cupped his face, her fingers finding his lips.

"What am I doing here?" he asked her in a harsh voice.

"It doesn't matter," she said. "We've found you."

She put her arms all the way around him. Elliot sank down into her, shuddering, his body so cold, and he clung to her as though he'd never let go.

⁓

Juliana made her calls later that afternoon, without Elliot.

She thought she'd be going by herself, with Hamish to drive her in the dogcart, but at the last minute, Mr. McGregor came barreling down the stairs and out of the house declaring he'd accompany her.

McGregor's kilt bounced above his bony knees, his coat collar half turned wrong. Komal came out after him, grabbed him by the arm, turned him around, and yanked his collar straight.

"Leave me be, interfering old woman." McGregor trailed off into mutters as he stamped through the mud to the dogcart. Komal threw up her hands and disappeared back into the house.

They went first to the neighboring estate of the man called McPherson. McPherson's house was a proper castle, dating to the fourteenth century, McGregor said, with all the drafts to prove it. The house stood on the edge of a loch between a fold of mountains, the road taking them to a drawbridge.

The drawbridge was up when they reached it. Hamish pulled the dogcart to a halt, and Juliana looked up at the round, squat castle. She'd been uneasy leaving Elliot behind, but Mahindar had promised to look after him, and Elliot himself had growled at her to go.

Shutting her out again, like the dark wooden drawbridge that now shut them out of Castle McPherson.

A man appeared on the battlements. He was large and bearlike, and wrapped in blue and red plaid. "Stop there, McGregor!" he bellowed. "I have twenty cannons trained on ye, unless ye can pay the ransom."

Juliana glanced at Hamish, but the young man appeared to be in no way alarmed at this. McGregor stood up in the cart.

"Open up, McPherson, ye daft bastard. I have the new Mrs. McBride with me."

McPherson peered down at them, shading his eyes. "Oh aye?" He looked down on his side of the wall. "Duncan! Wake up and lower the bridge!"

The drawbridge, which looked to be in good repair, cranked down on oiled chains. Hamish, without question, picked up the reins, and the dogcart rattled across the bridge.

On the inside, McPherson's house proved to be up-to-date and pleasant. McPherson had renovated the castle into a comfortable, habitable abode, with plenty of paneling, glass windows, drapes, carpets, books, soft furniture, and a staff of about a dozen to look after it. The castle also had a long gallery full of ancient Scots weaponry, paintings of McPherson ancestors, and relics not only of Culloden, but from clan wars from the more distant past.

McPherson, who met them at the door and proceeded to show Juliana these wonders, was a giant of a man. Where

McGregor was small and wiry, McPherson was tall and rotund, large with good meals and muscle. His red hair and beard were just going gray, and his face was northern Scots fair and freckled, tinged now with summer sunburn.

"I collect," McPherson told Juliana as she admired the historic pieces. "Real Scottish history, not the tartans and fake claymores shopkeepers sell to English tourists. I have mostly McPherson relics here, but some McGregor and McBride as well."

"He *collects*," McGregor snorted. "That's what he calls it. His clan were beggaring thieves is what he means. Raiders. Stole half of what the McGregors owned."

"Aye," McPherson said in a good-natured voice. "And the McGregors stole it back, and helped themselves to more." He laughed heartily. "Always been at it, his family and mine, from way back. His men kept stealing our women, and we stole theirs back, so we're probably related. Cousins eleven-ty times removed or something."

"Half this loot is McGregor," Mr. McGregor said. "That dirk, for instance."

Juliana studied it in its glass case. "He's keeping it well for you."

McPherson roared with laughter again. "I like this lass. What would happen to all this in that tumbledown ruin of yours?"

"She's going to renovate it." McGregor sounded half proud of Juliana, half grudging. "She'll have us eating off silver plates with snowy white napkins before we know it."

"Bloody good thing too." McPherson turned to Juliana as she finished studying the contents of the last case. "Tell your husband he's welcome to come here for shooting anytime he wants. Saw him walking around with a gun yesterday, but I know he found nothing in McGregor's hills. McGregor hasn't had a gillie to keep his game in thirty years."

"McBride will get his own gillie," McGregor snapped, as though eager to defend Elliot.

"Aye, but until he does, he's welcome to shoot on my land. My son moved to Edinburgh and has become a prissified city gent and won't dirty his hands on the land here. But he has sons," McPherson added with a twinkle in his eye. "I am corrupting my grandsons to love all the traditions of Highland Scotland. His father hates it." He bellowed a laugh.

"Mr. McBride will be grateful for your generosity," Juliana said. "He sends his apologies for not calling, but he has been under the weather."

McPherson's eyes lost their twinkle and sympathy took their place. He knew, drat him, exactly what had happened. News certainly traveled quickly.

McGregor broke in. "Aye, last night we spent a long time getting him acquainted with the McGregor malt."

McPherson burst out laughing again. "Ye need a strong constitution for that. He'll be all right, lass." He glanced again at Juliana, as though he knew full well about Elliot's breakdown but was willing to go along with McGregor's explanation.

Later, as a plump maid brought tea into the drawing room, and Juliana poured out, McPherson said, "Speaking of the McGregor malt, I suppose you'll be visiting the Terrells."

"The English family?" Juliana asked. "Yes, I ought to."

"They're not bad sorts," McPherson said. "They know they're incomers and don't try to be more Scottish than the Scots. But they have visitors, a lowland Scottish family of the stiff-necked variety, lately back from India. They say they know your husband. Or know friends of your husband, in any case."

Would wild Elliot likely be acquainted with stiff-necked, dour people who'd probably refused beautiful meals such as the one Mahindar had served last night? Then again, Elliot had hidden depths. She couldn't be certain of the sort of people Elliot would know.

"Sounds like we should bypass them today, eh, lass?" McGregor asked.

"No, indeed." Juliana watched the stream of tea as she refilled her cup, giving McGregor and McPherson time to sneak nips of brandy into theirs from McPherson's flask. "We will have to go and endure."

"You see?" Mr. McGregor said to McPherson. "Prim and proper. She wants to have a midsummer fête and ball. Just like when Mrs. McGregor, God rest her soul, was with us."

"In your house?" McPherson boomed. "She'll need a bloody miracle then."

"Not a miracle, Mr. McPherson," Juliana said. "Careful planning. With organization, one can do anything."

~~~

Juliana regretfully took her leave of Mr. McPherson soon after. The castle was a homey place in spite of its bulk, McPherson warm in spite of his.

After the maid helped Juliana into her light coat and gloves, McPherson, out of earshot of McGregor, said in a low voice, "I'm afraid you've got your work cut out for you, lass."

"Castle McGregor?" Juliana asked, straightening her gloves. "Yes, but as I said, organizing will solve most of the problems."

"I didn't mean with th' monstrosity he calls a house." McPherson took on look of sympathy. "I meant with McBride. Now, don't draw up all proud. He's been to hell and back, and that touches a man. I've scraped through some tough places in Africa, and I know what 'tis like. There are some horrors no man should have to live through." McPherson put a broad hand on her shoulder. "If it becomes too much for ye, or him, ye send him to me, and we'll have a nice day's fishing. Nothing calms the soul like a day on the river."

"Thank you, Mr. McPherson. You are kind."

"You're a proud lass, I can see. Determined to take care

of him. McBride's a lucky man. But remember—he's welcome here. Ye both are."

"Thank you," Juliana said again, and then McGregor was bellowing that they needed to get a move on.

They all worried about Elliot, Juliana thought as the dogcart bumped across the bridge and set off again toward the village.

The idea warmed her and at the same time bothered her a bit, because Elliot was not a pathetic creature of misery. He was stronger than all of them. The fact that after his ordeal he hadn't turned into a drooling lunatic chained to a bed attested to that strength. He knew madness could take him anytime, and he was fighting it. She'd not let anyone forget that.

Juliana's next call was to Mrs. Rossmoran's cottage, which was set far back into the woods near Castle McGregor. The house of whitewashed stone with slate roof looked in good repair, and a neat garden with rows of cabbages, carrots, greens, and other vegetables ran alongside it. A patch of pansies bloomed defiantly among the rest of the practical garden.

Mrs. Rossmoran's granddaughter Fiona—Hamish's cousin, a pretty girl about Hamish's age—told them that unfortunately Mrs. Rossmoran was laid up this morning, but would be happy to know they'd called. Fiona waved to Hamish, who returned the wave before he jerked the cart around and headed for the Terrells.

The Terrells occupied a much more modern house on a hill overlooking the village. The long, two-storied house was built of fine stone with a slate roof, black painted shutters, and square chimneys. Its garden was formal, with shrubberies, fountains, and summer flower beds in full bloom.

The drawing room was large, airy, and elegant, reminding Juliana of the one at her father's estate near Stirling. Another tea tray, more pouring out, this time by Mrs. Terrell. The gentlemen drank whiskey rather than tea, but they lingered in the drawing room, talking about masculine pursuits.

Juliana did not like Mr. and Mrs. Dalrymple. She wasn't certain where her dislike came from, because they were pleasant spoken and polite, despite McPherson's description of them.

Mrs. Dalrymple wore a rather prim gray gown, its bustle so small as to be only a nod to the fashion. Her hair was brown going to gray, dressed in a simple coiffure, and she wore no earrings or brooches, her one piece of jewelry the thin wedding band on her finger. No frivolity for Mrs. Dalrymple, her ensemble proclaimed.

She also confirmed that, indeed, she and her husband had met Elliot in the Punjab.

"We did not mix much, of course," Mrs. Dalrymple said. "Mr. McBride was a planter and a single man, while my husband had a position with the ICS."

"Indian Civil Service," Mrs. Terrell translated.

"We did not mingle much with the plantation owners," Mrs. Dalrymple went on, rather haughtily. "One didn't, you know. Planters were so apt to take Indian wives. Not that Mr. McBride ever exhibited that inclination," she said quickly. "But our dear friend Mr. Stacy unfortunately succumbed."

"I still cannot understand why your Mr. Stacy would want to marry an Indian woman," Mrs. Terrell said. "How positively awful. Imagine living in intimate quarters with a heathen."

Juliana thought of Priti, the daughter of the woman they discussed, and felt her temper stir. "One must have lived with Indian people all throughout the house, in India."

"Well, yes, the *servants*," Mrs. Dalrymple said. "One didn't *marry* them."

"Was she a servant, then?" Juliana asked, her heart beating faster. "This lady?"

"Good heavens, I have no idea. One didn't like to ask. I suppose she could have been from a good Indian family, but I doubt it, you know. They never let their women leave the purdah, and certainly not to marry into Scottish families."

"I see." Juliana clicked her cup to her saucer. "What happened to Mr. Stacy?"

Mrs. Dalrymple stilled. Her husband came alert on the other side of the room, ceasing his droning to Mr. McGregor.

Into the ensuing silence, Mrs. Dalrymple said, "Mr. Stacy was killed. I'm sorry to have to tell you this, Mrs. McBride, but we very much believe that your husband was his murderer."

Chapter 12

Juliana couldn't move. Her wrist hurt from the angle at which she held her teacup, but she could not unbend it to set her cup down.

"Killed?" she repeated, her lips stiff. "Yes, I heard that Mr. Stacy died in India, but in an earthquake."

"That is what Mr. McBride *told* you," Mrs. Dalrymple said. "We are taking steps even now to present the proof that your husband killed Mr. Stacy." She lifted her cup again. "There. I have warned you."

Mrs. Terrell looked faintly embarrassed, and Mr. McGregor slammed his whiskey glass to the table. "Bloody nonsense! McBride's a good lad, wouldn't hurt a flea. You're talking out your ass."

Mrs. Terrell gasped. "Really, Mr. McGregor, your language."

"Why mind my language when you are bandying about the name of a good Highland lad? Ought to be ashamed."

"To be honest, my dear," Mr. Dalrymple, more soft-spoken than his wife, said, "we don't know that he hurt our Mr. Stacy. We have only the rumor."

McGregor picked up his whiskey. "Well said. I like you, Dollimple."

"Dalrymple," Mr. Dalrymple corrected.

"Dull Pimple." McGregor drank down the rest of his whiskey.

Mrs. Dalrymple looked distressed. Juliana rose. "I believe we shall leave now. Thank you for the tea, Mrs. Terrell."

McGregor got himself to his feet, his kilt swinging. "Excellent, lass. All this liquid makes me have to relieve myself. Nice to have met you, Dall Blimple."

Juliana somehow got herself out of the room. She stalked out of the house, kindly thanking the Scottish maid who brought her things, resisting the urge to tell the girl to find other employment.

But, Juliana thought viciously, when Castle McGregor was ready, she'd offer positions to everyone in the village, and the Terrells and their friends would have to either scuttle back to England or fetch and carry for themselves.

Behind her she heard Mrs. Terrell admonish Mrs. Dalrymple in a low voice, and Mrs. Dalrymple's shrill reply, "He killed our Mr. Stacy. There's no doubt in my mind. And he should swing for it."

"Not to worry, lass," McGregor said cheerfully to Juliana as they climbed into the dogcart behind Hamish. "I got our revenge on them. I spit in the whiskey decanter."

⁓

Elliot walked. He hadn't brought the shotgun this time, to Mahindar's relief, though he'd never loaded it the last time he'd taken it out. Priti had been with him, and he hadn't wanted to risk the little girl getting hurt.

Today he tramped through bracken and mud, skirting small fields thick with summer grain. To the east, the land rolled down to the sea, which stretched wide and blue to be swallowed by the gray horizon.

He walked to forget the look on Juliana's face when they'd climbed up out of the cellars, her cheeks streaked with dirt and tears, her pretty gown ruined. She'd gazed at Elliot in anxiousness, fear even, a look he never wanted to see again.

She'd discovered today what Elliot truly was. If she'd known when they'd sat together in the dim chapel what she knew today, she'd never have made the smiling suggestion that Elliot marry her.

While in the cellars this morning, Elliot had truly believed himself back in that prison. All his senses had told him so—he'd heard the men speaking the dialect of the tribe, smelled the filth that accumulated in the holes, tasted the dust in the air. He had *been* there.

And yet, Elliot couldn't remember for the life of him why he'd gone into the tunnels beneath the boiler room or how he'd even found them. Exploring the house? Searching for something? He had no idea.

Being outdoors was safer. No danger of him confusing this country with the wilds in the northern Punjab and Afghanistan, where a knifelike wall of mountains marched across the horizon, and the sea was only a distant dream.

Here, conifers and leafy trees soared to the sky, covering the folds of mountain. Meadows full of wildflowers and wandering sheep stretched along the hills.

Elliot found himself emerging from the wood to a whitewashed cottage with a slate roof, a vegetable garden filling the side yard. A young red-haired woman tended the garden, crouching to pull weeds with her gloved hands. She heard Elliot's step and rose, smiling with delight.

"Mr. McBride. Ye've come. My grandmother will be that happy to see ye."

The young woman tugged off her gloves and moved quickly to the open door of the house, apparently assuming he'd follow. Elliot made his decision and stepped inside after her, ducking his head under a low, thick lintel.

The inside of the house was small but warm. This was an old crofter's house, which had originally had one large room and a loft, but in recent years, interior walls had been built to divide up the house. The front door opened into a kitchen and small sitting room, the sitting room containing cushioned armchairs and a wide hearth rug.

The walls were freshly painted, curtains hung in the windows, and a flower box outside the window overflowed with summer blossoms. Cozy. Juliana would like it.

The door to an inner room opened, and Mrs. Rossmoran, leaning on her black cane, emerged. Elliot offered Mrs. Rossmoran his arm, led her to the chair, and made sure she settled herself without harm. Her granddaughter Fiona moved to the kitchen, filled a kettle from the pump at the sink, and set the kettle on the small black stove.

"Thank ye, lad," Mrs. Rossmoran said. "Ye're a gentleman, even if ye're kin to McGregor." She thumped the seat of the second chair with her cane. "Sit there and let me look you over. Your lady wife came to call, but she was with McGregor, and I didn't want to see him. A lovely creature, is the new Mrs. McBride. Very proper too, paying me a formal visit. Her mother was a Duncan." Mrs. Rossmoran grunted as she moved deeper into the chair. "Daughter of one of my friends at school. Quite a featherhead was your wife's mother. Charming, but a featherhead."

Elliot had nothing to answer to this outpouring. He gave Mrs. Rossmoran a polite nod as he obediently took the seat, and she charged along.

"Juliana's mother charmed prim and proper St. John into marriage for his money all right, smooth as butter, then she ignored him, bought more clothes than any woman has need for, and completely neglected her daughter. Mrs. St. John let the servants do as they pleased, and mostly they didn't please to do anything. And so poor little Juliana was left quite to herself. It isn't good for a child to be alone like that. Oh, she had nannies, a proper governess, and finishing school—her father was not the sort to forget about her education—but her playmates were footmen and maids, her confidants the housekeeper and butler. Any polish Miss St. John acquired she managed to put on herself, never mind that fine academy she attended, which I thought a waste of time and money."

Elliot recalled how, the few times he'd visited Juliana's home with Ainsley in his youth, they'd been banished from any room Mrs. St. John might enter. Juliana had pretended she didn't mind—it was a fact of life that children did not mingle much with their parents—but Elliot had seen Juliana's hurt when her mother did happen to cross their path and never noticed her daughter in front of her.

"Don't look so surprised at my knowing all this, lad. I might be buried out here, but I know every Scottish family this side of the country and on up into the Orkneys, and I get stacks and stacks of letters."

Fiona brought over the tea tray and placed it on the table. "She does, Mr. McBride. Every day, letters and letters. And sends a pile out herself."

"So I know all about your young wife," Mrs. Rossmoran said, signaling Fiona to serve Elliot first. "She's a good lass, from what I hear. I did shake my head when I learned she was to marry Mr. Barclay. Not a good match for her. He's an incomer without much to recommend him, his family dull as ditchwater. Thank heavens he eloped, but with all things, a piano teacher! Well, may she have the joy of him."

Elliot accepted his tea. "I'm just as happy he stepped out of the way."

Mrs. Rossmoran took the cup Fiona gave her in both hands, but she didn't tremble. "Of course you are. I always thought you and young Juliana would make a couple. Helps that she's such friends with your sister, and your brother and her father thick in finance. Though why a man has truck with finance, I don't know. But these days, there's not much in the land anymore, and bankers and merchants rule the world. I hear *you* have quite a penny put by."

"A bit." Elliot drank his tea. Conversation with Mrs. Rossmoran was proving to be refreshing—Elliot didn't have to say a word.

"Made it out of the subcontinent, didn't you? So many go out there to make their fortunes, and they end up destitute, or dead of disease, or addicted to some noxious substance. But that never happened to you, eh? Ye kept your head and made money off foolish Englishmen who wanted you to teach them how to make money there." Mrs. Rossmoran chuckled. "Wise, lad. When I was a girl, I watched the Sassenachs drive away the Scottish farmers and burn out tenants so they could turn Scotland into one big sheep pasture. Fitting that one of our own took away the money all those sheep made for them."

It hadn't been quite that simple, but Elliot didn't bother correcting her. Her outpouring was lightening his darkness a little.

"So what are you going to do, eh?" Mrs. Rossmoran paused to take a sip of tea. "Young Hamish says you're mad as a hatter. You look sane enough to me, but Hamish says you're a raving madman sometimes. My grandnephew likes to exaggerate, but the core of what he says is true. Have you seen a doctor about it?"

"I have. He wasn't much use." Patrick had suggested a specialist, who'd listened to Elliot, taken his pulse, said *Hmm* a lot, and prescribed a course of barley water.

Mrs. Rossmoran sniffed. "Doctors only tell you what you pay them to tell you. I wager he gave you some foul muck in a black bottle that will do you no good at all. Or he says it's all nonsense and you need to stiffen your resolve. But doctors are too young these days, coming out of schools with highfalutin ideas about what goes on inside the body. They pay no attention to what goes on inside people's lives, do they?" She patted Elliot's kilt-clad knee. "What you're doing is grieving, lad. Grieving for yourself. Because what ye were is gone, isn't it? You've seen too much, and you've been hurt too much. The man you were will never come back."

All true. Every word was true. Hearing this blunt assessment coming out of Mrs. Rossmoran's small, pursed mouth was both startling and comforting.

"You've started off well, though, in your marrying," Mrs. Rossmoran said. "You stick with her, lad, and you'll do fine."

"Aye. I can agree with that."

Mrs. Rossmoran laughed, showing she'd lost a good many of her back teeth. "I thought you would. Saw the twinkle in your eye. That's what ye need, lad. Bairns. A good many of them. Ye get on home and get to it."

Elliot departed not long later, swimming with tea and full of shortbread that Fiona had served hot from the oven. Nothing for it but that Elliot should wrap up half of it to take home with him.

Mrs. Rossmoran might have something, he thought as he climbed along the side of a hill, well under the trees, heading in the direction of Castle McGregor. *Bairns.*

Elliot always felt better when he was with Priti. How much better would he feel if he and Juliana surrounded themselves with more wee ones, all red haired like their mother? A whole nursery of children for Priti to play with and for Elliot to bask in.

The steps he'd have to take in order to bring in those wee ones made his heart lighter.

His body warmed at the memory of Juliana in the dining room, her body under his on the table, how fine it had been to climb into bed with her later and draw her back against his body. He would have done more if he hadn't had to spend considerable time calming down McGregor. Tonight he would—

The woods didn't change, and only silence flooded it. But Elliot halted, every nerve alert.

He scanned the hill that rose to his left, its towering trees cutting off his line of sight in that direction. But he knew. The prickle in the back of his neck told him.

There was a watcher in these woods.

And he was watching Elliot.

The thought rose—*Please, not again*—but Elliot squelched it. He was mad, yes, but his madness couldn't make an entire wood go silent.

Woods teemed with life. Birds, beasts, and insects lived out their existence in their particular strip of territory— they were born, raised, ventured from the nest, found mates, raised their own young, and died. All that life made noise.

A silent wood meant a predator, one so deadly that all animals stilled, as Elliot did. That predator might be a bear, a wolf, or more likely these days, a human.

How long Elliot stood unmoving under the noiseless trees, he wasn't certain.

Gradually, the sounds began to return. A robin called, another challenged. Undergrowth rustled—squirrels or rabbits returning to their business.

Elliot scanned the hill again. Nothing had changed. But the animals knew, as Elliot knew, that the hunter had gone.

He remembered now why he'd gone to the boiler room, his excitement in finding the trapdoor. He remembered what he'd been looking for before his mind had seized him and transported him to the past.

Elliot started walking, fast, faster, until he was running down the slope, back to discover whether he'd been right.

⁓

Mahindar informed Juliana that Elliot was not there when she arrived home from her call to the Terrells, but before she had the chance to worry, Elliot came striding in through the open front door.

"Juliana, come with me."

He was out of breath and walking swiftly, but his eyes were alight with determination.

Juliana opened her mouth to ask where he wanted to take her, but closed it when he shoved a shortbread-scented package at Mahindar, grabbed Juliana by the hand, and started pulling her to the kitchen.

"May I at least take off my hat?" she asked.

Elliot frowned down at the hat's saucy tilt of brim, the feathers that curled over the crown, and the ruche of ribbon in the front. He wasn't studying the hat, Juliana realized, but deciding a way to conquer it.

His fingers made short work of the pins, then he lifted off the hat and tossed it into the hands of Channan, who'd hurried out of the kitchen to join them.

Elliot took Juliana's hand again and towed her onward, through the kitchen, down the stairs in the back of the scullery, and to the darkness of the cellar and the heat of the boiler room.

At least the boiler was working now. A red flicker came from the great hulk of iron in the corner, which would heat water for the kitchen, and with luck and time, the bathrooms upstairs. By this light, Elliot lit two candle lanterns and passed her one.

Mahindar appeared in the doorway. "Sahib, why are you down here again?"

Elliot handed Mahindar his lantern, shed his coat, pushed up his sleeves, and hauled open the heavy trapdoor.

"Because I remembered why I came down here this morning." He took the lantern back from Mahindar. "You stay up here," he told the man. "I want someone to know where we are in case the door falls closed, and I can't open it. Which is what happened to me this morning."

"Ah," Mahindar said, as though that explained everything.

"Juliana?" Elliot asked. "Are you willing to explore with me?"

"Perhaps the memsahib will want to change her dress," Mahindar said. "It is powerfully dirty down there."

Juliana glanced down at her rust-colored silk. She had liked the gown when she'd put it on, but now it was tainted by the fact that she'd worn it to meet the Dalrymples. Elliot was impatient, and Juliana didn't want to take the time to go upstairs and change.

"That's all right," she said. "After all, I've worn it once now."

The flippant remark did not have the desired effect. Elliot said nothing, and Mahindar looked distressed. "Wait, I beg you. Wait one moment."

He dashed off and came running back in less than a minute with a large, white, flapping garment. He set Juliana's lantern on the floor, bunched up the garment, and dropped it over Juliana's head.

It was one of Mahindar's, Juliana realized as she settled it, the long shirts that went over his white trousers. This one was clean and large enough to cover most of Juliana's gown.

"I don't want to ruin it," Juliana said.

Mahindar waved that away and shoved the lantern back into her hand. "I have many. Go. Go."

Elliot lowered himself into the hole, set his lantern on the edge, and reached up to lift Juliana down with him.

He had to stoop in the low room below, but this time, the closeness did not appear to worry him. As soon as Juliana had steadied herself next to him, Elliot led her onward.

"I have something I must tell you," Juliana said as she followed Elliot into the bowels of the old castle. "I'm afraid it concerns Mr. Archibald Stacy."

Elliot did not answer. He strode on quickly, despite having to bend head and shoulders, and Juliana hurried to keep up with him.

"You are most exasperating, Elliot McBride," she said.

He reached back and took her hand again. "I know."

His strong grip was a lifeline, pulling her through the dark. Their lamps were weak, candles illuminating only small circles of space. Hamish had promised that kerosene was on its way to the house, although perhaps wax candles inside tin lanterns were a bit safer down in this unknown darkness.

"Where are we going?" Juliana whispered. There was no need to whisper, but the dense warmth around them seemed to require it.

Elliot answered in normal tones, sounding perfectly sane. "When I was a lad, I found the plans of the old castle in one of the books in Uncle McGregor's library. The castle had been a giant of a place, with underground storage and living quarters, in case of siege. Uncle McGregor brought me down here and showed me a little of it then, and I started exploring it again after I bought the place."

"People lived down here?" Juliana shivered. Such a maze, the roof so low. It would have been appallingly dark, the inhabitants not having even the good candles she and Elliot carried now.

"They lived here when they had to," Elliot said. "Uncle McGregor says the McPhersons raided often in those days, and the McGregors would hide the women and children and anything else valuable down here."

"Mr. McPherson seems quite congenial to be descended from raiders. By the bye, he sends the message that you're welcome to fish or shoot on his estate anytime you wish."

"Six hundred years ago, the McPhersons were brutal warriors, and so were the McGregors. It was a long feud. Times change; people don't."

Whatever that meant, he didn't explain.

"Elliot," Juliana said as he took her onward through the darkness. "I know I am supposed to be an obedient wife, letting my husband decide my fate unquestioningly. But I'm afraid I never had good examples of obedient wives in my life. My mother did as she pleased. My stepmother is a bit more considerate of other people's wants, but Gemma makes no secret of her opinions. So I must ask you—do you intend to live at Castle McGregor for the rest of your life, exploring the old castle and walking about the Highlands? Or may we, at some point, return to civilization? If only for a brief interlude? My wardrobe will soon be depleted at the rate we are carrying on."

Elliot straightened abruptly, and Juliana realized they'd stepped into a room whose ceiling rose high enough for him to stand at his full height. Juliana's candle beam didn't reach the roof, but she felt the vastness of wherever they were, the cool draft that meant clean air flowed from somewhere.

"We won't be returning to Edinburgh yet," Elliot said absently, flashing around his lantern.

"I do understand that too many people at once unnerve you," Juliana said. "You have been out of the habit of seeing company, and people do tend to whisper about you. I know this. In fact, I'm very surprised you came to Edinburgh at all, though so fortunate for me to find you lurking on my wedding day."

"Of course I went to Edinburgh."

His voice held a sharp note, and Juliana found his attention fixed hard on her, his gray eyes glittering silver in the candlelight.

"To attend my wedding?" Juliana asked him, her voice faint. "How civil of you."

She'd sent the invitation to Rona inviting *The McBride Family*. Juliana had told herself that she'd worded the missive that way because she had no way of knowing whether the three younger male McBrides would be in the country for the occasion.

But Juliana knew she'd never have been able to pen an invitation to Elliot specifically. Keeping the request general, she'd avoided having to write Elliot's name.

Elliot's hand, still around hers, gripped harder. "I didn't

go to Edinburgh to attend your bloody wedding. I went to stop it."

Juliana blinked. "To stop . . . ?"

His gray gaze was so sharp it cut. "Of course to stop it, lass. Do you think I'd allow anyone but me to marry my Juliana?"

Chapter 13

"But . . ." Juliana's mouth went dry. His gaze was filled with hot determination, the Elliot who'd carved a place for himself in a faraway land and didn't let nearly a year of imprisonment kill him. "If you didn't want me to marry Grant, why wait until my wedding day to speak?"

"Because I knew I'd have the best chance to win you if I stood up in the church and told the world that I had reason not to let you be joined to Barclay."

"What reason?" she asked, barely audible. A person could stop a wedding if they could prove that one party was already married to someone else, or that the two in question were too closely related, or that the marriage had been forced—none of which applied in the case of Juliana and Grant.

"I would have said that Juliana was my lass, had always been mine. That I wasn't stepping aside for any other."

He had more in his eyes than he ever said in words—raw pain behind the gray, the loneliness of a man who thought he'd be alone forever.

"Why didn't you tell me?" Juliana asked, voice still soft but thick with emotion. "Why didn't you tell me when I was waiting to marry him, when I knew I couldn't have you?"

Elliot dropped her hand and flashed his lantern around again. "Because what would you have seen if I'd come crawling to you when I came home from India? A broken man, one afraid of the dark and equally afraid of the light. I was nothing." His voice was fierce. "You've seen what I still do. You wouldn't have wanted a husband like me—or ye'd have married me out of pity, and I couldn't have stood that. I wanted to have something to give ye. A house, a husband who could walk upright most days . . ."

Juliana stood still, unable to move. Her breath came sharply, cut off by the tight lacing of her corset. One thought stood out among the rest—she hadn't known how Elliot had felt about her. All these years, when she'd thought of him, craved to be with him, knowing he was wandering the wide world, out of her reach—he'd been thinking of her.

"You ought to have told me," she whispered.

Elliot didn't change expression, but she saw the windows to his soul shutter to her again. "You know now."

He turned away, moving off into the darkness.

Juliana hurried after him, her heart pounding. She moved back and forth between elation and anger, bewilderment and wild happiness. Elliot, handsome Elliot, the lad she'd loved from afar, had wanted her all this time. She'd watched him swarm up the tree to retrieve the kite, secretly admiring how athletically his limbs moved, while pretending no interest at all. The firmness of his cheek under her lips when she'd given him the rewarding kiss had been imprinted on her thoughts for weeks afterward. The kiss he'd stolen when they'd danced at her debut ball had lingered for years.

Her feet splashed in water, breaking her spinning thoughts. "Where are we now?" she asked, dragging up her damp skirts.

Elliot flashed his lantern around. "If I am right, a cave

in the side of the hill between the McGregors and the Ross-morans." He took her hand again, his fingers warm.

"Why is it wet?"

"The tunnel runs along the river. The river might even cut into it."

Elliot led her along at a slower pace, lifting his lantern high and studying the ground before he allowed Juliana to move forward with him. The floor of the cavern sloped downward, the gleam of water trickling across the bottom.

He moved confidently, and Juliana realized she should worry that Elliot wouldn't know the way back. But she didn't worry. He'd studied the plans, he'd previously explored the tunnels, and people in India had hired him for this very sort of thing—to explore, to discover things, to find the way for others.

This Elliot exuded capable, quiet competence. The broken, wild-eyed man who'd looked at her a few moments ago and confessed he'd gone to Edinburgh to break up her wedding had gone.

Elliot led her across the smooth stone floor to the higher end of the slope, the sound of water to their left. The draft Juliana had felt before strengthened, the breath of air refreshing after the dank warmth of the tunnels.

Elliot walked her unerringly to a hole to the outside world. The opening, at Elliot's head height, was covered with thick brush, bushes having grown right over it. Elliot blew out the candle in his lantern, handed the lantern to Juliana, and reached through the hole to break away branches.

He easily tore off many of the thinner pieces of the brush, but the trunks of two bushes had spread themselves across the hole. Climbing out this way would be possible but a scratchy, tight fit.

Elliot took both lanterns back from Juliana, blew out the candle in hers as well, and tossed the lanterns through the hole to the earth outside. He boosted himself a little way out of the hole then half climbed, half lifted himself over

the remainder of the bushes. The spindly branches caught
on his kilt and lifted it high over his hips as he worked his
way through.

"Elliot," Juliana said in a small voice. "You know you
are wearing nothing under that."

His taut thighs and strong buttocks worked to lift Elliot
out of the hole before his entire body disappeared. Juliana
stepped worriedly to the opening just as Elliot looked back
inside at her, his smile full of sin.

"I'm a Scotsman," he said.

Still flashing the wicked grin, he cleared more branches
from the hole and reached for her.

Juliana clung to him as she kicked and wriggled her
way out, Mahindar's shirt now torn and stained with dirt.

The hole opened onto the sheer side of a hill. Elliot leaned
against the almost vertical slope and helped Juliana find
footholds, tussocks of grass that wouldn't slip under her feet.

They'd emerged to a treeless heath that was filled with
rocks and bushes like those which had grown over the hole.
The slope on which they stood ran steeply down to the
rushing river below—one misstep could plunge her into it.

Elliot was not about to let her go. He held Juliana with
immovable strength as he guided her along their makeshift
path, until they came to a true path that had been cut into
the side of the hill. The sound of sheep bleating in the distance indicated what this path was likely for.

Elliot settled Juliana against a large boulder that might
once have been a standing stone, her feet on firm ground,
then he climbed back up the hill. Juliana watched him cover
the hole, replacing the branches and smoothing the earth.

He retrieved the lanterns he'd tossed out and made his
way back down to her, walking sure-footedly along the
ridge to the path, never a misstep. He might have been
walking on a wide, paved road for all Elliot noticed.

He returned to Juliana's boulder and leaned on it next to

her. "This valley would have been a good place for the McGregors to come to evade the McPhersons," he said. "The McGregors could have crossed the river and hidden in the meadows beyond without anyone realizing."

"But then they'd have abandoned the castle to the rival clan," Juliana said, following his gaze across river. "Do you think any of McGregor's wild ancestors would have done that?"

"No, but they'd have sent away the women and the wee ones. The families could have lived off the land in that valley a long time, in the warm months."

Juliana took in the beauty of the scene, the river rushing below them—the same one that had frightened Nandita so when they'd clattered over the bridge. Mr. McGregor and Hamish both claimed that the river teemed with fish, and in the folds of the valley, the McGregor women and children of old would have found berries and other sustenance. In peaceful times, they'd have explored the valley that rolled between the hills, and would have known exactly where to hide when battle came.

"I'll wager there are bushes plump with berries down there now," Juliana said, her mouth starting to water. "How about it, Elliot? Shall we bring back a bucketful and teach Mahindar how to make raspberry fool?"

"We don't have a bucket."

Juliana lifted the white shirt and made a bowl of it. "I used to do this with my pinafore when I was a girl at my father's manor house. I'd bring home plenty of bright red berries, half of which I ate on the way. Drove my governess wild."

Elliot didn't look at her, but a faint smile crossed his face. "The Juliana I knew always had her pinafore neat and clean. Never a hair out of place, following all the rules."

"That was the Juliana I showed to company. When I was alone in the woods, I was a bit more lackadaisical. No one to see me, you see."

"I wasn't company. I was the unruly brother of your friend."

"Perhaps, but when Ainsley paid a call, or I called on her, things had to be done properly. She laughed at my insistence on etiquette, but she played along."

"The fact that you convinced Ainsley to do anything by the rules is a bloody miracle," Elliot said, with the fondness of an older brother for a harum-scarum sister.

"I remember she rather enjoyed raiding the pantry when we were at school. I thought her audacious, but she never minded sharing the spoils. But she turned out all right, didn't she? Happily married now, with a child of her own and another on the way."

"I want children."

Elliot's blunt statement made her stop. The sun was descending behind the hills to their right, casting shadows over the river below. Elliot looked down the hill at the roiling water, bracing himself on the boulder. The sun slanted from the jagged mountain to sharpen his face and outline his body in a faint glow.

When he looked at Juliana again, the liquid light brushed the fine net of scars that ran from his temple into his hair. "Many children," he said.

"I see." Juliana's heart thumped. "Is *that* why you rushed to Edinburgh to stop my wedding and steal the bride?"

"No, to take you away from that twit, Barclay. Lucky for him, he'd eloped, so I didn't have to kill him."

"Kill him?"

"For his sake, I hope he took his pianist back to England. He embarrassed you, and I'm not forgiving him that." Elliot looked off into the distance again. "I didn't realize I wanted more children then."

"But you realize it now?"

"Something Mrs. Rossmoran said to me today put it in mind."

"Mrs. Rossmoran . . ." Juliana blinked. "You spoke to her

today? When I stopped, her granddaughter said she was poorly. Is she all right?"

"Mrs. Rossmoran is the hardiest woman in the Highlands. She had her granddaughter lie because she didn't want to see Uncle McGregor."

"Oh." Juliana rearranged her ideas about the frail old Highland rose. "I'll remember to make my next call alone, or with you. She apparently doesn't mind seeing *you*."

"Today, she didn't. Next time might be different."

Juliana waved her hands in exasperation. "*Anyway*, because I didn't see Mrs. Rossmoran, we went right on to the Terrells, and I need to tell you what happened there. The Terrells have some friends named Dalrymple, and I'm afraid they believe you killed Mr. Stacy."

He didn't look at her. The only indication that Elliot had heard her came from a faint twitch of brows.

"Elliot?"

"Who knows?" he said slowly. "I might have."

Juliana had opened her mouth to agree with him that it was absurd, and the words got tangled up. "I know . . . she could not . . . *What?* But you said yourself that Mr. Stacy had disappeared when you went back to your plantation, and you never saw him again."

"Never saw him again that I remember," he corrected. "Mahindar told me he'd been reported dead in Lahore, but that was when I was very ill, and I have little memory of anything I did during that time."

"But Mahindar would know," Juliana said. "He nursed you, didn't he? He's been with you through everything. Perhaps you ought to tell me exactly what happened to you."

Elliot paused, but when Juliana thought he would begin pouring out the whole tale, he only said, "Have Mahindar tell you. He will be more coherent."

"But if you *had* done such a dreadful thing, even if you didn't remember, Mahindar would know about it. And he'd have told you."

Elliot shook his head. "Mahindar might have kept it from me. From everyone."

"Why on earth would he do that?"

"To protect me. If I don't know what I've done, I won't rush out and turn myself in to the police."

He was far, far too calm about this. "Well, I refuse to believe it," Juliana said. "What reason would you have for killing Mr. Stacy?"

Elliot's shoulders went up in a small shrug. "Maybe I was taking my revenge on him."

"This is all absurd. I will ask Mahindar to tell me the truth."

"He lies for me very well. And *to* me."

Juliana lifted her chin. "Not to me, he won't. But we must do something about the Dalrymples. We cannot have the police rushing up here to arrest you."

Elliot's eyes narrowed as he at last looked at Juliana fully. "I agree. I've never heard of these Dalrymples."

"They claim they lived in India and were great friends of Mr. Stacy. And that they'd met you at least once."

"Stacy never mentioned them. And I never met them."

"Interesting." Juliana tapped her lip. "I believe we should learn more about them, and I believe I know who to ask. Now then, you said, before you dragged me through the caves, that you remembered why you'd come down to them this morning. What did you mean?"

"I'm not sure now. I had an idea, but . . ."

Juliana folded her hands. "I'd be ever so interested to learn, now that I've climbed through all the caves and am dirty and scratched."

Elliot turned and looked straight at her, all interest in Mr. Stacy, the Dalrymples, and their horrible accusation gone. "But I'd rather go back to talking about children." His focus was entirely on her again, penetrating any barrier Juliana might have raised, bypassing any stray thought.

"I want children, and I want them with you. Do you want them with me?"

His look was heart-stopping. Juliana's body warmed, the breeze in the shadows becoming nothing.

"Yes," she said. "I do."

Chapter 14

The little smile she gave him when she answered, half coy, half innocent, made his blood incandescent.

He did not want Juliana involved in his past, did not want it to touch her. Juliana was his now, his future.

Elliot turned to face her as she leaned against the boulder, one of his knees going between her legs, leaned down, and kissed her.

She tasted of dust and the wind of the late afternoon. Her skin was damp with perspiration, cheeks streaked with dirt. She was achingly beautiful.

Elliot hadn't bothered with breeches beneath his kilt, the weather being so warm. Juliana's comment on his naked state below the tartan had twisted heat through him. She liked to look at him, had no embarrassment about her husband's naked body. He'd always known she wasn't a vaporish miss, and he loved her for it now. His cock bumped Juliana's skirt through his plaid, wanting to be inside her, wanting them to be naked on the ground on this quiet, wild hill.

Dangerous. But he knew the watcher was gone, the noises of the countryside normal. Birds flitted in the brush and rabbits rustled, not worried about Elliot and Juliana.

Juliana's mouth held warmth, her lips more skilled at kissing him now. She shaped them to his, and her tongue flicked across Elliot's without him having to coax.

His cock tightened even more. He wanted her tongue on it, her lips closing around him while he skimmed his hands through her hair and thrust gently into her mouth. But that was the skill of a courtesan. Elliot would teach it to her, but not here, not yet.

Elliot broke the kiss, liking how Juliana kept her hands clasped behind his neck, her eyes half closed, as though not wanting to let him go. Her mouth was moist and red, and Elliot kissed it again.

Then he gently untwined her grip and sank down to kneel in front of her. Elliot bunched her skirt in his hands, the hem damp and muddy now, and pushed it upward.

Juliana reached down. "Elliot, what are you . . . ?"

Elliot lifted the skirt and petticoat all the way to her hips. The bustle she wore today was smaller than her evening one, the stiff shaper plumping her skirt out at the back with a soft linen panel in the front.

He unfastened the hooks and pulled the bustle from her. He'd have to start dictating that she didn't wear a bustle at all when they knew they'd be alone.

Elliot next undid the drawstring of her lawn drawers and tugged them down.

He barely heard her faint noise of protest. He studied his warm-scented Juliana, hair fiery red between her thighs, the curls already moist. He leaned forward and kissed her, breathing her in. "You're wet for me."

One slender finger traced his temple. "I cannot seem to help it."

"I like you wet for me." Elliot drew his tongue down the seam of her cleft. "I like tasting you."

Her fingers moved in his hair, less controlled. "Someone might come."

"Warn me."

Elliot didn't care if they did. Let these Highland people see him on his knees loving his wife. They'd know she belonged to him, know he'd go after them if they harmed her in any way.

Elliot held her skirts bunched in his hands. Smooth cotton brushed his face as he leaned into her, tongue dancing along her opening.

Juliana moved her feet apart without him asking. She smelled of honey and salt, and her own nectar. Elliot drew some onto his tongue, pausing to savor it.

Her little berry firmed as he breathed on it. Elliot, hands full of fabric, slid his tongue over her, opened his mouth to reach more of her. Her legs moved apart still farther, and there was her moisture, sweet and made for him.

"Dripping wet," he murmured. Her swift intake of breath made him ache.

He thrust his mouth over her and drank. His tongue moved, his throat worked as he drew her into him. This woman was beauty in all things—heat, sex, innocence.

When he and she had been young, and Elliot had first become aware of the amazing eroticism of women, he'd fantasized about her. The day he'd helped her with the kite in the tree, when they'd both been sixteen, and she'd raised on tiptoe to kiss his cheek, he'd not only fallen in love with her, he'd wanted her in the most basic, primal way.

Her demure look, the blush as she pulled away from the kiss . . . She'd been so innocent. He'd wanted her bodice sliding down to her waist, baring the pink of her nipples, wanted her flush to deepen as he pushed up her skirts and did what he was doing now. He'd wanted to lay her down in that meadow and show her what it meant that they were man and woman.

Elliot had watched her run off, back to the children she'd been entertaining. But in his mind, they'd remained hidden behind the shrubbery, Elliot thrusting hard into her, claiming her, marking her, making her his.

"Mine," he whispered now. He couldn't help himself.

He licked and nipped her, and Juliana made sharp little noises, feminine and sweet. Elliot's cock was pounding, but he ignored it to bask in the taste that was Juliana.

She rose on her tiptoes, her hands still in his hair, small fingers clenching. Elliot barely felt the tugs; he was surrounded by her and drowning in her. Her thighs were hot against his face, and he could scarcely breathe, but he didn't care.

With his eyes closed, there was only darkness and the scent and taste of Juliana, the sound of her finding her highest pleasure.

She arched against him, betraying that she wanted his mouth. Elliot rewarded her, flickering his tongue inside her until more of her liquid flowed into him.

"I can't . . . I can't . . ."

Elliot held the fabric of her skirts against her body, tightly out of his way, as he drank her down.

Juliana drooped against the boulder, her legs bending. She swayed, her hands landing on Elliot's shoulders to keep herself from falling.

Elliot finally granted her mercy. He wiped his mouth on a fold of his kilt and got to his feet, letting her skirts fall, and he plunged his mouth over hers. She kissed him back with strength that made his heart ache.

"We need to get indoors," Elliot said. He kissed her hair, her face, her lips again. He needed to be inside her, needed it now.

"We'll have to walk," Juliana said. "I do not believe I can crawl back through the tunnels."

"Then we walk."

Elliot snatched up her bustle, grabbed her firmly by the elbow, and strode away with her, in search of the shortest route back to the house.

~~~~~

The summer sun didn't set until after ten. Juliana lay naked in the big bed with Elliot, the last light of the day caressing the long planes of his body.

Elliot wasn't asleep. He skimmed his fingertips down her damp side and around her breast, thumb finding and teasing her nipple.

He'd brought her in here, stripped off her clothes and his, laid her on the bed, and made love to her for two hours.

Now he stretched out on his side, his half erection heavy against her thigh. Elliot's gray eyes were soft in the light, but he looked nowhere near tired.

Juliana said softly, "When I was told what happened in the marriage bed, my stepmother mentioned none of this."

Elliot lifted the weight of her breast, caressing the tightness of her nipple. "None of what?" His head was on her pillow, the covers long ago kicked off.

"None of what we've done today. I was told to lie quietly on my back and let you adjust me as necessary, and then you would come in on top of me." She smiled at her questions— *What will I do in the time between that and when he spills his seed?* The whole discussion seemed long ago and innocent now. "You would derive pleasure in the act, but I probably wouldn't. I was to hold and comfort you when you released, because at that moment, a man was, for the only time in his life, weaker than a woman."

Elliot laughed, a deep-voiced, masculine laugh. "Was this in a book?"

"I expect so." Come to think of it, she couldn't picture Gemma lying back so tamely, and Ainsley had said, with a twinkle in her eye, that the marriage bed could be a fine place. "But no one mentioned dining room tables, or what you did outdoors today, or me wanting to hold you in so many different ways."

"Mmm. What sort of different ways?"

Juliana ran her hand over his shoulder. "I never thought I'd need to touch my husband at all. But you are so very touchable." Juliana glided her fingertips across his knotted shoulders, tracing the scars that lined them. "I don't like that they hurt you."

"It doesn't hurt anymore."

But it had hurt him. Very much indeed. "You're safe now," Juliana said. "Here in this house, with me, you're safe."

"I know that."

"But this morning, you thought you were back in the prison."

Elliot twined his hand through hers, stilling her touch. "It happens."

"Quite often?"

Elliot's eyes lost their warmth while he kissed her fingers then let them go. "Not as much now."

Juliana skimmed her touch across the tattoo around his bicep then moved to his flat nipples, his wiry hair catching the last of the sunlight. "I want you to be well."

"I'm well when I'm with you, Juliana."

"I want you to be well even when you're not with me."

Elliot closed his hand around her wrist and gave her a heart-stopping smile. "Then you'll have to stay with me always."

"Well, of course. I did marry you. But seriously, Elliot, you know that some days I will have to leave you alone, and you, me."

He caressed her wrist, but didn't let go. "I don't know if I will ever heal as much you want me to."

"Perhaps if you talk about it . . ."

"No." His voice grew hard. "I don't want to remember, or talk it over, or dwell on it. I want to be in the here and now. They never knew about you. They could never take you away from me."

Juliana wasn't quite sure what he meant by this last, but it made sense to her that he would want to push aside bad memories to enjoy the safety and calm of being home. But she also knew that the distance she felt between herself and Elliot wouldn't lessen until she understood what had happened to him.

Or perhaps she expected too much. Many a husband and wife had distance between them that they never closed. The man stayed at his business or in his club; the wife made her calls and planned her social engagements. They came together when they hosted a gathering or attended one together, but only briefly. Juliana had friends who barely communicated with their husbands at all. They'd conceived children with these men but barely knew them.

Elliot said he wanted more children. Juliana had seen hunger in his eyes when he'd announced that desire.

She let her hand slide from Elliot's chest to his tight abdomen, touching the indentation of his navel. Elliot released her wrist as she traced below his abdomen to the organ that was again as hard as when he'd made love to her not a quarter of an hour ago.

Elliot laced his hands behind his head and rolled over onto his back, giving her full access to his body.

"So you find you want to touch me, do you?" he asked, sinful heat in his eyes.

Juliana had felt him wonderfully inside her, had seen his hardness dark and beautiful, but she'd not touched it until now. She daringly dipped her hand to his warm balls, which became tight against her palm.

Elliot lay rigidly, as though he forced himself to remain still, his hands tucked firmly behind his head. He made a noise of pleasure as Juliana drew her fingers up either side of his shaft, liking the satin smoothness of his skin.

In the dying light, he was dark with wanting, heavy in her hand.

She closed her fingers around him and squeezed, and a louder groan escaped Elliot's lips. The tip reddened as she drew her hand to it. The head was different from the shaft, she found as she traced it, more giving, but at the same time stiff and warm.

Juliana wondered what he tasted like. Her thoughts shot back to Elliot licking and drinking her on the path in the woods. She'd never felt anything like that in her life. The heat of his mouth, the friction of his tongue . . . she squirmed to remember.

She leaned down and licked his tip.

"God, Juliana, you'll kill me." The words were soft, tight.

Juliana brushed her tongue over him again, liking the warm salt taste of his skin. She enjoyed the various textures of him too, the slight sponginess of the tip, the edge of the head, the straight sides of the shaft. The coarse hair at the base tickled her tongue, his balls like warm velvet.

Elliot's abdomen rose and fell with his breath, and she couldn't resist moving upward to lick his navel. Her hair fell forward, pooling around him.

His breath went out in a grating sigh. One hand found her hair, bunching it in his fist. "No, they couldn't take you away from me."

The words were so soft Juliana wasn't certain she heard them. She circled his navel with her tongue then traced down the line of hair that led back to his staff.

She began tasting him again, moving her tongue up and down the sides of his shaft, dropping little kisses all the way up to the tip. Then she raised her head and smiled at him, thinking he'd laugh at how silly she was.

The look on Elliot's face made her stop. His eyes held pure carnality, raw need. He was a beautiful man, naked on his back, his tanned body spread for her on the sheets.

She had time for only one delicious glance before Elliot seized her under her arms and dragged her up his body. His mouth opened over hers, and his hands parted her legs.

Elliot lifted her hips a little, then sank her down onto him, his hardness entering her and rising high inside her. Juliana gasped, the position opening her, her body arching as more of him went into her.

Elliot's hips were moving then, his hands strong on her waist. Juliana felt joy build within her, the tight spiraling where nothing was real but Elliot inside her and the feelings in her heart.

As cries escaped her lips, Elliot rolled her over, the mattress crackling, and drove down into her. His eyes were fixed with a determined, almost mad light as their bodies came together.

Juliana remembered crying out, then Elliot shouting, then both of them collapsing onto cool sheets.

Elliot landed next to her, pulling her back into his embrace. Lassitude and peace struck her, and Juliana fell into a pit of sleep.

Elliot jumped awake.

Nothing had moved. Nothing had changed. And yet . . .

Moonlight mixed with lingering twilight outside the window, keeping darkness at bay. The half-light made Juliana's already pale skin white as marble.

Her quiet breathing hadn't woken him. Nor had any shout in the corridor—not McGregor and Komal in one of their English-Punjabi arguments, not Hamish bellowing something down the hall. The house was silent, the frogs, crickets, and night birds outside filling the dusk with soothing music.

A clock in the hall, which Juliana had insisted be cleaned, wound, and set, chimed twelve times. Midnight. An enchanted hour.

Elliot rose noiselessly from the bed. He could move like a ghost, skills learned as a tracker and hunter settling on him without him having to think about it.

Juliana slept on, undisturbed. Elliot pulled on his shirt, wrapped his kilt around his waist, grabbed his boots, and went into the hall.

He donned his boots at the bottom of the stairs then walked quietly along the flagstones to the kitchen. He found the shotgun Mahindar had hidden in the butler's pantry, and shells in a drawer high in a kitchen cupboard.

Mahindar was nowhere in sight, the family taking a well-deserved sleep. The likeliest person Elliot would encounter was McGregor, who sometimes wandered the house at night, but even he remained upstairs and quiet.

A cool breeze met Elliot when he stepped out the back door, but he didn't bother fetching a coat. He could wrap up in his kilt if need be.

A fox called in the distance, followed by the noise of small animals scurrying for cover. At the end of the garden, just outside the gate, Elliot stopped and loaded the gun, tucking spare shells into his sporran, along with the tin of biscuits he'd found in the cupboard next to the shells. He kept the gun open, slung over his arm.

He started along the path that would take him to the footbridge that led over the river to Rossmoran land. He and Juliana had used this route to return to the house that evening.

As Elliot walked, he relived the tactile sensations of being with Juliana—he inside her, she squeezing down without knowing she did it, the cushion of her breasts against his chest. He also remembered the delicious feeling of her tongue on his cock. Her hesitant little licks and kisses, growing bolder by the second, had him nearly crazed with need.

She was too innocent yet for the things he wanted to do with her. Her well-meaning stepmother had taught her that a man bedded his wife using one position, did his business quickly, and disappeared back to his club and his mistresses. Elliot would have to teach her that this was not necessarily so. Besides, he had no intention of spending days at a stifling club with hidebound men, nor did he intend taking a mistress. What idiot would, when he had Juliana?

Elliot reached the footbridge and the path that led to the steep hill where he and Juliana had climbed from the tunnels. He picked his way along, the moonlight giving him no need for a lantern.

The hill curved around into the fold of the valley, another hill rising beyond it. Elliot knew there must be more entrances to the tunnels—the McGregors of old would not have allowed themselves to be bottled inside if their enemies found and blocked one. He walked to the next hill, where trees began to rise around him again.

The woods went quiet, the watcher back.

Elliot snapped the shotgun closed and cocked it. "Come on out and face me," he said, voice loud in the still air. "If I like what you say, I might not shoot you."

Chapter 15

Silence. An owl hooted far, far away.

Only one man in Elliot's experience could track him in this way. But he was dead, gone, buried, forgotten by the world. Unfair that he was forgotten, because he'd been amazingly good at what he did, but the world was like that.

Stacy had to be dead. When Mahindar had told Elliot about the man's death, Elliot had accepted the story as plausible, because Stacy had been volatile and tended to provoke people.

Equally plausible was that Stacy had provoked Elliot, and Elliot had throttled him. Mahindar could have invented the story of Stacy dying in Lahore to spare Elliot—Mahindar was forever trying to spare Elliot.

The fact that Elliot had no memory of murdering Stacy meant nothing. He had no memory of many things, and Elliot had learned so well to be an expert at killing.

The watcher displayed skills very familiar to Elliot—he'd taught Stacy most of them.

Elliot was being stalked by a dead man. Or a man who was supposed to be dead and was not. Elliot still lived some of his days sunk in confusion, but his instincts, honed by months of animal-like existence, told him truths that his reason could not grasp.

"If I'm right," Elliot said to the night, "then tell your friends I didn't kill you. Keep them the hell away from me and my wife."

Wind sighed in the trees, last year's leaves scuttling in the dirt. It was dry now, no rain for days.

Elliot spoke again, keeping his voice level, no shouting. "If you're trying to take the child, I'm not letting her go to you. Priti is mine, and she's staying with me."

Silence. The watcher apparently did not intend to speak.

Elliot walked closer to the spot where he thought the next opening to the tunnels lay and set the tin of biscuits on a rock. "If you try to live off the land, someone will report you to the constable as a poacher. I'll have my lad bring you some food."

Still, nothing. The wind sighed again, and in the next instant, Elliot knew the watcher was gone.

He'd heard no branch moving, no twig breaking. Stacy was almost as good a tracker as Elliot. That had been the basis of the men's friendship at first.

Elliot waited for a long time after that. The noises of the woods returned to normal again, but not until the moon had moved well behind the hills in the west did Elliot snap open the gun and tramp back the way he'd come.

～～～

The next morning, Juliana emerged from bathing and dressing in the bedchamber to find the lower hall filled with men wanting work.

Hamish had spread the word with a vengeance. Men of all ages, shapes, and sizes had come from Highforth village and the outlying farms, from sturdy lads who should have been in school all the way to a stooped elderly man who'd come to give his decided opinions on everything. They'd arrived to put McGregor's house right.

Mahindar was a bit nonplussed about how he would feed them all, but Juliana had Hamish run to the village and see what he could find. Not only that, the farmers and crofters brought things with them—chickens, eggs, a nanny goat, cheese, bread, ale—gifts for the new laird and his lady.

Priti liked the goat, even though it immediately found and ate one of Channan's pretty silk scarves. The animal looked quite innocent when the discovery was made, despite the bit of indigo silk sticking out the side of its mouth.

McGregor sat down outside with the elderly man to chat and smoke a pipe with him, while Mahindar and Channan ran about the kitchen, Nandita tried to hide from all the strange men, and Priti played with her new friend the goat.

The day before, Juliana had begun lists of what needed to be done, but her round of calls, followed by climbing through the tunnels with Elliot and making love all evening, had kept her from finishing them. Mahindar's voice sounded down the passage as he tried to keep order, and Komal busied herself following people about and giving commands no one understood.

As Juliana tried to decide what they should do first, Elliot calmly walked in and took over.

He set men to repairing the roof, some to repairing windows, some to finding the wires and pulleys of the bell system, and some simply to cleaning. He gave orders clearly and without fuss, asking which would be the best men to do each job.

By midmorning, Castle McGregor buzzed like a hive, workers crawling all over it—raising dust, hammering, breaking away old things and putting up new. The kitchen overflowed with food, Mahindar, Channan, Nandita, Hamish, and Mrs. Rossmoran's granddaughter Fiona cooking up a storm and watching Priti at the same time. The nanny goat eyed Mahindar nervously as he approached her, but Mahindar only wanted a bit of milk.

Juliana commandeered a section of the dining room table, where she wrote letters, made her lists, and summoned Hamish from time to time with a handbell, which she'd found rolling in a drawer in the sideboard.

One of the smaller rooms on the ground floor, whose windows overlooked the land sloping down to the sea, would be sunny in the mornings, perfect as her writing room. The room next to it, large and airy, would be the breakfast room. She looked forward to mornings there with Elliot—he reading his newspapers, she reading and answering her correspondence.

Cozy, domestic, warm.

When the house was whole, she told herself, Elliot would no longer have his bad dreams and waking visions of the past. He was a natural leader—the way he handled the men working on the house told her that. He'd be himself again. They'd have summer fêtes and the shooting in August, Christmas and New Year's, and then return to Edinburgh or London—wherever her family and his decided to go—for the social rounds of the Season.

Mahindar fed them all lunch, mostly bread, meat, and cheese—probably Fiona Rossmoran's suggestion, though Mahindar brought Juliana a lentil and chicken stew with goat's milk that was seasoned to perfection.

The men worked throughout the afternoon, their banging and shouting somehow comforting. The old house had been quiet too long. Now it teemed with life.

Even McGregor was excited. He'd longed to repair the place, he'd said, for years, but he'd had no money, and he wasn't the sort of laird who'd force his tenants to work for no pay.

As the workday waned and the men went home with their families, Mahindar came to Juliana's dining room corner and cleared his throat. Juliana looked up from her list of supplies to find him curling and uncurling his large hands in nervousness.

"What is it, Mahindar?" she asked in alarm. "Is Mr. McBride unwell again?"

"No, no, the sahib is fine," Mahindar said quickly. "No, the thing I do not want to have to tell you is that we have a thief."

"A thief?" Juliana glanced at the jumble of furniture piled into the dining room, put there so the men could tear apart the other rooms. "How can you tell anything is missing? Or even what there was to be missing in the first place?"

"From the kitchen, I mean," Mahindar said. "Food."

Juliana's alarm dissolved. "You cooked many meals today. Food was going in and out. So many brought food— I doubt they were stealing it."

"Memsahib, please let me explain."

He had a point. Juliana closed her mouth and motioned for him to proceed.

Except that he didn't proceed. Mahindar stood still, his fingers curling again, his distress plain.

Juliana said, "I assure you that whatever you tell me will not leave this room. If you don't wish me to tell even Mr. McBride, I will not."

Mahindar sighed. "I wish to be mistaken about this. I very much wish it. I like him—he is so very eager even if he is clumsy sometimes. But he took a large plate of ham and six naan Channan had just pulled from the oven, and ran out the back door. He thought himself stealthy, and he was, because only my mother saw him. My mother, she told me."

Juliana had to smile. "If you are speaking of Hamish, perhaps he was simply hungry. He has been working hard."

Mahindar shook his head. "No, memsahib. He'd already eaten well. He wrapped these up and vanished with them, then came back soon after, trying to look innocent."

Hamish? Juliana wouldn't have thought it of him. Hamish had told her he lived with his mother, sister, and uncle on a small farm, his father having died a few years ago. Juliana hadn't heard that the McIver family was especially poor, but times could be difficult in the Highlands. Farming didn't pay what it used to, sheep were usually owned by the large landholders, and many crofters continued to stream to the factories in Glasgow and the north of England to find steady wages.

"Thank you, Mahindar," Juliana said. "I will speak to Hamish and sort this out." She put the lid on her inkpot and set aside her pen and her lists. "You need say nothing of this to him or Mr. McBride."

Mahindar looked both relieved and unhappy at the same time. "I do like the boy. He puts me in mind of myself as a youth. So eager to please, and I know that I was not always pleasing."

"I will take it up with him. You go and rest now. You've done so much today."

He looked surprised. "No, indeed, there is much more to be done. Much more. Thank you, memsahib."

Juliana waited until Mahindar had gone then went in search of Hamish.

"Juliana."

Elliot's voice rumbled through the narrow passage between main hall and kitchen as she walked there to look for Hamish. A moment later, Elliot was next to Juliana, pushing her up against the wall.

He curved his body over hers, warmth surrounding her. Instead of speaking to her, perhaps asking where she was going, Elliot put his fist beneath her chin, tilted her head back, and kissed her.

He crushed Juliana back against the wall, trapping her with his strength, and scraped his tongue between her lips. His mouth stole, commanded, left her breathless.

As abruptly as the kiss had begun, Elliot eased it to its

end. He looked down at her a moment, then he released her, dropped a kiss to the corner of her mouth, and faded away down the hall without saying a word. His kilt moved against his backside, the hem swinging with his stride.

Juliana remained against the wall, knees weak, her hands pressing the cold stone to keep herself upright as she watched him go.

She was still struggling for breath when Hamish himself came down the passage at his usual half run.

"Hamish." She made herself stand up straight. "Hamish, stop."

Hamish halted obediently, panting from his exuberant pace. "Yes, m'lady? Something I can do for you?" He sounded happy, not guilt stricken at all.

Juliana groped for a way to broach the subject tactfully but decided that asking straight out was best. "What do you know about some ham and bread that's gone missing?"

Hamish regarded her in surprise. There wasn't much light here, but Juliana could see by it that his blue eyes were guileless. "Nothing's gone missing, m'lady."

"I'm afraid you were seen walking out with a large plate of ham and fresh-baked naan." She gave him a little smile. "Or was Komal mistaken, and the goat ate them?"

Hamish looked even more baffled. "Not the goat. She's tethered in the kitchen garden, and I carried that food well away from her. No, I don't think the goat got any of it."

Juliana blinked at him. "So you admit that you took it?"

"Aye." Hamish seemed unworried.

"And what did you do with it?"

"Took it around to the footbridge path, to the hill above my great-aunt's cottage. Ye go around from the castle and cut left before the road reaches the river . . ." He pointed with his muscular arm down the passage in the general direction of Mrs. Rossmoran's cottage.

He was describing the path Elliot and Juliana had taken to walk back home yesterday afternoon. "You were taking the food to Mrs. Rossmoran? You ought to have asked me—I would have had a basket made up."

Hamish looked baffled again. "It wasn't for me great-auntie. I left it on the path, like he told me to."

"Like who told you to?"

"Himself."

Juliana stared. "Let me make sure I understand you, Hamish. *Mr. McBride* told you to take this food out to the path and leave it there? What for?"

Hamish gave her a shrug that said the ways of lairds were unfathomable to him. "Don't know. Me grandmum used to leave bowls of milk out for the wee folk. So they wouldn't steal nothing else if ye did, ye understand. The bowls were always empty in the morning."

"No doubt," Juliana said. "But a platter of ham and a pile of buttered Indian bread are a bit different from bowls of milk."

"Aye." Hamish's brows drew down again. "But I didn't ask. The laird's business is none of mine."

"Never mind, Hamish," Juliana said. "I will take care of it. But if Mr. McBride asks you to leave food out for the wee folk again, do come and tell me."

"He asked me not to, m'lady. Wouldn't have now, except ye pried it out of me."

"Nevertheless, you will."

Hamish met her gaze, weighing obedience to the laird against obedience to the lady. He heaved a sigh. "Yes, m'lady."

"Good. Thank you, Hamish."

Hamish's grin widened. He touched his forehead in a rough salute, turned, and galloped on toward the kitchen.

Juliana tamped down her misgivings and went in search of Elliot.

~~~~~

Uncle McGregor had all but dragged Elliot into the old billiards room at the end of the wing of the ground floor. Several billiards tables reposed here, only one of which was uncovered. The others were cloaked in huge dust sheets with accompanying layers of dust.

"While your wife is busy worrying about the ballroom and the reception rooms, let's not forget the refuge for the husbands, eh?" McGregor said. "When she has her grand fête, the put-upon clansmen will need a place to retreat."

Elliot opened cupboards in search of the cue sticks. He knew from the tedious balls he'd attended with his regiment that most husbands had no interest in gatherings that the ladies so loved, let alone any interest in dancing with their own wives. The gentlemen sought escape in cards and billiards, as McGregor said.

Poor bastards. The last thing Elliot wanted was escape from Juliana. He'd dance with her as much as she wanted. He felt whole and strong in her arms—why would he bypass any chance to have that? When he'd seen her in the passage earlier, he hadn't been able to resist stopping to steal a kiss. Why say an inane *Good afternoon. How are you?* when a heady kiss was so much more satisfying? The fact that Elliot *could* kiss Juliana any time he wished was a thing worth celebrating.

"Many's the night I whiled away the time in here, with my university mates," McGregor was saying, a wistful note in his voice. "I hated McPherson then, wouldn't let him in the door. Funny, he's the only one left now. Only one who stood by me when my lady passed on and the money ran out . . ."

Elliot found a wooden box of billiard balls along with the cues and carried them to the table. "My old mates are either dead or have buried themselves in the regiment, never to emerge."

"Aye." McGregor shook his head while he took balls from the box and rolled them onto the table. "When we're young, we think it will last forever."

Elliot wasn't ready to become moody and nostalgic yet.

He wanted many more years with Juliana before it was time to reminisce in the billiards room with the next generation.

Juliana walking in, her eyes bright, her cheek smudged with dust, was one of those things he planned to reminisce about.

"Mr. McBride," she said. "May I speak to you?"

Mr. McBride. So formal. Elliot thought about the billiards table behind him, pictured seating Juliana on its edge, her skirts up around her thighs. She could call him *Mr. McBride* all she liked while she smiled at him with desire in her eyes.

McGregor chuckled. "I told you, I swear by the conservatory. Nooks and crannies and comfortable benches."

Juliana sent him a surprised look. "The conservatory will not be ready for anyone for a time. I have sent away for many new hothouse plants. I assure you, it will be a fine place by the time of the midsummer fête."

McGregor kept on grinning. "I love a practical woman." He rolled the last balls onto the table and started out of the room. "You have your chat. Don't tear the cloth on the billiards table. It's the one thing I've kept intact."

He went off and shut the door behind him, his chuckles following him.

Juliana's rust and brown dress set off her red hair and blue eyes, even if the gown was buttoned to her chin. Juliana, who followed all the rules, would change into her evening dress for dinner, perhaps the off-the-shoulder shimmering blue one. Elliot could eat his dinner while imagining pouring another dollop of fine whiskey across her breasts.

Elliot couldn't stop himself going to her, meeting her halfway into the room, couldn't help brushing back a tendril of hair that had come loose. The kiss he'd claimed in the passage had fired his blood, and he'd not yet cooled.

"Elliot, did you hear me?"

"No. What did you say, love?"

"I said that Hamish has told me an extraordinary thing. He says you had him take a platter of ham out to the woods and leave it there. Along with some naan."

"Aye." Elliot nodded as he brushed back another tendril of her hair. "Good. I'm glad he remembered."

"But whatever for? Do not tell me you've put it by in case you grow hungry during your next tramp through the woods."

She looked so indignant that Elliot had to smile. "It's not for me."

"Who then? And anyway, animals will get it if you had Hamish leave it beside the path."

"He bagged it and strung it up in a tree. That is, that's what I told him to do."

Juliana's stare tried to penetrate his fog, to find its way to the real Elliot. He knew she wanted that, but the real Elliot had been lost a long time ago.

"Please tell me what for. A tramp?"

"For Archibald Stacy," Elliot said. No use in lying or telling Juliana pretty stories. "He's come for me."

Chapter 16

Juliana stared at him, worry in her pretty eyes. She was trying to decide whether to believe him. Didn't matter—Stacy was there, whether Juliana believed Elliot or not.

"Mr. Stacy is dead," she said. "You told me so. Mrs. Dalrymple told me so."

"I said that I assumed him dead because he'd vanished from his home, and Mahindar heard a story that he'd died in Lahore. Obviously the story was wrong."

"What about Mrs. Dalrymple? She is adamant that you murdered him."

"Mrs. Dalrymple knows damn all," Elliot growled.

Elliot watched Juliana try to catch her spinning emotions and make her practical nature deal with this new development. This made her the opposite of Elliot, who'd given in to letting his emotions do whatever the hell they wanted. Trying to suppress them only made him crazier.

Juliana didn't like her emotions slipping out at all, he'd

seen. She wanted order, not chaos. Elliot would have to show her one day that a little chaos wasn't so bad a thing.

"Well," Juliana said. "If Mr. Stacy is alive and has come to Scotland, then we must show him to Mrs. Dalrymple so she will stop putting about the preposterous story that you killed him."

"It might not be that simple."

"Why not? Presumably Mr. Stacy is hungry, or you'd not have left him the food. We'll invite him to the house for a meal."

She didn't believe him, or at least didn't believe in the danger. "Stacy has come to kill me. To hunt me. He hasn't shown his face to me yet, but I know it's him."

"But if you have not seen him, how can you be certain?"

Elliot turned away. He ended up at the billiards table where he rolled a white ball across with his hand, unerringly striking a red. "Difficult to explain, love. Stacy and I were trackers and sharpshooters in the army. Every tracker has a style, and I recognize his. I taught him most of what he knows."

"Do you mean like a hunter can tell what animal is in the brush from its spoor?"

He smiled at the billiards table. "Yes, but I'd rather not have to check his spoor."

"Elliot." Juliana came up behind him, her skirt rustling like soft leaves. "Are you certain?"

"Very certain, my love." Elliot turned and rested his hands on her corseted waist. "I wish I weren't."

"Well, if you are right that he is here, at least it means you didn't kill him."

"Yet. I might have to."

"No, you must call the constable and the magistrate. If you believe Mr. Stacy has come to harm you, he must be rounded up and arrested at once."

"No," Elliot said sternly. "The constable is a lad no

older than Hamish, and Stacy would make short work of him. If I start a manhunt, Stacy will either slip the net or hurt those who get in his way. I don't want anyone here in danger because of him. Let me do this my way."

"By leaving him food?"

Elliot knew he had to be patient with her. Juliana didn't understand, and he couldn't force her to understand. "You will have to trust me." He moved his hands under the swell of her breasts. "I'll let him harm no one. I know what he'll do, and I know how to coax him out."

Juliana wet her lips. Elliot knew the thoughts she struggled through. He'd seen it in the eyes of everyone he'd spoken to since he'd escaped from his prison, including Mahindar. The painful doubt, the question—was Elliot truly mad?

Elliot *was* mad; he knew that. Else he'd not have the dreams, the flashbacks, the certain panic that he was still trapped inside the cell, even after all this time. He couldn't explain that the thing he dreaded most was to wake up one morning and discover that *this*—what he had now—was the dream.

He was mad, yes. But not about this.

"Elliot?" Juliana's voice held a note of uncertainty. Elliot realized he'd gone stone still, staring past her at nothing.

He said, "McGregor and I today found all the entrances to the house from the tunnels below and stopped them up." In some cases, timber had sufficed, in others, he'd had the men screw down iron plates.

"Stacy will not get into the house," he continued. "Whatever he and I have to settle, we'll do out there. But you need to stay indoors, and not go out, not without me."

Her eyes widened. "My dear Elliot, I cannot remain confined to the house. I have too much to do. I will have to go into the village for things for the fête, or perhaps to Aberdeen."

Elliot shook his head. "Until this is resolved, send Hamish with instructions, or one of the other men."

"And when might everything be resolved?"

"I can't know. However long it takes me to find Stacy and face him."

Again Juliana gave him her assessing stare, trying to cover emotion and uncertainties with practicality. "In that case, please tell him to resolve this before my fête and ball. I'll not have him ruining my debut event at Castle McGregor."

Elliot touched his fingers to her chin and pressed a swift kiss to her lips. "I'll be sure to tell him."

Juliana softened her impatient look into a smile then made to turn and leave the room. Elliot stopped her with a firm hand on her arm.

"Do not go out exploring yourself, Juliana."

From the flash of guilt in her eyes, Elliot knew Juliana had been intending to do exactly that. He briefly wondered why the marriage ceremony bothered to contain the wife's promise to obey her husband—he hadn't met a woman yet who followed it.

"Pretend to believe me and stay safely indoors," he said. He'd already told Mahindar to keep a close watch on Priti, and not to let her venture out the back door alone.

Juliana studied him, her blue eyes drawing him in, then finally said, "Very well."

Of course, her ready capitulation, made in that soft voice, aroused his suspicions. "I mean it, lass. Whether you believe I'm insane or not, I want you safe."

Juliana's chin came up. "You asked me to believe you. Now I ask you to believe *me*. To err on the side of caution is not a bad thing. I wouldn't wander about the land alone, in any case. What if I fell into a bog?"

Elliot suppressed a shudder, not needing that worry to go along with everything else. He didn't fear so much what

Stacy would do to *him*, but if anything happened to Juliana . . .

He'd rather go back to his horrible dark cell and the tortures there than let Juliana come to harm.

Elliot stilled at the thought. This was the first time he'd ever considered such a thing. His body and mind had been broken, but he realized on a sudden that his physical pain would be nothing to what could be done to his heart if something happened to Juliana.

He leaned to Juliana and kissed her again, savoring the heat of her against the length of his body. If Elliot lost her, if she were hurt . . .

He'd die.

Elliot pulled her closer, caressing the tension from the back of her neck as he deepened the kiss.

Never let her go, never lose her. They hadn't been able to take her from him. He would let nothing take her now.

Elliot had to make himself release her. He knew Juliana wanted to get back to her organizing. She took refuge in her lists and schedules in the same way he took refuge in whiskey and in her.

Besides, keeping her here and playing out his fantasies *would* involve tearing the cloth on the billiards table, no doubt of that.

Elliot watched her walk away from him after she gave him one last kiss on the cheek, her small bustle swaying as she went. The driving need he felt to protect Juliana at all costs gave him several degrees of strength.

He remained staring for a long time at the door through which she'd strolled, examining this new feeling, watching the fragile spark of hope grow in the darkness like an ember gently blown to life.

~~~~~

Elliot did not come to bed that night. Juliana lay faceup on the mattress alone, contemplating the ceiling beams above her. She'd looked over swatches a draper from Aberdeen had brought her, trying to decide what to hang on the bed, once she could convince the mice to move out. For now, though, the bedposts were bare, like leafless trees.

The sun set and the moon rose, and still Elliot did not come.

She'd last seen him at supper, which McGregor attended. McGregor had glared suspiciously at the meal Mahindar had brought, declaring that lentils and curried chicken made a man weak. McGregor had repeated that several times as he ate every bite.

Elliot and McGregor had discussed shooting for the entire meal, and afterward, Elliot offered to show McGregor the Winchester rifle he'd ordered from America some years ago. Juliana had left them to their talk while she went on with her lists for the house, the fête, the ball, and the rest of her life.

Now she rested her hands on her chest and thought about what Elliot had told her about Mr. Stacy.

Juliana contemplated two choices. First, to believe that someone, whether it be Mr. Stacy or another, was indeed hiding in the woods east of the house, above the river. Or, second, to believe that Elliot was not quite sane after all.

She'd seen no evidence of the watcher Elliot had described, and he'd made her promise not to go out and look for any. This did not mean, Juliana thought, that she could not send others out to look for evidence for her. But then, if Mr. Stacy was as dangerous as Elliot claimed, she risked sending Hamish or Mahindar into peril.

Juliana had asked Hamish if, when he'd gone down to see his great-aunt after supper, he'd noticed whether anyone had taken the food he'd hung in a tree. Hamish had told her that the bag was still there, swinging heavy, untouched. He'd hung it well out of reach of foxes, he'd explained proudly, just as Mr. McBride had told him to.

So, there it was. Elliot was leaving food in the woods with no sign that anyone was there to take it.

Juliana had no idea exactly what he'd suffered during his capture in the Afghan mountains, or what he suffered now, or to what degree. She *had* seen Elliot sink into a stupor from which he couldn't be awakened, had twice seen him believe himself back with his captors and try to fight them.

Now Elliot believed a man from his past had returned from the dead to stalk him.

This belief, though, was a little different. Elliot had stood before Juliana, his eyes clear, fully aware he was in the here and now, and told her of his suspicions. He believed the man in the woods was a Scotsman he'd known in India, not one of his tribal captors. Elliot had warned her of the danger to her, and to Hamish and others—he was not focused on the danger to himself.

Juliana sorted her thoughts into neat lists, for and against. On one list, her husband was correct; on the other, he was letting the terror he'd suffered in the past guide his mind.

Tears slid from Juliana's eyes to the linen pillowcase as she stared up at the ceiling and made her choice.

Elliot settled himself into the tree he'd selected, and waited. He'd exchanged his working kilt and tough boots for the dark silk clothes he'd sometimes worn in India, and soft leather shoes, best for climbing.

The tree was wide, and the three-branch cradle he'd found supported him comfortably. He'd chosen with care.

On his lap, he held his Winchester Model 1876 lever-action rifle he'd purchased when he'd first left the army. He'd ordered a smaller bore, a .40-60, that they'd begun making in later years—though it was still called the 1876. Elliot had confined his shooting, once he'd left the army, to food game and target shooting, rather than big game—tigers and elephants were too beautiful in the wild, and what had they ever done to him?—and so saw no need for a larger caliber gun. Englishmen in India enjoyed shooting glass balls or plates out of the sky. Elliot, as a sharpshooter in a kilt, had been a favorite entertainment.

The rifle carried five rounds in the chamber, the lever action meaning he could pump the trigger mechanism after each shot to eject the cartridge and slide the next bullet into the chamber. He could fire all five rounds very quickly.

Stacy, of course, knew about this rifle and had a similar one of his own. What Stacy did not know about was the telescopic device Elliot had ordered before he'd gone back to India the second time. Snipers in the American Civil War had used such devices to bring their game into view—enemy officers rather than deer or bear.

Elliot had fitted the scope to the rifle before he'd left the house. McGregor had been fascinated with it, making Elliot promise to bring it with him the next time they went to McPherson's. McPherson would be green with envy, McGregor said, with glee.

Elliot lifted the rifle and sighted through the scope, the bright moonlight bringing the hanging bag of foodstuffs into sharp focus.

It still hung where Hamish had left it, full and untouched. Squirrels and birds would get it if he left it through tomorrow, but tonight, in the dead of night, Stacy might just come out for it.

Wind sighed in the trees, and scraps of clouds drifted overhead. The weather here, so close to the sea, was ever changing. A few miles north of McGregor's estate, the land curved and headed for the utmost north of Scotland and the stretch of water to the Orkneys.

Juliana would like a summer journey to the Orkneys, to watch from the boat as they slid past the Old Man of Hoy, standing sentinel over the islands. Elliot imagined her on the boat's deck, the wind in her fiery hair, her eyes filled with wonder as she stared at the tall pile of rock.

There were so many wonders in the world. Elliot wanted to show them all to Juliana.

His perch was cold, but he welcomed the wind. It erased the stifling heat of India from his brain, not that the Punjab couldn't turn bone cold in the winter.

Archibald Stacy. When the man had arrived in the Punjab with his young Scottish wife, looking to make his fortune, he and Elliot had resumed the friendship they'd begun in the army. When Mrs. Stacy soon died of typhoid fever, Elliot had nursed Stacy through his grief.

Then they'd met Jaya, the kin to princes of one of the native states. Elliot had not fallen in love with her as Stacy had, but Elliot had been young, lonely, and virile, and at the time, he thought he'd never make enough money to see Scotland and Juliana again.

Then when Jaya had played her game to make Stacy believe she preferred Elliot to him, Stacy had gone mad with rage. Elliot had been surprised. Stacy had always spoken of Jaya with indifference, having deeply loved his wife. Stacy had given no indication he'd been in a hurry to replace the first Mrs. Stacy, and so Elliot hadn't realized the man's true feelings.

They'd quarreled, and Elliot had relinquished Jaya back to Stacy, who'd promised to marry her. Elliot had thought the matter resolved.

Not long after that, Elliot and Stacy had been tramping together in the hills far to the north, never knowing that a tribal skirmish in the remote passes to the Afghan lands had begun. That was where Elliot had realized that Stacy still held a grudge, and held it with a vengeance.

The Highland moon sank behind the mountains, swallowed by the light that began so early in northern summers.

Strange that the sun stayed up so long in these latitudes but the air remained cool, while in the tropics, the sun sank quickly but the heat lasted far into the night.

As long as the darkness remained, Stacy never emerged, and the bag of food still hung untouched.

He doesn't like my Judas goat. Elliot allowed himself an inward smile. *My Judas ham.*

As the sun climbed out of the sea, Elliot lifted his rifle, aimed, and fired one shot. The rope holding the bag split and the bag fell with a thump to the path.

Elliot skimmed out of the tree, fetched the bag, and walked the few miles to McPherson's to give the contents to McPherson's grateful dogs.

~~~~~

Juliana stepped out to the kitchen garden with her basket, determined to fill it with the runner beans she'd spied yesterday. She looked up after picking the first handful to see her husband, clad in a short indigo jacket and dark pants that clung to his legs, walking up from the westward hills.

He was bareheaded, carried his rifle over his shoulder, and was followed by a long-haired red setter.

Chapter 17

Juliana watched Elliot come, her feelings a mixture of anger and relief. The shot that had awakened her at dawn had terrified her. Mahindar and Hamish had gone to investigate and returned saying they'd found nothing. No Elliot, no intruder, no bag of food, nothing.

Juliana had not been able to sleep again, fearing bloodshed and Elliot gone forever. Now she was sandy-eyed and a bit annoyed that Elliot should stroll casually through the garden gate as though nothing was wrong.

As Elliot neared her, Juliana admitted even in her anger that in the foreign clothes Elliot looked quite delectable. His tanned skin gave him an exotic touch, and the trousers, hugging him to his ankles, outlined every muscle of leg and buttock. The short jacket gaped open over a thin white shirt, which fit snugly to his tanned chest.

Juliana cleared her throat. "Good morning, Elliot."

Elliot lowered the rifle and stood its butt on the ground. "You're out early."

"I was awakened early. By a shot."

He nodded. "That was me. But the only casualty was a bit o' twine."

Juliana closed her eyes, letting out her pent-up breath. "Elliot."

Elliot touched her cheek, and she opened her eyes to find him gazing down at her, his gray eyes warm. "There was no need to worry, lass. I'm very good at taking care of myself."

"That might be true, but . . ."

"I hoped I'd find you in bed."

Juliana's heart jumped then settled down to a hurried thrum. She tried to shrug. "Vegetables still grow in this garden. They've gone a bit wild, but they're here. I thought I'd gather some. To help Mahindar cooking for everyone."

Babbling helped, but she could not stop gazing at his taut thighs and the thick bulge the trousers didn't bother to hide.

Elliot waited until she'd run down. "Where is Priti?"

"With Mahindar. Helping him with the goat."

"Make sure she stays with him or his family every moment of the day and night. Is Hamish here?"

"Banging around in the scullery. I don't think he ever sleeps."

"He's a lad." Elliot rubbed his chin, where golden whiskers had sprouted in abundance. "But I'll draw my own bath. Never mind."

Elliot made no move to go inside, however. He remained on the path, his hands on the barrel of his rifle.

"Elliot, you do know there is a dog following you, don't you?"

The red setter had sat down a few feet behind Elliot. When it saw Juliana looking at it, its tail thumped against the path.

Elliot glanced at it and the tail thumped double time. "She's one of McPherson's. She must be after more ham."

"Ham again? You're becoming quite obsessed with it."

"'Twas the same ham. I fed it to McPherson's dogs."

"So that's where you got off to so early? Fetching it?"

"Watching to see who took it. But no one did. I decided the dogs might as well enjoy it."

"Then you were mistaken about Mr. Stacy," Juliana said. "He isn't here."

Elliot shook his head. "I'm not mistaken. My experiment proved it to me."

"But if he didn't come out for the food . . ."

"If the man lurking in the woods had been a tramp or a Romany, he'd have come for the food. Stacy knows better."

"Oh." Juliana's nerves tightened again. "So by *not* seeing him, you know he is there."

"Yes."

Of course. So logical.

Elliot leaned to her, holding the rifle out of the way. His body heat touched her through his clothes, the cloth warmed by him. He kissed her, his unshaved whiskers rough on her lips, his skin smelling of wind, cold, and silk.

"Finish picking your vegetables," he said. He kissed her forehead, lifted his gun, and strode into the house.

Juliana watched him go, the silk trousers clinging to the finest male backside God had ever created.

⁂

Elliot, knees drawn to his chest in the old tin bathtub, scooped water into the brass bowl and poured it over his head. Warm water rained down his neck and back, washing away dirt and suds.

He felt the draft though he hadn't heard the door opening over the sound of the water. His head was bent over his knees, and he didn't look up. He scooped up more water, his skin heating as he poured the water down his back.

"Come in, Juliana."

The door closed, the draft vanishing. "How did you know it was me?"

He'd know her anywhere, anytime. "I recognize your step. I know what everyone's sounds like."

"I admit, there'd be no mistaking Hamish."

No, she certainly wasn't Hamish. As soon as Elliot had heard her walk into the room, as soon as her sweet scent had come to him on the draft, his erection had climbed high and stayed there.

Damn Stacy. Elliot could have spent the whole night wrapped around Juliana instead of sitting in a tree looking for the man.

Elliot's eyes were tired from lack of sleep, and his fingers were starting to shrivel from the water, but his cock was plenty awake.

He lifted his hand from the water, letting a stream of droplets fall on the rugs Mahindar had shoved around the bath. Elliot took Juliana's hand and placed it on his cheek.

"I've shaved," he said. "Not so much a barbarian anymore."

Her cheeks went pink. "I like you a barbarian."

Elliot's body went tight, and his cock was in danger of poking its way out of the water.

Juliana traced his cheekbone then moved her finger down to his lips. Elliot opened his mouth and gently bit her fingertip.

Juliana started, but she didn't pull away. She watched in fascination as Elliot closed his lips around her finger and sucked.

"Please tell me," she said, her eyes still on his mouth, "what happened to you in India. I want to understand."

The trickle of good heat in Elliot's veins started to ebb. He released her finger. "Not now."

"This isn't a whim of mine. I came up here on purpose to ask you."

Elliot returned his hand to the side of the tub and closed his eyes. "I don't want to go back there. I want to be here. With you."

"I won't insist on any detail that is too upsetting for you. But I want to know the gist. Please, husband. Let me understand."

The word *husband* made the heat return. But Elliot's fingers bit down on the tin bath, muscles bracing. "Mahindar . . ."

"I do not want to ask Mahindar. I want *you* to tell me."

Elliot pried his eyes open but slid down to let his head rest on the back of the tub. "Why?"

"Because Mahindar knows only the story you told him. I'm certain you left things out."

"Mmm. Probably."

Juliana put her hand on her chest, over her heart. Her wet hand seeped a damp handprint onto her blue bodice. "I know what you experienced was terrible. I know it will hurt your pride to talk about such things with your wife . . ."

Elliot laughed, letting his eyes drift closed again. "Pride? Pride was ripped away from me a long time ago. Pride is worth nothing. Nothing . . ."

The word spun the cold of the mountains toward him, the sound of gunfire, the endless skirmishes between people who cared nothing for borders drawn by governments—theirs or that of the British Raj. Elliot hid in a crevice in the rock, next to Stacy, neither man worried. They'd be able to slip away in the darkness, back down the hills to safer ground. Served them right for not checking local gossip first.

Then there had been the families. The two stupid Englishmen and their wives in their topees, bringing their children and a few Hindu servants with them to explore paths Alexander the Great had trod.

Stupid Englishmen who thought the color of their skin and their nationality would save them. They'd been cut off from retreat down the pass, targeted by one of the tribes who didn't give a donkey's balls about their nationality. The tribal men had lived in their rock fortresses in the hills for centuries—even Alexander, one of the greatest generals in written history, had turned back from them.

Elliot remembered the fear, the screams of the women, the cries of the children. He and Stacy had come out of hiding and cleared the way down the pass. He'd told the idiots to run—slow, too slow.

Shots had rung out, and one of the ladies had been hit. Only wounded, by the grace of God, but her terrified screams had split Elliot's ears for a long time to come.

He and Stacy had held a hurried conversation, deciding their strategy. They had to be drastic to get away at all. Elliot would hold down the tribesmen with his repeating Winchester, while Stacy herded the English families down the hill. Stacy would return when they reached safe ground, and cover Elliot's retreat.

Only Stacy had never come back. Elliot had held off the tribesmen for a long time, they determined to get the crazy shooter in the pass. But finally, Elliot had run short of ammunition, and the tribesmen had overwhelmed him.

Elliot's hands burned again as they wrenched away the rifle. They spit at him and called him a coward, then wiped the blood of their fallen comrades on him and tried to kick him to death. Stacy was gone, and rescue would not come.

Elliot flinched as the blows came down, feet and sticks, the butt of his own rifle.

His thrashing tossed water onto the floor, and Juliana's hands came to rest on his shoulders. "Elliot."

He opened his eyes to Scottish sunlight, tepid bathwater, Juliana sliding her arms around him from behind.

Juliana didn't ask why he'd started fighting, nor did she demand him to tell her what he'd remembered. She simply held him, never minding that her sleeves were getting all wet, the blue broadcloth becoming dark with water.

Elliot turned his head and kissed her cheek, liking how her breath felt cool on his damp skin. The screams, shots, and enraged shouts of men faded, to be replaced by the quiet sound of his lips on hers.

He reached his very wet hand up to undo the buttons of

her bodice, but his fingers were too slick. "Take this off," he said, tugging a button.

Her eyes widened. "Right now?"

"You charged in here while I was in my bath." Where Elliot couldn't walk away from her. "What did you think I'd do?"

He drew his finger down her closed placket, finding the damp spot where she'd pressed her hand. Her shoulder was also dark with water from where he'd rested his head.

"I am rather wet, aren't I?"

Juliana undid the first two buttons of the bodice, and Elliot's erection returned, harder than ever.

"Stand up," he said. "Bare yourself for me. I want to watch you."

Juliana's face flooded with color, but she rose, fingers still on her buttons. "Only a very wicked woman would do such a thing."

"Only wicked if the man is not her husband." Elliot laced his fingers behind his head, the warmth in his blood hotter now than the water. "But you're wicked, lass. You sat on a man's lap, in a chapel, and told him to marry you."

"That was not quite how it happened."

"'Tis how I remember it, love. Go on. Unbutton."

Elliot rested his hands on the sides of the tub again, but this time, his fingers were relaxed, warm.

Juliana, after a little hesitation, popped another button of her bodice. The linen corset cover beneath had a bow at the neckline, so fetching. Elliot watched her fingers, which trembled a little, as she unbuttoned the bodice all the way down.

"Take it off," he said.

Juliana slid the bodice from her body and draped it over a chair. Her arms were bare, the corset hugging her breasts and waist.

"Keep going," Elliot said.

Juliana flushed, pink spreading from her cheeks all the

way down her neck. In addition to the ten freckles on her nose, freckles also ran down her throat to her chest, the pattern forming a point between her breasts. The blush emphasized it.

She unhooked the corset cover and reached behind her to unlace the corset. That came off—she exhaled in relief—to reveal the little top of her combinations.

"The skirt as well?" she asked, setting aside the corset.

"And the petticoats and whatever contraption you're wearing beneath."

"I have to wear at least a small bustle with this, or the dress will sag." Juliana unhooked and untied the skirt from around her waist and pulled it away. She untied and stepped out of the petticoats as well as the bustle.

She stood bare but for her combinations, stockings, and low-heeled shoes. Her hand went to the fastenings of her combinations. "Shall I take this off too?"

Elliot's memories shot back to a time when he'd been painfully young and shipping back to India after brief leave. He and his mates had ended up at a cabaret in Marseilles, where young ladies pranced about a stage in their underwear and called out, "What shall we take off next, messieurs?"

That glimpse of blatant sin had been nowhere near as erotic as Juliana in her combinations shyly asking, *Shall I take this off too?*

"Shoes and stockings," Elliot said. His entire body was at peace, except for his cock, which was rigid as a maypole. But, after all, what did a maypole represent?

"Oh yes." Juliana slid out of her sturdy workday shoes and slipped off her stockings.

"That's enough," Elliot said when she finished. "Come here."

Juliana walked hesitantly to the tub. One step, two, three . . .

Elliot reached out, hooked his arm around her waist, and pulled her down to him.

No squealing when she got wet. Juliana laughed.

Her laughter was so dear to him. The fact that she laughed with him, better still.

Elliot pulled her all the way into the tub, onto his lap with its stiff erection, closing his arms around her and holding her close.

Juliana leaned against him and decided that Elliot wet was a grand sight. His eyelashes were beaded with water, his hair darker gold with it. From behind his lashes his light gray eyes were almost silver, his look heating her even in the cooling water.

Water droplets glistened on his shoulders and beaded in the hollow of his throat, sliding over the lines of his tattoo. Water curled the hair on his chest, darkening the golden strands.

Elliot stroked her with big hands through her wet combinations, molding her waist, her back, up under her breasts. His eyes were heavy with his lack of sleep, but his touch was sure and strong.

He cradled her in his hands, thumbs moving along her jaw to tilt her head back. He kissed her lips, his tongue taking the water from them.

Juliana lightly licked his cheekbone, liking the way her touch drew color across his tanned skin. He caught her mouth with his again, his kiss turning deeper, less playful.

She was soaking wet, her combinations forming to her body, the thin lawn hiding nothing.

Elliot slid his hands over her, cupping her breasts, her nipples tight against his palms. He kissed her with slow deliberation, a man seeking comfort.

He was aroused, the blunt hardness of his cock a firm line. Juliana wriggled against it, liking the feel of it.

"Wicked lass," Elliot whispered.

He skimmed his hands down her waist, tugging open her drawers and peeling them from her body. The drawers landed with a wet splat outside the tub.

There wasn't room for Elliot to make love to her here. He kissed her again, licking the water from her lips, stroking into her mouth. Juliana rubbed his slippery shoulders to his back, pulling him to her for a harder kiss.

Elliot's hands went everywhere—her thighs, buttocks, waist, breasts. He kissed her with longing, lips caressing then commanding.

He was lifting her up, up, rising out of the tub with her. Water crashed from their bodies back into the bathtub and all over the floor. Elliot pushed Juliana's camisole up and off, pulling her naked, wet body against his.

More kisses, Elliot lifting her against him, cradling her buttocks with one arm, while he hungrily took her mouth. He locked her legs around him, the ridge of his arousal nestled against her thigh, and stepped out of the tub.

Chapter 18

The bed was two strides away. Juliana landed on her back, ever so gently, then Elliot covered her, warm and wet.

He never stopped kissing her. He parted her legs, his callused hands rasping her skin, and entered her.

The bedsheets quickly became soaked as he moved inside her, his eyes darkening as he loved her as hungrily as he'd kissed her.

Elliot came apart in tight little jerks, Juliana's cries heartfelt. Elliot kept loving her, his eyes growing heavy, until he finished, gathered Juliana against him, and fell into an unmoving sleep.

When Juliana woke and ventured downstairs, the house was again full of men from the village, returning for another day of putting McGregor Castle to rights. Juliana had heard them arrive while she lay against Elliot, so she'd taken special care in front of the mirror to make sure her hair was perfectly to rights, the clean dress she put on nowhere near the water that coated the floor.

Elliot lay back in the bed and watched her, the sheets sagging down his hips. He regarded her with a half smile that was positively sinful.

"Go on," he said when she lingered. "Back to your lists."

Juliana smiled at him, her body happy, and made herself leave.

Mahindar passed her on her way downstairs, he heading up to Elliot. The man seemed to know exactly when Elliot would need him.

Juliana stopped him on the landing. "Mahindar," she said. "Thank you. For all you've done."

Mahindar blinked. "I've barely started, memsahib. There is much yet to do today."

"I meant about Elliot. For looking after him. For taking care of him. You didn't have to."

Mahindar shook his head. "He needed looking after. Still needs looking after. When we found the sahib, he was wandering miles from his house, half dead from thirst and exposure. We brought him home. We could not let him die."

"Not everyone would be that kind."

"I was raised to always give aid to the unfortunate. And the sahib, at one time, did me a good service. He took me away from a man who treated me shamefully." Mahindar smiled. "He even punched that other man in the face. My wife, she liked that. But we would have helped the sahib regardless. He is, in the truest sense, a good man."

"I've always thought so." Juliana paused. "You don't know how he escaped from whatever awful place he was in, do you?"

"No, memsahib. He has never told me the whole story. Only bits and pieces."

Juliana stood aside for two men who were waiting to

pass with a rolled-up carpet, and signaled them to proceed. Now was not the time to ask for Elliot's history, and besides, Juliana wanted Elliot to tell her himself.

"Thank you, Mahindar" she said again, sincerely, and went back downstairs to her lists and letters.

Juliana was pleased to find that while she'd been upstairs with Elliot, Hamish had brought in the post, including all kinds of news and notes from her family. Juliana took the post with her to the dining room, and settled in to indulge herself with it.

Ainsley wrote a nice long, chatty letter that only Ainsley could write. In it she said that she understood why Juliana had wanted them to stay away for a time, but that they'd be back for her midsummer fête, along with the entire Mackenzie family. She also reassured Juliana that the wedding gifts had gone back, except for those from people who were perfectly happy for Juliana and Elliot to keep what they'd sent. Those gifts would be arriving at Castle McGregor by courier later in the week.

Ainsley ended by professing gratefulness for Juliana marrying her troubled brother, and her certainty that Juliana would have a good effect on him.

Elliot's brother Sinclair wrote to both her and Elliot, declaring that he was happy with the turn of events. Sinclair, who was two years older than Elliot, said he would attempt to attend their midsummer fête, but he was always kept busy in London, not only in court, but in taking care of his two children. They went through a new governess every week. Sinclair would be kind and resist the temptation to foist the children off for the summer on Elliot and Juliana—Elliot and his new bride needed time to get to know each other before the holy terrors of the McBride family descended upon them. Sinclair concluded that he'd foist them off on Ainsley instead.

Juliana smiled as she finished the letter. Sinclair had always been good-natured, and he'd deeply loved his wife, who'd been taken from him so young, leaving him two children to raise on his own.

Juliana's father wrote in his understated way that he was glad that Juliana seemed to be happy. Implicit in the letter was the promise that, if Juliana should prove to become *un*happy, she could return home with no questions asked. Mr. St. John would even enlist the best legal help on her behalf in such a case.

Any other person might find this letter cool, but Juliana knew her father. He was a man of deep feeling, but he had decided long ago never to bother anyone else with those deep feelings. He was the epitome of the calm and stern Scot, expecting the worst, but quietly accepting the best if it should happen to come.

Gemma's letter was the longest. Juliana loved in Gemma the fact that she did not believe in keeping anything secret for anyone's good. She was forthright and honest, and if others found her opinions too abrupt, at least they always knew where they stood with her. The polite lie was not for Gemma St. John. She believed in unvarnished truth, for good or ill.

I must tell you what people are saying so you will be prepared upon your return to Edinburgh. Not everyone in the world believes this, but I have heard put about that your swift choice to marry Elliot shows that you are no different from your mother. All the work you have done throughout your life to prove you are not like her counts as nothing for vicious gossips such as Lady Gascogne and Mrs. Bassington-Smith and ladies of like mind.

I, being me, could not let that pass. I told Mrs. Bassington-Smith that your mother indeed was a scatterbrain, and we all knew it, but that you were as unlike her as a flower is to cheese. I said that you had been wise to accept Mr. McBride's timely proposal, and now have a husband and home of your own, and all's well that ends well.

Well, I shut her up, as you can imagine, but I know they rehearse this idea out of my hearing. One cannot have society without disparagers such as these, I know, but I thought I'd warn you. However, you do have your champions, including me, who believe you had a lucky escape from Mr. Barclay. As for opinion about Mr. McBride, everyone can only declare what a fine man he is, and no one can deny that he comes from an utterly respectable family.

Of course, they add, it's a pity that he's mad . . .

Juliana finished the letter, half uneasy, half reassured. She pictured the rather pretty Mrs. Bassington-Smith, wife of a high court judge, her black hair in its perfect ringlets, declaring over her waving fan that Juliana was no better than her mother.

Juliana's temper stirred. Really, it was no one's business why she'd married Elliot, or how they were getting on. Mrs. Bassington-Smith hadn't been on Juliana's guest list for the midsummer ball, and Juliana determined that the woman would not be added to any other list from here on out.

And Elliot wasn't mad. Not really. He'd been disturbed by the terrible things he'd endured, and he was trying to recover.

Juliana tamped down her irritation in order to answer the letters, soothing her temper by writing first to the people of whom she was most fond. She wrote also to merchants in Aberdeen and Edinburgh, ordering materials for the house, the fête, and the ball.

Elliot had told her, through Mahindar, that she could buy whatever she wanted or needed, with an open-ended account. Juliana, with the frugality and efficiency she'd strived to learn since girlhood, looked for the best things she could for the very best price.

By the time she'd finished her correspondence and emerged to have Hamish carry it to the village, it was time for luncheon, which she ate informally with Priti. Priti had been taught table manners, Juliana saw, holding her fork and spoon properly, eating only her bread with her fingers.

Juliana's heart warmed as she watched her. Who couldn't love this child, with her wild black hair and winsome smile, her prattling talk, in a mix of English and Punjabi? Her eyes were deep brown, but she had the look of Elliot. She would be lovely when she was grown, and Juliana vowed to watch over her every step of the way.

After their luncheon, Channan arrived to lead Priti back to the kitchen. Priti was glad to go, to play again not only with the goat, but with her other new friend—the setter who seemed to have no inclination to return home to Mr. McPherson.

Priti climbed onto Juliana's lap and kissed her cheek, and Juliana held her close. She was glad Elliot had brought her here from India, to a place where she could be safe.

Priti gave Juliana another sticky kiss, climbed down, took Channan's hand, and pulled the older woman away.

They had not been gone thirty seconds when Mahindar walked into the dining room, looking distressed.

"Memsahib, you have callers."

"Callers?" Juliana rose, dabbing with her handkerchief where Priti had left her honeyed kiss. "Good heavens, who would call while we're at such sixes and sevens?"

Mahindar presented the silver salver he held in his big hands. The two cards bore the names of Mrs. Terrell and Mrs. Dalrymple.

Chapter 19

"Oh Lord." Juliana sent up the fervent prayer. "I remember distinctly telling them the house wasn't fit for visitors, and wouldn't be until the fête. Where am I to put them?"

"Do not distress yourself, memsahib. The room you said you wanted for the morning room is clean and neat. I can bring you tea there, with little cakes. Miss Rossmoran has been teaching Channan how to make little cakes."

"Excellent, Mahindar. You're a wonder. Yes, put them there, and tell them I'll be right in."

Mahindar departed swiftly and quietly.

Juliana neatened her hair in the mirror. She was hardly dressed for accepting callers, in a workaday gown of brown poplin without much trim, though her Edinburgh dressmaker had always managed to make her dresses pretty even if they were inappropriate for the occasion.

They'll have to take as they find, Juliana thought irritably as she walked across the chaos of the house to the morning room.

Mrs. Terrell and Mrs. Dalrymple rose as Juliana entered. They took in her gown, glanced at each other, and kept their expressions fixed.

"I apologize for the dust and noise," Juliana said, her face heating. "We have the builders in, as you can see."

The ladies sat down, exclaiming that of course they expected nothing, that her morning room was lovely, had the best of views, would be splendid when it was finished. Mahindar glided in while they were chattering and set down the tea things, the ones Ainsley had given Juliana, plus a three-tiered tray filled with tiny cakes and petit fours.

Juliana poured out the tea.

"I wonder that your husband brought his Indian servants home with him," Mrs. Dalrymple said as she accepted a cup and plucked a cake from the tray Mahindar held. "One had to put up with them in India, of course, but I like plain Scottish servants now. The Indian ones do creep about so, and most of them are blatant thieves. It's unnerving."

Juliana looked at Mahindar, who kept his face completely blank. "Mahindar and his family are not thieves," she said. "They are perfectly fine people."

"Mark my words, they're not to be trusted," Mrs. Dalrymple said, waving her tiny cake. "What on earth Mr. McBride was thinking, I cannot imagine. The Hindus find it bizarre to cook a chop, can you imagine, Mrs. Terrell? They eat no meat themselves."

"Mahindar is not Hindu," Juliana said. "He's a Sikh."

Mrs. Dalrymple shuddered. "Even worse. They are so bloodthirsty."

"I have not found Mahindar to be bloodthirsty in the least," Juliana said. "What's more, he speaks perfect English." She gave Mrs. Dalrymple a pointed look.

Mrs. Dalrymple paid no attention, being busy taking a bite of her cake. She chewed a moment, then her face took on a peculiar expression, and she started to cough. "Good heavens, help us. He has poisoned us!"

Mahindar's eyes widened in astonishment. Mrs. Terrell, who had been staring out the window and paying no attention, jerked around. Juliana quickly handed Mrs. Dalrymple a napkin and tried not to cringe when the lady spit out the chewed cake.

"Poison," Mrs. Dalrymple rasped. "You must send for the constable at once."

"Nonsense." Juliana snatched up a cake from the tray and took a bite. The flavors were unexpected but ones she now recognized. "Cinnamon, cardamom, and a bit of black pepper, that is all. How lovely. Please extend my compliments to your wife, Mahindar." She smiled, trying to convey to Mahindar that if he valued his sanity, he'd flee the room now.

Mahindar made a polite bow. "Thank you, memsahib." With dignity intact, he turned and silently departed.

"You see what I mean about them creeping about?" Mrs. Dalrymple said. "And putting pepper into a cake? How ignorant. How foolish. Plain cooking is beyond them."

"Mrs. Dalrymple," Juliana said, no longer bothering to keep her temper in check. "If you have come here to insult my servants and disparage my food, I must ask you to leave."

"You know very well why I came today," Mrs. Dalrymple said.

Mrs. Terrell nodded. "We've come to give you another warning, is all, dear Mrs. McBride."

Mrs. Terrell was about thirty-five but she might have been fifty, round faced, her hair going to gray, a woman who would die rather than stoop to artifice to cover the gray threads. She wore clothes made well of costly fabric, but they were painfully, almost boastfully plain. Her entire being shouted, *My husband has money, but I am frugal and will never bring him shame . . . unlike some wives who wear gowns of dull poplin to receive guests.*

"Another warning," Juliana said. "Please tell me what you mean."

"Mrs. Dalrymple has telegraphed to Scotland Yard, and an investigation has begun. Murder is a very serious crime, Mrs. McBride."

"Indeed, yes," Juliana said in freezing tones. "So serious that one must prove it without doubt. It is not an accusation to be made lightly."

"And I do not make it lightly," Mrs. Dalrymple said. "Archibald was a fine youth. Almost like a son to my husband." She blinked her light blue eyes rapidly, though Juliana could discern no tears. "Mr. Stacy said he was off to visit your husband at his plantation one day, to see how he fared after his ordeal, and the next thing we know, Mr. Stacy is missing, presumed dead. A witness saw the two of them together, and then, Mr. Stacy was gone."

"What witness is that?" Juliana asked. "I would like to speak to him."

Mrs. Dalrymple gave her a wise look. "I will keep the name to myself. We have been advised to."

Juliana felt a cold chill but kept her tone confident. "Investigate away, Mrs. Dalrymple. Mr. McBride believes, however, that Mr. Stacy is still alive."

Mrs. Dalrymple jumped, and a bit of tea sloshed to the saucer. "Still alive? He can produce him, then?"

Juliana hesitated. "Not at the snap of a finger, no."

"There, you see?" Mrs. Dalrymple said. "Your husband has told you he left Mr. Stacy alive in India, and Mr. Dalrymple and I are going to prove that he didn't."

"She is adamant, my dear," Mrs. Terrell said to Juliana.

Juliana sat still and burned with anger. She had decided last night, lying in bed alone, to put her faith in Elliot. Yes, he might behave like a madman sometimes, but that did not mean he was wrong.

Her natural fear in the face of Mrs. Dalrymple was that Elliot *was* wrong, and that whoever he thought was lurking in the woods was not Mr. Stacy.

But no, Juliana had weighed all the arguments in her

head before drawing her conclusion. She would stand by Elliot. She would not be like her mother, who'd disparaged Juliana's father to all and sundry whenever she could. Juliana's mother, a beautiful woman, had been hopelessly spoiled by her own family and had chafed at the quiet decorum of the St. John household.

Juliana drew a breath to tell Mrs. Dalrymple to do her worst, when Elliot himself walked into the room.

Juliana nearly choked on her tea. Elliot wore a threadbare kilt, scarred boots, and a linen shirt, all covered with dust and plaster, because he'd been helping the men saw, hammer, and haul away debris. His hair was also coated with dust, as was his face, and from this mess his gray eyes blazed with a wild light.

"Juliana," Elliot said, then broke into a Highland brogue so broad Juliana herself scarcely understood it. "I heard ye had comp'ny. Are these th' wee lassies?"

Juliana cleared her throat. "Mrs. Terrell, our neighbor, and Mrs. Dalrymple, her friend from Glasgow."

"Och, aye," Elliot said. Then he spurted a string of words that sounded like, *Gae nae leaver due gran doch blochen.* Gibberish nonsense.

"Quite," Juliana said, pretending she'd understood every word.

"What's the matter, lass?" Elliot asked Mrs. Dalrymple. "Can ye nae ken yer own Scottish?"

"I learned long ago to speak plain English," Mrs. Dalrymple said. "That is the world today, Mr. McBride."

"Then it's a foolish world." Elliot went off into another speech that Juliana *truly* didn't understand. The soft consonants and long vowels were not from a language she knew, nor did they sound like the Punjabi dialect Mahindar and his family spoke. However, she continued to sip tea as though nothing were out of the ordinary.

Elliot had left the door open. Out in the passage, Komal's voice rose in Punjabi, and they heard McGregor's shouts.

"Bring those back, ye daft woman! A man's got a right to have a bottle or two stashed under his bed. That's single malt. Do ye understand me? Och, now ye've let that goat in."

Bleating sounded, followed by the noise of hooves on the flagstones, accompanied by the ripe smell of frightened goat, and Priti's laughing voice as she chased it down the hall.

"I was right," Mrs. Dalrymple said. "This is a madhouse."

Juliana rose to her feet. "Then the leaving of it will not pain you. Thank you for your warning, ladies. My husband and I will take it under consideration."

"You'll do a sight more than that." Mrs. Dalrymple slammed down her teacup and jumped up, Mrs. Terrell rising more decorously. "Mr. Dalrymple will speak to you, Mr. McBride."

Elliot nodded silently, as though he didn't care one way or the other. McGregor burst into the room, a bottle of whiskey in each hand, Komal trying to wrest one from him.

"Lassie, tell this woman t' leave a man be. Ah." McGregor stopped, his lively eyes taking in the shocked faces of the two visiting ladies. "Mrs. Dull Pimple. Taking your leave, were you? Good day, then."

As he bowed to them, Komal wrenched a bottle from McGregor's hand and held it aloft in triumph. Then she pulled her scarf over her face, and turned and faced the wall as the lady callers walked past her.

"Come along, Prunella," Mrs. Dalrymple said. "They've made their beds, and they must lie in them." She looked at Komal's colorful back. "You have to take a strap to them. It's the only way they learn to behave."

McGregor came alive with rage. "Ye even think about laying a finger on her, I'll shoot you dead. *I'm* laird here, and don't ye forget it."

Juliana hurried past Mr. McGregor, who was waving the bottle dangerously. "You had better go quickly," she said to Mrs. Terrell, half pushing the two women into the hall. "There's no telling what he'll do when he's enraged."

Mrs. Dalrymple scurried to the front door, narrowly missing two workmen who came in with a load of stone blocks. "Out of my way, if you please," she shouted. "You should be using the back door. The *back*."

She rushed out. There was bleating, and a scream, Priti's voice admonishing.

Juliana hurried out, followed by worried Mrs. Terrell, to find Mrs. Dalrymple in a tug-of-war with the goat. The animal had snatched at the fringes of Mrs. Dalrymple's silk shawl as she'd run by, and now the goat busily chewed as Mrs. Dalrymple struggled to pull the shawl out of the animal's mouth.

"No, no," Priti cried, shaking her finger at the goat. "Bad goat."

"Heathen child." Mrs. Dalrymple raised her hand at Priti, preparing to slap.

Rage flashed through Juliana, and she caught Mrs. Dalrymple's wrist in a tight grip. "Do not *dare* to strike her. How can you even think such a thing?"

Mrs. Dalrymple tried to wrench herself away, but Juliana was too strong. The goat, whether in disgust, or for reasons of her own, spit out the shawl.

Juliana picked it up and thrust it at Mrs. Dalrymple. "Never, ever come to this house again."

She expected Mrs. Dalrymple to exclaim that the shawl was ruined or demand the price of it, but the woman only gave Juliana another furious look and turned away. But the look held a flash of cunning, despite the woman's anger and fear, as though Mrs. Dalrymple knew something Juliana didn't.

Juliana didn't like the look, but she was too angry to worry about it at the moment.

"Mrs. Terrell," Juliana said, keeping her voice deliberately calm. "I am afraid that as long as Mrs. Dalrymple stays with you, I cannot receive you here."

Mrs. Terrell remained cool. "I am sorry to hear that, Mrs. McBride." She adjusted her gloves. "The ladies in this valley look to me for social leadership. I am afraid that they will follow my lead and not receive you. You've rather ruined yourself this day, I am pained to say."

She turned on her heel—taking care not to let *her* summer shawl flap anywhere near the goat—and followed Mrs. Dalrymple down to the gate, where an open landau waited.

"Oh, really?" Juliana said to the air. "Well, we'll see about *that*." She looked down at the goat, still chewing on whatever piece of shawl it had managed to tear off. Juliana gave its head a pat. "Good goat," she said, then took Priti's hand and led her back into the house.

She found McGregor prancing through the wide hallway. He linked his arm through a smiling Komal's and danced her around one way, then switched arms and went the other. She still had one of the whiskey bottles, and Mr. McGregor kept hold of the other, passing it from hand to hand as he danced.

Elliot was laughing.

"It is not funny," Juliana said with grim determination. "That woman is odious. But Elliot, she said she was having someone investigate you. She wants you charged."

"I can't be charged for murdering someone still alive."

"I do wish Mr. Stacy would make things easy on us and show himself. Rather obstinate of him not to."

Elliot shrugged. "He does as he pleases. He might go back to wherever he came from without ever revealing himself."

"Not very helpful."

Elliot lifted his gaze from her to McGregor. McGregor had stopped dancing and was patting Komal on the shoulder.

"Don't worry, lass," McGregor said. "I will never let that nasty female hurt you."

Komal actually smiled at him. Beamed, even. McGregor

turned brick red and started to stammer. Komal snatched the second whiskey bottle out his hand and ran for the kitchen.

"Blast you, woman!" McGregor rocketed after her, Priti happily following. They heard voices raised, in two different languages, down the echoing passage to the kitchen.

"Poor old devil," Juliana said, not stopping her smile.

She turned back to Elliot, who leaned his hips comfortably on the back of the empire sofa, his kilt outlining his thighs.

Even if he never spoke to Juliana of things important to him, she certainly could enjoy looking at him. And touching him. The wet heat of the bath hadn't left her all day.

"But, really, we must do something about the Dalrymples," Juliana said. "They could be dangerous to you."

Elliot shrugged. "Mrs. Dalrymple is not Scottish, whatever she claims. She didn't understand a word I said to her."

"My dear Elliot, neither did I."

He smiled. "In any case, I can't be tried for murder if there is no body, no grave, no marker."

"You can be tried if he continues to be missing, as the man suspected of making him *go* missing if nothing else."

"The great British system of law makes them have to prove it." Elliot went quiet. "But our Mrs. Dalrymple's not wrong, lass. I am a murderer."

"You're not," Juliana said stoutly. "Not if Mr. Stacy is alive."

"He is." Elliot's hands tightened on the back of the sofa, the knuckles whitening through his tan. "I'm not talking of him. I'm speaking of other men."

"You mean in the army. In battles."

He paused again, as though gathering thoughts he didn't want to think. "No. I mean when I was a prisoner. My captors taught me how to kill with my bare hands, and then made me do it for them."

Chapter 20

Juliana stared at him with the surprise she did so well, the expression of not wanting to believe the horrors he told her. Her blue eyes went a bit wider for a moment. Elliot hated that, with everything he revealed, he'd shatter more and more of her innocence.

Elliot lifted his hands and looked at them, callused and worn, the fingertips scarred where they'd been cut off, the nails surprisingly whole for having been pulled out and grown back.

"They taught me how to put my hands around a man's throat," he said. "How to use my thumbs to crush his windpipe. How to press my fingers into his eye sockets and pull his cheekbones from his face. A man will fight so hard to live when he's dying . . ."

Juliana's hand went to her own throat, slender with a sweet dusting of freckles. "You don't have to tell me, if you don't want to," she said.

"I helped them kill men in their rival tribe. They made me into an animal, and they laughed when their enemies died by my hands."

"Oh, Elliot."

At least she didn't say, with the superiority of Mrs. Dalrymple or Mrs. Terrell, that the men he'd killed were only heathens and didn't matter. They were men with lives and homes, with children and wives who'd wail in grief when they did not return.

"When it was over, they'd lock me back up again."

Juliana came to him with slow steps, her gaze never leaving his face. She closed her hands over his, lifted each, and pressed a kiss to his scarred knuckles.

"I know you had no choice," she said. "They would have killed you if you hadn't done it."

"But I should have refused. Obeying them makes me a coward by most standards. I should have resisted, even to death, before I did their work."

Her warm tear trickled to the back of his hand. "You had no choice," she repeated in a whisper.

It hadn't seemed real, those swift, silent battles in the night, Elliot chained and made to defend the camp from their rivals. In the cold blackness, Elliot had fought men who'd tried to thrust knives into him, his fear and obsessive need driving him on. He'd fought them because he'd refused to give up and die.

"I had to live," he said. "I was determined to live, whatever the cost." He released her hands and brushed back a tendril of her hair. "To see you again."

Juliana looked up at him, lips parted.

"It's what drove me to live, lass, every minute of the day or night. To see you again. To hear your voice. To touch you . . ." Elliot drew his finger down her cheek. "They wondered at my resilience. They called me a demon or the walking dead, because I wouldn't lie down and die. But I couldn't. Not until I saw you again."

More tears trickled down her cheeks. Elliot brushed one away with his finger.

"I didn't understand myself what you were to me," he said, "until I was in danger of never seeing your face again, or your sweet smile. Then I knew. You were my lass, Juliana. You always have been."

"But you came home." Juliana took a step back, pulled her handkerchief from her sleeve, and wiped her eyes. "You came home and never said a word to me."

"I didn't want you to see me until I'd healed. I was a broken man. But I realized I'd never heal until I returned to India and faced what I was, what had happened to me. Besides, Priti was in India. I didn't intend to leave her there to be raised without a father. I went back to settle everything for once and for all before I returned to Scotland forever."

"But I might have married Grant in the meantime," Juliana said. She sniffled, swiped at her nose, and tucked the handkerchief into her pocket. "I accepted his proposal because I thought I'd never see you again. You might have been too late."

Elliot let amusement slip through the shivering horror in his mind. "No fear of that. I had Ainsley keep an eye on you and tell me everything you did."

"But . . ." Juliana looked bewildered. "When on earth did Ainsley find time to be your spy?"

"My sister is amazingly resourceful. And cunning. If she couldn't speak to you herself, she'd recruit someone else to. And she reported everything to me. She didn't know the whole of what I was up to, and I asked her not to tell you I was asking about you, and to trust me. She did, bless her. I knew exactly when you were to marry Grant Barclay, and exactly how much time I had to return to Scotland and prepare things to scoop you up. I knew you'd never change the wedding date—you schedule your life to the minute and follow it exactly."

Indignation edged out her bewilderment. "Even so, you could have said something. When you were captured, when we thought you dead . . . They were the most awful months of my life. Nothing can compare. I cried all day in relief when I got Ainsley's telegram that you'd been found and were all right. And then you never wrote, never called on me, never spoke to me, never sent a message."

"I know I did it all wrong," Elliot said. "Ainsley would say I'm only a man after all. I did what I did because I didn't want to give you the chance to say no."

"So you came to my wedding to snatch me from the altar?"

"I'm a Highland barbarian. We steal our wives, didn't ye know?"

"You are horrible."

"I always have been." He managed a grin. "You knew that."

Juliana pressed her hands to her face. "Elliot, what am I to do with you?"

He couldn't stay away from her any longer. Elliot took her hands, tugged her against him, and closed his arms around her. He laid his cheek against her fragrant hair, and let her warmth soak into his body.

Juliana relaxed with a sigh, and Elliot closed his eyes, focusing only on the heat of her against him, the softness of her under the stiff fabric of her dress.

"Elliot," Juliana murmured after a while.

Elliot didn't answer. He kissed her hair.

"What *are* we going to do about the Dalrymples?"

Poor Juliana. So worried about trivial matters. Elliot tilted her head back and briefly kissed her lips. "I might know someone who can assist."

"Who?"

"Friend of a friend." He kissed Juliana again, tasting the tea on her lips, and the cinnamon and pepper of the cake she'd nibbled.

The stain of the past slipped away, once again. The darkness was still there, ready to flow out and twine him in its net, but for now, closing and locking the door then unbuttoning Juliana's dress was easing it away.

Elliot ended up sitting on the chair at the writing desk, she straddling his lap, he making made slow love to her, holding her.

In that quiet ecstasy, Elliot began to believe he could get well again. Maybe it would take a long while, and perhaps the memories would never entirely go away, but he would live. All he had to do was make love to Juliana, for now and for always, and he'd never fear anything again.

~

The work in the house continued through the afternoon and on into the evening. Elliot sent Hamish running to the village to telegraph London, then he took his rifle and went out looking for Stacy.

The red setter followed him, showing no sign of wanting to return to McPherson. Elliot didn't want the dog to be hurt, but he knew Stacy. The man had a soft spot for animals, and wouldn't hurt one to get to someone who'd enraged him. If he wanted Elliot dead, he'd confine his sights to Elliot.

Elliot found no sign of Stacy that day, however. Perhaps the man had given up and retreated.

Elliot had been keeping his ears open for news of any stranger staying in the area, but heard of no one unusual arriving of late, besides himself. He'd considered the possibility that Stacy might try to enter the house under the pretext of being a worker, but McGregor and Hamish knew every man for miles by sight, and Mahindar knew Stacy by sight. None of the men was Stacy.

When the workers went home to supper and bed, Elliot locked the doors of the castle with the giant keys then bolted them. After that he collapsed into bed and slept hard, his arms around Juliana.

In the wee hours of the morning, McGregor roused him to do some fishing.

Elliot took his rifle with him as well as his poles. He'd use the opportunity to search again.

McGregor took him along the river to the west, where it cut through the steep hills to fetch up into slower, more placid pools on McPherson's land. Here McPherson met them.

The setter, who'd followed Elliot, wagged her tail and sniffed McPherson, then went back to circle Elliot.

"I seem to have stolen your dog," Elliot said. "Or she stole me. I'm not sure which."

"I can spare her," McPherson said in his booming voice. "If she likes ye, why not? Ye need a dog in that great house of yours."

The setter followed Elliot to the deeply shadowed spot where he quietly cast his line. From there Elliot could see up and down the river and into the hills, where a hunter might sit with a rifle similar to Elliot's. The setter chased a few butterflies on the bank then settled down to watch the fishing with sleepy eyes.

The quiet of the valley was perfect. The river burbled into pools, the fish flipped and swam, and gratifyingly took bait. McPherson and McGregor caught several fish quickly, but Elliot had none.

Elliot didn't care. The point of fishing, he'd decided long ago, was to wait in cold water up to the knees and watch the eddies swirl by, the line dangle, and shadows move and dance. Fishing meant standing with a friend in silence with nothing needing to be said.

He saw no sign and felt no sensation of a watcher in the woods. Stacy wasn't there. Perhaps he'd given up and gone. Or perhaps Elliot was mistaken, and Stacy had never been there in the first place.

Elliot knew he had been, though.

"Who the devil is that?" McPherson's voice rang out over the water and the fish darted for cover.

McPherson was shading his eyes against the intense morning sun to watch a man walk down the hill toward them. The visitor wore a frock coat, trousers, and a stovepipe hat, a costume more suited to strolling about a city park than tramping through the wilds of Scotland.

"Dear God," McGregor said. "It's that Dull Pimple chap. Haven't we had enough of them?"

"*I* didn't invite him," McPherson said.

"Ye don't think I did, do ye? Here, you." McGregor cupped his hands around his mouth and shouted across the river. "Go away. Ye're upsetting the fish."

Ignoring McGregor, Mr. Dalrymple slipped and slid down to the bank and around a clump of trees to make straight for Elliot.

"Mr. McBride?" the man asked. "So pleased to make your acquaintance. George Dalrymple. Your boy said I might find you here."

Hamish. Well, the lad wasn't to know.

"I have something to discuss with you," Dalrymple said.

The man had a Scottish name, but he sounded as though he'd tried very hard to erase anything Scottish about him. Elliot resisted the temptation to speak to him in Gaelic for the humor of it, but he did let his Scots accent become broad.

"Do ye now?"

"Yes, and I think we both know what it is."

"I cannae think what."

McGregor and McPherson watched from across the river, standing side by side, but Elliot signaled them to stay where they were. He'd either send Dalrymple home or push him into the water, he hadn't decided which yet.

Dalrymple gave Elliot a pained smile. "My wife told me you seemed a rather simple man. And, by the way, you must excuse her for yesterday. She does get rather upset. We were both so fond of Mr. Stacy, you know."

"He never mentioned ye," Elliot said. "So he must nae have been fond of *you*."

"We became rather more attached to him when you . . . ah . . . disappeared. He was quite worried about you." Mr. Dalrymple's smile remained, but his eyes were hard. "I realize you claim not to remember anything about Stacy's death, but we are prepared to tell the police that you killed him."

"You're right. I *don't* remember."

"Nonetheless, we have ascertained that this is what happened. As my wife promised, we have begun an investigation."

Elliot cast his line into the water again, gently flicking his wrist just right . . . just right. The fish were nowhere in sight.

"Very civil-minded of ye," he said to Dalrymple.

"I understand, of course, dear fellow. You weren't right in the head at the time. There's speculation you still aren't, though you seem much better."

"Thank ye."

"And all this must be upsetting for your wife, who is from one of Edinburgh's most respectable families, I hear."

"She is, aye."

"I know you would like to spare her undue distress."

Elliot took his gaze from the gently bobbing line and looked fully at Dalrymple. The man's pale face was beaded with sweat in the sunshine, his features too perfect and delicate for this climate. If he'd been in India as he claimed, time had erased whatever effects the sunshine there had made on him.

"Be clear about what you're saying," Elliot said. "I'm interested."

Dalrymple smiled. "We're both men of the world, Mr. McBride. We've seen privation, and we've seen wealth, the extremes of each, haven't we?"

"Aye."

"I know that you . . . *acquired* . . . quite a bit of wealth for yourself. Hence your purchase of an estate in the Highlands."

"Aye." Elliot did not like the implication that he'd gained his fortune by anything other than backbreaking work, but he let it go. Not worth the bother.

"If you wish me to be plain, then I will be." Dalrymple cast a glance across the river at McPherson and McGregor, and lowered his voice. "You are unwell, and your wife is a pretty creature, and quite respectable. I'm certain that for a sum we can agree upon, the investigation into Mr. Stacy's death can lead nowhere in particular, or be withdrawn altogether."

Chapter 21

Elliot looked at Dalrymple for a heartbeat, then he drew back his fishing rod and sent the line over the river again.

"No," he said.

Dalrymple blinked. "Pardon?"

"I said no. You're not getting a penny."

Dalrymple blinked a few more times, as though surprised Elliot hadn't quickly begged the man to take all his money and leave him alone.

Dalrymple wet his thin lips. "Mr. McBride, your position is precarious. You killed a man and fled here to safety. You abducted his daughter and brought her with you. Now, while I agree that Mr. Stacy could be a hard man, and his daughter likely would have starved and died in India alone, I doubt you want this story to come out."

"She's not his daughter," Elliot said calmly. "She's mine."

Dalrymple stared. "Is she? Well, good God, man, in that case, I think we *had* better come to some sort of agreement. If your wife and her family find out about this by-blow, not only will they be shocked and upset, they might bring suit against you, do you not think?"

"I've already told my wife about the lass."

"Have you? Oh."

Elliot went on fishing. Beside him Dalrymple cleared his throat, started to speak, broke off, and cleared his throat again.

"Let me return to my original purpose," the man said after a time. "You murdered Mr. Stacy, and if you do not want to go to the gallows for it, you will make an arrangement with me."

"Stacy isn't dead."

"Pardon?" More blinking.

"I said, Archie Stacy isn't dead. He's alive and well."

Dalrymple actually smiled. "Ah, there we must differ. I have the death certificate."

He pulled a piece of paper out of an inner pocket of his coat, unfolded it, and held it up so that Elliot could see the printing and official seal.

Bang! Birds exploded into flight from the surrounding trees. Warm blood sprayed over Elliot's shirt, and he looked down in bewilderment at the filmy pattern of scarlet on linen. He felt no pain, and heard Dalrymple scream. The death certificate caught on the wind and fluttered gently into the river.

Elliot observed all this in one startled second, then he threw down his rod, stepped into deep shadow, and brought his rifle around.

Dalrymple remained in place, clutching his right hand and shrieking. McGregor and McPherson had disappeared into the shadows as well, only Dalrymple too far gone in pain to get himself out of the line of fire.

Elliot faded around the trees and moved swiftly and quietly in the direction of the shot. He ran up the hill, damp air forming droplets on his skin.

The scenario was eerily familiar, regardless of the tall

Scottish trees that marched around him. He fought off his mind's urge to take him back to the past, and ran on.

Elliot came out of the trees into a fairly flat clearing with an outcropping of bare rock. From the top of this rock, he had a perfect view of the river, the pool, and the exact spot where Dalrymple still stood.

Elliot pulled his rifle from his back and sighted down its scope. Dalrymple came into clear focus in the sunlight, his mouth moving as he swore in pain. Dalrymple had been facing Elliot, both of them in profile to this angle of the hill.

Stacy hadn't hit Dalrymple by mistake. The man was a crack shot, one of the best. The wind was strong here, but Stacy would have adjusted for that.

He'd shot at Dalrymple, not Elliot. One shot. A spent cartridge lay shining at the base of the rock.

Elliot picked up the cartridge and dropped it into his sporran as he scanned the hill around him. Nowhere did he see a man running away, or brush and saplings moving to show his passage. The grass around the rock was matted and flat—all of it. Stacy must have trampled it before he'd taken the shot to cover the tracks of his retreat.

Elliot slung his rifle over his back again and cupped his hands around his mouth. "Stacy!"

The word rang from the hills. The men below looked up.

The echoes faded and silence came back to him. If Stacy had been there, he'd vanished into the faint mist creeping down from the highest peaks.

Elliot climbed down from the rock and went in search of him.

⁓

Juliana spent the morning busy with preparations for the midsummer fête and making certain that the men worked in the most important areas of the house.

Because Elliot was off fishing with McGregor when the workers arrived, Juliana kept a special eye on Priti. She noticed the instant the little girl rushed out of the house on her own to play with the goat, and hurried out after her, welcoming the morning sun on her face.

Juliana relaxed as soon as she found Priti in the kitchen garden—Priti was talking to the goat tethered out of reach of the runner beans, and feeding it oatcakes.

She enjoyed a moment of watching the child. Priti was sweet-tempered, and yet had the impish determination of her father. She'd taken the upheaval from her home in stride, liked exploring Castle McGregor, and enjoyed following Hamish about, tugging on the lad's kilt when she wanted his attention.

The tranquil moment was disturbed when a man came out of the bracken at the foot of the garden. He was dressed the same as the workers—in kilt, boots, and shirtsleeves—his face covered with a rather tangled red-gold beard.

At the same time he didn't look like the other men. Something about him, something Juliana couldn't quite put her finger on, set him apart.

The man glanced briefly at Juliana, then his gaze went to Priti and stayed there.

Juliana stopped. A shout for Hamish worked its way up into her throat, but she bit it back, fearing what would happen if she startled the man. He did nothing, only looked at Priti.

Finally he turned slowly back to Juliana, met her gaze squarely, then turned and walked away.

Juliana started forward. "Mr. Stacy?"

The man didn't respond. Juliana followed him, staying well behind him, as he walked steadily down the path to the foot of the garden. He went through the gate then stepped into the woods and vanished from her sight.

Juliana hurried out the gate to the spot where he'd disappeared, but as much as she looked around, she couldn't tell which direction he'd gone.

She was still on the path when Mr. McGregor and Mr.

McPherson came puffing up from the direction of the river, both men agitated and out of breath.

"Did you see a man pass you?" she asked them, then looked at their faces. "Whatever is the matter?"

"It's McBride," McGregor panted. "Your husband, lassie, is running amok in the hills."

"Not running amok," McPherson corrected. "Chasing someone. A poacher, I'm thinking. An accidental shot."

"Shot?" Juliana touched her throat. "Elliot was shot?"

"No, no, lass," McPherson said quickly.

"He shot Dull Pimple." McGregor burst into laughter. "In the hand. That was a grand sight. The man dancing about, screaming like a banshee."

"Is he all right?" Juliana asked in alarm.

McPherson answered while McGregor kept chuckling. "Your kind heart does you credit, lassie. Dalrymple's fine. Bullet grazed him, the lucky bastard. My housekeeper is tending to him—she's a good nurse, but he's complaining all the way. Wants to bring a lawsuit against me." He laughed.

"What about Elliot? Where did he go?"

"Chasing the poacher," McGregor said. "I ran after him, shouted at him to leave the bugger alone, but he's gone. McBride didn't say anything, just dropped out of sight behind a rock and disappeared."

"We need to find him. Elliot, I mean. No, both of them."

"Dinnae worry, lass," McPherson said. "I know every inch of these lands, and your husband's only after a poacher, probably a lad from rougher country where the hunting's not so good. They don't have much up in the hills, and I don't begrudge them a hare or two."

"He's not a poacher," Juliana said. "The man Elliot is chasing is dangerous. I saw him."

Both men stopped. "Saw who?" McPherson asked.

"A man Elliot knew in India."

McPherson and McGregor exchanged a glance. "Lass," McGregor said. "I hate to say it to ye, but your husband's been acting a bit strange. Ye know he has. There's no one more dangerous in the hills than the pair of us. And him."

"But I *saw* him. Priti—you saw the man here, didn't you?"

Priti looked up from feeding the goat a fat head of cabbage. She nodded then turned her attention back to her more interesting friend.

"What did he look like?" McPherson asked, in the tone of someone humoring her.

"Like a Highlander," Juliana said impatiently. "In a kilt and boots, like one of the workers. But different. Like Elliot."

That's what had struck her—while the men here were sunburned pink from working in the summer outdoors, Mr. Stacy's skin had been burned deep brown, like Elliot's. Both men had lived a long time in a country where the sunlight was far stronger than that of northern Scotland.

"We need to find him," she repeated.

When the older men continued to look at her skeptically, she swung away in exasperation. "Fine, then I'll find someone who *will* help me. Hamish!"

She ran back toward the house. There were plenty of men there from the village and those who could be spared from their farms, all happy to earn the extra wages.

Juliana ran to the top of the staircase and shouted down at them all. "Gentlemen. Lads. Stop!"

One by one, they stopped hammering and pounding, looking around in curiosity to see what the lady of the house was screeching about. Hamish popped out from one of the upstairs rooms, hammer in hand.

Quickly Juliana told them what she wanted them to do. "An extra jar of ale to the man who finds my husband."

Tools were dropped, and booted feet hammered on the stairs and the flagstone floor. The men eagerly raced out the door, scattering as they ran into the sunshine and wind.

Juliana knew that they, like McGregor and McPherson, weren't particularly worried about Elliot, but why give up the easy chance for some fine brew? She followed them down and out, but swept Priti up into her arms when the little girl wanted to go with them.

"No, Priti, you stay with me."

Priti gave her a look of disappointment, then flung her arms around Juliana's neck and kissed her cheek.

Mahindar came out, followed by the three women, to find Juliana. "You are wise, memsahib. The sahib will not be in any danger now, not with thirty men searching the hills for him."

"Do you believe him, Mahindar? That Mr. Stacy has followed him here?"

Mahindar looked troubled. "I do not know. The sahib has had waking visions before. Certainties that he was being followed or hunted. When he first came home, he was so very ill."

"What does Mr. Stacy look like? Does he have red hair? Very light red?"

"Yes," Mahindar said cautiously. "But so does almost every man working here."

He had a point. Because a Scottish man had a fading sunburn from India did not mean he was Mr. Stacy. Many gentlemen from England or Scotland went to the Raj—with the army, the civil service, or on their own to try to make a living.

Then again, Juliana had made her decision what to believe, and she'd stick by it.

She carried Priti inside, with Mahindar and family, to wait for the searchers' return.

~~~

The men came back at sunset, Elliot with them. Hamish declared himself the winner of the ale. The others good-naturedly debated that, except Elliot.

Juliana had never seen Elliot furious before. When she'd known him during their youth, he'd been at his most smiling and charming, and since their marriage, he'd been quiet, or seductive, or silently withdrawn.

Now his gray eyes sparkled with rage, and he stormed past his rescuers, took Juliana by the arm, dragged her into the dining room, and slammed the door on prying eyes. The setter, who'd been following him, scratched at the outside of the door and whined.

Elliot ejected the bullets from his rifle, unloading it in angry silence.

"I'm sorry," Juliana said before he could speak. "I was worried about you. Mr. McGregor and Mr. McPherson said you'd rushed off into the hills after a man who apparently is not averse to shooting people."

Elliot slammed the unloaded rifle to the table. "And every single one of the men you sent after me might have been killed. Hamish might have. McGregor might have. What if I'd shot one of them by mistake? Or Stacy had?"

"I assumed they'd all make so much noise they'd announce their presence long before you saw them. Mr. Stacy would run away, and you'd grow exasperated and come back home with them. Which you have."

"Bloody hell, Juliana. What did you think I meant when I said Stacy was fucking *dangerous*? He could have shot any or all of the fools you sent after me, and they'd drop without knowing what hit them. He's a trained sharpshooter. Hell, I trained him."

Juliana lifted her chin. "I return to my theory that Mr. Stacy would find it more expedient to go back into hiding. And I was right."

"But you might not have been right, love. McGregor insists it was a poacher with a stray shot. It wasn't. No poacher around here uses bullets like this." He reached into his sporran and dropped a bit of metal onto the table. "This is a cartridge for a custom rifle, like mine, not a common shotgun."

Most bullet casings looked alike to Juliana, but she nodded at it. "Yes?"

"Your lackeys surrounded me and bade me come back with them like a pack of nursemaids."

"I can't help what they thought," Juliana said, still studying the shell casing. "And I'm sorry. But I would rather see you walk home, angry at me, than be carried home on a litter, hurt, maybe dead."

Elliot's silence made her raise her head. He wore a bleak expression, his anger winding down into weariness. "Ye don't believe me, do ye, lass? Ye think your husband's a madman, like they do. McPherson is ready to throw me into a padded room."

"No, I . . ."

His lips tightened. "Don't pretend, Juliana."

"I'm not pretending. I believe you. Now you need to believe *me*."

Elliot stopped, his expression still grim.

"'Twas not an easy decision," Juliana said. "You may believe me on that point too. But I weighed all the possibilities against what I had observed myself and drew the conclusion that you are not mad. Not about this anyway."

His eyes glinted. "Did you make a list?"

"In my head. Yes, I did."

"Not about this anyway?" he repeated.

"You know perfectly well what I mean. Whenever you talk to me of Mr. Stacy, you sound quite sane. Did he really shoot Mr. Dalrymple?"

"In the hand. It was a magnificent shot." Elliot reached into his pocket. "But I think he was anxious to get rid of this."

He dropped a piece of paper onto the table. The paper was damp, the ink blurred and illegible.

"What is that?"

"Death certificate. Dalrymple claims it is. It has to be a forgery, but it's hard to tell now."

Juliana touched it. "Mr. Dalrymple had this?"

"Mr. Dalrymple is a petty blackmailer. He wants money

out of me to keep quiet that I killed Stacy. He's gambling on me being so insane I don't remember anything I do."

"Well, it's nonsense. Mr. Stacy is alive and here. I saw him."

"What?"

"In the garden." Juliana told him of the encounter, and her conclusion that the man had been in India.

"Damn it."

"You can't be everyplace at once," Juliana said. "Besides, he did nothing. He looked at Priti, then looked at me, then ran off when I called him by name."

"Damn it to hell," Elliot said feelingly. He added a few more expletives that gentlemen should never use in front of ladies, and segued into languages she didn't know.

"He did nothing. He looked at me most peculiarly, and at Priti, but did and said nothing."

"Son of a . . ." More expletives. Elliot came to her. "Don't go near him. Don't leave the house. Give up your soiree until I've found him."

"Midsummer's Eve fête and ball," Juliana corrected. "Which is next week. And no, I won't give it up."

"Until I've found him, I said."

"Elliot," Juliana said with patience, though his warmth close to her was most distracting. "The supplies are arriving. The house—at least the public spaces—will be ready. The invitations have been sent and replies received. The villagers are excited about the fête. I cannot possibly cancel everything now."

"Postpone, I meant," Elliot said, his jaw tight.

"It amounts to the same thing. I have only just now finished sending out all the letters to my wedding guests, explaining my change of circumstance and apologizing for saying I'd marry one man and marrying a different one on the same day. Therefore I refuse to let one mad Scotsman—I refer to Mr. Stacy, not you—make me send out *more* letters explaining that, I'm very sorry, but the first event I am hostessing at my new home must be *postponed*. I will not do it. I will not let Mr. Stacy force me to do it. I will not let *you* force me to do it."

"Dear God, are you telling me that a bloody fête is more important than a sharpshooter hiding out in the woods?"

Juliana opened her eyes wide. "Yes. It is quite the most important point in our lives. If we let gentlemen like Mr. Stacy—and, I might add, Mr. Dalrymple—prevent us from carrying out events crucial to us and our marriage, then where would we be?"

Chapter 22

How do you wrap me around your finger, Juliana McBride? Her eyes sparkled with resolve and stubbornness, her lips quivering from her stout declaration.

I love you with every breath I draw.

Elliot caressed her cheek then leaned down and kissed the soft lips he'd been longing to taste all day.

"Then I'll just have to find him first," he said, his lips a breath from hers. "Don't send half the village after me this time."

Her stubbornness dissolved to worry, and that worry touched his heart. "Be careful."

"Always, love." He kissed her again, then released her with reluctance to retrieve his rifle.

Juliana believed him. Elliot's heart sang it as he left the room—finding the entire household, including the dog, gathered in the passage outside the dining room. They collectively tried to pretend they were doing something else when he emerged, but Elliot strode past them, unseeing.

She believed him. The rest of the world thought Elliot irretrievably mad, but Juliana had decided to trust his word.

She'd just given him the most beautiful gift he'd ever received.

⁓

The day of the midsummer fête dawned promisingly enough. The weather was calm, the sky arched blue overhead, and only a few white clouds drifted over the highest hills.

Juliana gave the fine weather the merest glance, relieved the rain had stopped. Rains had swept over the house two nights running, as had high winds and wild lightning. Hamish had been convinced he'd seen a ghost again and refused to leave the kitchen, despite all Juliana's efforts.

And Elliot had hunted Mr. Stacy. Elliot had gone out walking the hills, even in the bad weather, but he'd never found trace of his prey. Either Mr. Stacy had gone to ground, or he'd left the area entirely.

Juliana knew—and she knew Elliot did too—that Mr. Stacy wouldn't simply leave. He'd come for a reason, and while that reason was not yet clear, if Mr. Stacy were anything like Elliot, he'd stick to his purpose.

The fact that the house began filling up with guests also might have triggered Stacy's absence. First to arrive was Sinclair McBride and his two children, Andrew and Caitriona. Six-year-old Andrew took at once to Priti and her goat, while Caitriona, a dignified eight, preferred to sit in the drawing room and look at Juliana's ladies' magazines.

They were lonely children, Juliana sensed, though she soon learned why Sinclair called them ungovernable terrors. The day they arrived, Andrew managed to lure the goat upstairs and hide it in the tiny room Komal occupied. The shrieks and scolding went on for hours, the goat, bleating wildly, happy to escape. During all this Caitriona sat calmly in the drawing room, holding her large golden-haired doll, and quietly turned the pages of the magazine, uninterested in the entire affair—uninterested in everything.

Next to come were Ainsley and Cameron and their baby, Gavina. They were quickly followed by more Mackenzies—Lord Ian and his wife Beth, with their children, accompanied by Daniel Mackenzie, Ainsley's grown-up stepson.

A gentleman called Mr. Fellows arrived quietly and alone the day after that, to Juliana's surprise. She'd invited him, but he'd replied by return post that he might not be able to make the journey from London.

"I am so pleased you could come after all, Mr. Fellows," Juliana said, coming into the front hall to meet him. "Your caseload has lessened?"

"No," he said in the dry tone Juliana was to learn he used habitually. "Not really."

Lloyd Fellows, a detective inspector for Scotland Yard, was a half brother to the Mackenzies, and shared their looks—dark hair with a touch of red, hazel eyes with glints of gold. His stance, his quiet gestures, and the way he bent his head to listen to her, put her strongly in mind of Lord Cameron.

Mr. Fellows was quite a good detective, Juliana had heard, though she'd met him only once before, at Hart Mackenzie's wedding, and that only for a brief greeting.

"Well, I am pleased you took time from your duties for our first event as Mr. and Mrs. McBride," she said.

"I'm afraid I didn't come for pleasure, Mrs. McBride. I came in answer to your husband's telegram."

"Telegram?"

Mr. Fellows obviously had no intention of explaining what the telegram said. He looked about at the freshly cleaned stones of the hall and the varnished and repaired wood. "I heard the McGregor house was a run-down wreck. I'm pleased to see accounts were wrong."

"We've done quite a bit of work since moving in, that is certain. Now, if you are looking for my husband, I believe you'll find him at the river with Lord Ian. Fishing. A pastime they both enjoy, apparently."

"Thank you." Mr. Fellows gave her a little bow. "I will take myself there."

He withdrew without further word. Very polite, yes, Juliana thought, but with a hardness about him that told her he had to make himself remember to be polite.

Fellows went, and Juliana returned to her other guests and the ongoing preparations.

Elliot found Lord Ian Mackenzie to be one of the most refreshing men he'd ever met.

Of the Mackenzie family, Elliot had only ever talked at length with Cameron, his sister's husband, but he'd found Cameron too different from himself to form an instant friendship with him. He and Cameron could talk about horses, but Cameron raced expensive champions, while Elliot had confined his horse owning to useful farm animals. They both had traveled the world, but Cameron had always lived in luxury in the best hotels, while Elliot had eked out an existence either on army pay or on his own, living in hovels that he shared with reptiles and large insects.

Ian Mackenzie, on the other hand, was easy to be with. For one thing, the man didn't feel the need to *talk*.

Ian also knew what fishing was all about. A man stood on the bank and cast his line, then waited in silence. He might lend a hand to his fellow fisherman then quietly return to his own line when the task was done.

Everyone else Elliot met wanted him to make small talk. Even McPherson and McGregor, though both were good-natured, expected Elliot to contribute to conversations and looked at him with puzzled patience when he did not.

Ian, on the other hand, just fished. And shut his mouth. The two men hadn't said a word to each other since

Elliot had found Ian examining the fishing rods in the back hall of McGregor Castle that morning. Elliot had said, "Do you fish?" and Ian had nodded, brushing his fingers over a particularly good pole. "Come on then," Elliot had said.

The two men had chosen poles and nets and gone down to the river, where they'd stood in silence ever since. Elliot pushed aside thoughts of Stacy and the horde of people about to descend on his home. Nothing existed but the quiet plop of hooks into water, the faint hum of flies, the ripple of a fish going for the bait.

Elliot had caught two fish, Ian three, when a figure in a dark suit, a garb more common to the dingy streets of London than the open Highlands, walked down the path to the flat bank of the river.

"Mr. McBride." The man held out a hand. Elliot wiped the fishy dampness of his hand on his kilt and shook it. The man nodded to Ian, who acknowledged him only with a glance before going back to his fishing. "I'm Inspector Fellows."

"I gathered as much," Elliot said.

"I've looked into the matters you asked me to," Fellows said. "I can tell you here, or we can . . ." He motioned toward Castle McGregor, the top spires of which were just visible through the trees.

"Here, if you don't mind," Elliot said. "If we return to the house we might be recruited to round up things for the jumble sale."

Fellows acknowledged this with a half smile. "Ian can keep his own counsel," he said with another look at Ian, who was far more interested in the river than their discussion.

"Archibald Stacy," Fellows said. "Joined your regiment in 1874 and went to India. Was a subaltern."

"Two years younger than me," Elliot said. "I was a lieutenant by then. He was a good shooter already, so they had me help train him to be a sharpshooter. He learned quickly."

"Left the regiment four years later, decided to try his hand at civilian life in India. But you know this too."

"I had no trouble helping an old friend."

Fellows's expression didn't change. He was a man doing his job, an expert at turning up solid information. But Elliot sensed a curiosity in the hazel eyes that would lead the man to make more connections than someone simply taking down facts.

"Mr. Stacy was reported dead in Lahore, after an earthquake that unhappily took quite a few lives," Fellows went on. "Right before you returned to Scotland."

"He was gone from home before that," Elliot said. "I got back to my plantation after my escape in October of that year, and Stacy was already gone. So my manservant informs me. I don't have much memory of the time."

"Interesting that Stacy traveled to Lahore," Fellows said. "Your plantations were closer to Pathankot, nearer the native state of Chamba, to the east, is that right? I consulted a map," Fellows added in his dry tone as Elliot felt mild surprise. To many Englishmen, India was all one place, the same no matter where one traveled. They didn't know about the vast differences in climate, weather, vegetation, animals, and people. Englishmen were still shocked at the change when they traveled from someplace like Bengal to the northern Punjab.

"If you are asking me why he went to Lahore," Elliot said, "I have no idea. He had business interests in Rawalpindi, but none in Lahore as far as I know. As I said, I wasn't very coherent when I returned, and I'd of course been gone for nearly a year."

Fellows acknowledged this with a nod. He didn't exclaim in sympathy at Elliot's laconic statement of his time in captivity, which Elliot appreciated.

"An investigation was carried out when Stacy went missing after the earthquake, of course," Fellows said. "By the local British authorities. He'd been seen there quite obviously before the earthquake, but not afterward. Bodies were recovered from a collapsed building, but too battered to be identified, and witnesses put Stacy in that area that day. A death certificate was issued, and the case closed."

"How thorough was the investigation?"

Fellows shrugged. "From the report I read, and answers to cables, I'd say not very thorough. But I can't blame them—things must have been in chaos. But Stacy never came forward to announce he'd survived."

"A man can make certain he's presumed dead," Ian said, casting his line back into the water. "If he wants everyone to think he is."

Fellows looked at Ian in surprise. "You have experience of this?"

Ian pulled in his line and cast it out again, the quiet swish the only sound as they waited. Elliot thought Ian wouldn't answer, but then he said, "A man at the asylum had himself declared insane to get away from an uncle who was trying to kill him. The uncle wanted his inheritance."

"The uncle got it then," Fellows said. "If this man was declared mad, the money would be passed to the uncle as soon as he was committed."

"He didn't care. He wanted to stay alive."

"Hell of a way to do it," Fellows said. "Mr. Stacy could have done a similar thing—taken advantage of the confusion after the earthquake and lain low. If he knew the area and the people and how to blend in, no one might notice him slip away. A report would be filed declaring him officially missing or dead. End of the matter."

"Though I don't know why Stacy would want to be thought dead," Elliot said. He stood his fishing pole on its end and worked out a small tangle of line. "Or why he'd come here to watch me."

"That I don't know. Would you like to hear more?"

Fellows sounded patient, but Elliot knew that putting together what information he had gathered had taken the man much time and trouble.

"I would. I thank you for this."

"It is my job. And your sister can be . . . very persuasive . . . when she wants a thing done. A man calling himself Mr. Stacy and fitting his description took rooms in a boarding house in London a few months ago. He never gave the landlady any trouble, she says, and then one day he went out and didn't return, leaving his things behind. But he'd paid up a few more months in advance, so the landlady didn't worry."

"Did anyone see him leaving London? Traveling to Scotland?"

"Of course not. Only in fiction does the detective find the helpful porter who remembers every person who gets on and off every train between here and London."

"In other words, he's gone to ground," Elliot said.

"Waiting for your wife's fête to end before he hunts you again?" Fellows asked. "Kind of the man."

"I'm sure he intends to strike at the fête. Strangers roaming the grounds, everyone welcome, perfect opportunity."

"I suppose your wife cannot be convinced to cancel it."

Elliot let himself smile. "My wife is very determined."

From the water, Ian laughed. It was a warm laugh, though he didn't look up from his line. "My Beth is like that." The fondness in his voice could not be clearer.

Elliot and Fellows watched Ian until he turned away, his kilt moving in the breeze, to find another fishing spot a little way down the bank.

"He's a different man," Fellows said in a low voice. "Since he married."

Elliot could say the same about himself. In the scany fortnight he'd had a wife, the tightness in his body had begun to unwind. The nightmares still came, but he woke from them to Juliana's soothing hand, her voice, her kiss . . .

Fellows snapped fingers in front of Elliot's face. "You still with me, McBride?"

Elliot drew a breath, and forced himself not to slam the man's hand out of the way like an irritated tiger. "Thinking of wives."

"Hmm." Fellows's brows lifted and he looked away, as though he were thinking of someone too. "Do you want to know about this Dalrymple?"

"Yes. What did you find out?"

"Nothing. Absolutely nothing. I found no evidence that a George Dalrymple, married to an Emily Dalrymple, exists."

"Then who the devil is he?"

"Who knows? If he tried to blackmail you then he's a crook or a confidence trickster, and such people often take false names."

"Dalrymple somehow got himself a copy of the death certificate declaring Stacy dead, but Stacy shot him before he could give it to me." Elliot wondered whether Stacy had not wanted Elliot to see the paper or whether Stacy had just been annoyed at Dalrymple. He'd aimed for Dalrymple's hand, nothing more. "The Dalrymples have been keeping themselves to themselves since the event, I've noticed."

"I'll have a look at him, though," Fellows said. "I might recognize him. I have a good memory."

Ian laughed again from down the bank, this one short, and possibly ironic.

"Anything else?" Elliot asked.

"That is all I've discovered so far."

"That's a hell of a lot." Elliot started winding up his line. "I thank you."

Fellows watched him in surprise. "You are returning to the house? What about the jumble sale?"

"I've only been married a short while," Elliot said. "But I've learned the importance of keeping the lady happy."

Fellows nodded, brows rising, and Ian's laughter floated back at them once again.

Fellows fell into step with Elliot as he shouldered his pole and sought the path to the house, but Ian remained, fishing in silence, paying no attention to the others' departure.

The grounds were full of people when Elliot and the inspector returned. Hamish, out of hiding now that the storms were over, was busy walking about and glaring at everyone. Elliot had emphasized to Hamish that if he saw *anyone* at the fête he didn't recognize, he was to run and find Elliot.

"No one out of the ordinary," Hamish said as Elliot approached him. "No one I've never seen before."

"Good lad. Keep watching."

"Aye, sir. Mrs. McBride is looking for ye though. She's a bit upset."

Elliot handed Hamish his fishing pole and followed the lad's pointing finger to Juliana. She did look harried, tendrils of her hair sliding from her coiffure, her skirts whirling as she turned this way and that to direct, point, explain, argue.

Elliot watched her a moment, enjoying the sight of her flushed cheeks and excited eyes. Hamish might say she was worried, but Elliot saw a woman doing what she loved best.

"*There* you are, Elliot." Juliana swung to him as he approached. "I need you to man the jumble sale table. Mrs. Rossmoran is feeling ill."

"Is she all right?" Elliot asked, concerned, then twitched his brows together. "You asked Mrs. Rossmoran to run the jumble sale table?"

Juliana's look said that Elliot was a hopeless simpleton. "No, *I* was to look after it. But Fiona now must stay home and take care of her grandmother. Ill, my foot. Mrs. Rossmoran doesn't like fêtes and didn't want to be left on her own while Fiona came. Anyway, Fiona was to be the fortune-teller, and now I will have to do it, but I need someone to watch the table. Don't worry. The jumble sale is very simple. Stand behind the table, put the money in the tin, and don't let anyone walk off with the things." Juliana started for the house, and threw over her shoulder, "And *do* try to sell things. The money is for the church roof. You are charming. Charm them." And she was gone.

Chapter 23

Standing at the jumble sale table gave Elliot a fine view of the grounds and all the people on them. Juliana and her recruits had transformed the flat space below the house to a fair of booths, awnings, tables, ponies, children, men, women, dogs, and one goat.

The table had been placed on a little rise at one end of the grounds, and from there, Elliot could keep watch over every person who strolled about, played games, bought tea and real Scottish scones, or darted into shadows between tents. He saw Hamish in one of these shadows, but the lad was pointing out things to Nandita, his voice loud, words slow while he explained the fête to her.

The fortune-teller's tent, fully enclosed in bright red fabric, lay a few yards to the right of the jumble sale table. People lined up outside the tent, ducking in one at a time to have Juliana read their palms for a penny.

It was a fine idea, that tent. Elliot would like nothing better than to slip inside, pull the curtains closed against the world, and shut out all but himself and his beautiful wife.

Something cold and wet touched his palm. Elliot looked down at the red setter, who thumped her tail and grinned hopefully up at him.

"No scones here," he said. "Sorry."

He scratched her head. McPherson was generous to give him the dog, or at least let her live with them for the time. Elliot had decided to call her Rosie.

"How much is the pig?" a small voice asked.

Elliot looked down to see a girl child, her red hair as bright as Rosie's, staring up, wide-eyed, at Elliot, who towered over her.

What must she see? A huge man with close-cropped light hair, a hard face, and eyes like winter ice. Couldn't be a very pleasant thing for a child. Priti didn't mind Elliot, but Priti was used to him, and his daughter was worryingly fearless.

Elliot came around the table and crouched down to put himself at the girl's eye level. Giants weren't as frightening face-to-face.

Elliot lifted the little porcelain pig from the table. "This one? For you, nothing. Consider it a gift from Mrs. McBride."

The little girl shook her head decidedly. "No, me mum says I have to pay for it. It's for the church roof."

Elliot recognized Highland strength in her eyes—she was afraid of Elliot the tall McBride, but she would have her pig *and* contribute to the church roof, damn anything in her way.

"How much do you have?" Elliot asked her.

The girl opened a rather dirty palm with two coins on it. Elliot took one of them.

"A farthing for a pig. A perfect price."

He deposited the pig into the girl's hands. Satisfied, she gave him a big smile, turned around, and scurried back to her mother.

"Ye have the touch, ye do," a male voice said.

Elliot rose to his feet and faced the grin of his sister's stepson, Daniel Mackenzie.

Daniel was eighteen, broad and tall like his father, though he hadn't quite grown into the massive man Lord Cameron was. Daniel's body was still a little lanky, but in a few years' time, the son would closely resemble the father.

"I *used* to have the touch," Elliot corrected him. He rearranged a few things on the table to fill in the gap where the pig had been.

"I'd say ye still did. Ye've been recruited then?"

"Commanded. Got used to it in the army."

"No general can compete with our ladies, though, can they?"

"I've never met one who could."

Daniel's grin widened. He resembled his father, yes, but he didn't have the darkness in his whiskey-colored eyes that Cameron once had, a darkness that had been driven away by Ainsley. Elliot still saw the shadows in Cameron but not in Daniel.

But then, Daniel was young, and life hadn't thrown tragedy at him yet. Elliot had been much the same at eighteen.

Daniel looked over the collection of knitted pen wipers, doilies, an odd assortment of porcelain figurines, a clock that had stopped working, books without spines, and whatever other things people had found in their attics and contributed to the cause.

Daniel lifted the clock and looked at it with a practiced eye. "Ye have your work cut out for ye."

"Mrs. McBride will want it all gone."

"I'll take this off your hands at any rate." Daniel peered inside the clock. "I always need spare parts."

"For clocks?"

"For whatever gadget I'm trying to put together. I'm an inventor. I already have a patent on a new pulley system for trams."

A sharp mind. Elliot's mind at eighteen had been filled

with visions of glory in the regiment, of conquering a nation, of the praise of a beautiful woman when he finished.

"Five shillings for it," Daniel said, digging into his pocket and dropping the coins in the money box. He shrugged at his extravagance. "It's for the church roof, I'm told."

"I thank you," Elliot said gravely. "My wife thanks you. The church roof thanks you."

Daniel chuckled then studied Elliot with the same scrutiny he'd given the clock. "How is married life, eh? Ainsley said she's relieved you've got someone to look after you."

"Did she? But my sister enjoys playing nursemaid."

"Aye, she does. She's me mum now, and is good at it. I like to call her Mum in front of people. It makes her wild."

Ainsley was only eleven years older than Daniel. Elliot shared a grin with him.

He glanced again at the fortune-teller's tent, where lads from the village were waiting for the lovely Juliana to run her fingers over their palms, and his grin vanished.

"Daniel," he said. "Help me shift this lot."

Daniel followed his gaze to the tent. "Aye, Mrs. McBride is doing well in there. Promised me all kinds of riches and beautiful women. She's got the touch too."

"We'll sell everything on this damned table," Elliot said. "The minister will die of happiness." And then Elliot could go into the fortune-teller's tent and kick out the eager crofters' sons.

"The fair Juliana might kiss us," Daniel said. "Me on the cheek, of course, like a good auntie."

"Shut it, and sell things," Elliot growled.

Daniel joined him behind the table. For the next hour, the two of them held up objects and, like the best hawkers in Covent Garden, cajoled people to come and buy them. Daniel was good at it, and Elliot lost the avoidance of people he'd had since his imprisonment and remembered what it was to be young and brash.

"A pen wiper, dear lady," Daniel said, holding up a round

piece of knitting for a woman with a basket on her arm. "Why not two, or three? Ye have more than one pen, surely."

"A glass vase, lad," Elliot said to a young man. "To put wildflowers in for your lady. Ye can barely see the crack here. Ye fill this with flowers from yon meadow, and she'll be baking ye oatcakes in no time."

The table quickly became popular, the villagers drawn to Daniel's and Elliot's outrageous style. The ladies, in particular, flocked to them, blushing under Daniel's blatant flirtation.

The contents dwindled, and the tin box for the money filled up. When Elliot and Daniel were down to the last two or three items, they decided to hold an auction. They sold an old bonnet for thirty shillings, the most dismally cracked porcelain vase for twenty, and a pair of misshapen antimacassars for a guinea. Daniel raised his hands at the end.

"We're all done, ladies, thank you! And the minister thanks you."

"Yes, very well done, brother dear." Ainsley came out of the crowd, her little girl, Gavina, on her arm. She kissed Elliot's cheek. "Juliana will be pleased."

"'Tis what he's hoping." Daniel chortled.

Elliot secured the lid on the box of coins and handed it to Ainsley. "The villagers were generous."

"Of course they were. Two handsome Highlanders in kilts begging the ladies to give them their coin? They could not resist. You wouldn't even have had to give them the things. Which, by the way, they'll simply bring back to contribute to next year's jumble sale."

"Och," Daniel said in dismay. "I might go to America instead."

"If I'm recruited, you are too, lad," Elliot warned. He gave Daniel a thump on the shoulder, left the table, and headed for the fortune-teller's tent.

No one was waiting outside it at the moment—the villagers had all collected at the jumble sale table and hadn't drifted back to the tent yet.

Elliot raised the flap, walked inside, and found Archibald Stacy sitting on a chair in front of his wife.

～

Juliana watched Elliot change from her husband who'd obviously slipped inside to dally with her, to a cold being of ice. His warm smile vanished, and his gaze became fixed, every bit of heat in him dying.

He didn't ask how Stacy came to be there—Elliot would discern that Stacy had pulled up a stake in the back of the tent and ducked inside while Juliana was busy ushering out another villager.

Juliana had returned to the tent after walking out the young lady, who was happy to have been told that a young man of the village fancied her—not difficult to guess, because Hamish was friends with the lad in question—and found Mr. Stacy sitting at the table. He'd said, "Will you tell my fortune, Mrs. McBride?" and held out his empty hand.

Stacy said now, "Are you going to shoot me, McBride? If so, get it over with. I'm growin' too old for this."

"I don't have a gun with me," Elliot said, in a chill, dead voice Juliana had never heard from him before. "But I don't need one."

"No, they made you a savage, didn't they?"

The two men looked at each other, Stacy not rising from his seat.

Stacy was as tall as Elliot, but his red gold hair touched his shoulders, and he wore a short beard, somewhat unruly from his life out of doors. His eyes were pale blue but not soft—they were cool, like Elliot's. His nose had been broken once and so had the fingers on his left hand, all healed but a still little crooked.

Stacy locked his gaze on Elliot, and Elliot looked straight back.

"He has been telling me interesting things," Juliana said.

"I didn't come here to kill you," Stacy said.

Elliot didn't answer either of them. He stood rock still, his hands at his sides, his gaze on Stacy.

"I came here to talk to ye," Stacy said.

Elliot finally spoke, his voice cold. "Talk, is it? Ye've made a damn good pretense of wanting to kill me."

"No, I've been watching ye. Trying to decide how to approach ye. Because I knew the minute I showed myself to ye, you'd try to kill *me*."

"Give me a reason I shouldn't."

"I don't have one."

Juliana watched, her hands twined together on the table. She wanted to intervene in some way, babble that all would all be well if they only sat down and talked things through. But she also sensed that these were two very dangerous men, and for this moment, silence was best. She needed to discover the lay of the land now, offer advice later.

"If you touch Priti . . ." Elliot growled.

"I haven't come for the child. I know she's yours."

Stacy's eyes took on a vast sadness. He'd hoped, Juliana realized, that Priti was his, but now he knew she wasn't. When she'd caught him looking at Priti in the kitchen garden that day, he must have seen Elliot in her, and realized.

"Then what have you come for?" Elliot demanded.

"To reconcile," Stacy said. "Or try to. And to ask ye— beg ye—for your help."

Chapter 24

"Ye left me to die." Elliot's voice was soft but clear.

Stacy's face colored behind the beard. "I know. I can never explain to you how much I regret that."

"I cannae explain how much *I* regret it."

Stacy went quiet. Juliana saw the fear and guilt in his eyes, but he closed his mouth, a thin line behind his beard.

"Mrs. McBride," Elliot said. "Will ye tell this man his fortune?"

Juliana remained silent, Elliot's rage pressing on her like a humid summer night. Outside the tent children shouted, men laughed, women called to one another, and dogs barked—ordinary life in all its aspects. Inside the tent was a bubble of anger, old and new, and fear.

Juliana had dressed as a stage Romany, with silk scarves borrowed from Channan, bangles from Nandita. She'd spread a colorful silk cloth across the rickety wooden table and laid a brass bowl, into which people had been dropping pennies, at her elbow.

Stacy glanced at her then back at Elliot. Elliot didn't move. Still looking at Elliot, Stacy slowly stretched out his hand and put it, palm up, on the cloth.

"Tell him that he will die by the hand of one he wronged," Elliot said.

"Elliot . . ." Juliana began.

"Tell him."

Juliana got to her feet, her bangles jingling. "I think, Elliot, that you should listen to him."

"He told me he'd get them to safety and come back to help me fight. Together, we could have gotten away. Alone, I had no chance." Elliot pressed his finger to his temple. "Because of him, I live in darkness. It waits for me every day, not wanting to let me go. Because of him."

"Believe me, I had no idea what they'd do to you," Stacy said.

"You have no idea what they *did* do. When I was screaming in hunger, they cut off bits of my own flesh and tried to force me to eat them. They thought it was *funny*. They also thought it funny to shove me into a tiny hole for days and days and make me sleep on my own filth."

"I'm sorry," Mr. Stacy said in a hollow voice.

Elliot's eyes glittered, but he kept his tone even. "You were reported dead in Lahore."

"I know that. I was nearly beaten to death there. While I lay recovering in some back alley hole, I read in a newspaper that I'd been listed as one of the dead in the quake. I decided not to dispute it, and let it be official."

Elliot raked his gaze down his old friend's face, taking in the broken nose, the twisted fingers. "Who did that?"

"Jaya's brothers."

Jaya, Juliana said silently. *Priti's mother.*

"And you were in Lahore to . . . ?"

Stacy nodded. "Hide from Jaya's brothers. They came to my plantation with hired ruffians after she died, wanting to kill the one who, in their opinion, defiled her. I fled, choosing Lahore because I had little reason to go to that city. But they found me there, and their ruffians did me over and left me for dead. I hoped that when I was reported dead in the newspaper, they'd assume my body had been found and lumped in with the other poor souls lost in the quake. When I recovered, I left the Punjab and never returned. Had to abandon everything I had."

"Why are you here?" Elliot asked. "Wanting my help now?"

"They tracked me. Bloody persistent, Jaya's brothers—never offend an Indian prince. They found a boat I'd worked on and discovered that I was still alive, and where I'd gone. I left for England. There I read of your marriage and learned that you'd purchased this house. I came up here to ask you to help me go into hiding."

"But why should you have to go into hiding?" Juliana broke in. "They would not chase you all the way from India, surely?"

Stacy gave her a wry smile. "You would be surprised, Mrs. McBride. Jaya came from one of the native states. Small principalities surrounded by British India," he explained when he caught Juliana's puzzled look. "Her family was related to the ruling prince. She was rebellious and ran away from home, which ruined her forever. When I married her, I brought her under the protection of British law, but her family never forgave her—or me, the blackguard who ruined her. They decided to dedicate themselves to avenging her, once she was dead. They blamed me for her death as well. But they don't have to follow me here, in fact. They can afford to hire agents here to do the job for them."

Elliot's voice was cold. "So you've brought assassins down upon me and my family."

"Not necessarily. I managed to elude pursuit in Edinburgh. I'm asking for sanctuary here until I can decide what to do. You can tell your friends that I'm your distant cousin from Ullapool, or somewhere."

"No."

The word was as hard and icy as Elliot's eyes. Juliana rose again, supporting herself with the table. "Elliot . . ."

"No." Elliot's tight stare moved to Juliana. "I will not put my wife and my daughter in danger, nor my family and my friends, to harbor the man who destroyed my life."

"I don't blame ye," Stacy said. He curled his fingers closed. "I don't blame ye at all."

"Get up and get out. I want you miles away by tomorrow. Don't hide in my woods, or under my house, or above the river. I'll give you food, water, and money, and you get yourself away by foot, or horse, or boat, or whatever you want. Cross the ocean to Germany, hide in the Orkneys—I don't care. Just get away from me and mine."

Juliana had to press her hands together to stop herself from arguing. She had a decided opinion, but she knew that if she spoke it now, Elliot would storm away and not listen.

"Juliana, go back to the house," Elliot said.

"To the . . . No, I can't. The fête . . ."

"How did you get in here, Stacy? Through the back wall? Then that's how we're going out."

Elliot grabbed Stacy and pushed him toward the loose flap in the tent. As Stacy scrambled through, Elliot looked back at Juliana, his eyes like a winter storm. "Stay here if you won't go to the house. Don't move until I come back."

He followed Stacy out, then the tent wall fell back down to silence.

Juliana sat again in a rush, her breath leaving her. She had no idea what to do—stay here? Go after them? Try to talk to Elliot? And should she?

She didn't have lists or organized ledgers to help her deal with this. After she'd gotten over her fright of Mr. Stacy appearing out of nowhere, she'd had the idea that he and Elliot would talk, reconcile, become friends again. What had happened with Priti's mother was years ago—

Juliana liked it firmly in the past. They no longer needed to be angry at each other.

But then Elliot revealed that Mr. Stacy had been responsible for Elliot's being captured at all. Good Lord, if that were true, Juliana wanted to shoot Mr. Stacy herself.

How could he not have helped Elliot? Though he might not have known specifically what the tribesmen would do to Elliot, Mr. Stacy must have had some idea *generally*. And the tribesmen might simply have killed Elliot on the spot.

But then, Mr. Stacy had felt remorse and had gone back to try to find him. At least, he'd said so.

One thing shone in crystal clarity. Elliot was in a black rage, and there was no telling what he might do. Juliana shared a bed with him, and his powers of seduction were incredible, but she could not predict his path.

Juliana made her decision. She rose and stormed for the tent's entrance, lifting the flap to find a fresh-faced girl just reaching for it.

"Mrs. McBride, won't you tell my fortune?" The young woman had a few grinning friends behind her. "All of us? We long for tall, handsome husbands."

Juliana managed a smile, trying to mask her worry and rage. "I'm afraid that Madame McBride's head hurts too much, ladies. The fortune-teller's tent must close for now."

"Aye, we saw Mr. McBride comin' in to visit ye. No wonder ye look so tired."

"I tell fortunes." Channan's contralto cut through the girls' giggling. "I know how. Come."

She signaled with a dark hand, swept her scarves around her neck, and ducked inside the tent. Juliana thanked her silently and sped off in the direction of the house.

She found Mahindar in the middle of the lawn, showing children how to throw the balls at the bottles to knock them down. "Where is Priti?" she asked.

"With Lady Cameron," Mahindar said.

Juliana followed where he pointed and saw Priti peering at the baby Ainsley held down to her. The tall forms of both Cameron and Daniel Mackenzie stood guard behind them.

"Mahindar, please tell Lady Cameron that I want either Lord Cameron or Mr. Daniel with Priti at all times. Tell them she might be in danger."

"In danger." Mahindar's eyes widened. "In danger from who?"

"I don't know, and it might be all right, but please tell them."

"At once, memsahib." Mahindar dropped the ball he'd been holding and ran across the grass to the little cluster.

Juliana lifted the scarves that trailed down her gown and hurried on to the house. She found Komal in the kitchen, chopping vegetables, pots on the stove boiling, the fire high under the clay oven.

"Where is Mr. McBride?"

Komal still didn't speak much English, but she got the gist of Juliana's question. She pointed with the knife to the garden door and said something in Punjabi. Juliana nodded and rushed out to the gardens and down the path.

When she reached the gate, she saw Elliot returning up the path, his rifle slung over his shoulder. Elliot paused when he saw Juliana, then he came on.

"I remember telling you to stay in the tent," he said.

"Well, I could not, could I? What did you do to Mr. Stacy?"

"What I told you I'd do. Gave him provisions and money and sent him on his way."

"Could we not help him more? He seemed truly sorry."

"No." The word was as harsh as it had been in the tent. "He's let trouble follow him here. I will not let anything happen to you, or Priti, or Mahindar, or McGregor—*anyone*. If that means I throw Stacy to the wolves, then I throw him."

"It might be too late already, you know. We've been

insisting to the Dalrymples that Mr. Stacy is alive. While I cannot picture either Mr. or Mrs. Dalrymple as assassins, they might pass information to one."

"Possibly. Inspector Fellows told me they're using false names."

"There. You see?"

"I will deal with the Dalrymples."

"The point is, anyone looking for Mr. Stacy might already be here."

"Then it's a good thing I sent him on his way." Elliot took his rifle from his shoulder as they entered the kitchen, and opened it to unload it. "Where is Priti?"

"I told Mahindar to have Daniel or Cameron stay with her."

"Good." Elliot gave her a look of approval. "She stays either with them or with me." He put the rifle into its cupboard, locked it, and started out of the kitchen as though ready to return to the fête.

Juliana stepped in front of him. "Elliot."

Elliot halted, impatient. "I've done what I've done, love. That's an end to it."

Behind him, Komal kept chopping vegetables, watching in her quiet way. Juliana gathered strength from the woman's silent assessment and lifted her chin.

"I want you to tell me everything that happened to you, Elliot. When you were captured, what they did, and how you escaped. I need to know everything. Please."

~

She could have no idea how beautiful she was with the indigo scarf wrapped around her red hair, the blue and gold silks trailing down her shoulders. The head scarf brought out the blue of her eyes, which were now large in her ashen face.

"I don't . . ."

The words *I don't want to speak of it* came so easily to

Elliot's lips. So easily did they quiet the well-meaning questions put forth by his family, his friends, even Mahindar.

But Juliana had already heard what he'd spat to Stacy, the festering anguish that had welled up inside him. He'd stopped himself before he'd let worse come out—how he'd been used as a pack animal, the various forms of torture they'd tried on him simply to observe the results.

Maybe he could hold back the very worst. Elliot didn't want to watch Juliana's eyes change when she realized the full horror of it all. He didn't want to confirm that the lad she'd smiled upon at her debut ball was dead and gone. Juliana had asked to marry the young man who'd charmed her into the kiss, not the wreck of a man who'd dragged her to the altar.

But he would tell her a part of it. Juliana deserved to know something of the stranger she had married, and why he'd found it necessary to cast Stacy and his plea for help away.

Elliot gave Juliana a tight nod, took her hand, and led her up the stairs to their bedchamber, where he shut and locked the door behind them.

Chapter 25

Elliot told her. He started with Jaya and the fact that at first it had been almost a ménage à trois—he and Stacy had been young and found being lovers to the same woman exciting. Jaya had preferred Stacy, and when Stacy was slow to acknowledge his feelings for her, she came to Elliot.

Stacy had returned from a business trip to find Jaya giving him an ultimatum—he marry her or she would stay with Elliot. Stacy, realizing that he loved the woman, had grown angry at Elliot, thinking he'd tried to steal Jaya, then Elliot stepped aside and let Jaya leave with him.

Elliot had thought that the end of the matter. He and Stacy had gone north to Rawalpindi then to the borders of Afghanistan to meet with a trader who ran on up into the Hindu Kush and beyond to Samarkand. Elliot related to Juliana the attack on the English families, the plan to get them to safety, and Stacy abandoning Elliot to his fate.

As Elliot spoke it came back to him, all the things he tried so hard to push away. The beatings, the night they'd clamped his hands to a table and calmly pulled out his fingernails, one by one. How they'd beat him with metal rods until he couldn't stop the screams.

They'd sometimes take him out of his cell deep in the tunnels and talk to him. Elliot understood them a little—their dialect had been similar to those in the northern Punjab. They'd thought him a British spy, and asked when the soldiers would come marching. They hadn't believed Elliot when he said he knew nothing, neither did he care.

The torture, the alternate starvation and halfhearted feeding, the sleeplessness leading to long periods of unconsciousness had nearly killed Elliot. His captors expected him to die at any moment, they said, had even shown him the pit where they'd throw his body. Wild animals would find him there and tear him apart. They threatened to throw him in even before he was dead.

Elliot talked in a monotone, relating horror after horror, his eyes closing while his lips moved. He no longer saw the room, or heard the laughter outside, or felt the solidity of the floor beneath him.

He hadn't realized that his words had drifted to silence. His eyes remaining closed, his lids too heavy to open.

Then he smelled the rosewater soap Juliana liked so well, sensed the brush of her on his skin. Her warmth slid along his body, and still he couldn't open his eyes or reach for her.

"I never told them about you," he said, his lips stiff. "They questioned me and tortured me, but I never once said your name. You were mine, my secret. The one thing they could never take from me."

She skimmed her fingers up his arm under his loose sleeve. "I don't feel worthy of that."

"You were light and life. You are heat, and I'm so damn cold."

Elliot opened his eyes. Juliana a hairsbreadth from him,

surrounding him with her beautiful scent, her warmth. She was life, and home.

"How did you get away from them?" she asked, her voice holding a little tremor.

"They'd taught me to kill. When I helped kill some of their enemies, the leader started treating me better. Then one of the men became jealous of me, killed another, and blamed it on me."

"Oh." Juliana's hands came to rest on his chest, fingers points of warmth through his shirt.

"I knew they'd come for me right away. I hid in the dark. They sent in only one man to fetch me, because they didn't fear me enough. I had to kill him before he could make a sound. I dressed in his clothes. In the dark, I crept into the tunnel where they kept the guns and stole my Winchester back, and what was left of the ammunition.

"Someone saw me. I shot at him, and I ran. I disappeared into those hills so fast, I never looked back. I can't remember most of that run, but they were after me."

He felt a smile coming on. "But I was good. I always had been. I eluded them like an animal, laying false trails and crossing rivers, and praying I didn't step on a cobra and end everything. I had to get back home. I mean to Scotland. Had to." He brushed Juliana's hair back from her face. "I had to get home to you."

Tears trickled from her eyes. "I was so afraid every minute you were missing. I thought of you every day, every hour."

"I think I knew that. I could see you so clearly, even in the worst of the dark."

"How did you manage to get back to your plantation?"

"I haven't the faintest idea, love. At some point, I crossed the border back into the Punjab, and kept wandering. I suppose I simply knew my way home. Mahindar says he found me about ten miles away from my plantation, crawling, half blind with infection. But he knew it was me."

Mahindar had fallen to his knees and gathered Elliot, who was filthy and infested with vermin, to him and held him hard. The man had cried, rocking back and forth, saying over and over, *Sahib, I have found you. I have found you.*

Elliot vaguely remembered the kitchen of his plantation house, Komal and Channan exclaiming and crying, the three rushing to find water, food, clothing, a razor to remove the matted hair from his head and face. He remembered them showing him Priti, not two months old, and explaining that Jaya had died. Stacy had abandoned the child and gone who knew where, leaving Priti with Mahindar.

The weeks between then and Elliot's first convalescence in Scotland were a blur. Elliot moved in a daze, certain he was in the dream.

He'd realized one day, in Patrick's house in Edinburgh, that he couldn't hover in that bedchamber forever. He'd come up with a plan to bring himself back to life.

Juliana rested her head against his chest, her hands soft through his shirt, and Elliot rested his cheek against the scarf over her hair. She was everything he was not, whole and beautiful, kind and sensible. He might once have been charming as she'd claimed today, but he'd also been arrogant and confident that he could take on the world and win. Elliot had learned too late that he was as weak as those foolish English people who'd wandered too far into the Afghan hills, people he'd despised even as he'd helped them to safety.

"I'm not who I was," he finished. "Sometimes I thank God for that. I lost most of myself in those caves as a prisoner. I'm not sure who it was who came out."

"You're Elliot," Juliana said. "My Elliot."

"Not what you thought you were getting, eh, lass?"

She raised her head, her eyes still wet. "You are too hard on yourself. You are exactly what I wanted."

"I thought if I came here to this house and married you, I would get well." Elliot knew the rest with certainty. "But I might never get well."

"You will," Juliana said with conviction. "I know you will."

Elliot didn't share her confidence. Telling her the story had drained him, and he had nothing left for hope for the future. Tomorrow he could hope again. Tonight . . .

Tonight he had to be lord of the manor and let dozens of people into his house to see what he'd done with it. Tonight he'd dance with his wife and show the world the woman he'd caught.

He tilted Juliana's face up to his and kissed her.

Juliana rose on tiptoes into the kiss, seeking him, needing him. Everything Elliot had told her settled onto her like a black miasma. How a man could endure so much, how he could transition back to the calm, the everyday, was beyond her comprehension.

If she could wash it all away from him, she would. Juliana kissed his lips, running her hands over his broad shoulders. She marveled that such a strong man could have anything wrong with him at all. He'd returned to full health in the time he'd taken to recover and put his affairs in order. She couldn't ever imagine him weak.

Only a man as strong as Elliot could have survived the ordeal, in any case. His ten months as a prisoner might have taken away his youth but hadn't been able to break him, not completely.

Juliana sought him with hunger she didn't understand. Her blood burned for him, but not for the pleasure he could give her. She wanted to give to him, to heal him. She *needed* to.

Juliana tasted the desperation in him, the pain and the hunger, as his kisses turned fierce. He'd been alone in the dark for so long.

Elliot stripped the silken scarf from her head, then the one she wore like a shawl. The light fabric slithered to the floor, brushing her arms as it went.

He undressed her then, a layer at a time, kissing what

he bared as he peeled away her gown, her petticoats, her corset. His lips touched her neck, her shoulders, the inside of her wrists, her breasts, her abdomen as he knelt to loosen the top of her combinations. When Elliot slid her drawers from her, he leaned into her and kissed the join of her legs.

He got to his feet without continuing to explore her there, to her vague disappointment, and swept up the silk scarves on his way. Juliana expected him to carry her to the bed, but instead, he brushed the silk up over her bare buttocks and back.

The cool fabric whispered against her skin, her flesh rising in goose bumps. Elliot drew the silk down her breasts, his gaze dropping to them as her nipples hardened into tight points.

He guided her backward to the bed, then up onto the mattress, settling her on her back. He continued to glide the silk across her skin, teasing her nipples, her belly, the twist of hair between her legs.

He brought the silk to his lips and kissed it, then he laid it over her body while he shed his clothes.

The shirt and boots came off quickly, and Juliana watched with appreciation as he approached the bed, wearing nothing but his kilt. He unpinned it and let the folds drop, then slung the plaid on the bed to mix with the silk.

Elliot came down to kiss her. Juliana reached for him, but he evaded her, kissing her neck and throat, pinning her hands above her head to take his mouth down her body. He licked one nipple and drew it into his mouth, teasing with teeth and lips. He did the same to the other, taking more time with it. He lingered to nibble, tugging the nipple long, before he released it to lick it once more.

Elliot moved down to kiss between her legs again, but as her hips rose, Juliana wanting more, Elliot turned her over, to her surprise, and eased her onto her hands and knees. Her fingers and toes sank into the silk and wool on the bed, then Elliot came behind her, spreading her knees, his hand opening her, stirring her need.

Juliana felt his hardness against her entrance, strong and blunt, touching her lightly. She tensed, uncertain, then dragged in a sharp breath when Elliot pushed into her.

She felt not pain but impossible joy. He opened her, his hardness thick and long, the sensation incredible. Juliana uttered a cry, her climax already taking her, and Elliot had not even started to move.

He stilled inside her a moment, letting her get used to the fullness, the intense feeling of him in this position, then he began to move in and out.

Coherent thought deserted her. Juliana floated on feeling—of Elliot thrusting swiftly and fiercely, the pumping of his thighs against her buttocks, his fingers firm on her hips. Beneath her, both the rough of the kilt and the fineness of the silk rubbed her knees.

More sensations—his sweat dropping to her back, the intense heat of him against her legs, the sounds that came from his mouth. Not words, only sounds, a man in ecstasy.

Juliana's throat was raw, and she realized it was from her own cries. She pushed herself back into him, wanting him, and she heard herself begging him. "Please, please, *please!*"

Elliot went faster and faster, until Juliana thought she would die. He had to stop . . . She hoped he never stopped.

Their bodies were slick with sweat by the time Elliot's sounds became groans. The bed creaked, Elliot's body hard against hers, and Juliana breathed in long, shuddering gasps.

Nothing genteel or soft and slow about this lovemaking. This was raw, brutal passion.

"God, *Juliana*." Elliot's last thrust pressed inside her while her body squeezed back into his. He trailed off into beautiful, musical words she didn't understand.

Then he shuddered once, hard.

Juliana collapsed to the bed, her knees burning. Elliot withdrew from her and fell beside her, drawing her back against him with shaking hands.

He gathered her hair from her flushed face and kissed her cheek. She felt his pounding heart against her back, and his limbs, tangling hers, were hot.

The breeze from the window brushed their bodies, the sounds of the fête drifting to them.

Juliana drowsed, the brief lovemaking leaving her exhausted. Nothing had ever wound her up so intensely then released her so fast.

"What were you saying?" she asked. "The words?" He'd used the same language when he'd thrown phrases at Mrs. Dalrymple.

Elliot's voice went into mock broad Scots. "Och, lassie, do ye nae ken the language of your ancestors? 'Tis Gaelic."

"Is it?" She'd only ever been taught English, had been sent to an English school, and had been thrown together with people who wouldn't dream of speaking anything but English, the language of money and success.

"Aye. 'Tis."

Juliana traced his arm where it lay across his stomach, touching the tattoo. "How do you know it?"

"I know many languages. Gaelic, French, German, Urdu, Hindi, Punjabi. I never knew what I'd need to be speaking."

"What were you saying to me?"

Elliot kissed her temple, his lips warm and quiet with the intimacy of afterglow. "That ye were beautiful. And warmed me like nothing I'd ever felt. *An toir thu dhomh pòg?*"

Juliana smiled. "What does that mean?"

"Will ye kiss me?"

Her smile widened. "Yes."

She turned on the pillow, liking how his eyes were half closed and relaxed, like an animal in repose. Elliot kissed her softly, his lips parted, again with the warm intimacy.

"*Tha gaol agam ort,*" he whispered.

She traced his cheek. "What is that one?"

Elliot closed his callused hand over hers, bringing her fingers to his lips. "Someday, I'll tell you," he said.

～⁓

The midsummer ball went well until Mr. McGregor insisted he do a sword dance.

Juliana's guests had come from as far away as Edinburgh, including the rest of the Mackenzie clan and Gemma, even the formidable Duke of Kilmorgan and his recent bride, Lady Eleanor. They were not all staying in the house, as only a few guest rooms were yet habitable, but McPherson had volunteered to put up most of them in his giant castle.

The ball was a full Highland party, with all the Scotsmen in great kilts. Pipers and fiddlers had come from Highforth and the next village; village men and women had volunteered to help Mahindar and his family with cooking and replenishing food and drink; and many of them joined in the dancing outside on the lawn in the long twilight.

Elliot looked much better when he at last came down. He'd donned his great kilt, the swath of plaid looped over his shoulder. Unlike the Mackenzie brothers, he wore no coat, and looked like a Highland barbarian of old.

The guests poured in, anxious to greet the McBrides, welcoming Elliot as part of McGregor's family. It didn't take long for the dancing to begin.

What always made Juliana's heart swell about true Highland gatherings was that no one needed to be prodded to dance and have a good time. Partners were seized, circles formed, and dancing began.

As the newly married couple, Juliana and Elliot led the first reel. Juliana had only danced with Elliot once, at her debut in Edinburgh, where they'd done a stately waltz to the strains of Strauss. Now Elliot showed his true grace. He moved through the steps of the reel without missing a one, spinning Juliana and handing her off, and picking her up again without losing a measure.

The guests laughed and clapped, dancing around them. Daniel Mackenzie was the most enthusiastic, his youth letting him jump higher and swing ladies harder than his uncles, who were more absorbed in their wives. Only Ian Mackenzie didn't dance, preferring to sit with his wife and his children or hold his son's little hands when the boy wanted to dance to the music.

Mac Mackenzie joined his nephew Daniel in exuberance, his wife, Isabella, laughing at him, her color high and eyes sparkling. The duke, Hart, was quieter, but the look he gave Eleanor was so loving that Juliana's eyes moistened.

She wanted to have with Elliot what the Mackenzie brothers and their wives had. They had full trust, confidence, love. They enjoyed being together and watching each other. Yet, they didn't lose anything in each other, each of them having their own wants, their own enjoyments. But together, each couple seemed to be stronger than the sum of their parts.

Maybe, in time, she and Elliot could find that too.

The ballroom, still a bit barren with no drapes on the windows or pictures on the walls, resounded with energy. Music filled it with a wall of sound, the dancers' laughter resonating over it. McPherson danced with all the ladies, matching Daniel for enthusiasm.

McGregor, well gone in whiskey, shouted, "Bring the swords!"

Hamish fetched them from who knew where, a traditional claymore and scabbard he set in a perfect cross in the cleared corner of the ballroom. Elliot broke from his two brothers and Gemma to move across the room to it. Before he could reach it, McGregor motioned for the pipers to play.

He started off well enough. Mr. McGregor knew the steps, if he couldn't bounce very high, and touched his feet quickly and surely into the squares formed by the crossed blade and scabbard. But then the fiddlers sped up and the pipers followed suit, playing faster then faster.

McGregor roared as he tried to keep up, stamping to either side of the blade, jumping higher, the ribbon in his Scottish bonnet flapping. The guests applauded their approval.

Then his foot came down wrong, the sword skittered, McGregor's legs split, and he fell flat on his back with a grunt.

Juliana ran to him, but Elliot was there in front of her. McGregor allowed himself to be helped to his feet, then he threw Elliot off. "Leave me be, nephew. I'm fine."

But he did let Juliana lead him out of the ballroom, and when he reached the hallway, he began to limp. "Bloody sword. In my day, they were made so they didn't move."

Komal appeared out of the shadows to grab McGregor's other arm. She started scolding right away in both Punjabi and the few words she'd learned in English.

Juliana relinquished him. McGregor didn't seem to mind so much to lean on Komal while she led him down the hall toward the kitchen.

Juliana returned to Elliot, who watched from the doorway, and he put his arm around her to draw her back into the light and chaos of the room.

Debate had started about who should next attempt the sword dance. "Elliot," his older brother Patrick's voice rose. "You used to do it, and do it well."

"A dozen years ago," Elliot shot back, but the crowd took up the cause.

"Go to, McBride!" Mac Mackenzie shouted, and Daniel echoed him. Applause and yells urged him on.

"All right." Elliot held out his hands, motioning them to stop. "Play it slowly," he said to the piper.

The piper blew into the bag, filling the room with sound. When the musicians were ready, Elliot bowed, then he started.

He hadn't done this dance in years, but it came back to him. He leapt left, then right, his arm coming up for balance. Around the four sides of the sword and scabbard, outside the cross at first, left then right, his leaps high, kilt moving. Then inside the cross, toe and heel, flat foot stamp and toe. In and out, front and back, left and right.

The guests clapped along, and the men shouted encouragement. Elliot let himself rest on the cushion of music as his feet did the work.

The mind was a strange place. He hadn't done this in years, and yet, it all came back, steps learned long ago as a careless youth. His whole past was there, waiting for him to find it again.

The piper and the fiddler sped up. Elliot sped up too, to more applause and cheers.

Then the piper sped again. Elliot shouted, and he danced back from the swords, laughing and panting. "Enough!"

Juliana caught him as he backed away—what a fine feeling to yield to the softness of her. Daniel was pressed forward, told to show them what he could do.

Daniel made his bow, winked at the ladies, and proceeded. He began the dance as Elliot had, first outside the cross, then in between the blade and scabbard, his feet flashing back and forth. When the music sped up, so did Daniel, and Elliot joined the crowd in urging him on.

"Daniel does well," Juliana said into Elliot's ear as the piper played as fast as he could, and Daniel's feet moved precisely in the complicated jig.

"He's eighteen," Elliot said. "I'm thirty."

"Well, you did your best."

Elliot looked down at her sly smile and sparkling eyes and kissed her. The guests whooped. At the same time, Daniel finished the dance, bowed, and flashed his grin at every young lady in the room.

Juliana touched Elliot's arm. "He's going to break hearts. As you did."

"There was only ever one lass for me," Elliot said. He kissed the corner of her mouth, and the guests, watching avidly, cheered again.

~~~~~

Elliot thought about what he'd said again much later in the night, when the guests had returned to McPherson's or the village, and even Mahindar had been persuaded to bed.

Juliana smiled sleepily at him as Elliot made love to her, his need so great. The erotic feeling of her around him sent all other thought away. Nothing existed but the pleasure, her tightness, the scent of her, the heat of their bodies together.

Only ever one lass for me, he whispered to himself when he slid out of her and collapsed beside her, snuggling into her to sleep.

Elliot had met only one other woman as resilient as Juliana—his sister, Ainsley—and even Ainsley thought Elliot ought to be locked into a quiet room and fed gruel. Juliana had faced everything Elliot had thrown at her with head up and no complaints, taking it all in stride. She was strong, beautiful, and his. He slept.

Somewhere before the dawn, Elliot woke again. The night was still, the frogs silent, the room dark.

Elliot lay on top of the covers, Juliana now spooned back into him. Her warmth was all he needed in the summer night.

She was light. And life. He'd had a long climb and had a way to go still. But when he was wrapped in Juliana, all darkness vanished, unable to prevail.

He'd sent Stacy out into that darkness.

Rage answered. *He left me to endure torture and fear and starvation. And he brought danger to Juliana.* Stacy deserved whatever fate he found.

Elliot had taught the man, befriended him, grieved with him when he grieved. Stacy was never the same after his wife fell ill and died. Illness could come so fast in India, then infection, and swiftly, death.

Elliot remembered the night Stacy's wife had drawn her last breath, how Stacy, only a lad of twenty-three, had held on to Elliot and wept.

Stacy's grief had turned to rage, but he didn't have an enemy he could see to fight. Elliot had taught him how to turn his anger into honing his skills. He'd taught Stacy how to make the plantation work, which would have made young Mrs. Stacy proud.

So many nights they'd spent in quiet friendship, getting drunk on whatever fermented beverage they could get their hands on, or simply sitting on the veranda in the dark. They'd talk, or they'd be silent, either one companionable. They were friends who knew what each other thought even before they'd said it.

And then Jaya came and changed everything.

She hadn't meant to, Elliot knew now. But he and Stacy had been young, stupid, and arrogant, and they'd let her.

Now Stacy was out in the night, followed by people wanting to kill him.

Elliot let out a long breath. "Och, damn it," he whispered. He rose from the bed and began to dress.

Chapter 26

Elliot pulled on his boots in the hallway then walked softly down to the end of the hall and tapped on a door.

Fellows opened it almost at once, looking as though he hadn't been asleep at all, in spite of the dressing gown he wore.

"Come on a manhunt with me, Inspector?" Elliot asked.

Fellows nodded in silence, closed the door, and was out again, dressed, before Elliot had returned from the kitchens with his Winchester. The two men left quietly through the back door, Elliot moving the gate carefully so it didn't squeak.

Once they were down the path, toward the roar of the river, Fellows finally spoke. "Who are we looking for?"

"Stacy. And hired killers who want him dead."

"When we don't have to be quiet, you're going to explain to me why you know that and I didn't."

"Stacy himself told me," Elliot said. "Before I sent him to his death."

Fellows shot him a look out of canny hazel eyes but said nothing. They fell into step, Elliot leading the way along the river that led them to the house of Mrs. Rossmoran.

A light in the window of the cottage told Elliot that Mrs. Rossmoran or her granddaughter was awake. Mrs. Rossmoran wouldn't waste candles or kerosene on a sleeping house.

Elliot knocked on the door, not too loudly, in case the elderly woman would become alarmed. Hamish opened the door, his face like thunder.

"What de ye mean by it?" Hamish asked with a growl. "Sending that man here."

"He was here then?" Elliot looked around the small cottage, Fiona standing uncertainly in the kitchen, Mrs. Rossmoran sitting near the cold fireplace with a sharp expression.

"He was," Mrs. Rossmoran said. "I ken ye mean my lodger. Aye, he was here, but no more."

Elliot had thought as much when he'd logically run through the places Stacy could have hidden himself without starving. Poaching or hunting left a sign, and he'd not found a trace.

Elliot handed Fellows his rifle and sat next to Mrs. Rossmoran. "Why didn't you tell me he was here?"

"Ye never asked. And he begged me not to tell ye. He was worried you'd kill him or have him arrested. That's why he's run off. He seemed a kind man. And you, Elliot McBride, are a bit touched."

"That is true." Elliot shared a look with Fellows. "Mrs. Rossmoran, I want you and Fiona to come up to McGregor Castle. You'll be safer there."

"No, indeed, young man. McGregor and I never saw eye to eye. His wife was my sister, you know."

Elliot hadn't known that. "McPherson's then. Stacy is in great danger, and I don't want the people after him to come upon you."

Mrs. Rossmoran planted her cane. "This is my home. If

people come here while I'm out, they might harm the place. It's all I have."

Fiona watched worriedly from the kitchen. "Please, Gran."

"Hamish will send stout men to protect it while you're away." Elliot took her worn hand in his. "Please. I need you to be safe."

Mrs. Rossmoran watched him with shrewd blue eyes. "All right, lad. I'll go to McPherson's. But any man ye put in here to watch my house had better keep his hands out of the sugar barrel. Sugar doesn't grow out of the ground, you know."

"Actually, Great-auntie . . ." Hamish began.

Mrs. Rossmoran waved her cane at him. "Stop standing there with your mouth open and help me up. Bring all my shawls, Fiona. I don't trust McPherson to have enough bed-covers to suit me."

Elliot waited outside to see them on their way while Fellows scouted around the house. When Hamish came out, Elliot caught him by the shoulder.

"I know why your great-aunt said nothing. She does as she pleases. Why did *you*?"

"I didn't know." Hamish glared back at the house, his anger so apparent that Elliot believed him. "I'd have told you, right away. My great-auntie can be powerful stubborn."

Elliot had no doubt. Inspector Fellows returned, saying he hadn't found anything unusual near the house—no sign of hunters or intruders. They sent Hamish and his little party to McPherson's and went off into the woods.

～～～

Juliana awoke early in the morning to find herself alone. She wasn't alarmed—Elliot often rose before she did to begin working with the men on the house.

She went through her ablutions and descended the stairs.

The massive chandelier still hung in place. They'd tried to fix the mechanism to lower it to replace the candles, but it was frozen with rust. Juliana had decided that hurrying it for the ball might end in disaster, so she had a man up on a ladder each day, cleaning and oiling what he could.

As she reached the lower hall, she heard a knocking on the front door.

A lady never answered the door of her own house. The footman did it, or a housemaid if a footman was not available.

But neither Hamish nor Mahindar was anywhere in sight. The ladies of Mahindar's family were not allowed to answer, according to Mahindar, because letting them do so would mean Mahindar hadn't protected them from intruders.

Juliana ventured to the door, waving formality away. One could not stand on ceremony when one had no servants available. The visitor might simply be one of the guests returning from McPherson's.

Before she reached the vestibule, however, Mahindar hurried forward in a rush of cloth and soft footsteps. "Memsahib," he said in horror. "No. Let me."

Juliana stepped back to let him run past her to the vestibule. He flung open the door to the last person Juliana wanted to see. Mrs. Dalrymple.

"Morning, love," she said. "I need to speak to ye if ye don't mind."

Gone was the stiff-necked pose, the rather superior accent. Though Mrs. Dalrymple wore a well-made morning gown of gray cotton, she no longer looked like the prim and proper middle-class woman who'd tried to ignore everything Indian when she'd lived in India.

Her softly lined face looked more that of a harmless, middle-aged woman who went to the market with a basket on her arm. Also, her strained proper accent had gone, and now she sounded as though she'd come straight from the backstreets of Glasgow.

"Come in," Juliana said.

Mahindar looked unhappy, but Juliana wanted to hear what the woman had to say. She led Mrs. Dalrymple to the morning room and bade Mahindar bring them tea.

"I won't stay long," Mrs. Dalrymple said, sitting in the same chair she had occupied a week ago. "I just came t' give ye warning. Not that one," she said quickly as Juliana's brows went down. "Ye see, lass, I know ye've tumbled on t' us. Me husband came across Mr. Stacy's death certificate when he was working for the civil service in Lahore. He heard tell that your husband had turned up after being missing, crazy as a loon. So George stole the certificate. When we came back to Glasgow, me husband asked about and learned that Elliot McBride had purchased a house up here in Highforth. I'd never heard of th' place, but George says we were goin'. He decided that if your husband was out of his wits, maybe George could make you or his family believe he'd murdered Stacy and get some money out of ye."

"But Mrs. Terrell described you as a friend," Juliana said, keeping her anger in check with difficulty. "You knew her?"

"Mrs. Terrell." Mrs. Dalrymple dismissed her with a wave of her hand. "She's a simple one. I convinced her that her mother and mine had been great friends. Easy to do while I dithered at the post office and managed to steal letters of likely ladies in the area. So Mr. and Mrs. Dalrymple were invited to stay."

"Well, I am sorry we disappointed you," Juliana said stiffly. "Neither I nor my husband were willing to pay you any of your blackmail."

Mrs. Dalrymple winced. "Oh, I don't like that word, love. Sounds so nasty. Mr. Dalrymple and I, we provide a service. You'd be amazed at the things people get up to—rich ladies who steal from any house they enter, proper husbands who keep a bit on the side, upright clerks and bankers who skim out of the till. They get away with it—theft, adultery, embezzlement, and now we thought murder. The law can't touch these people, but we make them pay. 'Tis only right—they've committed crimes after all."

Juliana forbore to point out that blackmail was also a crime. In any case, the Dalrymples, or whatever their true names might be, never took the evidence of the wrongdoings to the police.

She grew impatient. "Why did you come to see me today?"

"Well, first I wanted to make my apologies. We had no idea that Mr. Stacy was alive, and your husband entirely innocent. We were so glad to learn it. 'Emily,' Mr. Dalrymple said to me, 'I'm that glad we were wrong about Mr. McBride. He's a fine Highland gentleman.'"

"What is this warning?" Juliana asked in a hard voice.

"Because we stole the death certificate and asked questions about Mr. Stacy and Mr. McBride along our way here, I'm afraid we inadvertently alerted some very bad men as to their whereabouts. But I wanted you to know that Mr. Dalrymple and I had nothing to do with that. We might ask people for what they can give—a contribution, if you like— to apologize for the wrongs they've done, but we never harm anyone. I know you have a man from Scotland Yard staying with you, but if anything happens to Mr. Stacy or your husband, it's nothing to do with us. That's why I want to warn you, to put you on your guard. I can tell that you are a sweet, respectable lady, and you and your husband should take care."

Too late for that. Hamish came barreling down the back hall, bellowing at the top of his lungs, "Mahindar! M'lady! Mr. McGregor! Mr. McBride went out to chase brigands in the woods!"

"There, you see?" Mrs. Dalrymple stood up. "Well, I've done me duty. 'Tis nothing on me and m' man, remember. I'll go and leave you to it."

"No," Juliana said. Her sharpness made Mrs. Dalrymple jump. Juliana pointed at the chair. "You will *sit down* and tell me every detail you know about these very bad men, and you will stay there until my husband and Mr. Stacy come home in safety. Hamish—run back to McPherson's and tell him all about it."

"I've just been. He's coming over. And all the Mackenzies."

"Good. Then wake up every man in this house and tell them to come and talk to me. We are going to find my husband and these assassins and end this, for once and for all."

Hamish's eyes rounded. "Aye, m'lady." He disappeared to do her bidding.

~

Elliot and Fellows moved swiftly and silently across the land, following the trail Elliot had picked up. Elliot's tracking ability came back to him as had the steps to the sword dance. Inspector Fellows had been hunting criminals in London for years and could move as quickly and quietly as Elliot.

The trail took them north across the hills and down into the next valley. The ocean was to the east of them, the land sloping out of uplands to farms and flat land by the sea.

Stacy would have led them that way and then doubled back, if Elliot were any judge. The rising sun spilled over the sea, anyone heading east walking into the large ball of light.

Elliot knew exactly where Stacy would head. A twinge of dread went through him, but Elliot motioned Fellows to follow him back toward the hills.

The trees closed around them again, cutting off the view of the cultivated lands and the cottages, civilization gone. The passes from Afghanistan to the Punjab were like that, knives of land that masked the view of anything but the steep cliffs to either side.

However, those roads came out of stark mountains to river valleys of amazing beauty. Elliot had been stunned by the glories that had existed outside the tunnels where he'd been buried, as he'd slunk back home like a wounded animal. Evil should not exist in that much beauty.

It had been cold there as well. Elliot had had only vague ideas of the seasons when he'd been held captive, but he remembered weeks of icy cold wind.

Here, summer made the air soft, but under the trees, cool mist gathered. The feeling of alertness as Elliot tracked was the same, though, the calm wariness, the warm sweat on his back, the controlled breathing that let him walk for long distances without becoming exhausted.

The fact that he was walking through damp leaves in Scotland instead of dry, cold mountains made no difference. Every rock and tree was either concealment or a hidden danger, each an obstacle to be assessed, traversed, then watched. All as quickly and thoroughly as possible.

Elliot made for the entrance to the tunnels closest to the edge of the hills. He knew Stacy had used them for cover and likely was there now.

He held a whispered conversation with Fellows about what he wanted to do, and approached the first tunnel cautiously. The entrance could barely be seen, covered with brush, weeds, and a fallen limb of a tree.

But Elliot had scouted these on his many walks around the estate in the last couple of weeks, taking note of every possible entrance to Castle McGregor. He knew he hadn't missed any.

The first sign that someone had passed that way came at the tunnel's opening. The brush had overgrown it, but someone had cut away the natural brush and replaced it with care.

Elliot moved the branches as quietly as he could, while Fellows kept watch. When Elliot had cleared a space, he dove inside in one quick movement, crouching beside the opening so he wouldn't be shown against the light outside.

Fellows followed, copying his movements. Elliot waited

until his eyes became used to the dark, then he walked forward.

As they moved through the damp caves, Elliot sensed the darkness inside him hunkering down in the corner of his mind, waiting to pounce.

His heartbeat quickened, and the perspiration that clung to his back began to trickle down his spine. The wet of it was clammy and cold, and his pulse pounded in his temples and made his head ache.

Not now. Right now, he had to find Stacy. He had to find Stacy and get the thugs chasing him arrested. Whatever was between himself and Stacy, they would have to work through it, but first he had to save the man.

Elliot hadn't had the chance to explore every bit of the maze of these tunnels. The ceiling on this part of it was low, and he and Fellows had to walk half bent over. Elliot's rifle would be useless down here, the walls too tight for any close shooting, but he had a knife, and Fellows was armed with a pistol, a good Webley.

Elliot knew men were down here with them. He found no sign, just as he'd never seen sign of Stacy in the woods, but he knew.

The darkness in his mind laughed at him. It was there, and it didn't care how dire was the situation. The waking visions or the sudden dizziness that stole his breath could rear up at any time, ripping away everything but stark animal panic.

Elliot drew a long breath and tried to fight it off. If killers were under the house, that meant that everyone in the house was in danger. Elliot had tried to seal off all entrances to the old castle from above, but that was before he'd known professionals had come here to kill Stacy. They might have been working at opening up those places while Stacy hid at Mrs. Rossmoran's and Elliot helped Juliana with her fête.

The thought of Juliana in danger, and Priti with her,

helped him push away the mocking voice inside him. He'd never let anyone touch them. Never.

A faint sound came down one of the tunnels. Elliot stopped, reaching back for Fellows in the dark, halting him.

Elliot heard it again, a footstep. Only one, probably misplaced. Elliot motioned Fellows to stay where he was, and crept forward, crouched almost to the floor.

He brought his rifle around, sighting down the barrel at the rough-hewn opening to the larger room.

Elliot saw them, or at least, saw the flicker of their lanterns. They were careful not to let the light fall on them.

He saw a flash of movement beyond them, which might be Stacy. Elliot had taught Stacy the trick of using just enough movement to entice an enemy out into the open, which was what they had done when they'd rescued the English family up in the Afghan mountains.

Stacy was drawing them into tight quarters, preparing the ambush. The problem with that plan was that there was only one of Stacy. In theory, a single man could hold off a platoon if he had the right kind of ground advantage, but in practice, many against a platoon was always better odds.

Elliot peered into the room again. If he and Fellows moved to flank, they could disarm both men, and Stacy would be safe. Elliot could go back home and feast on porridge prepared by Hamish or lentils and spices from Mahindar, whoever managed to get to the kitchen first.

He turned to creep back to Fellows to tell him his plan, when someone shouted deep in the bowels of the tunnels. The two assassins were moving forward in a flash, lost down the tunnel that led to the boiler room.

Elliot swore silently as he hurried back to Fellows. "The idiot Stacy is trying to lead them into a trap," he said in a low voice as he led Fellows forward. "They'll kill him instead."

"Then let us get there," Fellows said.

Elliot led Fellows up the tunnel and into the large room, the other man staying close behind.

Images of his last night in the caves came to Elliot, his desperate run down the tunnels, the churning in his stomach when he dared to crawl through the crack that led into the cave that held his rifle. At any moment, he'd be stopped and shot, or strangled, or beaten again. If they caught him, he'd never have another chance to get away.

He'd alternately crept on his belly like an animal and run like a rabbit. At every moment, he'd expected to feel shot ripping through his back, stopping his life in a wash of pain.

Elliot's breath came faster. If he didn't slow, if he didn't calm himself, he'd run in on a burst of panic and get Stacy killed.

He saw the flash of gunfire. Heard yells. Elliot's thoughts scattered, and he ran forward.

Stacy. Was he dead or alive?

A few more shots were fired, then silence.

Elliot moved on, Fellows behind him. Both men moved noiselessly on toward where he'd heard the shots.

Another flash of revolvers. Bangs echoed through the tunnels and made it impossible to hear. Fellows clapped his hands over his ears, but Elliot, trying to hold on to his rifle, didn't have that chance. His ears rang, and smoke choked him.

The barrage of bullets died, and Elliot moved quietly forward.

He finally saw his old friend Stacy at the end of the tunnel behind a crate, a lantern on the floor to give away his position. Two men rose from the shadows, revolvers cocked, and opened fire on Stacy.

Chapter 27

The light extinguished to blackness. Elliot sensed rather than saw Stacy rise, aim his gun with uncanny precision at the flash of one revolver, and shoot his assassin through the heart.

A marvelous shot, with only the tiny light of the gun's flash to guide him, but the problem was, the bullet that had left the assassin's gun hit Stacy. Stacy grunted, then went quiet.

Elliot could neither see nor hear. He crept into the end of the tunnel, shouldering his useless rifle again, trying to stay utterly silent.

On a sudden, he was shoved against the wall, a body rank with sweat and smelling of blood and smoke pushing past him. The second assassin, who fled down another tunnel.

Elliot heard the worry in the other man's running foot-steps, the growing terror. The assassin didn't know where he was, and his friend was dead. He was alone. In the dark. Under the earth.

Elliot let him go for now. He returned to the crate and the lantern, dug matches out of his pocket, struck one, and lit the lantern.

Stacy sagged against the wall, blood on his side. Another man lay stretched out beside him, facedown, unmoving.

Stacy lifted his gaze to Elliot, his eyes resigned. "I'm sorry, old friend. So sorry."

"Shut it," Elliot said. "Ye trying to die a hero?"

"Best way."

"You're an idiot. Stay still."

Fellows came into the light, shaking his head. "Heard him, tried to follow. Lost him."

"Never mind," Elliot said. "You don't know your way around down here. Stay with Stacy. I'll hunt."

He turned away and picked up the fallen assassin's pistol as Fellows nodded, Elliot's heart hammering, his skin hot.

"McBride," Stacy said.

Elliot looked back. Stacy was grim-faced, blood trickling from the side of his mouth.

"Get the bastard."

Elliot intended to.

~~~~~

Elliot could move like smoke when he wanted to, or a ghost in the night. He tracked the other assassin in silence and darkness.

The footsteps of the man ahead of him moved swiftly, then hesitantly, then swiftly again.

This was Elliot's territory, and here he was master. He'd learned his way around the tunnels of his prison on his own, sometimes hiding down there for days. Whenever his captors found him again, they beat him, but eluding them had given Elliot a small measure of triumph. He'd made his captors hunt *him*. He'd turned the tables and enraged them.

The unknown man in the dark was trying to kill Stacy for

defiling an Indian prince's sister. Never mind that the prince
had kept Jaya behind locked doors, never allowing her even
to look out a window. Jaya, as headstrong as her brothers had
been, had escaped. Jaya had been gifted in conversation and
intelligence, wasted, secreted in her luxurious home, waiting
for her brothers to marry her to some elderly wealthy man to
further their own power.

He couldn't help thinking that Juliana would have liked
Jaya in other circumstances and been indignant on her
behalf.

The man was slowing now, uncertain. He went one way,
then the other. Elliot followed, allowing his footfalls to
sound occasionally so that the other man would flee him.

Up through a tunnel, again with a low ceiling. A faint
light glowed at the end, and the man hurried forward.

The light was not daylight. It came from the cracks
around the trapdoor that led to the boiler room. Elliot's
quarry hesitated, then swarmed up the ladder fixed into the
wall.

They or Stacy must have found the entrance before and
worked on the door, because the man quickly pushed it
open and climbed through. Elliot rushed him, yelling.

The assassin turned around and shot once, but Elliot
had expected that. He threw himself out of the way, the
bullet missing him and pinging into the wall. The assassin
climbed desperately up into the house, Elliot after him.

The assassin burst out of the boiler room and through
the main cellars, up into the kitchen. Screams sounded,
and Elliot's throat closed up as he pounded after him.
Mahindar's family would be up there—with Priti.

Elliot was hard on the man's heels. He had his pistol, but
the assassin decided that using Channan then Nandita as
shields was a good idea. Komal, on the other hand, picked
up a long knife and went at him.

The man dropped Nandita, who, screaming, somehow found her way to Hamish as the lad barreled into the kitchen.

But the assassin was still running. He stormed into the main part of the house, where Juliana would be. Alone.

There she was, standing in the vestibule, looking down the hall at the approaching man with wide, frightened eyes. Priti was nowhere in sight, hadn't been in the kitchens either. Safe?

The assassin ran into the staircase hall. Elliot stopped, lifted his pistol, and took aim.

"Mr. McGregor!" Juliana shouted. "Now!"

A deafening roar filled the hall as McGregor, on the landing above them, aimed his shotgun at the ceiling and fired both barrels. The shots struck the plaster and stone around the great chandelier, which swung, groaned, and tore out of the ceiling with a rush of rock, nails, and rusted metal.

The assassin screamed. Flinging down his pistol, he leapt, rolling, as the monstrous iron thing plunged to the floor below.

He couldn't move quickly enough. The chandelier hit with a roar of broken metal. Juliana fled out the front door, shielding her face. The assassin managed to get his torso out of the way of the chandelier, but his legs were trapped. He struggled, then he fell, his face ashen. Defeated.

Elliot let out his breath. He kept his pistol trained on the man, made a wide berth around the wreckage, and knelt next to the assassin.

The assassin was an ordinary-looking man, with dark hair and brown eyes, a suit of such plainness that no one would have looked at him twice. He opened his mouth and spewed a string of invectives at Elliot, his accent pure Cockney.

Elliot unwrapped his hand from around the pistol—it hurt to open his fingers—and shoved it at Mahindar, who'd rushed into the hall followed by his family and Hamish.

Elliot turned his back on them all and walked out of the dim wreckage of the house to the light, and to Juliana.

~~~~~

Juliana shook all over as Elliot came to her and took her into his arms. She held him close, smelling the acrid smoke of pistols and the dank air of the cellars on him. The tightening of his hold on her for a long moment was the only indication of what it had cost him to hunt for Mr. Stacy and his killers in the dark.

Elliot drew in a shuddering breath and let it out again. "I have to go back down," he said. "Stacy's hurt. Shot. Fellows is with him, but he won't know how to get out."

"Yes, of course. Go."

Elliot touched his forehead to hers and drew another breath. Then he kissed her, released her, and strode away, calling for Mahindar and Hamish to help him.

Juliana watched him walk away with them, her knees weak with relief but her heart still beating hard. He was all right. He'd fought, and he'd won, against more than just the assassins.

But there was much to be done. Juliana hurried into the house. She had to prepare a bedchamber to receive the wounded Mr. Stacy, and they needed to send for a doctor or surgeon. And then there was the matter of an assassin lying in her hallway.

She entered the main staircase hall to the chandelier strewn across the floor, its giant wheel having gouged a small trench into the flagstone. Cameron and Daniel Mackenzie and some of the workers were trying to lift it off the poor man.

As soon as the ring of chandelier moved enough, Cameron grabbed the man under the arms and hauled him out. He was groaning, his legs bloody, his face wan.

"You'll have to put him in the morning room," Juliana

directed, "to wait for Mr. Fellows. Stay in there, and don't let Mrs. Dalrymple leave."

"Right ye are, ma'am," Daniel answered cheerfully.

Juliana skirted past the chandelier and the dangerous criminal and went on to the kitchen to enlist Channan and family to help fix a room for Mr. Stacy. Priti had been taken off to McPherson's after Hamish's bellowed announcement that Elliot was hunting assassins, to be watched by Gemma, and the ladies of the Mackenzie family.

Mr. McGregor was already in the kitchen. He was proudly showing the empty shotgun to Komal. "It was a hell of a shot, lass," he said loudly. "Boom! Then that great eyesore comes crashing down. Smash!"

Komal listened, actually smiling. She took the gun from McGregor's hands, checked that it was unloaded, then slapped him across the shoulder with her open hand. "Stupid old man," she said clearly in English.

McGregor chuckled. "She likes me."

Juliana recruited Channan and Nandita to go up the back stairs with her and make one of the rooms habitable. Not long after, Elliot came striding back, followed by Hamish and Mahindar carrying a large, flat board with Mr. Stacy on it, his torso stained with blood. Fellows, his face marked with dirt, broke off from the rescue party to enter the morning room and confront the assassin and Mrs. Dalrymple.

"Billy Wesley," Fellows said, sounding the most jovial Juliana had heard him since he'd arrived. "I've been looking for *you* for a long time."

Juliana left him to it and spent the next intense hours in Mr. Stacy's sickroom. The village doctor, used to dealing with gunshot wounds in a country upon which people descended every autumn to shoot things, knew what to do. Elliot helped him, the two of them performing the grim business of digging the bullet from Mr. Stacy's side and bandaging him up.

As a lady, Juliana supposed she should not look upon an undressed man's flesh, but Mr. Stacy was so pathetic, and someone was needed to mop up the blood as it gushed out.

Elliot held the wound closed while the doctor sewed it up. Stacy had been given a bit of laudanum for the pain, though he'd not wanted to take very much.

"Almost done," Elliot said to Stacy. "Bear up, man. I've seen you with worse."

"When I'm digging a needle through *your* flesh, ye can say the same of yourself." Stacy flinched as the doctor tugged the stitches through his skin. "I beg your pardon, Mrs. McBride, for bloodying up the sheets."

"I have others." Juliana wiped his brow. "What will stave off infection is rest and keeping your bandage clean. Mahindar is very good at changing bandages, I'm told."

"Yes, ma'am," Stacy said. "McBride, you're right. She would do well in the army."

Elliot didn't look up. "Aye, that she would."

Before Juliana could answer in indignation, Stacy lost his amused look. "I never should have brought this upon you."

"Save your breath for healing," Elliot said.

"I'll make sure it doesn't happen again. Satisfy the brothers' honor without you or your family getting hurt."

"Juliana, find a bandage for this man's mouth. Inspector Fellows will have Jaya's brothers dealt with when he returns to London."

Stacy subsided then, but mostly because the laudanum was having deeper effect, and the worst of the surgery was over.

The chaos lasted most of the day, but one by one, the guests left, taking the train back to Aberdeen, where they'd go their separate ways. Ainsley and her family and Gemma were the last to leave.

Ainsley hugged Juliana on the doorstep, while her husband, child, and Daniel waited to hand her into the dogcart.

"Whatever you have done, thank you," Ainsley said, kissing Juliana's cheek. "The change in Elliot is remarkable."

"Do you think so?" Ainsley hadn't seen Elliot on one of his bad days, or bad hours, since her arrival. He'd come through the rescue of Mr. Stacy and the flurried activity this afternoon without breaking stride.

"I do. Trust me." Ainsley gave her another kiss, patted her on the cheek, and was gone.

Juliana waved them away, and went to say her last goodbye, to her stepmother.

Gemma made her sit down for a moment in the morning room, now empty of assassins and blackmailers. "Well, Juliana? You've made your bed, as they say. Do you still want to lie in it?"

Juliana's face warmed as she thought of what she and Elliot often did in the bed upstairs. "I believe I do."

Gemma's businesslike look softened. "Don't stay away forever, love. Your father and I miss you—goodness, how he misses you. Every day he talks about how you used to walk about, so proud to wear your ring of keys as mistress of the house. How you'd make sure his tea was served at exactly six, that his study had the books he needed most within his reach, his ink bottle always filled. The housekeeper and I make sure of it now, of course, but it was special to him that you did it. That you took care of him."

Juliana's eyes grew moist. Her father was not a talkative man, and she'd not known he even noticed what she'd done. Juliana had told herself that the best sign of an organized household was that the hand that guided it was invisible, but she'd always felt a tiny bit of hurt that her father had never said a word.

"I didn't know that."

Gemma's hand was warm on hers. "I know, dear. Your father has never known much how to show his heart. Your poor mother was terrible at reading him, and so the match was doomed from the outset. I am a bit more shrewd than she was, and I know that your father is a man of deep feeling. His failure with your mother upsets him. He knows it was difficult for you. And he truly does miss you."

"Thank you." Juliana's chest felt tight. Her father had never gushed affection, but she'd known it was there, underneath, though she'd never been quite certain how much. "I'm sure that Elliot and I will be back in Edinburgh soon. We have been invited to stay there with Ainsley, and also to attend Lord Cameron's horse training in March."

Gemma gave her a knowing look. "Are you certain about that, my dear? Your husband does not look as though he's ready to share you with anyone yet. Ainsley and Rona told me of their visit here, how he tossed them out most unceremoniously. They couched it in terms that said they found it amusing—the newlywed husband wanting to be alone with his wife. I imagine there was a bit more to it than that, but of course, they had to explain their too-quick visit. Mr. McBride now looks happy to see the backs of us all."

"Because he is worried about Mr. Stacy."

"Humph. Your Indian manservant has already told me that Mr. Stacy is removing to Mr. McPherson's for his convalescence. I'd say that was best. McPherson's house is a bit more comfortable than this one."

"Only because I have not had the time to make the place more habitable. The rooms that are finished have turned out splendidly."

"How quick you are to defend." Gemma smiled. "I meant no offense. From what Ainsley told me about the condition of the castle when she visited before, what you have done to this house in the meantime is quite astonishing. I have often said that no one could be a better general than you—or perhaps a sergeant major. I'm sure you bullied everyone in your power to make this house shipshape."

"I've had to. If only you had seen what a nightmare it was."

"But, Juliana, *you* saw it, you laid your plans, and directed everyone in battle against it. Your need to be a better woman than your mother was is admirable, and I understand it, but you must not let it obsess you. Mr. McBride needs a wife, not a sergeant major."

Juliana bristled. "Gemma, you cannot tell me that this house does not need work."

"Of course it does. But your husband is not a house. Do not try the same approach with him. Believe me, it will not work. Now, don't open your eyes wide at me, child, and pretend you don't know what I mean. To you, disorder is anathema. You think that if you can bring order to Mr. McBride's life, he will be well. He is in disarray, and you must fix him. Perhaps you have not articulated it like that, but I see it. You did the same with your father. But people can't be fixed, especially not men like Mr. McBride. Not in the way you mean. You have to understand, and help him, dear. Not repair him."

Chapter 28

Juliana sat in silence, her hands folded on her lap. Was that what she'd been trying to do? Gemma was a wise woman—she always had been.

Had Juliana been trying to tear down and reconstruct Elliot in the way she'd remembered him? In the way she thought he ought to be? In the way she could understand him better?

"Oh, Gemma." Her eyes burned. "I have no idea what I am doing. I don't know how to love a man. I only know how to make lists."

Gemma's face softened. "My dear, your other fault is being too hard on yourself. You believed you needed to be the perfect daughter—now you're trying to be the perfect wife. You and Mr. McBride are two strangers attempting to learn all about each other. The process is slow. It took me twenty years to get to know your father, and ten of those years I've been married to him." Gemma placed a warm hand on Juliana's knee. "Besides, Mr. McBride doesn't look terribly put out that you're trying to repair him. He looks much better, even in these two weeks since the wedding."

Ainsley had said much the same thing. Juliana gave a faint laugh. "I doubt that is my doing. Elliot never listens to a word I say."

"You mean he does not snap a salute and obey you, like that Hamish does," Gemma said. "Or Mahindar Singh, who falls all over himself to please you. Your husband goes about his business, but he notices. He certainly notices you." Her smile turned sly. "Can I assume that within the year, your father will take on the happy title of Grandpapa?"

Juliana blushed. "It is far too soon to know that."

"But from your pink cheeks, I see that you and Mr. McBride are striving for the outcome." Gemma got to her feet in a rustle of crisp poplin. "I will leave you to your strivings, stepdaughter, and eagerly await the announcement."

Juliana rose with her and caught Gemma in her arms. Gemma stopped, pleased, and hugged Juliana back.

"Thank you for coming," Juliana said with sincerity. "I'm only sorry we did not have enough time to spend together."

"Of course we didn't. What with your planning, your house not ready, people shooting at one another, and crashing chandeliers, we did not have a moment to ourselves." Gemma kissed her cheek. "Next time, dear."

Juliana walked out with her stepmother, arm in arm, and put her into the dogcart that Hamish had driven back from the station, likely at his usual breakneck speed.

She waved at Gemma for a long time, blinking back tears, then she went back to the house, with much to think about.

Juliana amazed Elliot every time he looked at her. The day had been crazed, with getting the guests away, moving Stacy to McPherson's, and putting the house to rights—at least as much to rights as a run-down manor house-cum-castle could be.

Inspector Fellows had left with culprits in tow. He'd taken the Dalrymples to the nearest lockup for a hearing on a charge of blackmail, and the assassin back with him to Edinburgh. He, Elliot, and McPherson had arranged for the removal of the body of the fallen assassin in the tunnels, the man to be sent back to his family in London. Throughout it all, Juliana had helped, advised, and made little lists in her notebooks. Neat, efficient, cool, and lovely.

Juliana sat now at the other end of the dining table, the house finally emptied. She wore a blue satin tea gown that rode low on her shoulders, a cameo resting at her throat. She'd caught her curls up into a simple coil woven with a blue ribbon, fine curls framing her forehead.

Her notebook reposed next to her, with a Faber's pencil nearby, so she could add to her blasted lists as she thought of things. Her curls trembled a little as she bent her head to write, candlelight catching on her sleek hair.

Elliot's gaze went lower, to the shadow between her breasts. She'd worn the tea gown several times since their marriage, and Elliot decided he loved the dress. The satin hugged her body, and the décolletage put her breasts in tantalizing view. He would buy her a dozen such dresses and make sure she wore nothing else.

Elliot picked up his glass of wine. "What are you writing?"

Juliana looked up, pencil poised. "Hmm? What's next to be done, of course. The chandelier replaced. What a monstrosity. I'm rather glad it fell. We'll have something much more tasteful and charming in its place. I thought the drawing room carpet would be fine, but when we moved a chair to decorate for the ball, I found a very large hole all the way through to the floor beneath. I'd wondered why that chair was in such an odd place . . ."

Elliot rose from his seat, walked down the table, and

pulled the notebook out from under her hand. He snatched the pencil as well.

"Elliot, what are you doing?"

Elliot tossed book and pencil to the other side of the table. He decided to be kind at the last minute and not put them on the fire.

He pulled a chair to her corner of the table, opening his knees to make room for the table leg that butted in his way. Ignoring Juliana's splutters of indignation about her notebook, Elliot took her hand, turned it up on the table, and lightly traced a line that creased her palm.

"I'm going to tell your fortune."

He saw the shiver go through her, watched her gaze fix on his.

Elliot traced another line. "I see a young woman in a blue dress. I see her in a bedchamber, candles lit, the bed turned down."

"Do you?" Juliana wet her lips. "How very interesting."

"I see a man, kissing her."

"This grows still more interesting. Who is this man?"

The sly look she tried to assume had Elliot instantly hard. "He's a mad Scotsman, weather-beaten, has kicked around the world. He has shorn hair and colorless eyes, and he loves you."

"Loves." The word was breathless. "Your eyes aren't colorless. They're gray like stormy skies. They're the best color I've ever seen. *Loves?*"

"Loves." Elliot leaned closer, studying her red lips and the moisture behind them. Her mouth waited, a warm place of enchanting desire.

He touched one plump lip with his—

And the darkness took him. Just like that. One moment, he bent to kiss his wife in a place of warmth, beauty, and happiness, and the next, he was back in the caves in the craggy mountains, waking up from the dream.

He felt the cold darkness, the stone beneath him, his beard and hair scratching his face, his filthy clothes crawling with vermin.

"No!" Elliot stared at his hands in the faint light, saw the cracked, dry skin, the calluses so hard he could barely feel anything through his fingertips.

"No!" he shouted again.

He hugged himself, willing himself back into the dream. It was there on the edges of his vision, the candlelight on Juliana's hair, her eyes so blue, the same color as her gown.

He couldn't touch it. She wasn't real, none of it had been. The darkness mocked him, laughed at him for thinking he was well.

"Juliana," a voice said. He recognized it as belonging to one of his captors, the cruelest of all, who'd sometimes amused himself by stripping off bits of Elliot's skin with a jagged-edged knife. "The woman you love." He spoke in his rough Punjabi, in a dialect they both understood.

Not Juliana. They can never take Juliana.

"You love her," the man said. His knife went to the inside of Elliot's wrist. "Say it."

"I love her," Elliot whispered.

"Shout it. Tell everyone."

No. She was his secret. If they knew about Juliana, they'd threaten her, mock her, defile her memory, take her away from him. Elliot knew she was safe in Scotland, in her father's prim house in Edinburgh, with her family, her friends, her miles of lists, her laughter.

They'd force him to talk about her, to tell them every single little secret memory he had of her. They'd describe what they'd do to her, what they wanted to do to her, until any thought of her was mixed with something horrifying.

And then Elliot would have nothing. Nothing between himself and the darkness.

Juliana was light. He couldn't let them extinguish the light.

"No!"

"Say it."

"I love her!" Elliot dragged his hands from his face. "Don't take her away from me. *Don't take her away from me.*"

The man grinned, his teeth crooked and brown. "She will never love you. You are broken and ruined, dirt beneath my heel. We broke you. Juliana will never want that."

The mocking voice, the knife, the smile, her name on his lips, drove Elliot into the frenzy. He'd be beaten for it, he knew, but he couldn't stop.

"I'll kill you!" Elliot wrenched himself from his crouch and launched himself at his captor. His hands closed around the man's throat, fingers knowing what to do. He felt glee when the man scrabbled at his wrists, dark eyes opening wide.

"Sahib!" the man tried to gasp. "Sahib, it is Mahindar."

Liar. Mahindar was all that was kindness and goodness, and this man was evil incarnate. Elliot would choke Juliana's name from his throat, so he could never say it again.

"Elliot!"

Her voice came from his dream, which tapped at the back of his mind. The dream wanted him to relax into it, to slumber in its peace, to never wake again.

But Elliot had to stay awake. He had to escape. He had to get home. To her.

Other hands grabbed his, trying to break his grip. Strong hands, as large as his, the slimmer hands of a woman but just as strong, and then the soft touch he knew deep inside his heart.

"Elliot," she said in her musical voice.

The darkness cracked. Light came rushing at him, spinning in dazzling points, and then faces and voices. The wide, scared blue eyes of a Scottish lad, the dark face of a woman determined, the eyes of the man who'd helped him at every turn, and the sky blue beauty of Juliana's eyes. Juliana was the only one who didn't try to loosen Elliot's grip, who only touched, and asked.

The rest of the real world now crashed into him, and the spinning stopped. Elliot was standing in the dining room of his own house, his manservant Mahindar bent backward over the table, Elliot's hands around his throat.

Elliot swiftly lifted away from him. Nausea hit him right after that, bile shoving its way into his throat.

Juliana went to him, reaching for him. She closed her arms around Elliot, and he shuddered. He wanted to scoop her to him, to hold her, but he was going to be sick.

"No," he said hoarsely.

He broke her grasp and pushed her away. Mahindar, coughing, stood up, helped by Channan, who hovered worriedly.

"I am all right, sahib," Mahindar said, barely able to speak the words. "I will be fine."

He wouldn't be. There were bruises on Mahindar's throat, and he coughed pathetically.

Damn it. Elliot swung away from them all and strode from the room, Hamish scuttling out of his way.

Dear God, he had them terrified, and no wonder. He could have killed Mahindar if they hadn't been able to break Elliot out of his stupor.

What would have happened if it had been Juliana's slender throat under his hands? Or Priti's? What kind of monster had he become?

He heard Juliana calling after him. Elliot didn't pause but walked on out into the night, into cool twilight and misty rain that had begun to fall.

⁓

Juliana started after Elliot. Mahindar, helped by Channan, collapsed heavily onto the chair Elliot had vacated.

"No, memsahib," Mahindar said. "I told you. When he is like this, it is best to let him go."

The evening was darker than usual, clouds having gathered, a new rain falling. Juliana saw Elliot outside the open dining room window, his tall form disappearing into the mist.

He walked swiftly, his head bowed. The red setter, Rosie, loped out of the garden and went after him, but Elliot didn't turn to acknowledge the dog. He pressed on, swallowed by darkness.

"No," Juliana said. "I won't let him go. No, don't stop me, Mahindar. I can't let him be alone."

Mahindar's protests faded as Juliana rushed out the door. She noticed that Channan had not tried to stop her, the look in her wise eyes telling Juliana that she agreed.

Juliana ran out into the rain. She realized halfway down the path that she hadn't stopped for a wrap or boots, and that she sloshed through mud and wet in her tea gown and slippers.

What did it matter? Juliana gathered up her water-stained satin skirts and ran on.

Rain beaded on her bare head and shoulders, not strong enough to be proper rain, but steady enough to get her sopping wet.

Elliot walked fast. Juliana ran to keep up, panting, her corset stealing her breath.

He was heading not up into the hills as Juliana had expected, but along the narrow, rather precarious road to the river. That way lay the wooden bridge across which Hamish had driven them the first night from the train.

At least, Juliana thought that was where Elliot was going. She soon lost him in the lowering fog, the path and trees swallowed by the thickening mist. Even Elliot's pale hair and swirling plaid disappeared from sight.

A flash of red came to her, the setter, who rushed back at Juliana, tail waving. Rosie ran in a circle around Juliana then dashed on ahead again.

Juliana's heart thumped. She could see well enough to

keep her feet on the road, but the fog was descending rapidly. Soon, she'd be groping her way through the black, and the edge of this road plunged off into darkness.

The hollow thump of Rosie's feet on the wooden bridge gave Juliana a burst of vigor. The bridge rode high over the water, the river rushing and roaring below.

Juliana saw the form of Elliot in the mist, facing the rail, his kilt a smudge in the darkness. She hiked her skirts high out of the wet and ran the last few feet.

Chapter 29

"Elliot!"

Elliot didn't appear to hear her. He kept his face turned to the river, hand gripping the rail, as Juliana dashed to him, the boards hard under her thin slippers.

Her dress would be a ruin, Channan would shake her head at it, but Juliana didn't care. She'd shred the thing—she never wanted to wear this gown again. She wanted no reminder of the moment in the dining room when she'd seen her charming husband overcome with terror so great he'd slipped away from her. Right in front of her, he'd been taken away.

"Elliot," she panted.

He looked up. His face was so bleak, that Juliana's heart broke.

She feared he'd walk away from her again, but he hung on to the bridge's rail while he shook his head. "Juliana, I can't do this."

His voice was broken, rasping with despair. Juliana took

the last steps to him and closed her hand around his tight wrist.

"You can. I'll help you."

"You saw what I did. I've done it before. I'm hurting people—innocent people. And I can't *stop it*."

"But you do stop it." Juliana caressed his wrist. "You do. You stop in time. Have you ever truly hurt anyone in your fits?"

Elliot looked away from her, his winter eyes closing briefly. "No, but it has been damn close. Look what I did to Mahindar tonight."

"But you always stop yourself, Elliot. Something inside you tells you that you must."

"I stop because someone like Mahindar makes me. Or you do."

Juliana shook her head. "That's nonsense. We couldn't possibly hold you back if you didn't want us to. You're far too strong, stronger than any of us. Stopping the attacks is *your* choice."

When he looked at her again, his eyes were hot with rage. "What if I can't come to my senses in time? Dear God, what if I try to harm Priti? I adore her. She's . . . she's the spark that pulled me out of the blackness. She's why I finally got out of bed after my escape. I needed to take care of her. I need to take care of you." Elliot released his hold on the railing and caressed her throat with the backs of his fingers. "And what if I try to hurt *you*?"

"I am fairly resilient," Juliana said. "Not a porcelain doll. My mother used to disparage me because I was such a robust child. A lady is meant to be fragile and frail, but that's poppycock. I'd never get a lick of work done if I were frail."

She'd hoped to make him smile, but Elliot's eyes remained bleak. "You're not that resilient, lass." He ran his fingers up and down her throat, shaking his head again. "If I hurt you, it would kill me."

"What were you thinking of—when you went after Mahindar, what were you thinking?"

"What the devil was he even doing in there?"

"I called him." Juliana swallowed, his fingertips on her skin drawing fire. "When you sat back and went blank, I shouted for him. I was worried about you." She put her hand on his, stilling his touch. "What were you thinking of?"

Elliot closed his fingers around hers then seemed to realize that she stood there soaking wet. He released her, slid off his coat, and draped it around Juliana's shoulders. The trapped heat from his body embraced her, surrounding her with his warmth and scent.

"I was dreaming I was back in my cell, in the caves. Except that they made me say your name. I blurted out the secret of you. And they were going to take you from me." Elliot gripped her shoulders through the loose coat. "They were taking you away from me. I can't do this if they take you away from me."

"I'm here." Juliana looked up into Elliot's anguished eyes, his brows drawn down as though all the fury in the world coursed through him. "I'm here, Elliot. I've always been here for you. And I always will be."

Elliot gripped her shoulders even harder. His breath came faster, the fine rain dripping down his face.

"I'll always be here," Juliana repeated. "Always."

"Why should you? He was right. I'm broken."

Juliana didn't know who *he* was, but she knew the answer. "Because I love you. I love you my dearest, darling Elliot. I've loved you since the day you put the frog in my pocket, and kissed me to distract me from it." She turned her head and kissed the hand that rested on her shoulder. "I love you, Elliot McBride."

When she looked up at him again she found his gaze burning into her. The wild look he'd had in the dining room was back, but she could see that he remained in the present, no flashing back to the past.

A hoarse cry escaped his throat. Elliot dragged Juliana to him, his arms coming around her to hold her—tight, tight. He shuddered, then shuddered again, sobs choking out of him.

Juliana clung to him, pressing her cheek to his. He rocked her in his arms, his tears mingling with the rain to wet her face.

"Don't love me," he said. "Don't."

"There is no *do* or *don't*," Juliana whispered. The mists dissolved and the rain came down faster. "I love you because I love you. I can't help that."

His embrace nearly crushed her, his strong body shaking. "Never stop. Never stop loving me, Juliana."

"I never will."

Elliot raised his head. Tears streaked his face, his eyes were red-rimmed, and his face twisted in pain and hope. "I love you so much," he said brokenly.

Juliana's own tears came. She brushed away his and kissed his lips.

Elliot crushed her up to him, taking her mouth in a brutal kiss. Their mouths fused, heat to heat, lips touching, parting, gliding together. *Never stop loving me.*

Never. Never. Gemma had said Juliana shouldn't try to repair him. Juliana understood now.

She didn't need to be Elliot's caretaker; she needed to be his friend and guide, his lover. She would anchor him when he rode the storm of his fears, listen when he needed to speak, and provide a safe haven for him when his journey was done.

She loved him, and the kiss rode on the wings of their love together.

A dog barked. Rosie ran to them, her red body soaked, and shook herself out all over them. Juliana broke the kiss to laugh.

"No hope for this gown now," she said over the rising wind.

Elliot was looking up and past her, and Juliana turned. Down the path came lanterns, points of light in the darkness. They were all coming—Hamish, Mahindar, Channan, Nandita, Komal, McGregor, and Priti in Nandita's arms. Even the goat, who shook her head at the rain.

Their lanterns gleamed out in the darkness, falling on Juliana and Elliot in each other's arms on the bridge.

Mr. McGregor stopped the procession, holding his lantern high. "Well now," he shouted, his grin gleaming hugely from his bearded face. "It appears as though the lad's all right."

"Mahindar," Elliot began. He drew a breath to say more, but he arrested it, let out the air he'd drawn, and simply looked at the man who had been with him through so much.

"Come back to the house, sahib," Mahindar said, raising his lantern high. "Come back to the house with the memsahib. It is warm there."

Juliana locked her hands behind Elliot's neck and gave him another long kiss, her body warming at his hard kiss in response.

"Let's go home," she said.

The look Elliot gave her heated her to her toes. She snuggled into his coat, took his hand, and led him back toward the house, into its warmth and welcoming light.

~

"Say it again." Elliot heard the savagery in his voice, and he couldn't stop it. "Say it again."

Their bodies dripped, but with sweat now, not rain. Outside the wind had risen, the summer storm howling in to drive away the mist. Alone in their bedchamber, Elliot had stripped off Juliana's wet clothes, his own landing with hers on the floor. The bed rocked now with his onslaught, Elliot loving her with the fury of the storm.

"I love you!" Juliana cried.

Darkness swirled through Elliot's mind, but it was the

hot darkness of climax. Juliana's shout wound him tighter, Elliot barely hanging on.

"Again!"

"I love you!" Juliana opened her eyes, her laughter ringing up to him. "I love you, Elliot McBride."

"I love *you*." The words came out in a rush, wildness washing over him. "I love you, Juliana. My lass, my own sweet lass. Sweet, holy God."

His seed shot from him, finding home in Juliana. Elliot's hips rocked against hers, his sweat and her honey where they joined.

The wind slammed into the house, and Elliot thrust for the last time, burying himself inside her. He groaned again, fire flickering on the edges of his vision.

Juliana skimmed her hands down Elliot's body, touching him everywhere, her face relaxed in the warmth of passion. Her hair was a mess, curls awry, her naked body the best place his could be.

"Say it again," he said, kissing her swollen lips.

Juliana smiled, the smile languid now, and brushed her fingertips over the base of his neck. "I love you."

Did the words sound best when they burst out of her in passion, or said sweetly in aftermath? Or whispered into his ear while she'd held him as he'd wept?

Elliot would make her say it in all ways, in every room in the house—and on the grounds, in the dogcart, in the train when they finally went back to Edinburgh. In every place they ever were throughout their lives, Elliot would make it his quest to discover where and how the words *I love you*, from Juliana's lips, sounded best.

"I love you, my wife." He let his voice go soft. *"Tha gaol agam ort."*

A smile spread across her face. "Is *that* what that means? *I love you?"*

"It does."

"Then . . . *Tha gaol agam ort.* Did I say it correctly?"

Hearing the words, in beautiful Gaelic, while she lay under him in bed was undoubtedly the best of all.

"Ye did, lass. *Tha gaol agam ort-fhèin.* I love you too." He kissed the line of her hair. "Thank you."

"Mmm. For what? Letting you teach me Gaelic?"

"For all of it."

Juliana knew what he meant. Elliot loved that he didn't have to explain himself all the time to her. She understood.

Juliana touched the tip of his nose, and gave him her most beautiful, warm, and loving smile. "In that case, my love, my bonny husband . . . You're welcome."

Chapter 30

Elliot found Juliana in the morning room, July's warm air carried on a light breeze through the window. She was elegantly beautiful in her pale lawn gown buttoned all the way up her throat, her hair dressed casually in a twist of curls.

As usual, she had a notebook open on the table beside her and a pile of letters and cards on a second table. Ink, paper, and blotting paper were spread out before her, waiting for her to cover them with her practical words.

Elliot walked into the room and closed the door behind him. "Good afternoon, my wife."

Juliana scribbled something into her notebook and looked up at him. She took him in—his boots and kilt, a loose coat slung over a loose shirt—and flashed her beautiful smile. "Good afternoon."

"We're going on a picnic," Elliot said.

"How delightful." Juliana wrote down another note. "Who is going? You and Priti? Or Uncle McGregor and Mr. McPherson? Or—"

"You and I."

Juliana's brows rose, her pen stopping. "Are we? When?"

"Right now."

Juliana looked at him in bewilderment. "On the moment? I've just started my correspondence."

"On the moment. Right now. Put down your pen."

"But I have all this to finish."

Elliot started for her. Before he could reach her and snatch the pen from her hand, Juliana quickly laid it down and rose to her feet.

"Very well," she asked. "But may I ask why?"

"Why the picnic?" Elliot shrugged. "Why not?"

Juliana cast a glance at her paper-strewn tables. "I have much to do, Elliot. When I hire a secretary, perhaps I can leave whenever I like . . ."

Elliot caught her hands and pulled her away from the tables. "Not when you hire a secretary. Now. I'm going to sway you away from your papers, lists, and organization. I'm going to thoroughly seduce you from it, my wife. Right now."

He saw her soften, the desire glow in her eyes, the spark of mischievousness he'd always sensed in her, even when he was slipping the frog into her pinafore pocket. She hadn't screamed and tried to beat it away from her. She'd calmly dipped her hand into her pocket, released the poor thing into the grass, and walked away, giving Elliot a superior look over her shoulder.

Juliana still had the mischievousness, but her frantic fears that the world would condemn her if she slipped in any point had kept her from enjoying it.

Elliot wanted to teach her to find and revel in that part of herself again.

"All right then. A picnic." Juliana turned for the bellpull.

"I will have Mahindar fix us a basket. I'm sure he will make up a splendid one."

"No." Elliot stepped in front of her, blocking her way. "No basket. We see what we find on the way. No planning. No organizing. No lists."

Her lips parted. "Oh."

"Turn around." Elliot caught her shoulders and gently turned her in place. "Out the window. Pick a direction down the path. That is where we'll go."

She hesitated, ready to argue again. Elliot leaned down and bit the shell of her ear. "Go," he said.

Juliana sped away to the windows. She stepped out of the longest one and hopped down to the path that ran around the house. There she paused, looking around, trying to decide which direction to go.

Elliot stepped out after her, took her arm, and tugged her with him down an overgrown path leading east. "This way."

"I thought I was supposed to choose the direction."

"You were debating which was the best way to go. Making lists of for and against in your head. Weren't you?"

"Um. Yes."

"This direction is random. We go."

They couldn't walk side by side down the narrow walk, but Elliot didn't mind coming behind Juliana, where he could observe her small bustle swaying as she went.

The walkway led to the path that skirted the river and wended its way to the footbridge to Mrs. Rossmoran's cottage.

As they rounded a bend, Elliot caught sight of movement in the brush. He hesitated, the wary hunter in him returning, but then he recognized the rough McIver kilt Hamish liked to wear, and the colorful silks of Nandita's scarves. The two were standing in the shadows, very close together.

Elliot watched them for a moment, their innocence

reminding him of when he and Juliana had shared their first dance, then he turned away and caught up to Juliana.

The river rushed beneath them as they walked over the footbridge together, as strongly as it had the night Elliot had stood on the larger bridge, looking over the water in black despair.

He hadn't had any thought of ending his life that night— though he knew Mahindar still believed he had. Instead, the endless rush of sound had caught at him, making Elliot stare into the river's depths while he fought his demons in the dark.

Mrs. Rossmoran and Fiona were both home. "Bannocks?" Fiona asked in answer to Elliot's question. "Aye, baked this morning. And shortbread from yesterday."

Fiona made them up a bundle in the kitchen, while Mrs. Rossmoran sat in her usual chair and regarded them all imperiously.

"So, you've decided to live, have you, young Elliot?"

Elliot slid his arm around Juliana's waist. "I have."

"Hamish says you look much better," Mrs. Rossmoran said. "Act much better too. Haven't tried to strangle anyone in a while. You've made a good choice in wife." Mrs. Rossmoran gave Juliana an approving glance. "I said that from the start. And when you have a few babes in the nursery, 'twill be even better. But mind Hamish. He's growing smitten with that young Indian girl who came with your manservant. He brought her to visit the other day. Sweet young lady, after she got over her shyness. Her English is improving as well. I gather she had an unhappy time of it in India, poor soul." She sighed. "Why anyone wants to live any place but Scotland, I don't know."

Fiona brought them their package, giving Juliana a wink and a smile. "Off you go."

Elliot took charge of the bannocks and shortbread and led Juliana away.

As they headed for the path that ran along the Rossmoran side of the river, Elliot heard Mrs. Rossmoran say to Fiona, "Do you think she is increasing? She had the look of it. Next spring, there'll be a new McBride, you mark my words."

Elliot took Juliana's hand and led her on.

Elliot had lied when he'd said the picnic idea was completely spontaneous and unorganized. In truth, he had a goal in mind.

He'd found the place while exploring the land, looking for Stacy—who was still a guest of McPherson, though he was on the mend. Elliot and he had begun repairing things between them, talking of old times and new, Stacy planning what he'd do when he recovered. In London, Fellows had put in motion ways to keep Jaya's brothers at bay. Fellows's half-brother, the Duke of Kilmorgan, had much influence in politics, and ambassadors had talked to the ruling prince, who decided he didn't like members of his extended family going after Britons. Jaya's brothers had been called home, and there they stayed. Stacy could now live his life again, out of hiding. He would stay in Scotland, he said, and try to carve a place for himself.

Elliot found that talking to Stacy helped. He was learning how to remember the past without fighting it, without fearing it would destroy him. Perhaps one day, Elliot's memories would be distant enough to no longer threaten. He knew it would take him a long time to reach such peace, but he had everything he needed to begin.

The place Elliot had found was a hidden meadow, surrounded by thick trees. The last few days had been rainless, so the grass was dry though still a deep green. Heather swayed across the meadow, rippling purple, interspersed with tiny white and gold flowers to make the place seem to sparkle.

When Elliot folded back the last branch to let Juliana through from the overgrown path, she gasped in delight.

"Beautiful." She ran a few steps and spun around, laughing. "This was no arbitrary direction, Elliot McBride. You brought me here on purpose."

"That is true." Elliot walked unerringly to the base of a tree and fetched a bundle of blankets that he'd asked Hamish to leave there for him.

"Trickster," Juliana said, but she was still laughing.

"Only in part. I'm trying to demonstrate that you can throw off your shackles and enjoy yourself once in a while. The world will not stop if you do."

Juliana watched him spread out the blankets, her hands on her hips. "Oh, very well. I know I can be a bit zealous about organizing. But I like it."

"I'm not demanding you give it up every day." Elliot stretched out on the blanket. "Just every once in a while."

Juliana carefully collapsed next to him, leaned down, and kissed his lips. "I think I don't mind." She looked at their bundle. "We have food. But nothing to drink."

"We can take a drink from yon river," Elliot said. When Juliana blinked, he grinned. "Or wait for Hamish to bring the jugs of water and wine as I asked him to." He ran his hand down Juliana's bodice to rest his palm over her abdomen. "I told him to give us an hour or so alone, first."

Juliana's cheeks went pink. "An excellent idea."

"I brought something else." Elliot reached into the pocket of his coat for the box that Mahindar had handed him this morning and opened it.

Inside, on a bed of velvet, lay two rings. One was a wide gold band; the other, a narrower band encrusted with sapphires.

Juliana took a quick breath. "Ours?"

"I told Mahindar what to order the day of our wedding. They're finished, and here." Elliot drew out the smaller ring, lifted Juliana's left hand, and slid it onto her third finger. "With this ring, I thee wed."

Juliana studied the ring, her smile happy. She took the man's ring and slid it onto his finger.

"With this ring, I *thee* wed."

Elliot couldn't stop his smile. The cool band was heavy on his finger, clasping him just right, belonging there.

He took Juliana's hand again and kissed it, right over the ring. Then he pressed their hands together on her belly.

"Is Mrs. Rossmoran right?" he asked. "Is there a wee one?"

Juliana went quiet, and for a moment, Elliot's heart squeezed with worry. Then she smiled. "She is."

"Dear God." Elliot's lungs ceased to work. He tried to say a few more things, such as, *I'm going to be a father again. You've made me so happy, love. Do you think it will be a boy or girl?*

All he could do was roll onto his back and stare up at the blue sky and sunshine.

Priti's birth had occurred while Elliot had been imprisoned, her existence unknown to him until Mahindar had sprung it on him, releasing an ember of joy and wonder. This was the first time Elliot would be a father alongside the child's mother, watching Juliana carry it, being there when the baby came into the world.

It was too much to take in.

Juliana blocked the sun from him, curls escaping her pins. "Elliot, are you all right?"

"I am." Elliot sounded so calm. Inside him was a riot of noise, of joy, of beating drums and claxons, of all the sounds of India on a festival day. "I am fine. I never have been so fine."

He tugged her down to him, wrapping his arms around her and rolling her gently to the blanket, taking care. "I am everything that is all right."

Elliot kissed her beautiful smile, the dimple at the corner of her mouth, the tip of her tongue.

The darkness inside him, which had been reticent of late, reached for him with spidery fingers. Elliot moved his thoughts back to the little one nestled inside Juliana beneath him, and the darkness snapped away.

While Elliot had been imprisoned in the caves, thoughts of Juliana had given him the freedom he needed to keep himself alive. They hadn't been able to reach that corner of his mind, and so hadn't been able to imprison him entirely. Juliana had been his secret, his knowledge that no one could touch.

This child inside her was another knowledge that they could never take from him.

Elliot's home, his wife, his family. All his, and all real.

The darkness died with a whimper, and Juliana welcomed Elliot, unhindered by pain and shadows, into her arms.

Turn the page for a preview of the next
historical romance by Jennifer Ashley

The Wicked Deeds of Daniel Mackenzie

Coming soon from Berkley Sensation!

He doesn't have the ace.

Daniel held four eights, and had backed that fact with large stacks of money.

Mortimer thought he was bluffing. He'd been trying to convince Daniel that he'd drawn the straight, that he'd been given an ace from the young woman who dealt the cards at the head of the table.

The other gentlemen in the St. James's gaming hell called the Nines had already folded in Mortimer's favorite game of poker. They and the rest of the hell now lingered to see the battle of wits between twenty-four-year-old Daniel Mackenzie and Fenton Mortimer, ten years older than Daniel and a hardened gambler. So much cigar smoke hung in the air that any consumptive who'd dared walk in the door would have fallen dead on the spot.

The game of choice at this hell was whist, but Mortimer had recently introduced the American game of poker, which he'd learned during a yearlong stint in that country. Mortimer was very good at it, quickly relieving young Mayfair aristos of thousands of pounds. And still they came to him, eager to learn the game and try to beat him.

Ten gentlemen had started this round, dropping out one by one until only Daniel and Mortimer remained.

Daniel kept his cards facedown on the table so the nosy club fodder couldn't telegraph his hand to Mortimer. He gathered up more of his paper bills and dropped them in front of his cards. "See you, and raise two hundred."

Mortimer went slightly green but slid his money opposite Daniel's, his fingers shaking a little. Daniel picked up another pile of notes and laid them on the already substantial stack.

"Raise you again," Daniel said. "Can you cover?"

"I can." Mortimer didn't dig out any more notes or coin, but he obviously hoped he wouldn't have to.

"Sure about that?"

Mortimer's eyes narrowed. "What do you take me for? I can cover the bet. If you'd like to question my honor in a private room, I will be happy to answer."

Daniel refrained from rolling his eyes. "Calm yourself, lad," he said, making his Highland accent broad. He lifted a cigar from the holder beside him and sucked smoke into his mouth. "I believe you. What have you got?"

"Show yours first."

Daniel picked up his cards and flipped them over with a nonchalant flick of his wrist. Four eights, one ace.

The men around him let out a collective groan, the lady dealer smiled at Daniel, and Mortimer went chalk white.

"Bloody hell. I didn't think you had it." Mortimer's own cards fell faceup—a ten, jack, queen, seven, and three.

Daniel raked in his money and winked at the dealer. She really was lovely. "You can write me a vowel for the rest, Mortimer."

Mortimer wet his lips. "Now, Mackenzie . . ."

He couldn't cover the bet. What idiot wagered the last of his cash when he didn't have a winning hand? Mortimer should have taken his loss several rounds ago and walked away.

But no, Mortimer had convinced himself he was expert at the bluffing part of the game, and would con the naive young Scotsman who'd unashamedly walked in here tonight in his kilt.

A hard-faced man on the other side of the room sent Mortimer a grim look. Daniel guessed that the ruffian had lent Mortimer cash for this night's play and wasn't pleased that he'd just lost it all.

"Never mind," Daniel said. "Keep what you owe as a token of appreciation for a night of good play."

Mortimer scowled. "I pay my debts, Mackenzie."

Daniel glanced at the bone-breaker and lowered his voice. "You'll pay more than that if ye don't beat a hasty retreat, I'm thinking. How much do ye owe him?"

Mortimer's eyes went cold. "None of your business."

Daniel shrugged. "I don't wish to see a man have his face removed just because I was lucky at cards. What do ye owe him? I'll give ye that back. Ye can owe *me*."

"Be beholden to a Mackenzie?" Mortimer's outrage rang from him.

Daniel filled his pockets with his winnings and took his greatcoat from the lady dealer. She ran her hand suggestively across Daniel's shoulders as she helped him into it, and Daniel tucked a banknote into her bodice.

"Aye, well." Daniel took his hat from the lady who gave him an even warmer smile. "Hope you can find tuppence for the ferryman at your funeral. Good night, man."

He turned to leave and found Mortimer's friends standing in front of him.

"Changed my mind," Mortimer said. "The chaps reminded me I had something worth bargaining with. Say, for the last two thousand."

"Oh aye? What is it? A motorcar?"

"Better. A lady."

Daniel hid a sigh. "I don't need a courtesan, Mortimer. I can find women on me own."

Easily. Daniel looked at ladies, and they came to him. Part of his attraction was his wealth, part of it was the fact that he belonged to the great Mackenzie family and was nephew to a duke. He never argued about the ladies' motives; he simply enjoyed.

"She's not a courtesan," Mortimer said quickly. "She's special. You'll see."

An actress, perhaps. She'd give an indifferent performance of a Shakespearian soliloquy, and Daniel would be expected to smile and say she was worth every penny.

"Keep your money, pay your creditors," Daniel said. "Give me a horse or your best servant in lieu—I'm not particular."

Mortimer's friends didn't move. "I think I must insist," Mortimer said.

Seven against one. If Daniel argued, he'd only end up with bruised knuckles. He didn't particularly want to hurt his hands, because he had the fine-tuning of his engine to do, and he needed to be able to hold a spanner.

"Fair enough," Daniel said. "But I assess the goods before I accept."

Mortimer agreed. He clapped Daniel on the shoulder as he led him out, and Daniel stopped himself from shaking off his touch. Mortimer's friends filed around them as though in a defensive flank as they made their way to Mortimer's waiting landau.

Daniel noted as they pulled away from the Nines that

the bone-breaker had slipped out the door behind them and followed.

~~~~~

Mortimer took Daniel through the misty city to a respectable neighborhood north of Oxford Street, stopping on a quiet lane near Portman Square.

The hour was two in the morning, and this street was quiet, the houses dark. Behind the windows lay respectable gentlemen who would rise in the early hours and trundle to the City for work, while their gentlewomen wives readied themselves for calls to other ladies of the neighborhood.

Daniel descended from the landau behind Mortimer. "She'll be asleep. Leave it for tomorrow."

"Nonsense," Mortimer said loudly, with drink in his voice. "She sees me anytime I call."

He walked to a black painted front door and rapped on it with his stick. Above them a light appeared and a curtain was drawn back. Mortimer looked up at the window and tapped on the door again.

The curtain dropped, and the light faded. Mortimer waited with ill-concealed impatience, letting his stick continue to tap lightly on the wood.

Daniel folded his arms and leaned against the door frame, stopping himself from ripping the stick from Mortimer's hands and breaking it over his knee. "Who lives here?"

"I do," Mortimer said. "I mean—I own the house. At least my family does. We let it to Madame Bastien and her daughter. For a slight savings in rent, they agreed to entertain me and my friends anytime I asked it."

"Including the middle of the bloody night?"

"Especially the middle of the night."

Mortimer smiled—self-satisfied English prig. They had to be courtesans. He'd reduced the rent so he could obligate them to pay in kind, so he could rub their noses in his power anytime he wished.

Daniel turned back to the landau. "This isn't worth two thousand, Mortimer."

"Patience, patience. You'll see."

The rest of Mortimer's friends had arrived and hemmed them in, blocking the way back to the landau. The bone-breaker was still in attendance, hovering in the shadows a little way down the street.

The door opened. A maid who'd obviously dressed hast-ily stepped behind the door as she opened it wide and let the stream of gentlemen inside. The drunker lads of the party wanted to pause to see what entertainment she might provide, but Daniel planted himself solidly beside the door, blocking their way to her. They moved past, forgetting about her the moment they turned away.

Mortimer led the way to double pocket doors at the end of the hall, and pushed them open. Daniel caught a flurry of movement behind them, but by the time Mortimer beck-oned Daniel in, stillness had taken over.

A fire danced on the hearth behind a long, empty table, the walls covered with a pale blue, gold, and burnt orange striped wallpaper. The gas chandelier above the table hung dark, and one solitary candelabra with three candles sat on the table. A young woman was just touching a long match to the candlewicks.

When the third was lit, she blew out the match and straightened up. "So sorry to have kept you waiting, gentle-men," she said pleasantly enough in a voice very faintly accented. "I'm afraid my mother is unable to rise. You will have to make do with me."

She bathed them in a smile.

Whatever Mortimer and the other gentlemen said in response, Daniel didn't hear. He couldn't hear anything. He couldn't see anything either, except the woman who stood poised behind the candelabra, the long match still in her hand, the smile of an angel on her face.

She wasn't beautiful. Daniel had seen faces more beautiful in the Casino in Monte Carlo, at the Moulin Rouge in Paris. He'd known slimmer bodies in dancers, or in the butterflies that glided about the gaming hells in St. James's and Monaco, smiling and enticing gentlemen to play.

This young woman had an angular face softened by a mass of dark hair dressed in a pompadour, with ringlets trickling down the sides of her face. Her nose was a little too long, her mouth too wide, her shoulders and arms too plump. Her eyes were her best feature, set in exact proportion in her face, dark blue in the glint of candlelight, and framed by lush black lashes.

They were eyes a man could gaze into all night and wake up to the next morning. He could contemplate her eyes across the breakfast table and then again at dinner while he made plans to look into them all through the night.

The young woman wasn't a courtesan, however. Courtesans began charming from the moment the gentleman walked into the room. They leaned slightly forward, they gestured with graceful fingers, implying that those fingers would be equally as graceful traveling a man's body. Courtesans drew in, they suggested without words, they used every movement and every expression to beguile.

This woman stood fixed in place, her body language not inviting the gentlemen into the room at all, despite her words and the smile she'd thrown at them. If her movements were graceful as she turned to toss the match into the fire, it was from nature, not practice.

She wore a plain gown of blue satin that bared her shoulders, but the gown was no less respectable than what a lady in this neighborhood might wear for dinner or a night at the theatre. Her hair in the simple pompadour had no ribbons or jewels tucked into it—the unaffected style hinted that the dark masses of hair might come down at any time over the hands of the lucky gentleman who pulled out its pins. She wore no jewelry at all, in fact, except for one silver locket that nestled at her throat.

The young woman spread her hands at the now-silent men. "If you'll sit, gentlemen, we can begin."

Daniel couldn't move. His feet had grown into the floor, disobedient to his will. They wanted him to stand in that place all night long and gaze upon this woman.

Mortimer leaned to Daniel, his eyes glittering. "You see? Did I not tell you she'd be worth it?" He cleared his throat, straightening up. "Daniel Mackenzie, may I introduce Mademoiselle Bastien. Violette is her Christian name, in the French way. Mademoiselle, this is Daniel Mackenzie, son of Lord Cameron Mackenzie and nephew to the Duke of Kilmorgan. You'll give him a fine show, won't you, mademoiselle? There's a good girl."

~~~~~

The man Mortimer called Daniel Mackenzie came around the table and boldly stopped right next to Violet.

Scottish, she thought rapidly, taking in his bright blue and green plaid kilt, fashionable black suit coat, and ivory waistcoat. *Rich*, went her assessment, noting the costly materials and the way in which the coat hugged his broad shoulders. Tailor-made, and not by any cheap or apprentice tailor. A master had designed and sewn those clothes. *Used to having the very best*.

The other word that came to her was *dangerous*. Violet didn't know why she should think this, but every inch of her flesh itched with it, every breath threatened to choke her.

Mr. Mackenzie topped most of the other gentlemen here by at least a foot, had a hard face, a nose that would be large in any other man's face, and eyes that made her stop. Violet couldn't decide the color of them in this light—hazel? brown?—but they were arresting.

So arresting that she stood there staring at him, not taking the hand he held out to her to shake in greeting.

"Daniel Mackenzie, at your service, mademoiselle."

He gave her a light, charming smile, his eyes pulling her in, keeping her where he wanted her.

Definitely danger here.

He kept a barrier in place behind his eyes, she saw when she risked a look into them, a closed door. This man gave up his secrets to very few. He would be hard to read, which could be a problem.

He did nothing but stand waiting with his hand out. Violet finally slid hers into his gloved one, making the movement slow and deliberate.

"How do you do," she said formally, her English perfect. She'd discovered that speaking flawless English reinforced the fiction that she was entirely French.

Daniel closed his giant hand around hers and raised it to his lips.

The quick, hot brush of his mouth to the backs of her fingers ignited a spark to rival that on the match she'd tossed away. Her nerves tightened like wires, forcing the deep breath she'd been trying not to take.

The little gasp sounded loud to her, but Mortimer's cronies were making much noise as they shed coats and debated where each would sit. Daniel's gaze fixed on Violet over her hand, challenging, daring, knowing.

Show me who you are, that gaze said.

Violet was supposed to be thinking that about *him.* Whatever the world believed about the talents of Violette Bastien, medium and spiritualist, she knew that her true gift was reading people.

Within a few moments of studying a man, Violet understood what he loved and hated, what he wanted with all his heart and what he'd do to get it, what made him happy, and what hurt him. She'd learned these lessons painstakingly from Jacobi in the backstreets of Paris, had been his best pupil.

But not Mr. Mackenzie. He did not let anyone behind his barriers, not easily. But when he did . . .

When he did, worlds would unfold.

Violet snatched her hand from his grasp. "Please, gentlemen," she said again, striving to maintain the cheerful note in her voice.

She moved to sit down and found Daniel Mackenzie's hand on the back of her chair. She forced her gaze from him and seated herself, trying to ignore the warmth of his body at her side, the fold of open coat that brushed her shoulder. The breath went out of her again as Daniel eased her chair forward, his strength unnerving.

Violet laid her hands flat on the table, trying to use its cool surface to calm herself. She needed to appear utterly composed, sugar-sweet and ready to help.

"Will you all give me a moment to prepare myself?" she asked, throwing out an appealing look.

The gentlemen readily agreed. Most had been here before, most often as Mortimer's guests, but some returned alone for private consultations with Violet and her mother.

Only Mr. Mackenzie kept watching her, leaning on the table so he could look her in the eye. "Prepare yourself for what?" he asked.

Mortimer answered him from down the table, "To contact the other side, of course."

Daniel kept his gaze on Violet. "The other side o' what, mademoiselle? The room?"

"The ether," one of the other men said in a superior tone. "She's a spiritualist, man. Didn't you know that? Madame and Mademoiselle Bastien are the most famous spiritualists in London."

The flash of disappointment in Daniel's eyes stung Violet. Stung her hard. Why she should care what this gentleman she'd never seen before should think of her she didn't know, but she did.

Plenty of people didn't believe in spiritualism and scoffed at what she did. They didn't believe that a trained medium could contact the departed beyond the veil, to let the dear departed send comforting messages to the survivors, warn of impending danger, or just have a little chat with those who remained behind.

Just as well, Violet's inner voice drawled. *You don't believe it either.*

Violet had never felt the cold touch of the otherworld or the trembling ecstasy her mother found in her trances. She'd never seen a ghost or a spirit, and had never had one talk to her, or knock at her, or do any of those other useful things spirits could do.

But she'd become very, very good at pretending she had.

That Daniel Mackenzie didn't believe shouldn't bother her. Jacobi had told her never to argue with an unbeliever, but to move on to the next mark. She should close to him and concentrate on the other gentlemen, to make Mr. Mackenzie feel that he was somehow left out, to make him doubt his disbelief just a little bit.

So why couldn't she turn away with her superior little smile, her amused disdain? Why did she keep wanting to look at him, to explain that she did this for survival, and beg him not to dislike her for it?

Daniel leaned his elbow on the table, stretching the fine cloth of his coat. "The other side of the ether, eh? I'd like to see that."

Mortimer said, "You're in for a show then. That's why I said she's worth more than a motorcar or a horse."

Violet suddenly wished she *did* have the powers her mother claimed to, so that she could curse Mortimer into living out his life as a rabbit—or at least being a disappointment to any ladies he took to bed.

The room at last quieted, the gentlemen calming down to watch her prepare. Violet knew why they liked to watch her—when she closed her eyes and drew long breaths to calm herself for her trance, her breasts rose to press tightly against her décolletage. Distracted the clients wonderfully.

This time, however, when she opened her eyes again,

she found Mr. Mackenzie not distracted in the slightest. Instead of letting his gaze drop to her chest, as the gazes of the other gentlemen had, Mr. Mackenzie smiled straight into her eyes.

Never let a skeptic make you nervous, Jacobi had said. *Give them a show in spite of their disbelief. Make them doubt their own doubts.*

Violet drew on the techniques the middle-aged man had painstakingly taught her. A glance around the table, ignoring Daniel. A small smile, the look of inner serenity, soft movements of her hands as she spoke.

"All is calm tonight, and very clear. Mr. Ellingham, I believe we were very near reaching your father the last time. Shall we try again?"

Before eager Mr. Ellingham—who was trying to find out where his now-deceased father had hidden away about ten thousand pounds of the family money—could answer, Mortimer broke in.

"Contact someone for Mackenzie. He's my guest tonight. His dear old mum, perhaps."

Violet turned without hurry back to Daniel. She didn't miss the flicker of disgust at the mention of his mother, disgust aimed at both Mortimer and the mother in question.

"Perhaps that would not be for the best," she suggested gently.

Mr. Mackenzie gave her a guileless look that masked his growing anger. "Let me mum rest in peace," he said. "Why don't you contact me dad, instead?"

Too transparent. Violet gave him a sweet smile. "You are trying to trip me, Mr. Mackenzie. If you wish me to contact your father, I suggest a telegram, because that gentleman is very much still living."

Daniel gave her a look of new assessment, then he burst out laughing. His laugh was deep and true, a man who knew how to laugh for the joy of it. "Fancy you knowing that. You are right, Mortimer. She has the gift."

"I don't need the gift to read the newspapers," Violet said. "Your father appears in many of them, especially the sporting news. Now if he'd like me to tell him which of his racehorses will do the best this year, he is welcome to join us."

Daniel wound down to a chuckle. "I'm starting to like you, mademoiselle."

She let her eyes go wide. "I am pleased to hear it, Mr. Mackenzie. However, if you have come tonight only to mock me and my work, I will have to ask you to depart. Or at least wait in the hall."

"Why?" His eyes took on an impish twinkle. "Does my mockery disturb th' spirits?"

"Indeed, no. Those on the other side can be quite forgiving. But *I* find it a bit distracting."

Daniel's laughter rang out again, and he raised his hands in surrender. "Forgive me, lass. I'll be the model of goodness from now on. Promise."

Violet knew better than to believe him, but she returned her attention to the others. "Shall we simply see what spirits are close tonight?"

The other men, laughing along with Mr. Mackenzie, or perhaps at him, agreed enthusiastically. They liked the show.

"Then, as you know, I must ask for silence."

Violet closed her eyes again, and thankfully, the gentlemen quieted down, their guffaws finally dying off.

She went into the movements she'd rehearsed so many times. She let her breathing become slow and deep, spread her hands on the table, and rocked her head from fully bent forward to all the way back, her face to the ceiling. Violet kept her eyes closed as she let her breathing become more rapid, faster, faster, twisting her face as though something pained her.

Soft noises escaped her mouth, and she moved her head the slightest bit from side to side, making sure she didn't overdo it. Too much gyration looked fake. A little bit was far more frightening, a person in the grip of some force she didn't quite understand.

Violet also knew bloody well that a woman moaning, perspiring, and letting her breasts move with her panting breath froze a gentleman in place.

A large, warm hand landed on hers, and Mr. Mackenzie said in a quiet voice, "You all right, lass?"

Violet froze. For a moment, her rapid breaths choked her, and she couldn't find air.

His voice was filled with concern. That concern sent a shock through her. No one had ever spoken to her like this—not her mother, not even Jacobi, who'd been closer to her than a father. Daniel Mackenzie, a stranger, a man of warmth by her side, touched her in worry, and asked after her with a kind of protectiveness she'd never experienced before.

It nearly broke her. A moment ago, Violet was priding herself on being able to handle a roomful of half-drunk, unruly gentlemen who'd come upon them so rudely in the middle of the night. Her mother had been too upset by their arrival to rise from the bed, and Violet had said she'd take care of everything.

The moment Mr. Mackenzie voiced concern, Violet felt herself shattering, the façade she strove to maintain crumbling to reveal the lonely and weary young woman behind it—nearly thirty years old, unmarried and unlikely to be, taking care of an ill mother, living by her wits and her skill in hiding her lies.

She found it easy to keep the barrier between Mortimer and his ilk, but she recognized that Daniel Mackenzie could rip her to shreds with one touch.

She tried to catch her breath, tried to keep her persona in place, but for a moment, she was only a frightened young woman angry at a man for exposing her.

Mr. Ellingham, oblivious, broke the tension. "Damn it, Mackenzie. We'll never get a contact if you interfere with the medium's trance. Everyone knows that."

Daniel kept his gaze on Violet. "You sure you're all right, love?"

Violet moved her hands to the table again, pressing them down to stop their trembling. "Yes. Yes, I am fine, thank you."

"You're an ass, Mackenzie," Mortimer said, his voice tinged with brutal anger. "Now we'll have to start all over again."

"No, we won't," Daniel said, still looking at Violet. "We'll go and leave Mademoiselle Bastien to her sleep."

"The hell we will," Mortimer said, standing up. "We're not leaving this house. Not until we have satisfaction."

An imperfect pair . . .
perfectly matched.

FROM THE *USA TODAY* BESTSELLING AUTHOR

JENNIFER ASHLEY

The Duke's Perfect Wife

❦

Lady Eleanor Ramsay is the only one who knows the truth about Hart Mackenzie. Once his fiancée, she is the sole woman to whom he could ever pour out his heart.

Hart has it all—a dukedom, wealth, power, influence, whatever he desires—and every woman wants him. But Hart has sacrificed much to keep his brothers safe, first from their brutal father, and then from the world. He's also suffered loss—his wife, his infant son, and the woman he loved with all his heart though he realized it too late.

doorstep, with
ken long ago.
—and aroused
n—Hart won-
. . . or save him.